Josie had written an article on kissing once and knew the signs that a man wanted to lock lips.

"Maybe if we just got it out of the way," Tuck suggested, "then it'd be over and out of our systems."

She felt him tug, and she gave in, melting into his body as their lips met. *Yeah.* This is exactly what she needed. Wanted.

Tuck cleared his throat as he took a small step backward, giving her space.

She almost felt shy as her eyes fluttered open to meet his. "Yeah," she said, feeling the need to say something. "I'm glad we got that out of our systems."

"Me too."

She searched his face, wondering if he was as big a fibber as she was. Because now that she'd kissed him, she only wanted to do it again. And again. "Liar," she whispered, calling his bluff.

"You too," he whispered back, heat and mischief molten together in his gaze.

Then they pulled each other in for a second kiss.

PRAISE FOR ANNIE RAINS AND HER SWEETWATER SPRINGS SERIES

"Top Pick! Five stars! Romance author Annie Rains was blessed with an empathetic voice that shines through each character she writes. *Christmas on Mistletoe Lane* is the latest example of that gift."

—NightOwlReviews.com

"The premise is entertaining, engaging and endearing; the characters are dynamic and lively...the romance is tender and dramatic...A wonderful holiday read, *Christmas on Mistletoe Lane* is a great start to the holiday season."

—TheReadingCafe.com

"This first installment of Rains's Sweetwater Springs series is cozy and most enjoyable. A strong cast of supporting characters as well as expert characterizations and strong plotting will have readers looking forward to future installments."

—*Publishers Weekly*

"What a sweet Christmastime romance! *Christmas on Mistletoe Lane* was a fun series starter, and I am looking forward to see where the Sweetwater Springs series goes!"

—The Genre Minx

"Settle in with a mug of hot chocolate and prepare to find holiday joy in a story you won't forget."

—RaeAnne Thayne, *New York Times* bestselling author

"Annie Rains puts her heart into every word!"

—Brenda Novak, *New York Times* bestselling author

"How does Annie Rains do it? This is a lovely book, perfect for warming your heart on a long winter night."

—Grace Burrowes, *New York Times* bestselling author

SPRINGTIME AT HOPE COTTAGE

ANNIE RAINS

FOREVER

NEW YORK BOSTON

Copyright © 2019 by Annie Rains
Preview of *Snowfall on Cedar Trail* © 2019 by Annie Rains

Cover design and illustration by Elizabeth Turner Stokes
Cover copyright © 2019 by Hachette Book Group, Inc.

"Last Chance Bride" copyright © 2012 by Robin Lanier

Forever
Hachette Book Group
1290 Avenue of the Americas, New York, NY 10104
read-forever.com
twitter.com/readforeverpub

First Edition: March 2019

Forever is an imprint of Grand Central Publishing. The Forever name and logo are trademarks of Hachette Book Group, Inc.

The publisher is not responsible for websites (or their content) that are not owned by the publisher.

The Hachette Speakers Bureau provides a wide range of authors for speaking events. To find out more, go to www.hachettespeakersbureau.com or call (866) 376-6591.

ISBN: 978-1-5387-1398-3 (mass market), 978-1-5387-1399-0 (ebook)

Printed in the United States of America
OPM
10 9 8 7 6 5 4 3 2 1

For Vic Rains, in loving memory.

Acknowledgments

This book wouldn't have been possible without the help of so many. I'd like to thank my family, who put up with me working in the mornings, at night, on car rides, and all the times and places in between. Your patience and understanding, support and encouragement keep me going. Also, thanks to my husband, Sonny, who bounces ideas around with me for these imaginary characters that I love so much (but I love you more, of course).

I want to send out a huge thank-you to my talented editor at Grand Central / Forever, Alex Logan, who makes my work infinitely better. Thank you to the entire Grand Central / Forever team, including sales, marketing, production, and the art department, for all your hard work! And to my tireless agent, Sarah Younger of Nancy Yost Literary Agency, for believing in these books and in me. ♥

Thanks to my critique partner, Rachel Lacey, and to my other #GirlsWriteNight ladies: April Hunt, Tif Marcelo, and Sidney Halston. I'm so glad we're in this together.

A very special thanks goes out to Julie Bailey for reading this book and making sure I got Tuck and his Cherokee family just right. I so appreciate your time and feedback, and I appreciate having you as a reader!

And as always, my books wouldn't be possible without all my wonderful readers who invest their time and hearts in these stories. From the bottom of *my* heart, THANK YOU!

CHAPTER ONE

Definitely not in Kansas anymore.

Or, in Josie Kellum's case, New York City. She'd barely stepped off the jet bridge and into the airport before she'd realized she was in for a culture shock. And that was saying a lot, considering her home state was a proud blend of people from around the world. All cultures and people except perhaps the sort that lived deep in the mountains of North Carolina.

Readjusting the carry-on bag on her shoulder, Josie weaved her way toward Baggage Claim. Just looking around, she could guess who the locals were, arriving back home from their travels. They didn't seem to be in a rush to go anywhere unlike the travelers she'd seen just a couple of hours ago at LaGuardia Airport. Even now, Josie was rushing, though her flight had landed early, and for the first time in ages, she wasn't chasing a deadline.

She stopped at Baggage Claim and retrieved her brightly colored luggage.

Understandably, her best friend, Kaitlyn Russo, couldn't meet her here today. Kaitlyn ran a successful bed and breakfast, which demanded someone always be there to play hostess. When Josie had assured Kaitlyn she could grab a cab to Sweetwater Springs, Kaitlyn had only laughed.

"A forty-five-minute drive will cost you those red-soled shoes you love so much."

"Christian Louboutins," Josie corrected. "And they're more than shoes." They were one of her only indulgences. "So I'll just rent a car, then."

"When was the last time you actually drove a car, Jo?"

Kaitlyn raised a good point. Josie took public transportation everywhere she went. She didn't own a car, and she'd never driven one down the side of a mountain.

"Don't worry," Kaitlyn told her. "I'll find someone to pick you up. Mitch has a friend that drives that way all the time. Maybe he can swing by and drive you in."

Mitch's friend. That was the extent of Josie's knowledge on who she was looking for right now as she scanned the surrounding area. There were a few people standing against the wall near Baggage Claim. An older man with white hair. A middle-aged guy in a uniform of some sort. Maybe Josie should've thought to make a sign to hold up that read MITCH'S FRIEND.

As she was pondering what to do next, someone grabbed her left shoulder. Reflexively, Josie whirled around, catching one heel of her Christian Louboutins on the wheel of her rolling luggage. She tried to steady herself with the handle but it retracted with her quick movement.

Am I being mugged? Her gaze darted to her checked laptop bag as she stumbled. Luckily the front flap was still open from where she'd grabbed a breath mint earlier. Grabbing her can of pepper spray, she righted her body and met two darker-than-night eyes cast in a tanned, angular face. The man had shoulder-length, silky black hair, and he was, for lack of a better word—which was saying a lot for a journalist—gorgeous.

She held up the spray, targeting the man's face. She'd purchased the can after taking a self-defense class recently. It'd been research for an article that her new boss had shot down with sniper efficiency, saying it wasn't sexy enough. What did Bart know though? Protection in all senses of the word was *very* sexy.

"Whoa!" Her attacker took several steps backward and held up his hands. "What are you doing?"

"Defending myself. You grabbed me from behind."

His brows gathered. He could be a model. He didn't need to attack innocent women if he was struggling financially. This guy was far better looking than some of the models in the popular magazine that she worked for.

"I didn't grab you from behind. I tapped your shoulder... Are you Kaitlyn's friend?"

Josie swallowed hard. "Are you... Mitch's friend?"

He gave a small nod before glancing back down at the pepper spray still primed at his face.

"Don't you know you're not supposed to touch strangers without a proper greeting?" she asked, shoving her can into her luggage. "That'll get you killed in some places."

"And evidently blinded here," he muttered, rolling out his shoulders. "No good deed goes unpunished."

Josie cringed. "I'm sorry. I just... I was expecting you

to be holding a sign and standing over there." She gestured toward the small group of people along the wall.

The man followed her gaze. "Okay. Any other expectations I should know about?" he asked, looking back at her. "Because I happen to like my eyes. I prefer to keep them."

She kind of liked his eyes too. And his face. His skin was a perfect bronze color, which, coupled with his high cheekbones, made her suspect that he had American Indian heritage. "Um, no. Well, yes. I guess we should make proper introductions since we'll be spending the next forty-five minutes in your vehicle together." She held out her hand. "I'm Josie Kellum. Aka Kaitlyn's friend."

He took her hand, and a shock wave of warm tingles slid up her fingers and down her spine. "Tuck Locklear. Mitch's friend." He looked down at her luggage. "I'd like to help you with your bags, if that's okay."

Her cheeks flared hot. "Um, yes. That would be great. Thank you."

Way to go, Josie. She tended to get a little high-strung after pulling several late-nighters in a row. It was a combination of not enough sleep, too much caffeine, and too little human interaction. She'd needed to finish up edits on a few articles before this trip though. That way she could relax a little bit and let her hair down, so to speak. There was also her overactive imagination, a hazard of being a writer, that had made her leap from an uninvited touch to the assumption that she was being mugged.

Tuck led her to a blue Jeep Wrangler Sahara in the parking lot and loaded her luggage into the back while she climbed into the passenger seat, where a large chocolate Lab lifted her head from the floorboard behind her.

"Oh, hi there. And who are you?" she asked, turning to pet the dog's head.

Tuck climbed into the driver's seat. "This is Shadow," he told her before addressing the dog. "Lie down."

Shadow looked at Josie once more and then did as Tuck asked.

Josie noticed the dog's harness read THERAPY DOG in large block letters. She wondered why Tuck needed one, but considering they'd only just met and she'd already tried to single-handedly blind him, it was probably best not to pry. "Thank you again for picking me up," she said, facing forward and pulling on her seat belt.

"It's not a problem."

She waited for him to say more. When he didn't, she filled the silence with the next obvious question. "So, what do you do?"

"Do?" He glanced over.

"For a living. I'm the executive editor for the lifestyle section of *Loving Life* magazine."

Work was always her crutch in social situations. Other people tended to tell tales of their latest vacation. Or they whipped out pictures of their significant other or their pair of angelic-looking kids. Some even had cute, far too-spoiled dogs that they showed off proudly on their cell phones. Everyone had someone, even Lisa Loner, the woman who'd been dubbed the office's wallflower. Just last week, Josie had been cornered by Lisa in the hall while going for her third cup of coffee. Lisa had been bubbling with excitement to show off her new engagement ring and tell the dramatic story of how the guy she'd just met had proposed.

Even though Josie was skeptical of the whirlwind relationship, she also found herself feeling a void in some way. She'd chosen her career over chasing dreams of romance and a family of her own. A successful career is what she'd always wanted but somehow, lately, it didn't seem to be enough.

"I *do* physical therapy," Tuck said.

"Oh." Josie looked over, trying to fit her driver into the mold of all the physical therapists she'd met before. Most of them were clean-cut ex-jocks wearing khakis and polo shirts. Although handsome, Tuck had hair that scraped along the tops of his shoulders and his muscles were lean rather than bulky. He wore a relaxed pair of jeans and a gray T-shirt. "Kaitlyn said you come this way often. Do you work at a hospital nearby?" she asked.

"There you go with those expectations again." A smile lifted his defined cheeks. "No, I see patients in the wild, meaning at their homes, out in public, and sometimes literally in the woods. It's more natural than using exercise machines in an air-conditioned building with a TV mounted on the wall."

"Sounds interesting," she said, keeping to herself the fact that, if she were a patient, she'd prefer the machines and daytime television.

"Shadow is my partner. She works alongside me most of the time."

Hearing her name, the Lab lifted her head once more.

Josie was about to pet her but then pulled her hand away. She'd written an article on canine-assisted therapy once. There were rules about socializing with the dogs.

"It's okay," Tuck said. "Shadow isn't working right now."

"Oh. Good." Josie moved her hand and petted the top of Shadow's head. She was soft and leaned into Josie's touch. "What a good girl you are." Even though the dog wasn't working right now, Josie felt herself immediately relax.

Then her cell phone dinged loudly from her purse. She faced forward, pulled the phone out, and checked the caller ID. Her stress level immediately jumped right back up—both because work was a major stressor these days and because she'd taken that moment to glance out her window at the steep drop of the mountainside.

She turned away from the window only to lay eyes on her driver, which spiked her blood pressure for a whole different reason.

* * *

Tuck knew the type. Work obsessed, self-absorbed, and judging by her luggage and fancy leather purse, materialistic.

Not *his* type.

He listened as Josie talked on the phone, suddenly sounding firm and a tad bossy. His own phone vibrated in the middle console. He shifted his gaze for just a second as he navigated down the mountain. Sweetwater Springs was only another ten miles away, and he couldn't get his passenger to her destination soon enough.

Tuck recognized the number on his caller ID as the same one that had called earlier in the day. A Beverly Sanders had left a message asking him to call her back. He hadn't yet. He wondered if the woman was a prospective patient. If so, she should've called his office number. He had a secretary that he shared with the local home-health occupational and speech therapists in Sweetwater Springs. Only current patients got his cell number, and only to use during emergencies.

After a moment, his phone dinged with another voice-mail. He'd check it later. Right now, his passenger was still talking on her own phone.

"All right, Dana. Yeah. I'll take care of it...I know I'm on vacation but this can't wait. Uh-huh. Bye." Josie clicked a button on her phone and placed it on her lap.

From the corner of his eye, Tuck caught her looking at him. She opened her mouth to speak. *Can't we just ride in silence the rest of the way?*

"So, Kaitlyn and Mitch are happy, huh?" she said.

Tuck gave a small nod. "Mitch is happier than I've seen him in a long time." And Mitch deserved it after all his years of running from the ghosts of his past. Tuck, on the other hand, was faced with his late wife's ghost every day. Even now, after moving to a new home on Blueberry Creek last winter, Renee seemed to be everywhere.

His fingers gripped the steering wheel tightly as he refocused on Josie.

"Kaitlyn seems happy too," she said. "I miss her back home in New York. We used to have lunch together at least once a week."

Tuck guessed that Josie had to schedule those lunch dates in her calendar. She probably had to schedule her showers too.

And he shouldn't be thinking about her in the shower. While they might not have clicked personality-wise, her looks hadn't gone unnoticed. Although a widower, he was still a red-blooded male who hadn't had sex in over two years. Josie had long, blond hair that was pulled back in a tight ponytail at her nape. Her skin was smooth and creamy. When she'd captured his attention with a can of pepper spray primed at his face, he'd stared at her long enough to see that her eyes were almost a turquoise blue.

Her phone made a ridiculous, high-pitched meow from her lap.

Shadow stood at attention in the back seat and gave a soft *woof*.

"Sorry. That's just a text message alert," she told Shadow. "I don't have any cats stowed away with me—I promise." She read the text and started laughing to herself.

In contrast to the meow, this was a pleasant sound. Tuck caught himself smiling for a moment.

Then Josie's phone meowed again. And again. It continued to meow while her fingers tapped along the screen rapidly in response until he turned his Jeep onto Mistletoe Lane where the Sweetwater Bed and Breakfast was located.

He pulled into the driveway of the two-story Victorian house that his friend Mitch and his fiancée, Kaitlyn, had inherited last October and parked. "This is it."

"Wow." Josie stared out his windshield at the inn for a moment. "I can't believe Kaitlyn owns this place. It's amazing."

"You should see the inside. She's a talented interior designer."

Josie turned to him. "She's the best at everything she does, including being a friend."

The warmth in her voice and her eyes intrigued him. Maybe there was more to her than fancy clothes and luggage. Not that it mattered.

Tuck looked away to keep from staring. "I'll, uh, get your bags and help you in." He hopped out and walked around to the back of the Jeep.

Josie was standing beside him before he knew it with her laptop bag thrown over her shoulder along with that expensive-looking purse. "I got it," she said. "Thanks again for the ride."

Without waiting for him to respond, she grabbed the handle of her luggage from his hand and smiled up at him. Fresh faced and beautiful. She didn't wear a lot of makeup, which was a quality he liked about a woman.

"You sure? I don't mind," he said.

"Positive." She held out her other hand.

"What's that?" He looked down at the folded cash in her palm.

"For your troubles."

He lifted his gaze to those turquoise eyes. "I'm not a cabdriver, and it wasn't any trouble."

She tilted her head to one side, revealing the delicious curve where her neck met her shoulder. "I know, but you didn't have to go out of your way for me."

If he couldn't tell by looking at her, this would have given away the fact that she wasn't from around here. People in Sweetwater Springs didn't mind helping each other out. It was one of the things he appreciated about his hometown. He'd seen the stark contrast of other communities when he'd gone away to college, first for his bachelor's degree and then for his doctorate of physical therapy. As far as he knew, there was no other town quite like this one, which was why he was never leaving again.

He pushed her money toward her, his hand sweeping over hers in an unexpected touch. Her skin was soft, and he didn't pull away immediately.

Josie's eyes widened just a fraction, and something buzzed between them. Whatever it was, it was unwelcome.

"Josie, you made it!" Kaitlyn called out as she headed down the porch steps of the house.

Josie turned her attention to Kaitlyn, and both women squealed with delight. Tuck imagined that Shadow was standing at alert in the back seat again, his cue to get back in the Jeep and leave.

"Thank you, Tuck!" Kaitlyn called.

"No problem." He waved and quickly shut the door behind him, barring any further encounters he might have with Josie. Besides, he was running late for dinner with his friend Alex Baker, the police chief in Sweetwater Springs. Before going to the Tipsy Tavern, however, he needed to drop Shadow off at home.

Tuck was almost to his cottage on Blueberry Creek when his phone started to ring. The caller ID showed the same number that had called before. That woman was bent on talking to him tonight. He moved to connect the call and find out why but stopped short when he heard a high-pitched meowing from the passenger seat. It meowed a second time, and Tuck couldn't help grinning. Josie Kellum was undoubtedly losing her mind right about now.

He parked in his driveway and commanded Shadow to follow him into the backyard. Then he returned to his Jeep and wavered only momentarily on which direction to drive. Back to the inn to return Josie's cell phone or to his dinner destination? He couldn't keep the chief of Sweetwater Springs police waiting, now could he?

There was something about Josie Kellum that left him unnerved and restless; he didn't want to see her again tonight. Besides, maybe it would do her good to disconnect from her busy city life for just a while longer.

CHAPTER TWO

*J*osie felt naked.

She never went anywhere without her cell phone, and now she'd been without it for almost three hours. She'd used Kaitlyn's cell phone to call at least a dozen times already with no success. "Where is Tuck and why isn't he answering his phone?"

"He's probably out grabbing a bite with Mitch and Alex," Kaitlyn said, as she pulled various items from her cabinets and fridge. Mr. Darcy, Kaitlyn's golden retriever who lived at the inn, wagged his tail expectantly at her feet, as if hoping that some bread crumb would drop. "Don't worry. As soon as he realizes he has your phone, I'm positive he'll return it."

Josie wasn't so sure about that. She hadn't exactly made the best impression on the man. Maybe he was getting payback for when she'd pulled a can of pepper spray on him. But instead of voicing her concerns, she simply nodded from the kitchen island where Kaitlyn had set her up with a deep glass of red wine—*bless her*—and watched as her friend prepared some kind of delicious pastry that she planned on serving for tomorrow's breakfast.

Josie's stomach grumbled softly. The only thing she'd eaten today was a pack of graham crackers that the flight attendant had handed her. "Speaking of food…"

Kaitlyn glanced over her shoulder. "I thought we'd order pizza tonight if that's okay."

"You don't cook for the guests?"

"Breakfast, yes, but other than some finger foods, they're on their own after that. Most guests go out, which we can do if you'd rather. I figured, after your flight, you might just want to settle in though. We can eat, watch romantic comedies, drink, and catch up. Just like the old days."

Mr. Darcy woofed softly.

"Yes, you can come too," Kaitlyn told the dog with a grin.

The old days had only been last year but it felt like forever ago. Josie missed having her best friend nearby. FaceTime or Skype didn't compare. And watching chick flicks was lonely without Kaitlyn laughing beside her. "Sounds nice."

"Great." Kaitlyn pulled her gaze from the dog back up to Josie. "I'll order the pizza as soon as I get these pastries wrapped and put away in the fridge."

Unlike Kaitlyn, Josie was pretty sure she didn't have any hidden domestic side. Pressing a few buttons on her microwave was as much cooking as she did. And anytime someone handed her a baby, she felt like she could barely breathe.

Josie lifted her glass of wine back to her lips and took a large sip. She was having a great night. There was no reason to spoil it with thoughts of the past. Especially not when Tuck Locklear was doing a fine job putting a damper on it himself. Unable to help herself, she grabbed Kaitlyn's cell phone again and tapped the redial button. She'd already left Tuck several messages but one more wine-induced threat wouldn't hurt.

"Me again. You have my phone, and I *know* that you know. Please bring it back or I will text my phone all night and the meows will haunt you in your sleep."

When Josie clicked End, she looked up at Kaitlyn, whose brows were raised over wide eyes.

"The meows will haunt you in your sleep?" Kaitlyn asked, her mouth twitching in a half grin. Then the two of them burst into laughter, causing Mr. Darcy to run in circles and yap excitedly between them.

"I might have to cut you off early tonight," Kaitlyn remarked when she could breathe again.

This. This is what Josie had missed. Since Kaitlyn had left, her life had become a tad boring. She still had friends and went out but it wasn't the same. She missed having someone to laugh with and talk about everything and nothing at all with.

After finishing off a bottle of wine and a nineties-themed movie marathon, Josie retreated to her room. Every room at the inn was named after a romantic couple from books and movies. The room that Josie was staying in was coincidently themed with one of her favorite Jane Austen novels, *Pride and Prejudice*.

Josie closed the door and lay back on the queen-size bed. Without thinking, she reached inside her pocket for her phone, feeling the phantom vibration that had irritated her all evening. Right. Tuck had never returned her call or her cell phone.

With a frustrated groan, she sat back up and retrieved some sleepwear from her luggage. After washing her face and letting her hair down, she climbed under the rose-print comforter and waited for sleep. It was too quiet for her body to settle down though. In the city, there was a constant buzz of energy, even when you were tucked away in your own little apartment.

Sweetwater Springs didn't have that. Behind these closed doors, she was alone with herself and nothing else. And being alone with herself was just a little too close for comfort.

* * *

Tuck arrived at the Tipsy Tavern to not one but two friends. "Hey, Mitch. Didn't expect to see you here."

Mitch Hargrove had returned to Sweetwater Springs last fall and now worked at the local police department with Chief Alex Baker.

Tuck turned to Alex. "How'd you wrangle Mitch away from Kaitlyn long enough to grab a meal with us?"

"I may have threatened jail time," Alex said, lifting a longneck bottle to his mouth.

They all chuckled as Tuck slid into the booth across from them.

"Kaitlyn is otherwise occupied by her friend Josie tonight," Mitch explained.

"Ah, yes. The princess from up north."

Mitch raised a brow. "I only got to spend a few minutes with her but she seemed nice enough."

"Try a forty-five-minute ride down Mount Pleasant

while she talked and texted on her phone the entire time."

Alex's face scrunched up. "Knowing you, that didn't go too well."

"Not especially." Tuck hadn't gotten a cell phone for himself until his wife, Renee, had gotten sick. He'd needed to be reached quickly in case of an emergency. Before that, any messages could wait until he got back to his office or home. He wasn't a fan of this age of immediate information. And watching people walk across the street with their gazes pinned to their screens was infuriating, even if it did account for at least some of his physical therapy business.

"That's a shame," Mitch said. "I was thinking we might enlist you to take Josie out on the town one night. She's beautiful, and you, my friend, have been celibate too long."

"Beauty doesn't make the woman," Tuck pointed out. "I've known far too many women who were nice to look at but I wouldn't want to spend any amount of time with them." Renee had been one of the exceptions. She had it all. Beauty, depth of character, and a kind heart.

"He's right," Alex agreed, taking a sip of his drink. "I can vouch for that truth."

Mitch shook his head. "I don't think so in this case. Kaitlyn wouldn't have a friend that wasn't also a good person. You two just got off on the wrong foot—that's all."

Tuck considered this. He'd seen a shimmer of something surprising when Josie had spoken about Kaitlyn. She'd been warm, sincere. And that smile of hers when she'd looked at him . . . yeah. Maybe there was more to her than what met the eye. "She's only here for a week, right?"

Mitch nodded. "Which makes that perfect if you're just looking for a casual hookup."

Tuck lifted his brows.

"I'm just saying it's been a while," Mitch said.

Tuck was just about to respond when a waitress stepped up and took their orders. Afterward, they fell back into easy conversation that thankfully didn't return to Josie. He didn't want to talk about his sex life, or lack thereof, or admit to the guys that he was holding Josie's phone hostage, which seemed both immature and completely unlike him. But he'd already gone out of his way for her today.

Ten minutes later, the waitress arrived with their burgers and fries and slid a plate in front of each of them.

When she was gone, Alex looked at Tuck. "So how's the new place working out?"

Tuck twirled one of his sweet potato fries in a dab of ketchup. "Good. A little big for one man." At least in comparison to the home he'd shared with Renee, which had seemed to be closing in around him since her death. "I'm considering renting out the room above the garage. It's just more space than I know what to do with." He reached for his glass of water and took a sip. "Then again, I like the peace and quiet of Hope Cottage. I'm not sure I want to disturb that by becoming someone's landlord."

"That's the nice part about the B and B," Mitch offered. "It's just for a couple of nights and then the guests leave. If you get someone who's rude or loud or plain unbearable"—he shrugged—"it's not much of a commitment. Renting a room long-term, however, could be miserable if you get the wrong tenant."

Alex lifted his brows with a slight nod. "Just ask Simon Griffin. I had to remove his renter by force last week because he wasn't paying. And the place looked like it hadn't been cleaned since the tenant moved in three years ago."

Tuck's mouth puckered as if a lemon slice had been shoved in. "That's terrible."

"And it's not that uncommon." Alex sandwiched his burger between his hands and took a bite.

Tuck took a bite out of his own burger, reconsidering wanting to do something with his garage apartment after all. He didn't have the time or energy for any kind of drama right now. He was finally in a place where he was enjoying life again. He loved his work, his home, and his dog. Adding a few horses to the stables out back would make things just about perfect.

After their meal, all the men said their goodbyes, and Tuck got into his Jeep to drive home. Shadow was likely ready to go outside again, and Tuck couldn't wait to lie on the couch and finish the murder mystery he'd been reading for the last couple of days.

When he pulled into his pebbled driveway, he grabbed his cell phone from the console and saw that he had five missed calls with voicemails. He listened to them one by one while he opened the back door of his house and watched Shadow dart out into the darkness. He didn't have a fence but she was an obedient dog. One command would send her sprinting back in his direction.

The message that Beverly Sanders had left earlier when he'd been driving Josie from the airport played first.

"Hi, Mr. Locklear. This is Beverly Sanders again. I called yesterday and asked you to contact me. You don't know me but I would really like to talk to you."

He'd call her first thing tomorrow, he decided.

The next voicemail played.

"Me again. You have my phone and I *know* that you know. Please bring it back or I will text my phone all night and the meows will haunt you in your sleep."

This pulled an unexpected laugh out of him, a sound that sent Shadow running back in his direction. He let her inside, and then he locked the door, making a mental note to turn the volume off on Josie's cell phone tonight.

* * *

Josie inhaled deeply as she set out on the walking trails behind the B&B. *Wow.* If she could bottle up this fresh mountain air stuff, she could make enough income to quit her job. Then she wouldn't have to tolerate her new boss and his horrid article ideas.

She was a serious journalist. She wrote things that mattered. Since Bart had taken over *Loving Life* magazine, he'd been pressuring her to write trash.

Josie continued forward, following the cutesy signs staked in the ground that pointed the way. She'd only been in town for twenty-four hours, and she was already going slightly stir-crazy. Kaitlyn seemed to be in her element though. By the time Josie had climbed out of bed this morning, Kaitlyn had a full breakfast spread on one of the dining room tables. The other guests were chatting and making nice, and for a moment, Josie had felt this warmness spreading through her like the hot molasses on her stack of pancakes. That had quickly passed, however, when the cozy conversation at one of the tables had turned to her, the only single person in the room.

"Do you have someone special in your life, dear?" a woman in her mid to late sixties had asked.

The question didn't used to bother Josie so much. She

was proud of her career at a well-known magazine. Or she had been until Bart took over.

Josie picked up her pace now, forcing herself to soak in her surroundings. The tall pines with their sappy scent. The chill of the spring air. Mountains towering in the distance. She was walking in a postcard right now. The article she'd written about Sweetwater Springs being a romantic holiday retreat last December hadn't been a fabrication by any measure. This was a beautiful town. She could only imagine what a wonderful place it would be to spend Christmas and New Year's.

Bart had suggested titling the follow-up article that Josie wanted to write "Sex in the Sticks." He'd clarified that she didn't actually have to have sex. Nice of him, considering having sex wasn't part of her job description.

A bird fluttered by. She stopped in midstride to watch. Its feathers were a perfect blend of purple and pink, like a ripened raspberry. Josie had never seen a bird quite like this in the wild or otherwise. Not that she spent much time outdoors.

"Beautiful," she whispered, finding herself following it off the path. The bird dipped between trees, almost as if it were teasing her, luring her to whatever secret place it was going. Hopefully not into a lion's den.

No, there aren't lions in the North Carolina mountains. But there were definitely bears.

Her breath seized in her chest, and her feet froze. Perhaps following a bird off the path wasn't such a great idea. Her gaze stayed on the vividly colored creature until it fluttered out of sight. Then she turned to head back to the trail.

As she did, her foot caught on a knobby root that poked out of the soft ground, and her body went flying forward.

Her right knee hit another hard root in the ground, taking the brunt of the fall. Then the rest of her body followed, making a forceful impact that shot the air right out of her lungs. She struggled to breathe for a moment as her world shifted and settled.

Birds tweeted in the tree limbs above, and it occurred to her that they might be laughing at the spectacle she'd just made of herself. Thankfully, no human was around to witness it.

"Ouch," she finally muttered. Her body was already aching three seconds after falling so this didn't look good for the rest of her day.

She reached for her phone to call for help, and then, adding insult to injury, she realized she didn't have her phone, thanks to Tuck. She was beginning to think she would've been better off hitchhiking down the mountain than accepting his ride into Sweetwater Springs yesterday.

This trip was supposed to be relaxing, and some parts had been so far. She and Kaitlyn had chatted and watched a couple of movies last night, and they'd gotten more time to catch up after breakfast. But now Josie had reached her limit being unplugged. She needed her phone back, and once she found Tuck, she intended to give him a piece of her mind.

Josie sat up on her bottom, feeling pain spark behind her right knee. She pulled her leg in front of her to take a better look. A bright purple bruise was already forming around her inner knee, reminding her of when she'd taken a bad spill on the track in high school.

This isn't good.

She looked up at the path ahead. How was she supposed to walk back to the B&B like this?

Glancing around, she found a stick that she could use as a cane. It was thick enough to hold her weight and long enough so that she didn't have to hunch. She moaned and squeaked in pain as she unfolded her body to stand. She took one baby step forward and heard the stick crack under her. Her arms flew out as she toppled side to side, desperately trying to stay upright on one good leg. After a moment, she placed just the big toe of her right foot down to balance. Instantaneous pain rocketed up through her knee and settled in her forehead.

She stared down the path. How far had she gone? Maybe a mile. She'd seen those shows on TV where people got lost in the woods. There was a slew of things that could happen from this point on, and none of them were on her to-do list for this minivacation.

There was no way she was going to be able to walk back so she'd just...scoot along on her butt like a crab. It would be dirty and more than a little embarrassing if Kaitlyn or any of the guests saw her. She'd just stop scooting and yell for help once she was close enough to the inn for people to hear her, she decided. *Yeah.*

They didn't call her the queen of good ideas for nothing. Actually, Kaitlyn was the only one who called her that, but it was true. In times of stress, Josie was the one who could find a solution, and considering her limited options right now, lowering to her bottom and dragging herself back to the inn was her only choice.

CHAPTER THREE

There were two items that Tuck had been avoiding all morning, and he was about to check them off in quick succession. Call Beverly Sanders back and see why she wanted to talk to him, and return Josie's phone, which was now dead.

He climbed into his Jeep and glanced over at Shadow in the passenger seat, giving her a gentle pat on the head. Seeing that she was secure, he backed out of his driveway and headed toward Mistletoe Lane and the Sweetwater B&B. He'd already pulled up Beverly Sander's contact information and only needed to tap Dial as he drove.

As he listened to the phone ring, he readied his greeting. The call went straight to voicemail. *Even better.*

"Hi. This is Tuck Locklear returning your call. I'll be home after five o'clock this evening if you would like to talk to me then. Have a nice day."

He disconnected the call and enjoyed the remainder of

the quiet drive. As he pulled into the driveway of the inn, an uneasiness spread through his gut and chest. Perhaps he should've swung by before his first appointment this morning.

He checked the watch he wore on his wrist. It was just after noon. Maybe he'd taken this little irritation too far.

"Tuck!" Kaitlyn said when she opened the door with her young golden retriever at her side. Mitch had brought the dog to Tuck's place for a sort of playdate with Shadow a few weeks ago.

The pup brushed against his jeans, no doubt leaving behind a scent that would leave Shadow restless all day. Tuck dipped to pat the pup's head and then returned to standing. He faced Kaitlyn, whose smile had now twisted into a stern line.

"I told Josie to give you the benefit of the doubt, that you didn't realize you still had her phone."

"Pleading the Fifth," Tuck muttered. He pulled at the thin silver chain he wore around his neck as if it were suddenly choking him, even though he'd been wearing it since his grandfather had given it to him as a child. The circular pendant held an engraved image of a bear, reminding him of his character—temporarily derailed by his beautiful passenger yesterday. Releasing the chain, he pulled Josie's phone out of his pocket. "Will you return this to her, please?" If he was lucky, he could sprint back to his Jeep and avoid any altercation.

"Actually, I need your help. Josie went for a walk on the trails out back over an hour ago and hasn't returned. I'm starting to get a little worried about her."

Tuck stiffened.

"Mitch is working at the police station, and Gina is out doing errands this morning." Gina was Mitch's mom, and she helped run the bed and breakfast. "I'm all alone here so I can't really leave the guests. Mr. Cooper is on oxygen, and he keeps trying to light up a cigarette. I'm afraid he'll burn down the inn when I'm not looking."

"You want me to look for Josie on the trails?" Tuck asked. He was never one to turn down a request for help but his mind was thinking in sonic speed about a way to say no to this one.

"Please," Kaitlyn said. "I walk the trails every afternoon, and it shouldn't take more than an hour. The path is clearly marked so I can't imagine she veered off."

"Maybe she's just nature-watching," he suggested.

Kaitlyn frowned. "Josie doesn't nature-watch."

Tuck's mom, who educated the community and anyone who'd listen on the Cherokee culture, would call this justice. She always taught him that good deeds were rewarded and that the bad were punished. Having to meet a woman scorned on a beaten path alone was some form of karma.

Tuck massaged his forehead and then reluctantly agreed. "Let me grab Shadow from the vehicle. She'd probably love to take a hike anyway."

"Thank you so much. I'm sure Josie is fine, but…"

"But she's new here and doesn't have a phone." He shoved Josie's cell phone back into his pocket. He'd grab his own from the Jeep's console just in case.

A couple of minutes later, with Shadow at his side, he set off behind the Sweetwater B&B. It was a beautiful March day. From the hiking trail that Kaitlyn and Mitch had added here, one could appreciate nature at its finest. And from various breaks in the trees, Mount Pleasant could be seen reaching up into the low-hanging clouds. Maybe he should start using this trail for some of his physical therapy patients. He had his own path along Blueberry Creek but he'd found that a variety of environments made for good distraction when someone was in physical pain. He'd talk to Kaitlyn and Mitch about it later.

But first, he needed to find the city princess.

After another ten minutes or so, Shadow paused, probably sensing a squirrel or rabbit, and then took off running around the next bend. Tuck kept his pace steady until he heard a woman's shriek. Breaking into a jog, he stopped short of a disheveled Josie on the ground. Judging by the markings on the dirt path behind her, she was dragging herself.

She looked up with a dirt-smudged face and a fiery glint in her blue eyes. "You!"

Shadow, always eager to help, nudged her damp nose to Josie's cheek, the equivalent of a canine kiss. Josie pushed the dog away from her face and then grimaced.

"Are you hurt?" He'd tried not to notice her soft curves yesterday but now it was unavoidable as he scanned her body for the source of her pain. These were the mountains. It was only March so he doubted she would've been bit by a rattlesnake, but there were other critters that could've snapped at her flesh.

She was wearing shorts that stopped midthigh, giving him a delicious view of her toned legs. There was no question she worked out in some way or another. Guessing by the shape of her calves, she was a runner.

"It's my knee," she huffed, pulling her right leg out in front of her. "I tripped on one of the tree roots out here."

Tuck closed the distance and squatted in front of her to get a better look. He gently touched the flesh along the inner kneecap.

She clutched the back of her thigh. "Ow!"

"You'll need to take a trip to see Dr. Miles to make sure you haven't torn any ligaments. He's a good doctor. I work with him a lot." Tuck looked around. "I'm surprised the path had any roots. It seems pretty smooth out here."

Josie averted her gaze. "I might have stepped off the path."

"You what? Didn't you see the signs telling you not to? You could've gotten attacked by a wild animal or gotten lost out here. There are stories of people vanishing out in the mountain forest, you know?" Although every time Tuck heard those stories, he'd wondered if the lost people just didn't want to be found. On occasion, he'd thought to himself how wonderful it would be to disappear from the world himself. He had survival skills though, and he seriously doubted that Josie did.

"If I had gotten lost, I'd just call someone," she said, her expression now tight with more than just pain. "Oh, wait. I couldn't because *someone* stole my phone."

Tuck sighed dejectedly. "I didn't steal your phone. You left it in my Jeep. And it wouldn't have done you any good out here anyway. I doubt there's reception." He pulled her cell phone from his pocket and handed it over.

When she took it, she tapped the screen quickly and then huffed. "We'll never know because it's dead."

"Of course it is. It meowed with your incoming text messages to me all night." Tuck took that moment to straighten and return to his feet, just in case Josie decided to attack him like a feral animal.

"Not all night," Josie objected. "Kaitlyn took her phone with her to bed."

He laughed and then asked, "Can you walk?"

"If I could walk, would I have been scooting on the ground?"

Tuck massaged one side of his temple. He was going to have to carry her the half mile back to the inn. That presented all kinds of problems. He doubted she was heavy, but he was attracted to her, even if he didn't want to be. And she smelled like a field of honeysuckle. Holding her close wasn't a good idea, and he suspected she'd hate the suggestion as much as he did.

"Why are you staring at me like that?" she asked, narrowing her eyes.

He hadn't realized he was. "I have to get you back down the trail. If you can't walk, then I'll need to do it another way."

Josie seemed to process this. "Don't Mitch and Kaitlyn have a golf cart or something you can use to come pick me up?"

He resisted explaining to the city princess that this wasn't a golf course. "No. And they don't have a horse and carriage either. My Jeep won't fit down these trails so it looks like I'll have to carry you."

"Carry me?" Her eyes widened, and her pretty pink mouth popped open. "No, no, no, no. I'll walk."

"You just said you can't."

"I was mistaken. *Can't* isn't in my vocabulary." She shifted around, grimacing and squeaking in pain until she was on her feet. At least she was wearing sneakers. The pallor of her skin told him there was no way this woman was going to make it down that path without him though, no matter how determined she was.

Not waiting for her to come to her senses, he grabbed her arm and draped it around his shoulder, pulling her body flush against his side as she stood. A buzz of awareness came alive in his stomach, like a beehive disturbed.

"What are you doing?"

"Helping you. Again."

"I don't need—" She stopped talking when he turned and leveled her with a look. Their faces were so close that it would have been all too easy to find a different method to silence her. Without thinking, his gaze dropped to her deep-pink lips. Did she taste as sweet as she smelled?

He quickly looked away. Mitch was right. He'd been celibate too long. Long enough to be at risk for making a paramount mistake—because that's exactly what kissing Josie would be.

* * *

This must be what natural childbirth feels like.

Josie had been walking for nearly half a mile, doing her best not to limp and make unattractive noises every time her right foot went down.

Instead, she was distracting herself by stealing glances to the side and admiring Tuck's profile. His silky black hair was pulled back today, making a short ponytail. And there was no doubt about it—a man with a ponytail was hot.

"I thought you said we were only half a mile away," she said in a strained voice.

"We were. We're almost there. See?" He pointed at a bend in the path. "Once we round that corner, we'll be able to see the B and B."

If she weren't in so much pain, she might have jumped for joy. Instead, she felt like collapsing. For a moment, that's what she thought was happening when her body was swept up in Tuck's arms and secured against his chest. He was gentle, keeping one arm under her knee to keep it extended.

Shadow woofed from the ground below.

Josie looked up at Tuck, whose face was only inches from hers. At this distance, she could peer into the depths of his eyes. There were splinters of light brown softening the deep-cocoa color.

"You were starting to lean into that knee," he explained. "I don't want you to make it worse."

"Oh. Thank you." She hesitated on her next comment because she was still upset with him about her phone. "And I'm sorry," she finally said. "You must have things to be doing right now other than rescuing me."

"It's okay. I'll call my patients once I get you settled inside and let them know I'm running late."

Patients. Guilt flooded through her. She hadn't even considered that he might be missing work because of her. "I saw a bird," she heard herself say.

His gaze lowered to hers, and at this distance, just a look felt strangely intimate for two people who barely knew each other.

He lifted a brow without saying anything.

"It was pink and purple. Gorgeous," she said. *Why am I so nervous all of a sudden?* "That's why I stepped off the path. I've never seen a bird like that one."

"A purple finch," he said.

"Oh." Some part of her had thought the bird was one of a kind. That no one would believe her when she said she'd seen a brightly colored, magical little bird. Now she felt a bit silly. "So, there are lots around here?"

He nodded. "There are a lot of great birds around here if you want to take up bird-watching."

Take up bird-watching. There was an idea for a future article. She'd likely have to head off into the country to find a multitude of birds though, and who had time for that?

"Here we are," Tuck said.

Josie blinked the bed and breakfast into focus and smiled.

"We need to get your leg up and put some ice on that knee. Hopefully Kaitlyn has some NSAIDs."

"NSAIDs?"

"Aspirin or ibuprofen. If not, I'll go get you some from the first-aid pack I keep in my Jeep."

Kaitlyn flew out the back door when they were only a few feet away. "What happened?" she asked, searching Josie frantically. "Why are you carrying her?" she asked Tuck.

Instead of immediately responding, Tuck walked past Kaitlyn into the living area of the inn and then gently placed Josie on the couch.

Both relief and disappointment swam through her. Josie had gotten quite cozy in Tuck's strong embrace.

Josie looked past Tuck at Kaitlyn. "I'm fine. I just tripped and busted my knee."

Kaitlyn gasped. "Did you step off the path?"

"She was following a bird," Tuck said, one corner of his mouth drawing up in a half grin.

"A very pretty bird," Josie defended, but the corners of her mouth pulled up as well.

"Oh, there are some great birds down here." Kaitlyn grabbed a couple of pillows and helped Josie position them behind her head. "The bluebirds are my favorite."

"You've only been here a few months, and you're already one with nature?" Josie asked teasingly.

"I put out bird feeders so the guests can watch them. I have a book that tells you what they are, if you're interested."

Tuck had walked out of the room. He reappeared now

with a glass of water and two white pills. "Here." He handed her the water and medication. Then he sat on the edge of the couch and gently felt around her kneecap.

Josie gritted her teeth, even though he was gentle. "You're good with your hands," she found herself saying. "But I'm not flirting, just pointing it out."

Those brown eyes of his seemed to dance as he looked up at her. "You need to get checked out by Dr. Miles. It looks like more than a contusion to me. Are you able to take her?" he asked Kaitlyn.

She shook her head. "Gina went grocery shopping. She won't be back for at least an hour. Can it wait?"

"You guys, this is silly. I don't need a doctor," Josie said, even though her knee begged to differ.

"I'll take you myself," he told Josie and then turned back to Kaitlyn. "Can Shadow stay here with Mr. Darcy?"

"Of course. Mr. Darcy has been needing another playdate. I'm sure the guests would love an extra dog to love as well."

Tuck pulled his cell phone out of his pocket. "Great. I just need to cancel the rest of my appointments for the morning and then we can go. I'll call Dr. Miles and let him know we're coming."

Josie inwardly grimaced. She hated for Tuck to cancel his work on her behalf but what choice did she have? She was out of her element here in the North Carolina mountains, in more ways than one.

* * *

Tuck had been sitting in the waiting room of Dr. Miles's office for almost an hour. Going into an examination room with Josie had felt a little too personal for two people who only just met yesterday. Then again, he'd already held her in his arms, memorized her smell, and was having fantasies about the feisty city princess.

The waiting room door opened, and Josie hobbled clumsily out with a bulky air splint around her right knee. Dr. Miles followed behind her and smiled at Tuck.

Tuck rose to his feet. "How is it?" he asked Josie, knowing Dr. Miles couldn't tell him directly because of patient confidentiality laws.

She sighed. "I sprained my knee. Not bad. Dr. Miles says rest and ice should do the trick."

Relief flooded through Tuck on her behalf. Josie didn't seem like a woman who liked to slow down, which is exactly what a more serious injury would've done.

"It's just a grade one sprain of the medial collateral ligament," Dr. Miles confirmed. "I expect, as long as you take it easy, Josie, your knee will be as good as new in a week's time. Use the crutches today. After that, the knee brace I've given you should be sufficient."

Tuck took a closer look at the brace encasing her joint.

"I'm also prescribing physical therapy to teach Josie some strengthening and stability exercises that she can do on her own to tighten up that MCL. Do you know any good PTs?" he asked Tuck.

Tuck looked up. "Not in New York I don't."

"Josie says she's staying for a week. She only needs a couple sessions to get her started," Dr. Miles said. He handed Tuck a prescription with "Physical therapy" scrawled in classic doctor's handwriting. Tuck swore that doctors took a medical school course on the fine art of barely legible script.

"Tuck is the best PT in town, if you ask me," Dr. Miles told Josie, who was leaning heavily onto her crutches.

She was no doubt tired and needed to go back to the inn and rest.

Josie looked at Tuck. "I'm not sure if he has room in his busy schedule," she told the doctor.

"I can fit you in," Tuck answered with a small nod.

"Oh, good." Dr. Miles turned to Josie and patted her back softly. "You're in good hands."

That was part of Tuck's hesitation. His hands were itching to get hold of Josie's curves, and now he had doctor's orders to do so.

After helping her to his Jeep, he got behind the wheel and started driving back to the inn.

"I've been a huge inconvenience to you since I got here," she said after a few minutes. "If you want to back out of therapy, I understand."

He glanced over and saw vulnerability flash in her eyes. It surprised him that she cared about messing up his schedule or making him go out of his way. Perhaps he'd misjudged her based on a false first impression. Granted, she'd pulled a can of pepper spray on him. "It's okay. And Dr. Miles is right. You need to learn some stability exercises to keep you from injuring it further. I just discharged a patient on my caseload so I have a spot for you in the mornings this week. I'll swing by, and we'll get started tomorrow. How does that sound?"

"Great. Thank you."

He saw her shake her head from his peripheral vision.

"I just can't believe this is happening. It was so stupid to follow that bird," she said.

Tuck laughed softly. "Next time, follow the signs."

"I promise. I guess this'll keep me from my daily jogs, won't it?"

"I'd stick to walking for the time being," Tuck advised. "And keep your bird-watching strictly on the trail."

Josie laughed. The sound made him glance over just in time to see her lips part and her head tip slightly back, elongating her neck.

His heart thumped to life at the sight of her. The tight ponytail she'd had earlier was loose from her struggle on the trail and her visit to see Dr. Miles. For a moment, Tuck imagined pulling the tie away and letting her hair spill over her shoulders. Then kissing that neck of hers until she forgot all about the pain in her knee.

He turned into the driveway of the Sweetwater Bed and Breakfast, hot and bothered. He needed to go for a walk himself tonight He got out of the Jeep, retrieved Josie's crutches, and helped her make her way back inside to the couch.

"Mitch can help her get upstairs to her room tonight," Kaitlyn told Tuck. "Thank you so much. Why don't you come to breakfast tomorrow before Josie's appointment? It's the least I can do to thank you for taking such good care of my best friend."

"I'll take a rain check on that," he said. "I have a patient at seven a.m."

"That's so early," Josie said from the couch.

"I'll be heading here after that," he told her. "Be up and ready to work. Until then, keep it iced and elevated on a pillow."

"Got it."

Kaitlyn walked him and Shadow to the door and showed them out. As Tuck got into his vehicle and settled Shadow in the passenger seat, he found himself dreading tomorrow's appointment with Josie almost as much as he was looking forward to it.

* * *

Later that evening, Tuck grabbed some meat from the fridge and carried it to the grill on his back deck. He'd been waiting all afternoon to sit out here with his perfect view and grill a steak. Then he and Shadow would play a little fetch, watch the sunset, and go to bed—his idea of a perfect day.

His cell phone buzzed as he lit the charcoal. It was Beverly Sanders's number again. Time to unravel this mystery of why she seemed so intent on getting hold of him.

"Hello," he said, focusing his gaze on the horizon.

"Hi, is this Tuck Locklear?"

"That's me."

"This is Beverly Sanders," she said. "I got your contact information from an acquaintance and was hoping that you could help me." She was interrupted by a cough that seemed to carry on for a solid minute. "I'm sorry," she finally said. "I'm afraid I've been quite sick these days."

"I'm sorry to hear that."

"Thank you. My eleven-year-old granddaughter, Maddie, was in a car accident with her mother last fall. Her mother, my daughter, died, and Maddie was injured very badly."

Tuck walked to a nearby chair and dropped down in it. "I'm so sorry, Ms. Sanders."

"Please call me Beverly. And thank you." She paused. "Maddie broke her collarbone and right leg in several places. She stopped seeing her first physical therapist soon after the accident. She refused to go to her appointments. If she doesn't start back up, her doctor says that she might cause herself further damage. I was hoping you would agree to work with her."

Tuck stared out at his backyard. "I'll need to have access to her files."

"Of course. I have copies of everything," the grandmother said eagerly.

He absently pulled at the chain around his neck, fidgeting with its charm. "I can't make any promises but I'll do what I can. She might not work for me either though."

"I think she's ready. Thank you so much," Beverly said.

Tuck enjoyed working with children. He and Renee had always hoped to have two or three of their own. Instead, his wife was gone, and he was here. "You're welcome. I can come to your home for the first visit if you'd like."

"No, I think Maddie would work better for you somewhere else."

"Okay, then you can come to my place. I work with several patients on my personal property. It's right on Blueberry Creek."

"I think Maddie would like that."

They arranged the first appointment and hung up. Then Tuck returned to his grill, thinking about the day and his patients. His mind kept circling back to one patient in particular. It'd been two years since Renee had died, and none of the women he'd dated recently, while nice, had made him feel anything. Josie wasn't at all the kind of woman he usually found himself attracted to. But there was something about her that energized him in a way he hadn't felt in a while. He liked the feeling but he guessed it was as short-lived as her time in Sweetwater Springs.

CHAPTER FOUR

*J*osie had barely touched the delicious breakfast Kaitlyn had prepared this morning in anticipation of this exact moment.

Tuck walked through her bedroom door and pinned her immediately with that dark gaze of his. They were about to have their first physical therapy appointment, and her stomach was a bundle of nerves and butterflies. She'd had physical therapy before but the therapist she'd had in high school had been older and not nearly as cute. Tuck had a Jacob-from-*Twilight* vibe going for him, and she'd always been on Team Jacob.

"Did you sleep well?" he asked.

Josie nodded. She was alone in her bedroom with a man right now. This hadn't happened in ages. She couldn't very well do therapy on the couch downstairs, with the inn's guests rotating in and out. This was the most private place at the B&B but it felt much too intimate.

Her heart pounded, and she felt breathless and a little dizzy as he stepped closer. Maybe it was the pain medicine that Dr. Miles had prescribed but she didn't think so. "Yes, I slept very well, thank you." Except for the wee little fantasy she'd entertained about being with Tuck in this very bed. Why had she let her imagination even go there? Now she was going to have to block the fantasy out of her mind for the next hour. "Did you? Sleep well."

He smiled at her. Forget Team Jacob, she was Team Tuck all the way. She wasn't even upset anymore that he'd kidnapped her cell phone the day before yesterday. "I'm not the one with a knee injury. I slept like a rock."

Josie swallowed. "Right."

"How's the knee? Ready to get it moving?"

"It's sore and no," she said honestly. She'd kept ice on it since yesterday, and every time she'd even moved it slightly, it had throbbed. That was the whole point of the knee brace Dr. Miles had given her, she guessed. To keep it from moving too much.

He grabbed a couple of pillows from the other side of the bed and brought them around. "Here." After guiding her to sit up, he placed the pillows behind her back. Then he sat down on the edge of the bed and pulled her leg into his lap. He grabbed the top edge of her brace and pulled it down. It wasn't like he was pulling down an article of clothing, but still it was strangely sensual.

Josie sat up straighter as he pressed his fingers into the puffy skin around her kneecap. "What are you doing?"

"Palpating your knee."

Her skin came alive under his touch, sending shock waves through her body. She shifted restlessly.

"Does that hurt?" he asked.

"A little."

"You know what they say: no pain, no gain. But don't worry—I'll try to go easy on you."

"I'd appreciate that," she said.

He put a hand under her knee and used his other hand to bend her leg just a little bit.

She flinched, hoping she didn't look like a big baby. Usually, she considered herself to have a high pain tolerance.

"We're just going to hold this stretch for a moment." After a few seconds, he straightened her leg and repeated the process several times. Each time, it was less painful. "This will get the swelling out of the joint," he told her.

"Is there a less painful way to do it?" she asked, trying to keep her breathing under control.

"I'm afraid not. Sorry." He released her leg and stood. "Okay, now I want you to sit on the edge of the bed."

She did as he asked, cringing as her knee bent in an almost ninety-degree angle for a fully seated position.

Tuck sat beside her on the bed again, close enough to where his thigh brushed against hers just slightly. "Watch me." He straightened his knee, lifting one of his legs out in front of him. "We're just going to do a few active knee extensions." He crouched down on the floor and helped her with the first few and then removed his hands as she continued on her own. "Great. That's perfect." He gave her an approving look.

Meeting his eyes did something to her insides. She didn't want to explore what or why. If she was going to be working with this man in such an intimate way, she needed to turn this silly attraction off. A fling on a mini-vacation might be appropriate in some circumstances but not in this one.

He grabbed the knee brace that Dr. Miles had given

her, wrapped it around her joint, and stood. "You ready to stand? I still don't want you putting a lot of weight on your leg today. But moving around your room and to the bathroom is necessary."

He offered his hand to help her stand.

Josie took it, the motion bringing her face-to-face with him. "Hi," she said, not knowing what else to say. He was standing right in front of her with his hands steadying her waist. They were in her bedroom with the door closed; under any other circumstance, making out seemed like the right next step.

"Ow." She bent to grab her throbbing knee.

"You're putting too much weight on it. Here, lean on me," he said, moving to her left side.

They took a few steps, turned around, and walked back to the bed. He kept his hands on her until she was seated again.

"You okay?" he asked.

If she wasn't, she wouldn't tell him. "Yeah. Feeling better already."

He nodded. "I want you doing the seated knee extensions ten times on the hour today. Keep the joint moving. When it's not in motion, keep it iced. Tomorrow, I'm guessing you'll feel a whole lot better."

"Okay," Josie said, fighting her pain and attraction.

"I'll be back in the morning for your next session. Wear something comfortable. We'll be going outside."

"We will?"

"Nature's rehab. I'll bring my binoculars in case we see a bird." He winked. "But we're staying on the path this time."

"Ha-ha," she said sarcastically.

Then someone knocked on the door. "Hey, you two.

How's it going in here?" Kaitlyn asked as she stepped inside.

"We're finished until tomorrow," Tuck told her.

"If you're done, I'll see you out." Kaitlyn led Tuck out of the room like the good hostess she was. Josie listened to their retreating voices and glanced at the brace on her knee. She'd worn something similar when she'd injured her knee in high school. With track and field on hold back then, she'd joined the journalism crew after school, and thus her love for stories had begun. She'd considered the injury an act of fate somehow, leading her in a new direction. That wasn't the case this time. Now it was just a hindrance.

Kaitlyn reappeared in the doorway a few minutes later. "Since we can't walk around downtown like I'd planned, I'm taking you for a brief driving tour. Then we can grab takeout on the way back. Sound good?"

Josie grinned. "Sounds perfect. I want to know everything there is to know about Sweetwater Springs."

Kaitlyn's excitement seemed to funnel out of her. "Wait a minute. That sounds like Journalist Josie talking."

Josie pulled her lower lip between her teeth. "Nothing wrong with a little research while I'm here, right? Readers wanted to know more about Sweetwater Springs so I thought I'd deliver."

Kaitlyn's brows lowered over her narrowed eyes. "But you're supposed to be relaxing and enjoying yourself. I want you to have a good time."

"And I will. But another article means more business for you and your new friends. You can't argue with that, can you?"

Kaitlyn seemed to consider this. "You are impossible, you know that? Carry your little notebook if you must, but it's my duty as your best friend today to show you a good time while you're here."

* * *

"You're almost there," Tuck encouraged Mr. Sajack late that afternoon as they walked to the elderly man's mailbox. After seeing Josie this morning, Tuck had been hiking with a patient with neuropathy, swimming with a man three months out from a rotator cuff surgery, and bicycling with a woman who'd had a total knee replacement a few months ago. All in a day's work.

Daniel Sajack was a below-the-knee amputee. He kept his body upright, just like Tuck had taught him, and continued forward on his prosthetic leg. His breaths came out in labored bursts.

"Gotta breathe, Mr. Sajack," Tuck instructed. "If you turn blue and pass out, then I have to carry you back inside the house. Just five more steps and we can see what's in that mailbox. Who knows? Maybe it's a big check."

Mr. Sajack started laughing, which rocked his balance slightly. Tuck reached out and steadied him. Shadow watched the two men from the grass, waiting where Tuck had ordered her to sit. Tuck didn't want her getting under Mr. Sajack's feet accidentally.

"I don't get big checks anymore," Mr. Sajack spit out. "I get medical bills now. Lots of 'em. If I'd have known it would cost so much to cut my leg off, I'd have done it myself with my grandpa's old pocketknife."

Tuck cringed. Part of him suspected Mr. Sajack was serious. "The hospital allows you to make small payments so don't let it worry you."

"Oh, I know." The older man lifted his prosthesis and

carefully pushed it forward for another step. "I'll be dead before they get a full payment out of me," he said. Then he let out a war cry of sorts as he reached for his mailbox.

Tuck watched satisfaction crawl through his patient's features. "You did it."

"Darn straight. Now open that box up and hand me those big checks you promised."

Tuck chuckled. "I didn't promise anything." He did the honors of opening the mailbox because having Mr. Sajack do so would require him to step on uneven terrain, and his patient wasn't quite ready for that. Tuck grabbed the mail and started thumbing through the envelopes, reading off the senders' names.

Tuck took his time. After all that exercise, this was a small break. For a new amputee, something as mundane as walking to the mailbox was a lot of work. When he was done, Tuck checked his watch. "All right. Let's get you back inside. If you hustle, you'll be there in time to see the five o'clock news."

Mr. Sajack frowned. "I never miss watching Serena Gibbs on the news. You better get me there."

Tuck shrugged. "I'm not picking you up and carrying you." He'd already carried one person this week, and Josie was considerably lighter than his current patient would be. "Let's go."

Fifteen minutes later, Tuck helped Mr. Sajack lower himself to his couch and handed him the remote. "T minus two minutes. I'll get you some water." After handing him a glass, Tuck spoke to Mrs. Sajack for a couple of minutes with Shadow at his side.

Mrs. Sajack offered Shadow a dog biscuit as usual, which Shadow held between her teeth. "Please stay for dinner. I always make too much," Mrs. Sajack insisted.

"Thank you but I can't tonight. I have plans."

The older woman smiled, making wrinkles fold deeply at the corners of her eyes. "All right, then. Another time." She patted Shadow's head and then walked them to the door and thanked Tuck for putting up with her "goat of a husband" one more time.

"Come on, Shadow," Tuck called as he headed down the porch steps toward his Jeep. When he opened the door, his partner in crime jumped into the passenger seat, and Tuck closed her in. Then he got behind the steering wheel and pointed his vehicle toward his sister Halona's flower shop.

* * *

Tuck never tired of walking into Little Shop of Flowers on Main Street. His every sense was accosted. The smell of fresh flowers, the blanket of cool air that kept them looking beautiful, and the explosion of color. Halona always had soft music playing in the background too. If Tuck couldn't be out in nature, this was the next best thing.

"Hey, stranger," Halona said, walking out of the back room. She wore an apron with a fancy rose print. Her long dark-brown hair was pulled back into a low-hanging ponytail, the same as she'd worn it since she was a little girl bugging the heck out of him. "Done for the day?" she asked.

"Just finished working with Mr. Sajack."

"Aw. How is he?" she asked.

"Grumpy as ever."

Halona laughed as she peered at him from behind the counter. "Are you going to the cemetery this afternoon?"

"Planning to."

It was Wednesday, and she knew him all too well. For the past two years, his routine had been to stop in here on the pretense of saying hello and to get a bouquet to bring to Renee's grave.

"Come on back. I'll get an arrangement started for you." She motioned for him to follow her to the back room.

Tuck walked behind the counter where there was a table and chair set up for his nephew, Theo, to play after school. "Where's Theo?" he asked, taking a seat.

"With Mom and Dad. Mom is trying to teach him the Cherokee language." Halona shook her head. "I tried to explain that his first language is English. If he won't even speak that anymore, why would he repeat anything she says in Cherokee?" Halona picked up her shears and started nipping the stems off a handful of flowers.

"No progress yet?" Tuck asked.

Halona blew out a heavy breath. "Not much. Theo is still waking up crying for his dad most nights, and I wouldn't wish that away for anything because that's the only time I hear his sweet little voice."

Tuck's heart felt like someone had given it a swift kick. His nephew had been diagnosed with selective mutism after his father, Ted, died the winter before last. Before Ted's skiing accident, Theo had been a typical boy. The death of his father had shaken him though. It'd been hard on Halona too, even though she and Ted were already divorced when the accident happened. Irreconcilable differences, which Tuck still didn't understand.

"Still taking Theo to counseling?" he asked.

Halona nodded. "I'm not sure it's doing any good. Since Theo doesn't talk, they just build with different types of blocks. Theo seems to enjoy it though, which is why I continue to take him."

"Well, let me know if you need a break. I can watch him one night for you. Give you a chance to sleep without having to get up with him."

Halona looked up from the arrangement that she was quickly pulling together. "Have I told you lately what an amazing brother you are?"

"No, I don't believe so."

"Well, you are. And I might just take you up on that offer. Being a single mom is no joke."

"I'm sure."

Halona narrowed her eyes. "What's going on with you anyway? You have that look."

Tuck raised a brow. "What look?"

"The one that says you have the weight of the world on your shoulders and you're pretending like you don't. You and Theo are a lot alike in that way, you know. You both internalize things. Maybe you should join in on his LEGO sessions. It might help."

Tuck smiled. "I just have a lot on my mind. I have a couple of new patients on my caseload. One is the woman staying at the inn with Kaitlyn Russo."

"Oh? I had heard Kaitlyn's friend from New York was in town. Did she get hurt?"

He nodded. "Yep. And now I'm her physical therapist."

"You make that sound like a bad thing. Is she hard to work with?" Halona asked.

Tuck thought about his answer. Josie was feisty but the hardest part was the fact that he was unreasonably attracted to her. He didn't have any experience providing therapy to a woman he had chemistry with. It was hard to touch her in a strictly platonic way when his mind was being less than professional. "She's only here for a few days. I can handle it. I'm also picking up an eleven-year-old girl as a patient. Her mom recently died in a car accident, and there's no dad in the picture. She's living with her grandmother just outside of town."

"Poor thing," Halona said. "You really do have the weight of the world on your shoulders. That's why you need someone special in your life."

Tuck rolled his eyes. "Or maybe that's why I *don't*. I have enough to deal with right now, don't you think?"

Halona wagged a finger before pointing it at him. "Oh no you don't. You're not pulling that with me." She had been his biggest cheerleader for getting back out there in the dating world over the last year. She'd tried to set him up with a number of her friends and was still trying every chance she got. "Renee would've wanted you to find love again."

He knew that was true. Renee had even told him so before she'd died. Finding love again had seemed like an impossible request two years ago but now he was beginning to reconsider. He might never find the kind of love he had with Renee but maybe he could find someone he enjoyed spending time with, to share life's events with. That wasn't so far-fetched.

Halona cut some ribbon and tied it around the floral arrangement. "So when are you meeting this little girl?" she asked, thankfully dropping the subject of his dating life.

"Tomorrow afternoon at Hope Cottage. She's my last patient of the day."

"Well, I expect to hear all about it." She handed the arrangement to him.

"Thanks. They're beautiful."

Halona nodded. "Of course they are. I'm the best florist in town. Also the only florist, but..." She shrugged as she trailed off. "Good luck with Kaitlyn's friend and the girl. Just remember: If it's going badly, compliment her hair or her shoes. If that doesn't work, have chocolate on hand. It works with any age group."

"That is not sound physical therapy advice," Tuck said, pushing back from the table and standing.

"No, it's advice on females." Halona pointed at her feet. "Shoes or chocolate."

Tuck scrutinized his sister's feet. "You're wearing flip-flops. I can't condone that kind of arch support when you're standing on your feet all day. And I'm afraid I'm fresh out of chocolate."

Halona grinned and wrapped her arms around his neck. "Then I'll take a big-brother hug instead."

* * *

"Popcorn—check. Wine—check." Josie grinned at Kaitlyn in the sitting room at the inn.

"Don't forget our movie," Kaitlyn said.

All the guests were upstairs, Mitch was working at the police station, and even Mr. Darcy was snoring on the floor below them. It was just Josie and Kaitlyn, like the old days.

"What are we watching?" Josie asked. She hadn't even cared to wonder until now. All she knew was she was having a girl's night with her BFF. They were going to eat, drink, and be merry.

"*Sleepless in Seattle.*" Kaitlyn flashed a Blu-ray cover as she walked to the entertainment system and then slid the disc inside the player.

"You have a thing for Tom Hanks," Josie accused as she laughed. She'd already had a full glass of red wine over pizza. "I'm not sure I understand it."

Kaitlyn giggled, more than a little tipsy now too. "He's adorable."

"Don't let Mitch hear you say that."

"Mitch has nothing to worry about. We're solid." Kaitlyn came to the couch and plopped down beside Josie. "And if we're talking crushes, *you* have the hots for your physical therapist."

Josie hid her smile behind her wineglass. "No I don't," she lied. "Okay fine, I do, but it's all very innocent. I mean, look at him. He's stupidly gorgeous. It's not even fair how good-looking he is."

Kaitlyn grabbed a handful of popcorn out of the tub between them. "I've heard that women around here actually get hurt on purpose so that they can be his patient."

Josie laughed until her ribs ached. "You're kidding!"

"No, it's true. They don't seriously injure themselves. It's mostly exaggerated sprains, kind of like yours." Kaitlyn raised her brows.

Josie's mouth fell open. "I didn't fake my fall."

"That's what they all say," Kaitlyn teased. "But seriously, he's hot and he's a really nice guy."

"True, but I'm not looking for any kind of relationship, short-term or long-term," Josie said.

Kaitlyn gave her a long look. "Don't you think it's time to let go of the past?"

Josie glanced over. "I have let it go. Really," she added when Kaitlyn narrowed her eyes. "I gave up a child in college because I wasn't ready to be a mom. Elizabeth is beautiful, smart, and healthy. She seems happy with her adoptive parents. It was the right thing for both of us."

"Why are you holding yourself back from finding a guy who can make *you* happy, then?" Kaitlyn asked.

Josie sighed. "I don't need a guy to do that. I am

happy." But she understood her friend's question. She just didn't have a good answer for it.

"Fair enough." Kaitlyn held up her hands. "Tuck probably isn't your Mr. Right anyway."

Josie reached for a handful of popcorn. "Why is that?"

"Well, for one, he's a widower."

Josie gasped, letting the popcorn fall between her fingers and onto her lap. "What?"

"He lost his wife before I knew him, and he only recently started dating again," Kaitlyn told her. "A man with a broken heart and a woman with a guarded one probably aren't the best match."

"My heart isn't guarded," Josie said, a little defensiveness rising in her tone.

Kaitlyn reached for another handful of popcorn. "Well, it's certainly not available."

Josie's good mood suddenly dulled. "I never would've guessed that about Tuck. He seems so . . . normal."

"Well, of course he is. Losing your spouse doesn't make you an outcast."

"I know that," Josie said. "I just mean he smiles and jokes around. He seems happy."

Kaitlyn tossed a piece of popcorn into her mouth. "Mitch says he's doing okay. As okay as someone can be after losing the love of their life."

"I can't even imagine." Josie blinked up at the TV menu screen for *Sleepless in Seattle*. "I don't think I can watch that movie now because Tom Hanks loses his wife. It's too sad."

Kaitlyn nodded in agreement. So instead, they continued to eat, drink, and chat, their laughter eventually starting back up, making Mr. Darcy lift his head with an annoyed look.

"I'm thinking I need a change," Josie finally admitted, two glasses in. "And no, not in my love life."

"What kind of change, then?" Kaitlyn asked. The popcorn bowl only held a few unpopped kernels now.

Josie lifted her shoulders, sloshing around the contents of the wineglass in her hand. "I'm not sure. I'm just not happy in my job since Bart took over."

"That's no secret."

"And New York isn't the same without you," Josie said. "I'm thinking about applying for a new job. I want to write about something more serious than dating trends and makeup." Or, if Bart had his way, articles that might be titled "Sex in the Sticks."

"Your article about romantic retreats last winter was good," Kaitlyn said.

"Thanks. But that was with Gary as my boss. Now that Bart has taken over, I just..." She shook her head. "I think it's time for me to move on, you know?" The idea had been niggling around in the back of her mind but this was the first time she'd said it out loud. She didn't like change. Keeping things the same was so much easier but she wasn't satisfied anymore. Going to a job she didn't love, writing articles that didn't excite her, and coming home to a lonely apartment wasn't fulfilling.

"Well, this is exciting. And worthy of a toast." Kaitlyn lifted her glass with an unsteady hand.

Josie's buzz from the wine was dulled by the adrenaline and excitement now shooting through her. She'd made up her mind and had said it out loud. She'd continue to work at *Loving Life* magazine while applying for other jobs as soon as possible. She was going to find a job she loved even more than when she first started working at *Loving Life*. It was time.

She lifted her glass and touched it to Kaitlyn's with a soft laugh.

"To new dreams and new beginnings," Kaitlyn said. "And hot physical therapists."

* * *

The next day Josie met Tuck outside on the trail behind the B&B. She was wearing yoga pants, a T-shirt, and a pair of tennis shoes—her typical wardrobe for an early morning jog. She missed those jogs, but walking alongside Tuck was nice too.

For the first few minutes, all she could think about was what Kaitlyn had told her last night. Tuck had lost his wife. Josie didn't know the details but it was tragic nonetheless.

"You okay?" Tuck asked. "You're quiet this morning."

She offered up a smile. "Just enjoying nature."

He gave her a curious look. "You are the same city girl I met a few days ago, right? The one who tried to kill me with a can of pepper spray?"

That made her laugh. "The very same. Maybe I hit my head when I fell too."

Tuck grinned. "I could take you back to Dr. Miles."

"Not necessary." She gulped in a deep breath of the fresh air. "I'm shocked that my knee is already doing so well. The swelling was nearly gone when I woke up this morning."

"I told you it'd heal up."

The tension she usually carried between her shoulder blades was less too. She'd slept like a baby last night and hadn't rushed off this morning to get on the subway and get to the office early as she normally did in the city. "It's so peaceful here. I should really start taking a vacation more often."

"Some vacation. You hurt your knee, and now you're doing physical therapy with me."

"And yet I feel more relaxed than I have in a while. I even decided to start looking for a new job last night," she told him.

Tuck looked at her from under the ball cap he was wearing. "That's a pretty big decision."

"It is. And it's long overdue. I'm not leaving *Loving Life* magazine until I line something else up, of course, but I'm going to start putting out feelers." Excitement zipped through her all over again.

She'd also decided, as she lay awake in bed last night, that she might put up a profile on an online dating site too. She wasn't looking for anything long-term. No, she'd decided a long time ago that she was married to her career and always would be. But she enjoyed going to cultural events in New York. She loved festivals and the theater, and hated going alone, which was more often the case now that Kaitlyn had moved away.

"So this is what you do all day, huh?" she asked once they'd rounded the trail and were heading back to where they'd started.

"Partly. I do a lot of stuff. Sessions usually consist of stretching, exercises, and something functional like walking." He shrugged. "It all just depends on what my patient needs."

"I can tell you what I need," she said without thinking.

He looked at her with interest, his eyes narrowing just a touch. "What's that?"

Oh, there were so many things that came to mind. Things that Kaitlyn had warned her off of concerning Tuck.

"A drink. I'm leaving to go back to New York

tomorrow, and you've done a lot for me. Why don't you let me buy you a drink to say thank you?" It rolled off her tongue casually, as if the invitation were no big deal. And it wasn't, she told herself. Kaitlyn had already told her that Tuck wasn't really on the market. She just enjoyed spending time with him. Indulging in a little more flirty banter before she went home was innocent enough.

Tuck averted his gaze and focused on the trees. She watched him fidget with the silver chain around his neck, toying with a little charm that dangled at his chest. After a moment, he released it. "That's really not necessary," he said. "I've only been doing my job. You don't need to thank me or buy me anything. It might look bad for me to be seen out on the town with a patient anyway. Unprofessional."

Josie forced a soft laugh even though the skin on her chest was burning hot. "Right. I understand. I hear that you have quite a lot of patients who want to date you."

"Oh?" Tuck looked over.

"Yep. That's what Kaitlyn says. I was just suggesting a drink, not a date though. *Definitely* not a date." Because he was a widower. And she was leaving. And...

"I see. Well, that's good because I don't date patients." His gaze clung to her. "But if I wasn't your physical therapist..."

She blinked him into focus, her heart suddenly beating as if she'd downed three cups of espresso. *That* was an incomplete sentence. The writer in her wanted him to finish it. The woman in her wanted it too.

CHAPTER FIVE

Tuck looked at his watch. Beverly Sanders and her granddaughter Maddie were running a few minutes late. He was glad they were meeting here at Hope Cottage because it was close to their home, and he found it to be an inspiring setting for the most unmotivated of patients.

It certainly inspired him. That's why he'd moved here. The little house and surrounding property on Blueberry Creek had awakened something inside him when he was newly widowed and looking for a fresh start. Ancient Cherokees had a practice of going to the water for purification. Coming from a mixed home, with a Caucasian dad and an American Indian mother, he didn't exactly practice all the tribal traditions, but his mom had made sure he knew them inside and out.

Coming to live on Blueberry Creek had been a type of spiritual cleansing for him. All the regrets of his past—his worry that he hadn't been a good enough husband to

Renee, that he hadn't fought hard enough to find a cure—were washed away. An added bonus was that he could work with patients out in nature. Hopefully, his young patient would be a nature lover too.

A silver sedan drove up the road and turned into his driveway. Tuck watched it head toward him and come to a stop beside his Jeep. He waved and headed over.

Beverly pushed her driver's-side door open and smiled at him. "Good afternoon," she said. The woman had long white hair and smooth, pale skin.

"Good afternoon to you." Tuck watched Beverly pull a wheelchair out of the driver's back seat before they walked around to the passenger side. She opened the front passenger door, and Tuck met the gaze of a sullen little girl.

"Maddie, say hello to Mr. Locklear," Beverly prompted.

Maddie didn't budge, keeping her arms tightly folded across her chest.

Tuck also had a hard time saying hello for a moment. Maddie didn't look at all like her grandmother. Instead of pale skin, she had a deeply tanned complexion. The girl had long, silky black locks with thick eyebrows to match. He suspected that, like him, she had American Indian blood running through her. If so, coming to the water was the perfect place for her therapy.

"Hello, Maddie." He reached out his hand for her to shake.

Maddie stared at him for a moment, not making any move to put her hand in his. Then she huffed dramatically. "Fine. I'll do this but it's not going to change anything. I can't walk."

Beverly maneuvered the wheelchair to the car, and Maddie independently reached for the arm of the chair and then pushed her body up and transferred into it.

"Looks like you've mastered getting around," Tuck noted. "That's good. Means we can get straight to working out that leg."

Maddie didn't acknowledge his comment. It appeared the biggest challenge today was going to be for him. He couldn't help Maddie until she trusted him.

He steered the wheelchair down a narrow, beaten path along the creek. The ground was as smooth and flat as tile here, perfect for wheelchairs and walking. He stopped at a shaded spot beneath an old oak where he had several outdoor chairs set up for his patients. Then he took a seat in one and gestured for Beverly to take another.

Maddie used her arms to maneuver the chair and position herself just close enough to hear what they were saying but far enough away to make it clear she didn't want to be involved.

"So tell me what's going on in your own words," he said to Beverly. Usually he'd address the actual patient but he had a hunch that Maddie wasn't going to give him anything today except a surplus of attitude. "I've already scheduled a time to talk to Maddie's last physical therapist later this evening. Mr. Andrews couldn't talk to me before now," Tuck explained.

Beverly lifted her slight shoulders. "I already told you on the phone. Maddie had a good prognosis for walking after the accident, but you can't force someone to do something they don't want to do."

"You forced me to come here, didn't you?" Maddie said, keeping her eyes on the creek. Shadow took that moment to get up from where she lay next to Tuck and trot over to Maddie. Maddie looked down at Shadow and, almost reflexively, reached out to pet the dog.

This was exactly the reason Tuck had Shadow. She

was therapeutic in a way that some patients weren't even aware of.

"I didn't force you to come. You're too big for me to pick you up anymore," Beverly argued. "You got in the car with me of your own free will." Beverly turned to Tuck. "Do you see what I'm dealing with?"

He did. Something about Maddie reminded him of his sister, Halona, at that age. She'd worn a constant scowl during that time period too. Remembering Halona's advice, he glanced at Maddie's Converse sneakers. "Nice shoes," he commented.

Maddie seemed thrown off by his remark. "That's a weird thing for a physical therapist to say. What kind of PT are you anyway? You do therapy out here? Don't you have an office like a real PT?"

He laughed unexpectedly. "My office is the great outdoors, and I *am* a real PT. I can show you my degree if you need proof."

Maddie didn't look impressed.

"Are you keeping up with the exercises your last physical therapist gave you?" he asked.

"No."

"Why not?"

"Because they're hard," Maddie said. "And what's the point?"

"Do you *want* to walk, Maddie? Because if you don't, your grandma is right. I can't help you."

Something flickered in the muddy color of the girl's eyes. She was quiet for so long that he thought maybe she wasn't going to answer. Then she shifted and cleared her throat. "What if my leg just doesn't work anymore?" she asked quietly.

There. That told him everything he needed to know.

She was scared. Fear was her invisible enemy but he was going to help her slay it.

"What if it does?" he asked.

* * *

Almost done.

Josie had been locked away in her room all afternoon working on her follow-up story for Sweetwater Springs. There were a few minor details she needed to pass by Kaitlyn and then some polishing touches to be done.

She let out a contented sigh and put her laptop on the bedside table. Draping her legs over the side of the bed, she completed a round of knee-extension exercises like Tuck had taught her before standing on her own two feet. Her knee took her full body weight with little complaint. She walked slowly to the bathroom to freshen up and then poured herself some water at a table that was set up with a pitcher and glasses. There was also an arrangement of flowers there, which Josie thought was a nice touch.

Her cell phone meowed from the bed.

She didn't have a cat. Never had. But she'd always wanted one. Thus the cat ringtone. It was supposed to make her feel like she had the company of a pet without the upkeep. Maybe she should add that to her list of changes that she suddenly wanted to make in her new life. A new job, a dating life (*not* with her hot PT), and a pet. Surely that would fill the void her life seemed to have lately.

The text tones stopped, and then her phone started ringing instead. She walked to her bed, her knee aching just slightly inside its brace, and answered the call. "Hello."

"Josie? This is Ms. Plummer."

Even if the caller hadn't identified herself, Josie would've immediately recognized her landlady's crunchy voice, a product from decades of smoke exposure.

Josie frowned. "Hi, Ms. Plummer. How are you?"

"Good enough," the sweet older lady responded. Josie could picture her landlady in her gold jumpsuit that she wore almost daily. Ms. Plummer either had several identical jumpsuits or she wore the same one day after day. It was a mystery that still begged Journalist Josie to investigate.

"I'm not behind on my rent. It's not due until next week," Josie explained.

"Yes, yes, I know, dear. And you won't be required to pay it next month either."

"Oh? Why is that?" Josie asked, suspecting she wasn't going to like the answer. A free month's rent for no reason was unlikely.

"Well, there's been a little fire in the apartment next to yours, I'm afraid. Your place got a bit of damage as well. The fire marshal says no one can live in the space until the smoke has cleared and the damage has been fixed, which could take a while."

Josie covered her mouth with her left hand. "A fire? Is everyone okay?" She didn't hang out with the tenants who lived next door but she always thought she'd like them if she did. They were a nice couple who always gave her a holiday card and a paper plate of homemade cookies. The husband had helped Josie break into her apartment once when she'd accidentally locked herself out.

"Oh yes. Thank goodness everyone's fine. And don't worry about your belongings. I walked through your place and most of your stuff wasn't damaged. I posted NO TRESPASSING signs on your door too. No one is going to touch your stuff while you're away. But you'll need to find a place to live for the next couple of weeks, I'm afraid."

"Couple of weeks?" Josie repeated.

"Could be as long as a month."

Josie plopped down on the edge of the bed as her racing thoughts overwhelmed her. She didn't have anywhere else to go. Her mom and stepdad's home would be a two-hour commute to her office, and living with them would drive her nuts after a couple of days, much less weeks. She had acquaintances in the city but Kaitlyn had always been her closest friend there and the only one she'd even consider moving in with.

Maybe she could stay here at the inn while her apartment was being fixed. As a writer, she did most of her work in private anyway. Bart shouldn't mind as long as she met her deadlines. She could even Skype with the team for their weekly meetings. *That might work.*

"So save your rent money, dear, and use it to house yourself," Ms. Plummer continued. "I'm very sorry. Freak accidents happen sometimes."

This statement perked Journalist Josie's interest. "What kind of freak accident?"

"Oh, you know, some kind of kinky use of candle wax in the bedroom. I guess Mr. Diaz dropped one of the candlesticks in all his excitement."

Josie's imagination filled in the blanks. Well, that story would be one that Bart would definitely be interested in—"Freak Accidents in the Bedroom: How to Come Out Unscathed"—not that she'd ever pitch or write it.

"It seems like Mr. Diaz would've been able to put the fire out fairly quickly," Josie said.

"Well, yes, if the candle hadn't fallen next to the gas

heater. The Diazes didn't even have time to get dressed before they came running out."

That was quite a visual. "Well, thank you for letting me know, Ms. Plummer. I'm in North Carolina right now, and I might just stay here awhile longer. Can you keep me updated on when I can return?"

"Of course, dear. Thank you for being so understanding. I'll be in touch."

"Okay. Bye."

Josie disconnected the call with a heavy sigh. So much for going back to the city tomorrow and turning over a new leaf.

Someone knocked on Josie's bedroom door.

"Come in," she said, already knowing it was Kaitlyn All the other rooms were filled with guests now—several had arrived today—but Josie wasn't expecting any of them to visit her.

Kaitlyn peeked inside the doorway. "Hi. Just checking to see if you want to come downstairs and enjoy tea and cookies. I just set some fresh ones out in the dining area for the guests."

Josie sighed. "I could use a few cookies right now. Maybe half a dozen."

"Something wrong?" Kaitlyn asked, opening the door wider and stepping into the room.

"You could say that. I just spoke to Ms. Plummer. There was a fire in the apartment next door to mine."

Kaitlyn gasped. "What? Is everyone okay?"

"Sounds like it."

"What about your apartment?" Kaitlyn asked.

Josie pulled her lower lip between her teeth. She really didn't like to make herself an imposition on others. But that's all she seemed to be doing since she'd arrived. "My apartment has fire damage, and I can't return for a couple of weeks. I was hoping you might be able to let me stay here awhile longer. It'll be fun," she said, intentionally adding a little cheer to her voice. "Like a prolonged sleepover."

Kaitlyn didn't look as excited about the idea. "Well, there's only one problem with that. The inn is booked solid for the next couple of weeks leading up to the Sweetwater Springs Festival. Unless one of the guests cancels their stay, I don't have a room for you."

Josie had made her reservation months ago. She should've known staying here wouldn't work out. "Great. What am I going to do now? Finding a temporary dwelling in New York will be next to impossible if I go back."

"I'm sure you can find something in Sweetwater Springs though. I'll help you. And Mitch can ask around the police station. Really, things will work out just fine. And you and I can have more time together." Kaitlyn grabbed hold of Josie's hand and tugged her off the bed.

Josie's knee complained a little but not as much as the rest of her.

"Come on. We'll problem solve while we eat Grandma Mable's famous cookies," Kaitlyn said. "They make everything better."

* * *

Tuck sat in one of the chairs set up under the oak tree outside and looked out on Blueberry Creek. He studied the movement of the water, the sound, the birds singing somewhere in the background.

The physical therapist at Mount Pleasant Children's Hospital had agreed to call him back at five p.m. to discuss Maddie's condition. He'd gotten Beverly to give written permission to access Maddie's medical files prior to their session today. Since receiving the digital file, Tuck had studied every word of every report. Like Beverly had told him, Maddie had broken her collarbone and right femur in the accident. She'd had an open reduction and internal fixation surgery to fix the bone in her leg, but her injury left resulting nerve damage that might never correct itself. Maddie had also refused most attempts at physical therapy, causing muscle atrophy, or in layman's terms, wasting.

There were obstacles in his young patient's path to getting better, for sure, but Maddie was young and Tuck had seen patients with worse injuries who were now running marathons.

He realized he was holding his breath as he sat on the edge of the creek, waiting for Maddie Sanders's previous therapist to call. Shadow lifted her head to look at him with worried eyes. He leaned forward and gave her a gentle pat. "It's okay, girl. Just a little anxious—that's all." Maddie had been through so much. He wanted to help her in any way he could.

His phone buzzed, and he efficiently tapped the screen to answer. "Hello?"

"Mr. Locklear? This is Chad Andrews."

"Yes, hi. Thank you for calling me back."

"Of course." Tuck had researched Chad online earlier in the day. Maddie's former PT had been working at the children's hospital since his internship there in college a few years ago. "Mad Maddie, as we liked to call her, was only a patient here for two months but I remember her well," he said. "She had a lot of potential hiding under all her anger."

"Then why did you discharge her?" Tuck asked, working to keep his voice neutral. He didn't want to judge this guy without giving him a chance to explain.

"Well, I didn't want to but her grandma said the girl was refusing to come. If I had it my way, Maddie would have been up on her legs every day, no matter what. But I can't work with someone who doesn't show up. If a patient misses more than five treatments in a month, they're discharged out of our system."

Five treatments in a month?

Tuck's jaw tightened. He might not have any better luck than this guy, but a child shouldn't be able to make a decision that would affect the rest of their life. Beverly should have pushed Maddie and demanded that she worked harder.

"I'm glad to know she's starting back up with physical therapy," Chad said.

"Yeah. It looks like it's been four months since you last saw her." And Maddie had probably used her right leg very little since then.

"The wheelchair was only meant to be a temporary option. Her broken collarbone was still healing from the car accident so crutches weren't an option. I hope you can motivate Maddie to work this time."

"Me too. I'll go to her house for the sessions if I have to."

Chad laughed softly. "You might be exactly the guy Mad Maddie needs. Good luck."

"Thanks." Tuck disconnected the call and continued staring straight ahead. Maddie would be a challenge, that was for sure, but hopefully nothing he couldn't handle. He'd had lots of challenging patients over the years.

Josie sprung to mind. She was challenging in a whole

different way. It was all he could do not to say yes when she'd offered to take him out for a drink earlier. Even now, he was halfway tempted to call her up and change his answer. They were finished with their physical therapy sessions but she was still a recent patient of his, which meant she was strictly off-limits in his book. And even if she weren't, she was leaving town tomorrow.

CHAPTER SIX

Home sweet not-home," Josie said, shutting the inn's door behind her and dragging her tired body into the front room the next day.

Kaitlyn looked up from the book she was reading and frowned. "Any luck?"

Josie shook her head. She was supposed to be leaving Sweetwater Springs today. Not going all over town in Kaitlyn's car and looking for a temporary place to live. "None. Everywhere is booked for the upcoming Sweetwater Springs Festival. And if there are vacancies, then the very apologetic landlords want a permanent renter, not a stranger who'll only be in town for a couple of weeks."

Kaitlyn laid her book down on the coffee table and stood. "I'm sorry. Come on. I'll make you a cup of hot tea. Then we'll get you an ice pack for your knee and get it elevated."

"You take such good care of me," Josie said, barely even limping as she walked down the hallway toward the kitchen. "Can you and Mitch just adopt me?"

Kaitlyn laughed. "I'm not sure he'd agree to that. We're not planning to start a family anytime soon."

A little ache pinged in Josie's heart, competing with the dull throb in her knee. It was inevitable that Kaitlyn and Mitch would have kids one day. Kaitlyn was the type of woman who would make a great mother.

And Josie wasn't.

Josie cleared her throat as she sat on a stool at the kitchen island. "I mean, I know this town is small but I couldn't find anywhere with an availability," she continued, roping the conversation back to something that didn't make her heart ache.

"Hello, ladies," Mitch said as he walked into the room. He headed immediately to Kaitlyn's side and gave her a kiss on the cheek. Josie could see the attraction for men in uniforms. It was hot but, in her opinion, not as much as sexy American Indian physical therapists in jeans and T-shirts.

"No luck, huh?" Mitch asked Josie, when he finally pulled away from Kaitlyn. "I overheard when I walked in."

Josie shook her head. "None."

"Well, if nothing else, we can pull out the air mattress and set it up in our room," Kaitlyn suggested. "We won't let you go homeless."

Mitch's expression pinched.

Josie didn't blame him for being less than thrilled by Kaitlyn's offer. He and Kaitlyn were a new couple. They didn't need her crashing their love nest. "Don't worry about me. I'll figure something out. And I'll be out of

here by tomorrow for the guest who's reserved my room."
Even if she had no idea where she'd go.

Kaitlyn grimaced. "I wish I'd known. I wouldn't have
booked it."

"Who would've predicted I'd be staying here for any
length of time? Certainly not me," Josie said.

Mitch braced his body weight on the kitchen counter in
front of him. "I *might* know of a place you can rent," he said
hesitantly. "But I need to see if it's actually available."

"Where?" Kaitlyn looked up at him. "And why haven't
you mentioned this sooner?"

Mitch shrugged. "It didn't occur to me. Honestly, I
thought Josie would have no problem finding a place.
And I didn't realize you were going to move her into our
room if she did."

Kaitlyn punched his shoulder playfully. "Where?"

"Well, Tuck has been thinking about renting out his
garage apartment. He hasn't listed it yet, and he might
have changed his mind."

"Oh, that's perfect!" Kaitlyn clapped her hands together at her chest. "He has an empty room, and Josie
needs one. And they already know each other."

"No." Josie was already shaking her head. "I've already
imposed on him so much. I'll keep looking."

"Nonsense," Kaitlyn objected. "Call Tuck now," she
said, turning back to Mitch. "Unless you want me to pull
out that air mattress for the next couple of weeks. Could
even be a month."

Mitch stiffened and pulled out his cell phone. "Okay,
okay. I'll ask and let you ladies know." He walked out of
the kitchen.

Josie guessed it was because he didn't want them to
hear Tuck's loud objections through the receiver.

"I can't stay with Tuck," Josie muttered.

"What? Why not? He's a great guy. You already know that."

"Yes, and he's not on the market, remember?"

Kaitlyn laughed. "What does that have to do with anything?"

Josie cringed. "I may have invited him out for a drink yesterday," she admitted.

"What?" Kaitlyn squeaked. "You asked him out?"

"No." Josie covered her face. "Maybe. Kind of. It was just a casual invitation. I thought I was leaving so I put the idea out there. He rejected me though. He doesn't like me. Not in that way, at least."

Tuck's words begged to differ in the back of Josie's memory though. *If I wasn't your physical therapist.*

Heat swam through Josie's body, starting at her toes. She never should've asked him out. It was foolish. She wasn't what he was looking for, and she wasn't exactly looking. Not in Sweetwater Springs at least.

"It's his garage apartment," Kaitlyn said. "It's not like you'd be living with him. And maybe you can get a little extra physical therapy while you're there." She bounced her brows playfully. "Tuck might not be a dating option for you but it doesn't mean you can't hang out and enjoy the view."

Josie laughed and shook her head. Her best friend was right though. Josie needed a place to stay so, if Tuck agreed, she'd be adult about moving in temporarily. But there would definitely be no more physical therapy between them. Dr. Miles had recommended only a couple of sessions anyway and her knee was doing so much better. If Tuck agreed to house her, she'd just do her best to stay out of his long, sexy hair altogether.

* * *

Tuck wiped a hand across his brow.

Since Josie was no longer on his caseload, he'd used the open hours in his schedule to begin work on the stables behind Hope Cottage. They were empty right now but he'd already contacted a few people with horses for sale.

In the last hour and a half, he'd fixed a broken gate to one of the stalls. Now the door swung easily. He still wanted to give the outside a fresh coat of paint—maybe this summer—but otherwise, the stables were ready to house his therapy horses once he found them.

Temperament was key in buying a therapy horse. Not just any horse would do. It needed to be a horse that didn't get spooked easily. One that provided a smooth, steady ride for his patients. A cousin of his was a trainer who'd already agreed to help him prepare the horses to work with patients after Tuck got them settled into their new home.

As he exited the barn, buzzing with excitement, his cell phone rang. "Hello?"

"Tuck? How are you, buddy?" Mitch asked.

"Pretty good, I guess. Not really in the mood to meet up for drinks tonight, if that's why you're calling." Tuck cut through the field and headed into the kitchen for a cool glass of green tea.

"That's not why I'm calling. But you might change your tune about that drink after you hear my reason."

Tuck chuckled dryly as he pulled a glass from his cabinet. Then he opened the fridge door and grabbed the pitcher of tea. "Go for it."

"Are you still thinking about putting your garage apartment up for rent?"

Tuck paused in filling his glass. He'd had so much going on this past week that he hadn't given the idea much more thought since dinner with the guys the other night. "Yeah, eventually. To the right renter." The extra money would be helpful for purchasing the horses and their supplies. Later, it would help with upkeep costs.

"This person wouldn't be any trouble, and she'll only be here for a couple of weeks."

"She?" Tuck's brain was already connecting the dots. "You're not talking about Josie, are you? I thought she left town today."

"Yeah, about that. There was a slight change of plans," Mitch said. "She'll be staying a little longer, and the inn is booked up for the upcoming festival. She's great, man, but I don't want her sleeping in my and Kaitlyn's room for the rest of the month."

"Thought you said two weeks."

"Probably."

Tuck was shaking his head, causing Shadow to go on alert at his feet. "I don't think..."

"Everywhere in town is full."

"Sorry," Tuck began again but Mitch cut him off.

"Okay, I didn't want to have to do this, because I don't believe in having your buddies pay off their debts to you, but you owe me," Mitch reminded him.

"Owe you?" Tuck reached out to pet Shadow's head, letting her know that everything was okay. Just fine. But there was no way he was going to rent his garage apartment to Josie. Living with that kind of temptation might be more than he could handle.

"That's right—you owe me big, buddy. Remember that time you were out past curfew and freaking out because your mom was going to kill you?"

"High school? You're reaching as far back as high school?" Tuck asked in disbelief. He walked over to the kitchen table and sat down.

"You would've been grounded for months, and Dustin Robinson would've taken Renee to the prom instead of you. You always said that's what would have happened, and that you were indebted to me for life."

It was true. That night was the reason that Mitch had been Tuck's best man at his wedding. Well, that and the fact that Mitch was one of his best friends. Mitch had saved the day when Tuck would've otherwise been locked in his room for the rest of his senior year. Instead, Tuck had gone to the prom with Renee, and they'd fallen in love under the silvery strobe lights that night. Tuck's entire life had changed, and in some way, he had Mitch to thank for it.

Tuck closed his eyes. Was there a way to get out of this without Josie coming to live at Hope Cottage? It wasn't that he didn't like her but more that he did, and that was a little scary.

"She'll be in the garage apartment tapping away on her computer. You probably won't even know she's there. She's been with us all week, and I've barely noticed. Granted, I've spent a lot of time at the police station. Plus, she'll pay you rent. Extra money is always nice, right?" Mitch added with a note of desperation in his voice.

"The room doesn't compare to the ones you have at the bed and breakfast. It isn't even furnished but I do have a bed and dresser in storage that I can put up there."

"Perfect. Give me the keys to your storage building, and I'll set it up for you myself. So it's a yes?" Mitch asked, hope lilting in his voice.

Tuck leaned forward in his chair, propping his elbows

on his knees. "You're not going to take no for an answer, are you?"

"No. And after this, *I'll* owe you. I'll let the women know you agreed. Then I'll drop Josie off tomorrow afternoon. Kaitlyn is letting her borrow her bike too. Your place on the creek is only a mile's ride to anything she needs so it should be fine," Mitch said, seeming to have all the answers.

The physical therapist in Tuck wondered if bike riding was a good idea for Josie. It would be fine if she didn't overdo it. The last thing she needed was to reinjure her knee, which would put her back under his care. That wouldn't be good for either of them because *he* needed to keep his eyes and hands to himself.

"Fine," Tuck relented.

"Thanks, bud. See you tomorrow."

The call disconnected, and just like that, Tuck had a woman coming to live in his garage apartment. And not just any woman—the only woman who'd sparked his interest since his late wife.

* * *

Josie stared out Mitch's car window, memorizing the path to her new home. At least temporarily. They'd passed a grocery store, turned right, and were now on Blueberry Creek Road. The creek bordered her on the right side with tall pines and sweeping willows interspersed alongside it. The water was a murky brown color, and she wondered where it ran to. Maybe into Silver Lake downtown?

It was beautiful but everything inside of her was still fighting this. Living above someone's garage? Out in the middle of nowhere?

"Where will I get coffee?" she asked, turning to Mitch with sudden worry. Because she couldn't work without coffee. It was crucial for lubricating her creative gears.

Mitch turned to look at her. He had mirrored sunglasses hiding his eyes, which she guessed would be rolling at her panicked voice. "I set you up a pot in the apartment. Found it in Tuck's storage building. If that doesn't suit you, it's about a one-mile bike ride to the Sweetwater Café. Not sure what Emma's secret ingredient is but it's coffee on steroids. You'll be hooked."

Josie nodded on an inhale. Okay, coffee crisis averted. She had a place to work and coffee at the ready. There was also a place to walk and clear her head. Maybe she could even take her laptop and sit beside the creek. Sometimes a change of scenery refreshed the mind.

Yes. Everything will be okay. I can do this.

Mitch slowed his truck as they passed a large fenced-in field of wildflowers with a rust-colored stable set in the back. Then he pulled into a driveway in front of a beautiful one-story red cottage that sat inside that same fence. Flowers of every kind and color bloomed along the pebbled walkway leading up to the front door. They even climbed up the front of the house.

Josie blinked, hoping her eyes weren't playing tricks on her. The image in front of her was absolutely charming. And not at all what she was envisioning. "Tuck lives here? All alone?"

Mitch nodded. "Nice, isn't it?"

"Nice is an understatement." It had a large front porch with swings that hung from the roof of the veranda. The home was capped off with a white tin roof that she imagined made a delicious sound in a rainstorm, *not* that she'd be sleeping under that roof. To the left of the home was a disconnected garage with stairs leading up the side to what she guessed was the apartment where she would stay. "What is a single man doing living in a place like this?"

Mitch grinned and gestured behind them. "See that creek back there? Tuck may as well pitch a tent and live right next to it. The man loves his nature." He nodded his head at the window over the garage. "You'll have a nice view of Blueberry Creek too."

Personally, she would've preferred to look out over the field of wildflowers near the stables. They looked like something straight out of a magazine ad, inviting people to the simple mountain life.

She pushed out of Mitch's truck and stood for a second as he went to grab her bags from the back. Voices caught her attention from the other side of the house. Male and female. Josie craned her neck, and her heart jolted at the sight of Tuck. He was talking with a young, dark-haired girl on crutches. Off to the side of them was a wheelchair.

"Tuck sees some of his patients out here. He likes to use the great outdoors as his gym."

"Well, he certainly has a lot of that to offer."

"He's planning to add a couple of horses too," Mitch said as he carried her luggage to her temporary dwelling. "Tuck told me to show you up since he's seeing patients. He'll probably stop in and officially welcome you to Hope Cottage later."

She attempted to take one of her bags from him. "I can take that."

Mitch didn't release it to her. "You shouldn't carry these with that knee of yours. I'll do it."

"Right. Thanks." She followed him up the set of steps.

She'd nearly forgotten that her knee was even injured. She'd been icing and doing her exercises faithfully, and everything had settled almost back to normal just like Dr. Miles said it would. She'd probably still be sticking to flats and sneakers for the rest of her time here though, which was just fine with her. She mostly wore heels in the office, and only so she was taller than the guys who tried to push her around, aka Bart. She'd found she got a little more respect when she added a few inches of height.

Mitch pulled out a key, turned it in the lock, and the door released. Then he gestured for her to enter ahead of him.

Stepping over the threshold, Josie glanced around the open space. The front room held a single foldout chair and a small dining table. The living room blended with a minute-size kitchen. On the tiled countertop, she saw the coffeepot that Mitch had set up for her alongside a dorm-size refrigerator. Two doors exited the far side of the room.

Mitch pointed. "That one leads to the bathroom. That one to your bedroom."

She walked toward the bedroom and flipped the light switch, taking in the twin-size bed with a solid blue comforter. "At least there's a place to sleep," she said more to herself than Mitch.

"I pulled it from Tuck's storage yesterday. If you need something more, I might be able to find it in there. He has a lot of stuff. Couldn't find a TV though. Sorry."

Josie shook her head and turned back to Mitch. "I don't watch anyway. I'll be mostly working so this should be great. Thank you again."

"Anytime. Call if you need anything," he said as he headed for the door. "Reception is a little squirrelly here.

At least, that's what Tuck always claims, and I think he has the best carrier for the area. If you don't have any cell phone bars, you might have to hunt around for a signal."

Josie whipped her cell phone out to check. "Zero bars?" She looked up at Mitch, suddenly in a panic. "Zero bars? There's no phone reception?" she asked in disbelief.

"I'm sure there is somewhere. Just need to find that magic spot. Good luck." He crossed the threshold and closed the door behind him as if she might protest and climb back into his truck to leave with him.

Surely, there was reception somewhere, right? She couldn't stay here without a line to the outside world. She'd go crazy.

She stepped to the window and looked out on the creek and then to Tuck on the front lawn with the little girl. Staying in close proximity to him might be enough to drive her crazy as well.

CHAPTER SEVEN

Over the last forty-five minutes, Tuck had realized that Maddie was eleven going on fifteen. She'd used every muscle in her face to relay her irritation with him but hadn't flexed a single muscle in her right leg in response to any of his requests.

She was unmotivated and likely depressed, with good reason. Maybe she was having a bad day and her next scheduled visit would go better. He could only hope that was the case because this had been the longest physical therapy session of his career.

"Here. This is a printout of the exercises I want you to do." He placed it in Maddie's lap when she didn't move to grab it. "You won't get better unless you try, Maddie."

"I know that," she muttered.

It was just the two of them this afternoon. Beverly had dropped Maddie off so she could go to her own appointment in town. Tuck wasn't sure how serious Beverly's condition was but she'd taken to wearing a bandana over her thinning hair. Tuck had overheard her telling Maddie it was the hip grandma thing to do but he remembered when Renee had done the same. His late wife had been weak after her chemo treatments. She wouldn't have been able to care for a child in a wheelchair, especially not at Beverly's age.

"You're the only patient I'll be working with five days a week," Tuck told Maddie. "That's because I believe in you. But you have to believe too, okay?" He felt like he was talking to himself until Maddie gave a slight shrug.

"I'll do the exercises in my room so no one can laugh if I fail."

"Who would laugh? Not me." He sat down in a foldout chair beside her. "Not your grandma."

"I dunno. The kids at school are real jerks," she said. "Mean girls exist, and they're all in my class this year."

"Don't listen to them."

Maddie rolled her eyes before letting them narrow in on him. "You don't understand."

"I do, actually. When I was your age, I got picked on a lot too. It was right along that time that I started collecting pets. I got along better with animals than I did people." And he'd never lost his affection for four-legged creatures. "Eventually I found some kids who were nice enough, and we're still friends today." He was talking about Mitch and Alex, the best guys he knew. When kids had been mean to Tuck growing up, Mitch had threatened to beat them up. And Alex, true to his love of the law even back then, had threatened to tell the school's principal.

Maddie reached out to pet Shadow, a cascade of hair falling over her eyes. Shadow leaned into Maddie's hand, providing calming pressure through her palm. "I love animals but Grandma won't let me have pets. Not even a fish."

Tuck frowned. "Well, I'm sure you can make your case when you're able to do all the work that comes along with keeping a pet yourself. Do your exercises." He tapped the sheet on Maddie's lap. "Then we'll work on warming your grandma up to the idea of a cat or a dog."

"A cat," Maddie said with the smallest of smiles. "Shadow is great but I've always wanted a kitten." In this moment, it was all he could do not to go get her one, or two or three, from the local rescue shelter.

They both turned to the sound of a car coming up the driveway.

"I guess our time is up." He reached into his pocket and pulled out a foil-wrapped piece of chocolate. He'd gotten a whole bag at the grocery store the other day, taking his sister's advice on females.

Just as Halona had said, Maddie smiled widely. *Well, what do you know?* Chocolate was the way to a girl's heart. He'd have to remember that.

"Thanks," she said.

"You're welcome." He walked behind her chair and pushed her through the grass toward Beverly's parked vehicle. Judging by the looks of the older woman who didn't move to get out, he wondered if she should even be behind the wheel.

"You okay?" he asked, dipping inside the passenger door after he'd helped Maddie into the seat.

"Just a little green," Beverly said shakily.

"Ginger is good for nausea." Tuck had learned that while caring for Renee. "Need me to follow you home? To make sure you get there okay?"

"No, that's not necessary. We live just a couple of

miles away. We'll be there in a flash." She looked over at Maddie. "I'm sure you're tired too. We'll eat and rest. How does that sound?"

"Like every other night," Maddie said, her voice thick with sarcasm once again. Tuck guessed chocolate didn't fix everything. Maddie looked up at him. "And I might do these exercises before bed."

"Good idea. See you on Monday."

"Reese's Peanut Butter Cups are my favorite," she added.

"Good to know." He stepped away from the car and waved as Beverly drove off with Maddie. Then he turned toward the house, desperately wanting to go inside and have a tall glass of tea, or something stronger after the day he'd had. As he walked, his gaze wandered to the garage apartment. He'd seen Mitch drive up with Josie half an hour earlier. She was here, and the right thing to do was welcome her and see if she needed anything.

With a sigh of resignation, he veered toward the garage and climbed the steps, making a mental note to hammer in a few loose nails. The last thing he needed was to have Josie trip and need more physical therapy.

At the top of the staircase, he knocked twice on the door. It swung open on its own.

"Josie? It's me, Tuck," he called, poking his head inside the living area. "Josie?"

The front room was empty. The door to the bathroom was open with the lights off. Same with the bedroom. She wasn't here. The only evidence that she ever had been was her red luggage set sitting in the middle of the floor.

Where is she?

He headed back down the steps, looking out along the creek. Not there either. His gaze traveled to the field of wildflowers, the stables, and the storage building beside the barn. He was about to turn toward the other side of the house when he saw movement behind the building. Josie turned the corner and appeared to be dancing. Left, right, spin.

What is she doing? And why was she doing it near his storage building? They hadn't established rules yet but the building was off-limits. He'd okayed Mitch to go in and get a couple of things but that was it. Renee's stuff was inside, and while he couldn't live with it, he wasn't ready to part with her things just yet either.

Tuck picked up his pace, heading in Josie's direction. Unaware of him, she continued whatever she was doing. From a distance, it looked like one of the tribal dances his mom liked to teach at the community center once a month. As he got closer, he realized she was taking a few steps and holding up her cell phone. A few more steps, forward and back, left and right, holding that phone of hers overhead and craning to look at the screen.

"You won't find reception out here," he said once he was only a few feet away.

Josie jolted and yanked her phone to her side.

He almost laughed, which seemed to happen a lot when he was around her. "You won't find anything you need out here. No need for you to come this far out."

Josie blinked at him, her mouth tightening. "Is that how you welcome all your renters to your home?"

"You're my first renter so, yeah, I guess so." He held open his arms. "Welcome to Hope Cottage."

Her demeanor softened as she looked around. "It's beautiful here." Her gaze swept back to meet his. "But I don't think I can stay somewhere without phone reception. I have work to do. That involves checking in with my boss regularly."

"Don't worry. You can get cell reception on my deck. I'm not sure why but the signal is perfect there. At least for me."

"I can use your deck?" she asked, walking alongside him toward the house.

"Of course. The only place I'd rather you not go is that shed back there." He glanced over at her, and his pulse quickened. *She* was a lot more beautiful to look at than this field of flowers. It was more than that though. There was something about her eyes and her smile, confident and unsure at the same time. There was also the anticipation of what she'd say next, because her words never ceased to surprise him.

She met his gaze and gave him a questioning look. Then she stumbled forward.

His arms went out to catch her, snatching her from her free fall and pulling her body firmly against him. He didn't move for a long moment. She didn't either. They just stood there in a field of wildflowers, holding each other with their eyes locked.

Suddenly his mouth was dry, and his heart was thudding painfully against his ribs. Agreeing to have her live here was a bad decision. He was dipping his toe back into dating but a simple glance at Josie felt like dipping a hell of a lot more than that.

Josie's lips parted to say something but no noise came out.

"Looks like we, uh, might have ended our physical therapy sessions a little too soon," he teased.

"No, I'm fine. The ground is just a little uneven here." To prove her point, she pushed off him and started walking again, hurried now as if he were a threat, when it was exactly the opposite. *He* was the one in danger here.

His eyes lowered to admire her curves. Then he blinked, roped in his gaze and good sense, and followed her. "If you need anything, don't hesitate to come knock on my door."

She glanced over her shoulder, still moving hurriedly. She was definitely trying to get away from him. "Great. Thank you."

She veered toward her apartment, and he retreated to the house, where Shadow was resting near his chair and waiting faithfully for Tuck's return. He patted her head and then finally went into the kitchen to get himself that glass of green tea he'd needed half an hour ago. His parched throat needed it even more now.

A soft knock on his door drew his attention.

Shadow ran to the door with an answering *woof*. Tuck set his glass down and went to see who it was, already knowing. He'd just left Josie not two minutes ago. Or rather she'd left him.

When he opened the door, she was standing there, hands wringing in front of her. "Something wrong?" he asked.

She nodded quickly. "Spider. A big one."

Doubtful. He'd spent half the night cleaning the apartment. There were no eggs or evidence of any spiders or insects. It was spotless up there. "Where?"

"Blocking the doorway. I can't get inside."

He lifted a brow. "It's *outside* the apartment?"

"Yes, blocking the door. I move, and he moves."

"He?" Tuck couldn't help grinning.

She scowled back at him—almost as well as Maddie had earlier. He was half-tempted to reach into his pocket and offer Josie a chocolate too.

"If you don't get it, I'm going to set up camp down here at your place."

And that ultimatum sent his mind on a dangerous path. Josie spending the night under his roof was the last thing he needed, and the only thing he wanted.

* * *

"We just don't have big, furry spiders like that where I'm from," Josie explained as she followed Tuck over to the detached garage. "The spiders in New York stay hidden in the gutters. You never see them."

She felt a little silly but spiders jumped. And she didn't want to smoosh it with her tennis shoe; it might haunt her forever. But if it lunged at her and bit her, well, people died from spider bites, right? She'd read all about it as research she'd once done for an article on glamping, which was the glamorous version of camping.

She stayed at the bottom of the steps while Tuck and Shadow climbed to the top. He appeared to move his foot and chase the thing away. Then he looked down at the bottom of the steps where she was cowering. He turned her doorknob, opened her front door, and gestured for her to go inside.

"What if it comes back?" she asked.

"It won't," he said, not budging from the top. "But if it does, you can call me, and I'll come get it."

"I don't have phone reception up there, remember?" She started up the steps, drawing closer to him and ready to jump into his arms if the arachnid pounced.

"Hmm. That is a dilemma." He gave her a wide grin. "I'll look into getting a signal-booster device for up here. Future renters will need one anyway."

"Thank you," she said, deciding to worry about more spiders if and when more eight-legged critters actually appeared. Right now, Tuck was the obstacle in her path.

"You're welcome. Since I'm already up here, is there anything else I can help you with?"

Her overactive imagination took off running. "Um, nope. I don't think so. I plan to order takeout, maybe Thai, and work for the rest of the night."

His grin fell away.

"What?"

· "Well, even though we're only a mile from downtown, Blueberry Creek is technically outside the city limits. Boondock territory is the technical term around here."

"No deliveries?" she asked.

"And no Thai, I'm afraid. Not unless you want to drive up the mountain."

Her heart sank. All the comforts of home were being stripped away one by one. Takeout was what sustained her in New York, and good Thai was her go-to when she was having a bad day. Or a good one. Or when she was feeling lonely and missing Kaitlyn. Pretty much any time her emotions were unraveling at all—like now.

"I'm going to grill some chicken on the back deck. I have more than enough thawing if you want to join me. Then you can go to the grocery store tomorrow and stock your minifridge."

She really was trying to be good when it came to him. She only checked him out when he wasn't looking, and she was keeping her comments as innocent as possible. She couldn't cut off the buzz of awareness between them though. Did he feel it too? "A girl's gotta eat, I guess. Thank you."

"No problem." He started down the steps and then

turned back. "Maybe we can have that drink you suggested the other day."

She'd hoped he had forgotten about that. "Sure."

"Give me about an hour?" he asked.

"It's a date," she replied without thinking. That seemed to be a habit of hers when he was around. Before he could respond, she stepped into her apartment and shut the door behind her, barring sexy physical therapists and big, hairy spiders. Was she this socially inept in New York? Or was it just here, with this man?

* * *

An hour later, Josie stepped onto Tuck's back deck. The sun was already down behind the pinewood forest, giving it an inky contrast.

He looked up from the grill and nodded as she approached. "Hey."

"Hi." Josie took a moment to pat Shadow's head. "Hello to you as well. Do you get grilled chicken too?" she asked the dog.

"She wishes," Tuck said.

Josie smiled, feeling a little flutter of nerves in her belly. "Can I help?"

"No, it's almost done. Just sit down and relax. You get cell reception here so you might want to pull out your phone." He glanced up and winked at her.

It wasn't a bad idea.

She pulled her cell out and saw that she'd missed several texts from Kaitlyn already.

How is it?

Are you okay?

Need anything?

There was also a text from her mom: Did you make it home safely?

Right. Josie had forgotten to tell her mother about her change of plans. She tapped her index finger along her screen and responded to that inquiry first.

I'll be staying in Sweetwater Springs for a few more weeks. Long story. I'll tell you tomorrow. But I'm okay. Don't worry.

As long as you're okay, her mom replied quickly.

Josie smiled to herself. Her mom had worked full-time until Josie's senior year when she'd married Josie's stepdad. Since then, her mom had become more doting. She'd even had a few of Josie's friends over for holiday meals, something she'd never had time for during Josie's younger years. No matter what though, her mom had always done the best she could—even when it didn't seem like enough.

Love you, Mom, she texted and then set her phone on the outdoor table in front of her. She could respond to Kaitlyn later.

"Did the world fall apart while you were out of reach?" Tuck asked, sliding a bowl of grilled potatoes to the table's center. A moment later, he slid a plate of chicken breasts onto the table and one with bread slices beside it.

"No. It's still spinning on its axis for the moment... Mmm, that looks delicious." She breathed in the aroma of grilled food, feeling her mouth salivate.

"Hope so. Be right back." He walked inside the house and came back out with a pitcher. He lifted her empty glass and filled it to the brim and then poured himself a glass too. "This is green tea," he told her. "I swear by it."

"For what?" she asked as he sat down.

"For everything. Health, mood, sleep."

She nodded and lifted her glass. "Well, I take my physical therapist's orders very seriously." She sipped generously. "Wow, I'll have to get some of this when I'm back to real life."

"So your boss is fine with you staying longer in Sweetwater Springs?" he asked.

She lifted a shoulder in a half shrug. "He doesn't really have a choice unless he wants to fire me. I can work away from the office. Bart and I probably need space from each other right now anyway."

"Why is that?"

She chewed and swallowed a bite of chicken. "Well, my new boss and I don't see eye to eye on what makes a good story." She shook her head. "Bart has no idea what *Loving Life*'s readers want."

Tuck was watching her as she talked, which made her blood pressure rise. She felt the heat fill her cheeks even though the night air was cool and refreshing. She reached for her glass of green tea, also cool and refreshing, and took a sip to quench the sudden dryness of her throat. "What I'm really irritated by is the fact that Bart is changing everything at the magazine now that he's in charge. He's probably thrilled that I'm out of his way while he does it." She popped a piece of chicken into her mouth as she thought. "Bart's father was my former boss, and we were pretty close."

"Oh," Tuck said knowingly.

"Noooo." She laughed. "Not close in *that* way. Gary was more like a father figure to me, and he always told me I was like a daughter to him. We worked well together. Bart didn't even have a job at the magazine until his dad had a heart attack last month. Bart doesn't know anything about the culture we've created. He's inexperienced, and frankly I'm shocked that Gary put him in charge."

Anger knotted at the center of her chest. Not at Gary, whom she loved. She was mad at the situation that she had absolutely no control over. "Anyway, I'm going to make the most of it. I'll finish writing this follow-up article on the town and look for something else in the meantime. I've already perused job possibilities a little bit."

"Yeah? Anything good?" Tuck asked.

"Nothing that jumped out at me."

"Unlike hairy spiders," Tuck teased.

She laughed, nearly choking on her bite of chicken. "That's not funny. Did you see how big it was?"

"I did. Almost the size of my thumbnail."

"Don't make me come over there," she warned, even though scooting closer seemed like a really good idea as far as her libido was concerned.

Tuck held up his hands in surrender. "You're right. It was gigantic. The King Kong of spiders."

"That's better." She reached for a piece of bread and started buttering it. "And you fought it off like a true hero."

* * *

Tuck was enjoying tonight just a little too much. The more time he spent with Josie, the more things he discovered he liked about her. She was ambitious and conscientious.

She flirted just enough to pull him in but kept him at arm's length, which seemed to fuel his interest in her.

Alex had set him up with Sophie Daniels, the sister of one of the station's police officers, a couple of months back. Sophie was the owner of a boutique on Main Street and was not only successful but also pretty and sweet natured. That date had gone well enough but there was no chemistry between them. To be fair, it was his first date since Renee, and he'd felt a little guilty the entire time. Then the speech therapist he sometimes worked with had set him up with one of her friends last month. That one had been a disaster of royal proportions, and he'd sworn off dating for a while after that.

But this was nice. Not that being here with Josie was a date by any means. She was still kind of his patient. And his renter.

And the woman of my fantasies. At least his recent ones.

Josie set her fork down and sat back, pulling her hands to her stomach. "I'm done. I can't eat another bite but it was delicious. Thank you."

"Knee's okay?" he asked.

She nodded. "I'm even thinking I'll test it out on the bike tomorrow, if you think it's ready."

"Should be fine. If it starts to hurt, just get off and walk. You can call me, and I'll come get you if necessary."

"I'd hate to interrupt you from anything. I'm sure it'll hold up. I might even swing in to Dawanda's Fudge Shop and get a cappuccino reading. Kaitlyn told me I needed to while I was here."

Tuck groaned. "Are you sure you want to do that?"

"I don't know. It might be a nice element for my article. What's more personal than someone reading my fortune?"

Tuck frowned. "I have no idea. Truthfully, I don't buy into that stuff."

"No?"

He shook his head. "Someone I used to know had her fortune read by Dawanda once. The cappuccino told Dawanda a bunch of stuff that never happened." He looked up. "That person died young so I can say with all certainty that it never will."

He looked away and took a breath. The memory of Renee always seemed to knock the air right out of him. "Anyway," he said, forcing a shift in his tone of voice to lighten things up, even though his heart felt heavy again, weighed down by the grief that was always a memory away. "Just take whatever Dawanda tells you with a grain of salt."

"Noted." Josie pushed back from the table and stood. "Let me help you clean up before I go back to my apartment."

A few minutes earlier and he probably would've agreed just to be able to spend more time with her. Now, he just wanted to be alone. "Not necessary. I've got it. I'll see you tomorrow."

"Oh. Okay." She looked disappointed for a moment. "See you," she said softly, turning to head down the deck steps.

He watched her for a moment and then called after her. "Let me know if there's a big, hairy spider blocking your door."

Her laugh lifted his spirit and stirred a longing inside him to pull her back onto the deck and into his arms. He'd been alone long enough, hadn't he?

Instead of stopping her, he watched her walk away.

* * *

On Monday morning, Tuck saw Josie hop on her borrowed bike and set off. She'd been quiet for most of the weekend after their dinner together. He'd barely seen her but he'd known she was up there. His one-track mind hadn't let him forget.

Tuck refocused on his patient, who usually did his therapy here at the creek. Jeffrey Simmons was recovering from a stroke that had affected his left side. Since Jeffrey liked to fish, Tuck usually had him walk down the creek to their "spot" and then pull out his pole, bait the line—which wasn't easy because Jeffrey's fine motor control still wasn't great—and toss it into the water.

"Think I got one!" Jeffrey slurred, a remnant of his stroke. "Yoo-hoo. Earth to my PT. Said I got one."

Tuck pulled his gaze from watching Josie pedaling off down the road on her bike, telling himself it was just because he was concerned about her form and the possibility of her reinjuring her right knee. "Sorry, Jeffrey."

"I can't reel this one in on my own, boss. Think it's the big one." Jeffrey chuckled.

He probably wasn't right about that. Jeffrey's muscles were still weak. That, along with his balance, was what Tuck was focusing on. Even a small fish, like the one they eventually pulled from the water, probably felt like a monster to the expert angler these days.

"That thing is what caused all that commotion?" Jeffrey squinted at the fish, barely the size of Tuck's hand.

"Yep. Too small to keep. We'll toss her back and let her fatten up some more," Tuck said.

Jeffrey nodded. "Good idea. Then I need some help

sitting in that chair over there. Catching that sucker drained every drop of energy I had."

Tuck released the tiny fish back into the murky creek water and then assisted Jeffrey to the chair that Tuck kept set up for just this reason. "Easy does it. Keep your control all the way down."

Not heeding Tuck's advice, Jeffrey plopped down into the seat like a dead weight.

"We're going to have to work on that landing, Jeffrey." Tuck pulled up a chair beside him. "But first rest. Are you doing your stretches and exercises at home?"

"Every morning after my first cup of coffee. Janet sees to it."

"Good woman."

"I've been singing your praises all over town too. I thought my fishing days were over till I met you." Jeffrey smiled as he stared ahead. "I actually look forward to these sessions, which is more than I can say for a friend of mine who goes to some clinic up on the mountain."

"I'm glad you're happy with your improvement."

"I saw that you have a lady friend living here now," Jeffrey said.

Tuck shifted and directed his gaze to the steady flow of the creek's water. Anytime Tuck so much as spoke to another woman, people wondered if he was finally moving on. The attention made him a little bit uncomfortable. He felt like he was under a microscope or the subject of some romantic movie that everyone in town was tuned in to. "She's a renter in my garage apartment," Tuck explained. "She's only here for a couple of weeks."

"Ah, too bad. She was a looker from what I saw."

Tuck stood and patted Jeffrey's back. "If you have enough energy to talk about pretty women, then you have enough to keep working. Let's practice sitting without falling. What do you say?"

Jeffrey grunted. "You're as bad as the drill sergeant I had in boot camp. That's what I say."

"Then I'm doing my job correctly." Tuck offered a hand and helped Jeffrey to his feet. They did several rounds of standing and sitting and then walked back to Jeffrey's car, where Janet Simmons was waiting.

"Of all the fish in the sea, *she* is my perfect catch," Jeffrey said as his wife kissed his cheek.

"Nuh-uh. I caught you. Not the other way around."

Tuck loved the older couple. They had four grown children in town. By this stage in his life, Tuck would have imagined he'd have the start of what Janet and Jeffrey now had. Of what Tuck's parents had. Family was the most important thing. That's the mind-set that had been drilled into him since he was a child. But instead of having his own family, he had a dead wife and a dog. How was that for trampled expectations?

"Thanks, Doc," Jeffrey called out the window.

Tuck had explained many times to Mr. Simmons that he wasn't even close to being a medical doctor but Jeffrey insisted on using the nickname anyway.

"Good luck with your new lady friend," he called as the car started rolling forward.

Tuck blinked. He'd also made it clear to Jeffrey that Josie was just a renter. Evidently the old man didn't accept that explanation either. Janet and Jeffrey Simmons were central to the town's gossip vines so that didn't bode well for lying low.

Shadow barked.

"Exactly," Tuck said, looking down. "By the end of the day, I'll be married to Josie with twins on the way."

On a sigh, he grabbed the keys to his Jeep. His next appointment was taking place downtown. Claire Donovan was a late-twentysomething event planner who had a reputation for being smart, professional, and a bit of a shopaholic. Tuck didn't usually look forward to this weekly appointment but today he kind of did. Maybe he'd see Josie while he was out.

Woof.

Tuck looked down. He swore the dog could hear his thoughts sometimes. "I know, I know. She's all wrong for me." But that didn't change the fact that he still wanted to see her.

CHAPTER EIGHT

Josie couldn't remember the last time she'd been on a bicycle. Maybe when she was twelve?

She felt foolish and free at the same time as she breezed down Main Street. *Just like riding a bike* is what people liked to say about everything. Well *they*, whoever they were, were right. She'd mounted the Schwinn and taken off as if this were her normal form of transportation. Maybe when she got back to the city, it could be.

The gears were well-oiled, and they moved effortlessly, not requiring her knees to push too hard. The back of the bicycle had a wire basket, reminding her of the *Wizard of Oz*. Instead of Toto, she'd placed her carrier bag with her laptop and her purse inside. This would be great for her article. She'd traded the subway for a bike and was making her way past scenic buildings, all of which were only one or two stories high.

She passed a business called Blushing Brides and then

the Sweetwater Café. She'd be stopping there in a bit for that addictive coffee that Mitch had told her about. Next was a post office. From her brief glance through the plate glass window, Josie saw that there were only two people in line. That would be an anomaly in the city.

Josie slowed her bike and parked it in a freestanding rack for public use. She didn't have a lock but she doubted one was needed here, even though Kaitlyn had told her about a crime spree that had taken place this past Christmas. A teenaged boy had robbed several of these downtown shops to help his mom, who was battling cancer.

Josie draped her messenger bag over her shoulder along with her purse. Maybe she could interview that mom while she was here. It had all the makings of a great story, although not the kind that Bart was looking for. But maybe the kind that her next employer would like.

A door swung open to her left, and Josie paused to let a woman with a large bouquet of flowers pass. Josie turned to the store window of Little Shop of Flowers. When Kaitlyn was giving Josie a driving tour of Sweetwater Springs last week she had mentioned that Tuck's sister owned this place.

The front entrance door opened again, and a beautiful woman with long, brown hair came out holding a large evergreen wreath. When she saw Josie, she smiled brightly. She looked a lot like Tuck with her dark hair and high cheekbones.

"Hi," the woman said.

Josie realized she was staring. She blinked and forced a smile. "Hi. Sorry. I was just, um, admiring your shop window."

"Oh." Tuck's sister nodded. "Thank you. I'm working

on it for all the tourists coming in for the Sweetwater Springs Festival." She held up the wreath. "Thus the new wreath."

"It's beautiful. Did you make it?" Josie asked.

"Yep. I make all the arrangements." The woman shifted the wreath to one hand and held out her other. "I'm Halona Locklear."

"Josie Kellum."

"Nice to meet you, Josie. I haven't seen you around here before. Are you here for the festival too?"

Josie shrugged. "Not really. I'm a friend of Kaitlyn Russo's. I was just planning a short visit but now I'll be staying a little longer than expected."

Halona's eyes narrowed. "Wait. Are you the one staying with my brother?"

Josie swallowed, wondering if being here made her look like a stalker. She hadn't intended to be standing outside the florist shop. "I am," she admitted.

"Well, what a coincidence. I was hoping to stop by his home and introduce myself to you but now I don't have to."

Josie smiled. "That's so nice of you."

"Well, I know my brother can be lacking in good host skills."

"Actually, he's done well so far. He even made me dinner last night."

Halona's mouth fell open. "He what?"

Josie shrugged, feeling her cheeks warm. "I mean, I didn't have any food in the apartment so I guess he felt sorry for me. But he was the perfect host."

"Wow. Well, that's good to know. Feel free to step inside and look around the shop if you want. I'm just going to hang this wreath and then I'll be right in."

"I'd love to." Stepping inside, Josie found herself breathing in the intoxicating scent of fresh flowers of every type. There were flowers everywhere. An explosion of beautiful color made her freeze and just stare. She'd always been a lover of words. That's why she'd gone into journalism. But there were no words to describe just how breathtaking the inside of Little Shop of Flowers was.

A jingle bell rang above the door, and Halona reappeared. "What do you think?"

"I think it's incredible in here."

Halona shrugged slightly and looked around too. "I've always loved flowers. Don't tell anyone but I used to steal our neighbor Mr. Jenson's flowers growing up. He had a pretty little flower bed, and I'd sneak into his yard and pick them." She giggled as she crossed the room toward the front counter. "Mr. Jenson is fairly old now. I still think he blames all those missing flowers on the deer." She made a gesture like she was zipping her lips. "I believe in honesty but that's one secret I'm taking with me to my grave. Mr. Jenson is known for his temper, and I don't want to be on his bad side."

Josie laughed. "Well, your secret is safe with me."

"You're not local. That's why I divulged that tidbit."

Josie stepped closer to the counter. "What do you mean by that?"

"Well, Sweetwater Springs is a small town, as you can see. And it's true what they say about small towns."

Shaking her head, Josie asked, "What do they say?"

"That there are no secrets. You can't pass gas around here without someone hearing about it."

Josie let out a surprised laugh.

"But the mystery of the missing flowers in Mr. Jenson's rose garden—*that* is something that has evaded

Sweetwater's gossip chain." Halona looked proud of her small accomplishment.

They chatted for a little while longer. Josie liked Tuck's sister. Halona was a breath of fresh air, just like the flower shop itself.

After saying goodbye, Josie headed out of the florist shop and past the café—she'd be back in this direction in a bit—and started toward a fashion boutique she'd passed on her bicycle. She hadn't packed nearly enough clothes for a month's stay, not that she ever needed an excuse to shop. She may have to limit her shopping habit if she got a new job that paid less but she wasn't going to think about that right now.

"Welcome to Sophie's Boutique!" a woman said from behind a rack of clothing as Josie walked in. "Let me know if you need any help."

"Thanks, I will." Josie veered toward the closest rack and started browsing. She loved the smell of new clothes almost as much as flowers. She was entering a Zen state only comparable to what she achieved during writing when the boutique's door opened and she heard a familiar deep voice.

All the hairs on her arms stood at attention. *What is Tuck doing in a women's boutique?*

* * *

Tuck had heard of shopping therapy before but he'd never thought it was congruent with physical therapy. Apparently it was, in Claire Donovan's case.

His noontime patient had insisted this was her favorite pastime, and Tuck wanted her to return to being independent at doing what she loved. Claire had taken a nasty fall last month while planning a retirement event and had fractured the tibia in her left leg. As a result, she was seeing him for her injuries. They'd done some stretches and exercises in the courtyard and would now be working on walking and standing balance while perusing the clothing racks.

"Hey, you two," Sophie said, heading toward them with a sunny smile. Thankfully, she didn't seem to hold his lack of interest, after their date a few months back, against him. When he'd run into Sophie since then, she'd made polite chitchat as always.

"Hey, Soph," he said.

"Hi." Claire held up her arms to hug the shop owner and wobbled on her right leg.

Tuck stepped up to balance her. "No quick movements. Slow and controlled," he advised. That had been Claire's main issue in recovery. She was very animated, using her arms and body every time she spoke. With her injured leg, talking and walking, or even standing, was often a hazard.

"Oops. Sorry," Claire said sheepishly and then hugged her friend anyway. "What would I do without Tuck around?"

Sophie looked at him curiously, and he knew exactly what she was wondering.

"As your physical therapist," he said. Claire wasn't even on the market these days. She was dating Bo Matthews, and according to Claire, they were already talking marriage. "I'm hoping you'll be strong enough to be walking in and out of these stores on your own this time next month."

"Oh, that's right," Sophie said with a nod. "You fell a few weeks ago, didn't you?"

"In the line of duty," Claire said.

"Well, then it's *my* duty to give you a discount on whatever you buy today," Sophie said. "Twenty percent off. How's that?"

Claire beamed. "Sounds like I'll be taking my time on this shopping trip, Tuck."

Tuck swallowed a groan. *Torture.* A lot of his patients called him the torturer, and now he understood their pain. "I have another client at one," he reminded her.

"Oh, darn. Well, that gives me an hour to impulse shop." Claire started going through the rack in front of her. As she did, Tuck glanced around the store, his gaze landing on another shopper in the corner.

The woman waved shyly.

He only gave a head nod, careful to keep his arms ready for any of Claire's unexpected movements. His heart, however, gave a hard blow to his ribs.

Josie's gaze moved to Claire and then skittered back to the rack of dresses she was looking at.

Tuck looked at Claire too. She was a young, beautiful woman. He could only guess that Josie had come to the same conclusion that Sophie had before he'd clarified that he was only here providing physical therapy. But Josie wouldn't have heard that on the other side of the store.

So what if Josie thought he was here with Claire. He shouldn't worry about that. *So why am I?*

Josie headed to the cash register a few minutes later, and Tuck watched her talk to Sophie. They giggled, which he'd never found remotely attractive in a woman, but he did this time. Then Josie paid and turned toward the exit. She'd have to pass right by him to leave, and he wasn't about to let her walk out of here with any kind of misunderstanding in her mind.

"Josie," he said as she crossed his path.

She turned hesitantly, looking like she wished she could've escaped without any kind of real interaction. "Hi." Her gaze slid to Claire, and he recognized the look. Guilt. Did she think this was why he'd turned her down when she'd asked him to have a drink with her? They'd also had dinner together Saturday night, which, if he were dating Claire, would've been all kinds of wrong, especially with the way they'd flirted. He'd felt like he was cheating a little bit that night but it was on his late wife, Renee, not his patient Claire.

"Josie, I want you to meet a patient of mine. This is Claire Donovan."

Claire stuck out her hand, another quick, uncontrolled movement, and Tuck's hands went to her waist to steady her. "Nice to meet you, Josie. Are you new in town?"

Josie's brows furrowed above eyes as blue as Silver Lake. "Kind of. A temporary transplant."

"Oh, one of *those*." Claire nodded knowingly and tossed a glance over her shoulder at Tuck. Good thing he was still securing her to the floor, because he had a feeling that move would've shifted her off balance too. "Temporary. That's what they all say." She turned back to Josie. "Heed my warning. People fall in love with this town. They can't resist our charm down here. Isn't that right, Tuck?"

He nodded. "Claire and I are, uh, doing her therapy in what I would call her natural environment," he explained, in case Josie was still confused. She shouldn't be though. He'd done the same with her last week, although his motives and secret thoughts when working with Josie had been nowhere near the same.

Claire laughed. "Oh, you are so obvious, Tuck Locklear. You might as well say what you mean. We're not dating,"

Claire told Josie. "That's what he's trying to make sure you know. I'm just his annoying patient who insisted on having some retail therapy mixed with my PT."

Tuck didn't embarrass easily, and with his complexion, he didn't blush. But if he did, this would do it. "You're not annoying," he clarified, because the rest was pretty much true. That is exactly the message he was trying to relay.

"Oh." Josie looked between them.

"I can see why you care. She's pretty," Claire said.

Now Josie looked embarrassed. And her complexion didn't mask the flush of her cheeks. "Tuck is ... *was* my physical therapist too. I injured my knee last week."

Claire nodded. "Well, he got you up and about fast, didn't he? He's a good one."

"My knee wasn't too serious," Josie said, "but you're right. He is very good." She gestured behind her. "I'll let you two get back to work. See you tonight, Tuck."

Claire's lips went from a smile to a rounded little O. "Looks like you're offering more than retail therapy to some patients these days, Tuck." She swatted his arm and then let out a small scream as she went free falling toward the floor.

Tuck tried to catch her but this time he missed.

Claire hit the floor and then howled in pain while clutching her leg. Tuck was down by her side in a heartbeat. "Where does it hurt? Right here?" He peeled Claire's hand off her calf. "Take a couple of deep breaths."

"Do you need an ice pack?" Sophie asked, running over toward the commotion.

"Yes, that'd be great," he said. He looked up at Sophie, and then his gaze jumped to Josie's.

"What can I do?" she asked.

"Nothing. You've already done enough," he said, not

meaning to snap at her or give her a hard look. Why had she mentioned seeing him tonight? Didn't she know how that sounded? Not that this was completely Josie's fault. It wasn't. He should've stayed focused on his patient and not gotten distracted. He should've kept his attraction to Josie in line instead of letting it put the safety of his patient in jeopardy.

"Here!" Sophie held out the ice pack to Tuck. "I keep one in my minifridge just in case something happens. Nothing ever happens here though. This is the first time I've ever had to use it." The frazzled shop owner was talking a mile a minute.

Tuck rubbed a hand on Claire's back and used his other hand to secure the ice pack along her lower leg. When he looked up, Sophie was still watching with large, worried eyes.

But Josie was gone.

* * *

Well, that was a disaster.

Josie climbed onto her bike with her shopping bags secured in her wire basket and took off down Main Street, careful to pedal with smooth, controlled movements so she didn't aggravate her knee.

The rest of her, however, was fully aggravated. She hadn't done anything wrong. Tuck had called her over to talk to him and his patient, and she had only politely responded. Maybe she'd stayed a touch too long. For that matter, maybe she'd stayed in Sweetwater Springs too long.

When she reached Hope Cottage, she leaned her bike against the exterior garage wall. She still needed to work, and the only place here with viable reception was still on his back deck. He'd likely be gone for hours so she headed in that direction and settled in at the outdoor table where she'd enjoyed a quiet meal with him over the weekend. A meal laden with flirting. The air had crackled between them, and if she'd have stayed much longer, she might have shimmied right over to his lap and kissed him, despite knowing about his past.

She never should've had dinner with him Saturday night. She should've opted to starve in the safety of her apartment and continued working. Work was always the better choice. Speaking of which...

She yanked her laptop out and pulled up her work email inbox. As always, there were a handful of messages from readers about articles she'd written. She loved those, unless of course they were criticizing her work. Sometimes a reader called her out on some trivial little detail that she'd gotten wrong. And, of course, there was an email from Bart waiting for her. At this point, she'd rather read the critical-reader emails than those from her new boss.

She sucked in a deep breath of fresh mountain air and clicked on his name. Tuck had already fouled her mood at the boutique so she might as well let Bart finish her off.

It was a message to the entire staff. Josie scrolled through the names of those on the receiving end, noting several that she didn't recognize. That didn't make sense, because she knew everyone on staff. Or she had. Missing from the list was her junior editor, Dana Malchak. Also Allison and Pete from the magazine's food section. Had they been let go?

Josie scrolled down to read the email as dread swelled inside her chest.

Hey gang!

Josie frowned. *Gang?* As in the type that haunted certain areas of the city, or the Get Along Gang of her childhood, who spread cheer everywhere they went?

I know there's been a lot of change over the last month. Thanks to those who've accepted the challenge of bringing our magazine from mediocrity to excellence.

Seriously? She was going to combust into flames of fury at any moment. Bart's father, Gary, had run a good magazine. It wasn't mediocre by any means.

She continued reading.

And on that note, I have another change to announce. *Loving Life* magazine will now be called *The Vibe*. We're moving away from cutesy and charming. Sex sells, you guys. And we need sales!

The Vibe will encompass our new vision for the magazine. No more recipes, unless they're for mixed drinks or aphrodisiacs. We're also starting an e-zine to reach digital readers. More to come on personal expectations for each of you as we move forward.

Catch *The Vibe*!

Bart

Josie nearly gagged. Bart's father was on this email. Why wasn't Gary doing anything about this? The entire magazine was being uprooted. This wasn't what *Loving Life* readers had subscribed to.

Josie pulled a hand to her chest and gulped in more fresh mountain air. In. Out. In. Out.

"Everything okay?" a voice asked beside her. It sounded far away though because she was currently on the edge of losing it.

She whirled in her seat to look at Tuck. "What are you doing here?"

"I live here," he said hesitantly as a slow smile moved across his mouth. "I came to check on you. You ran out on me back there."

"You told me to leave."

He frowned. "No I didn't."

"You might as well have." She crossed her arms at her chest, feeling like a shaken bottle of soda inside, thanks to earlier and the email she'd just read. Closing her eyes, she sucked in more deep breaths.

"Can I get you something?" he asked. "Some tea?"

"I just need a moment."

Shadow brushed up against her leg and propped her chin on Josie's knee. Without thinking, she reached out to pet the dog's head as she breathed. After a minute, she opened her eyes, feeling slightly better.

She gave Shadow a curious look. "Wow, I need to take you back to the city with me." Her gaze moved to Tuck, who was now sitting beside her at the table.

"I'm sorry about earlier," he said. "I didn't mean to sound so harsh."

She gave a curt nod. "It's okay. How is your patient?"

"Spunky and she talks too much. But her leg should be fine. Rest and ice."

"Ah, I know that prescription well." A genuine smile stretched across her face. "I'm glad she's doing well."

"Aged me fifteen years but"—he shrugged—"I guess

I'll survive." He looked at Josie's computer. "Does work always make you hyperventilate?"

"I wasn't hyperventilating. And no. Only recently." She closed her laptop.

"Don't quit on my account. I have a patient coming in the next half hour."

"The little girl you were with the other day?" Josie asked.

"She may be little but she's tough," he said. "Every session with her feels more like a wrestling match."

Josie laughed out loud. It felt good, as therapeutic as petting Shadow's head. When her laughter died, she realized that the look on Tuck's face had changed. He was watching her with desire darkening the brown color of his irises. His gaze dropped to her mouth, making her heart quicken.

She'd written an article on kissing once and knew the signs that a man wanted to lock lips. Judging by the look Tuck was giving her now, that's exactly what he wanted. And what she wanted too.

"Maybe if we just got it out of the way," he suggested, "then it'd be over and out of our systems."

"Got what out of the way?" she asked.

"A kiss." His gaze stayed pinned on her lips. "Maybe then we could focus on something else."

"What if we kiss and it only makes us want to do it again?" she asked, feeling dizzy and breathless.

"Then that might be a problem."

She was sick of thinking about problems though. She had enough at work. She wanted to stop thinking for a moment. Everything inside her was frustrated, and kissing Tuck might just make her feel better somehow. "I could promise to kiss badly," she said. "Maybe I could even bite your lip or something."

The corner of his mouth quirked. "I could do the same. Bite you back."

And that didn't sound so bad at all. A shiver of warm tingles ran up her spine.

"I'd probably kiss badly anyway," she said, filling the space between them with nervous chatter. "It's been a long time since I've shared a kiss." In fact, she couldn't even remember the last time. Her dating life had circled the drain with her busy work schedule. What was the point? She wasn't the kind of woman who settled down to play house anyway.

"I haven't kissed in a while either," he confessed as he stood.

His wife. She should put a stop to this right now. Instead, she allowed him to reach for her hand and pull her to her feet as well. The movement brought them close, their faces only inches apart. Josie met his gaze, struck by the way he was looking at her, like she was the most desirable thing in his world. Could he feel her heartbeat wracking her body right now?

"I like your idea. We'll just get it out of the way. We'll both be awful kissers and be done," she whispered. Her gaze dropped to his mouth. Then she felt him tug, and she gave in, melting into his body as their lips met. His were warm and inviting. She parted her lips, feeling her entire body sigh with relief. *Yeah.* This is exactly what she needed. Wanted.

She curled her fingers into his T-shirt, clinging to him and this kiss. A gentle breeze wrapped around them, sending her hair flying in the wind. Maybe she was flying too.

He nibbled slightly on her lower lip as promised, and it was the exact opposite of bad. In fact, she involuntarily sighed into his mouth. If she had any blood flow left for her brain, she might've been embarrassed, but all her blood was currently pumping through her heart with enough force to knock her right off her feet.

Shadow barked below.

Tuck cleared his throat as he took a small step backward, giving her space. He didn't let go immediately, which was a good thing because she might not have been able to stand.

She almost felt shy as her eyes fluttered open to meet his. "Yeah," she said, feeling the need to say something. "I'm glad we got that out of our systems."

"Me too."

She searched his face, wondering if he was as big a fibber as she was. Because now that she'd kissed him, she only wanted to do it again. And again. "Liar," she whispered, calling his bluff.

"You too," he whispered back, heat and mischief molten together in his gaze.

Then they pulled each other in for a second kiss.

CHAPTER NINE

What am I doing?

When he'd first met Josie, he'd resolved that even though he was attracted to her, she wasn't right for him for more reasons than he could count. He wouldn't act on his desire. What he'd done on his back deck half an hour ago, however, had been the opposite of not acting on it.

"Where is your brain today?" Maddie asked.

Tuck blinked his young patient back into focus. "Hmm?"

"You're not even listening to me. I told you my leg is hurting and I want to stop."

Tuck had her standing on a level area of ground near the creek. He didn't use much in the way of traditional equipment, but Maddie's legs were weak so he had an aluminum walker in front of her. When he'd manually tested her leg muscles, they'd registered the same strength as some of his ninety-year-old patients whose muscles had atrophied from lack of use. Even so, most of those ninety-year-old patients could stand, and so could Maddie. She'd lost muscle strength and range of motion in her joints but it wasn't anything she couldn't get back. The prognosis for her nerve damage, however, was still uncertain.

He was sure Maddie also had a good bit of pain with movement. Depending on the patient, Tuck would tell them to work through any discomfort. The look on Maddie's face told him she'd reached her limit though. He pulled a chair over and helped her sit down. She groaned slightly in pain, which signaled Shadow to her side.

Maddie reached over and petted her.

"You sure you like cats better than dogs?" Tuck asked, pulling his own chair up.

"Dogs are good too. Especially ones like Shadow."

"After you're up and walking, we'll start working on your grandmother's rule." He handed Maddie a ball. "Just don't toss it in the creek. I don't feel like toweling off a wet dog this afternoon."

Maddie grinned and launched the ball in front of her. Dutifully, Shadow darted forward, retrieved it, and carried it back, laying it in Maddie's lap to repeat. After about five rounds, Maddie looked up at him. "I want to go to the Sweetwater Dance next week but Grandma says it's too much trouble."

Next week was the Sweetwater Springs Festival, which accounted for most of the town's tourism during the year. At least until last Christmas, when Josie's article had named the town one of the most romantic holiday retreats in the US. Leading up to the festival were all kinds of events. Outside movie screens and kite flying would be set up along Silver Lake. There'd be live bands and the

Sweetwater Dance for all ages that Thursday night in the local high school auditorium. Tuck had never been one to attend such events in the community. He preferred nature to crowds of people, and serenity to loud music and dancing.

"Why do you want to go to the Sweetwater Dance?" he asked.

Maddie's cheeks seemed to darken a shade, and she swept her gaze down at her lap and then to the creek. She launched the ball again. "I don't know. Maybe because I'm a girl. There'll be boys there and girls my own age." She shrugged. "I don't really get to hang out with anyone anymore. I barely have friends since, you know, the accident."

Tuck guessed that was partly Maddie's doing. From what he'd gathered, Maddie had shut down and pushed away everyone who'd tried to help her. That probably included any friends she had. It was progress that she was even interested in going to the Sweetwater Dance. "Do you want me to talk to your grandma?"

Shadow laid the ball in her lap, and Maddie threw it even harder this time. "She'll say no. I want to be able to go on my own. And I want to walk."

Tuck choked on a cough. "You want to be up and walking by next Thursday?" he asked.

She glared at him. "Thought you said that I can if I'm motivated and work hard."

"And with time. I said *with time*."

"Whatever." Maddie looked down at the ball that Shadow had laid in her lap. Instead of grabbing it, she began picking at an invisible piece of skin alongside her fingernail.

Tuck sensed that maybe her eyes were also welling

with tears. He absolutely did not want to make her cry. He'd been sensitive about moving too hard, too fast and causing her to give up. Evidently, she was ready to push herself though, but now she had unreal expectations.

"Forget I said anything." Maddie edged toward the end of her chair and put her hands on the armrests. "I'm ready to stand again."

"You sure?" he asked.

"Yep," she said in that clipped voice that the opposite sex got when they were ticked off.

"You'll get there but you need to pace yourself," he said.

Maddie wasn't looking at him anymore though, and he wondered if she was even listening.

"Maybe advance from a wheelchair to a walker or a cane first," he added.

Maddie's eyes slid to meet his. "A walker is for old people . . . But maybe I could use a cane if it's a cool one." The corner of her mouth quirked as she met him halfway. "Like Johnny Depp when he played Willy Wonka. He kind of made it look cool."

Tuck had carved a cane from cedarwood and given it to Renee when she'd been too sick to stand on her own. At the memory, his heart stung like salt water had washed up on an open wound. He hadn't thought about that cane in ages. It was in the storage building somewhere, collecting dust.

"I think I know where there's a cane that will work perfectly."

* * *

Josie closed her laptop and looked out the window of her apartment. The sun was on its descent. She must've worked hours, writing something that felt dull and flat. She'd tried to piece in her trip downtown, riding a bike through the scenic streets of Sweetwater Springs. How the store owners had been so friendly, inviting her in and making chitchat. Bart wasn't going to care one bit about any of that though. Maybe no one would.

When she'd run out of things to write about for her follow-up article, she'd started a list of future ideas to possibly pitch as freelance articles for other magazines. The list was long but none of the things she'd written down jumped out at her.

Now she was spent and frustrated as she stared out the window. A flurry of movement caught her eye. Blinking it into focus, she saw that it was Tuck and Shadow crossing the backyard toward the storage building where she'd gone to find cell phone reception on Saturday. She watched as he opened the door to the building and disappeared inside.

Leave him be, Josie. Because obviously, her resolution to keep things platonic wasn't exactly working when she was with him. She'd been wondering if Tuck had a lamp hidden away somewhere that she could use though. The overhead light in her main room was too much. In her own apartment in New York, she often just used a small table lamp, and having things as close to normal as possible would help with the flow of her writing. When things were off, *she* was off.

So there it was. She *had* to go.

Slipping her feet into a pair of flip-flops, she headed down the stairs of the garage apartment and toward the storage building. Shadow must have heard Josie coming, because when Josie was only a few feet away, the dog bolted out of the storage building and ran toward her.

Josie could tell when Shadow was working and when she wasn't. When on duty, Shadow stayed at Tuck's side. Now she ran and propped her feet up on Josie's thigh, smudging her jeans with dirt.

Tuck poked his head out of the building, presumably looking for Shadow. "Hey."

She offered a small wave. "I saw you out here so I thought I'd come see if you had a lamp in storage."

"Lamp?"

She nodded. "I'm used to working by lamplight." She was still petting Shadow's head, finding comfort there because her heart was thundering so forcefully that it threatened to knock her over. That kiss hadn't gotten anything out of her system. Instead, it'd been like an injection of desire flooding her veins.

"I might have a lamp. Let me see." He turned back to the contents of the building.

Josie stepped closer. She remembered that Tuck had seemed territorial the other day when she'd been walking around back here. He didn't seem as bothered today though. Maybe he'd been worried that she'd help herself to the contents inside.

She propped herself against the front of the shed and peeked her head through the doorway to watch as he searched through neatly labeled boxes of various sizes. There was furniture covered with blue tarps in the back. "Wow. A bit of a hoarder, are you?"

He glanced back at her but there was no humor in his eyes. "This was my wife's stuff. Late wife," he corrected.

Josie's lips parted. She'd been careful not to mention his wife. But now it was front and center in the form of a dozen or more marked boxes. *He still keeps them?*

Guilt consumed her in one big tidal wave, followed by regret. She'd kissed him but he was married. Granted, he was widowed, but his heart still belonged to his late wife. That was obvious. "I'm sorry, Tuck. I didn't mean to bring it up."

"You already knew?" he asked, a little surprise playing in his voice.

She nodded, feeling even guiltier for some reason.

"Right. Everyone knows. I considered moving to escape the kid gloves everyone puts on around me, but…" He sighed heavily. "It's my story. Leaving Sweetwater Springs won't make me forget."

He met her gaze, and sadness crossed his expression, like a storm cloud rolling through to the next location. "It's been two years. I suppose it's time I go through her belongings and give them to someone who can use them. It's been on my to-do list."

Josie also kept a to-do list but it didn't have nearly such heartbreaking items to check off. "Do you mind if I ask what happened to her?" She covered a hand to her mouth. "I'm sorry. That's too nosy, isn't it?" Kaitlyn hadn't known when she'd asked.

"It's okay. You're a journalist. Aren't you all nosy by nature?"

Josie tilted her head. "I would take offense to that if it weren't true."

The corners of his mouth twitched into a soft smile. "She died of leukemia. By the time she was diagnosed, it was too late to do much but watch her health decline." His smile vanished along with his gaze. Then he turned his back to her to continue searching. "Anyway, that's my story," he called over his shoulder.

Josie longed to step inside and wrap her arms around

him. To comfort him this time and take away the hurt for just a moment. "So you've moved to Hope Cottage since she passed away?"

"Yeah. I needed a fresh start and a big dose of hope. The place's name seemed like a sign of some sort." He continued rummaging through the marked boxes.

"What are you looking for?"

"A cane for one of my patients."

"Maddie?"

"Yep." He took a few steps farther into the building, obviously not finding what he needed.

Josie followed him inside and leaned against the inner wall.

"Ah-ha!" He turned and held up a lamp for her. "Will this meet your needs?"

That question opened a can of dirty thoughts. Seriously? What was wrong with her? They'd just been talking about his wife not three minutes ago. *No more drooling, no more kissing.*

"Yep. That'll work," she said, forcing a smile.

"Great." He brought it to her and went back to searching.

"Can I help?" she asked.

"No. It's in here somewhere. I'll find it."

"Why does Maddie need a cane?" she asked, knowing she should leave. She wasn't in a hurry to go back to her empty apartment alone though. She had a microwave dinner waiting for her that she'd purchased while out in town earlier, and that was all.

"She was in an accident six months ago and hurt her leg pretty badly. An injury like that requires lots of rehabilitation." He opened a large box as he talked. "Her mom died in the accident so Maddie hasn't exactly been in the mind-set to work until now."

"That's awful."

Tuck nodded. "Her grandmother doesn't appear to be in the best health either so she hasn't pressed Maddie to go to therapy. They've wasted all these crucial months."

"What about Maddie's father?" Josie asked.

Tuck shrugged as he continued shifting boxes around. "He isn't in the picture from what I've gathered. It's just Maddie and her grandma right now."

Josie shook her head. "That's not easy."

"Sounds like you're talking from experience." He glanced up.

"It was just me and my mom when I was growing up but at least I had one parent. She worked hard, and I was the latchkey kid who came home to an empty house and made my own dinner every night. Not that I'm complaining. She did the best she could when she was around." Josie had just wished she'd been around more.

Tuck looked at her for a long moment, which made her squirm. Then he returned to searching. After a moment, he pulled an object wrapped in a white cloth out of a box. He peeled the fabric away and revealed a wooden cane.

"Wow. That's beautiful." Josie leaned closer to see the cane, which looked more like a piece of artwork than something one would use to get around.

"Thanks," he said.

That was a curious response. "Wait. Did you make that?"

He ran a hand along the red-and-white-streaked wood. "It's cedar. The Cherokee consider cedar trees to be sacred. In the ancient days, we used it to carry the honored dead."

"So, you're Cherokee Indian?" she asked. She'd been wondering but it'd felt rude to ask.

"Half. My mom is Cherokee but my dad is a balding white man. I get my hair from Mom, as you can see." He offered a fleeting grin. "I made this cane for Renee. She was weak during her last few months."

"And you're going to give it to your patient?" That seemed like quite a sacrifice. Giving Josie a lamp was one thing. Giving a little girl a hand-carved cane that carried so much sentimental value was another.

Tuck closed the box and gestured that it was time to leave. "Maddie needs it, and I don't."

Josie stepped outside with her lamp and waited for him to lock up.

"She wants to go to the Sweetwater Dance next week," he said, walking back toward the house. "She actually asked me to have her up and walking on her own so she could go."

Josie shifted the lamp to one arm, letting it rest on her hip. "I've heard about the dance. It sounds like a lot of fun, especially for a girl Maddie's age."

"Yeah, well, her grandmother said no. She doesn't have the energy to take her right now."

"Then why don't you do it?"

Tuck looked over. "Do what?"

"Take Maddie to the dance. You two have a relationship, and she needs you. She can try out this cane you're giving her."

"No, those community events are not my kind of thing," Tuck said.

Josie frowned. "I missed most of the dances when I was growing up because my mom couldn't take me, and I didn't have a car."

"See? You turned out just fine," he said.

Josie chuckled and then went in for the kill. "Actually, I'm traumatized. I still have very deep emotional wounds about it."

His gaze hung on hers, and her body sizzled. "Is that so?" he asked, obviously not believing her. And if she wasn't mistaken, his tone was a wee bit flirtatious once again. How was she supposed to resist him when he turned on his charm?

"It is. I'll go with you if you want," she offered.

He hesitated.

"For Maddie," she added. "It can be part of your therapy with her."

He seemed to consider this and then sighed. "Okay. But only if you come along. This town has more than its fair share of matchmakers. Going to a community dance pretty much ensures that I'll be targeted if I don't bring a date."

Josie swallowed. First a kiss, now a date? What in the world was she doing? Tuck wasn't available, and she wasn't staying.

"Great," she said. "An added bonus is that it'll be great research for my article."

* * *

The following day, Josie decided she couldn't stay in her apartment for one more second. It was a beautiful day outside, and she wanted to get some fresh air in her lungs. It would be good exercise for her knee and maybe clear her head as well.

After pulling on her sneakers, she headed down the steps of her apartment and glanced in all directions as if looking for oncoming traffic. Instead, she was watching out for Tuck. As she tossed and turned in her small twin-size bed last night, she'd decided that it was best to avoid him when possible. She'd already agreed to go to the

Sweetwater Dance together but there'd be a crowd and no chance that she'd find herself lip-locked. She was the last thing he needed after what he'd been through. And she didn't need any more complications in her own life while she was here. Kissing a sexy widower would definitely be considered a complication.

With no sign of him in either direction, she bypassed Kaitlyn's bicycle and continued down the driveway on her walk along Blueberry Creek. After watching the water for several minutes, she turned to admire the neighboring houses. Some were big, some small. Each was different and charming in its own way. She imagined who lived behind the closed doors. So far, she'd liked all the people she'd met here in Sweetwater Springs. They'd all been so welcoming to her.

A quaint little log cabin stood out as Josie strolled. It had roses of every color climbing to the top. Josie's fingers itched to get one of those roses, reminding her of Halona's childhood story. Perhaps that was Mr. Jenson's house, the man whom Halona had taken roses from and who she claimed had a bad temper. Even as a child, Halona had shown an inclination toward flowers. For Josie, her passion had begun when she'd written her first book report. She loved writing down the facts. Loved moving words around until they flowed perfectly.

Josie's cell phone buzzed inside her pocket. She'd brought it out of habit but hadn't really thought it would work out here. Retrieving it, she checked the caller ID to make sure it wasn't Bart before tapping the screen to answer. "Hi there."

"Hey, friend. How's life at Hope Cottage?" Kaitlyn asked.

"Well, I'm staying in the apartment *beside* Hope Cottage," Josie reminded her.

"Same thing," Kaitlyn said. "Are you still crushing on Tuck hard?"

"He's a widower, Kay. As you pointed out, he's look-but-don't-touch territory." Josie nibbled at her lower lip, unable to not give all the facts—a hazard of her occupation. "At least from this point on."

"From this point on?"

"I may have kissed him the other day."

Kaitlyn squealed into the receiver. "You *kissed*?"

"Once. Okay, twice. But it's not happening again."

"What do you mean? Why not?" Kaitlyn asked.

"Because I've realized that he's not over his wife."

"Sure he is. He's moved, and he's even started dating a little bit. Mitch says Tuck is doing great these days."

Josie frowned to herself. "I just don't like being the rebound girl, even if it's a casual thing. I like to be with someone who's thinking of me and not the woman before me. I agreed to go to the dance with him next week but it's strictly as friends and nothing more."

"Uh-huh. Good luck with that," Kaitlyn said.

"Besides, I don't even have time for a casual relationship right now. I have articles to write"—even if she felt uninspired to write them—"and a new job to look for."

"You can have a career *and* a personal life, Josie," Kaitlyn told her for the millionth time over the course of their friendship.

Josie swallowed painfully. "I know." At least in her head, she did. Her heart told a different story. "So, are you calling to tell me a guest has canceled their reservations and I can come back to the B and B to stay?" Her eye caught sight of a squirrel poking around by the creek. She stopped walking for a moment and watched it scramble a couple of steps and then sit up on its hind legs. It repeated the actions, keeping a steady eye on her as well.

"No, unfortunately. Just missing you. The inn has been so busy. If I'd have known you were staying longer, I would've made arrangements to have more help at the inn so we could hang out more."

"It's okay," Josie said. "I've been hard at work too."

"Well, let's make time for coffee or lunch sometime this week. Then you can tell me more about this thing with Tuck that you insist isn't a thing."

"Sounds good." Josie watched the squirrel scamper away. If she kept her distance and her hands to herself at the dance, that would be true. Things would fizzle out like they always did. That's what Josie needed to happen with Tuck, even if another part of her wanted something entirely different.

CHAPTER TEN

The following Monday, Maddie wobbled slightly as she shifted her weight onto her good leg and pushed her right leg forward.

"Good," Tuck encouraged. "Do you like the cane?" he asked.

"I love it. It's actually kind of cool. A few kids at school even said so. I just wish I could use it all the time."

"Slow and steady wins the race," Tuck reminded her.

"I'm not a turtle," she quipped. "But I get what you're saying. I'm just tired of using the wheelchair."

"Once your legs are stronger, you'll be ready to stay upright all the time. First with the cane and then on your own."

Maddie smiled and continued for a few more steps. "I'm tired," she finally admitted. "Can we sit down?"

"Sure." Tuck gave a longing glance at the chair they'd left behind when Maddie had started walking. Beverly had dropped Maddie off again today, claiming she had another appointment, so it was just him and Maddie. He'd have to step away from the girl to get the chair or they'd have to turn and walk back. He wasn't sure Maddie had the strength to do the latter though.

From the corner of his eye, he saw Josie walking toward her apartment. "Hey," he called. "Can you help us out?"

She stopped walking and headed in their direction. "Sure. What do you need?" she asked once she was closer.

Josie was wearing yellow pants and a white top today. She was the very picture of a spring afternoon and just as pretty as all the flowers blooming around his cottage. It'd been all he could do to keep his distance over the past few days. They'd kissed and then her body language had made it clear that she didn't want it to happen again. Some part of him wondered if it was because he'd told her about Renee. Apparently she'd already known but maybe seeing the storage building full of Renee's things had made it more real. Or perhaps he hadn't hidden his raw feelings as well as he'd thought when she'd asked him questions.

"Can you grab that chair?" He gestured with a tip of his head, keeping his arms ready in case Maddie's balance wavered.

"Sure." Josie grabbed the chair and carried it over, placing it behind Maddie. "There you go."

Maddie reached a hand behind her to find the armrest, just like he'd taught her to do, and then slowly lowered her body until she was seated. She looked at Josie curiously through a lock of dark hair that had fallen into her face. "Thanks."

"You're welcome," Josie said with a bright smile. She

wore her hair pulled back in a loose ponytail today, accentuating her long, kissable neck.

Tuck roped in his gaze, wishing he didn't find this woman so irresistibly attractive. It wasn't like him to get his head spun around like this.

Josie offered Maddie her hand. "I'm Josie."

"Maddie." His patient continued to stare at her. "Are you Tuck's girlfriend?"

Josie's eyes flitted up to meet his. "No. I live in the garage apartment." She pointed to the door at the top of the stairs beside the garage. "Up there."

"Oh." Maddie's gaze stayed there a moment as if noticing the garage for the first time. "Tuck is my physical therapist," she said.

Josie nodded. "He was mine too before I came to live here. Now my knee is good as new. You're in good hands."

Maddie cast a look at Tuck. "He's going to have me up and walking for the Sweetwater Dance this Thursday."

Tuck flinched. There was no way Maddie would be up and walking on her own by Thursday. "I'm going to have you *attending* the dance with your cane," he corrected for the millionth time, "and a ready chair for you to sit in for most of the event."

Maddie's lips puckered. "He's taking me, and he's staying the entire time," she told Josie.

"I know. I'm actually going too," Josie said. "As *his* chaperone."

This made Maddie laugh. "Tuck needs a chaperone? Why?"

"Well, because I'm an awful dancer," Tuck admitted. "Josie will ensure that I don't have to embarrass myself."

"Oh no." Josie wagged her finger. "That was not part of the agreement. I love to dance, and I'm not saving you from the dance floor. In fact, I think there's a story there somewhere. Maybe it'll lead to my next article."

"You're a writer?" Maddie asked with a touch of awe laced in her voice.

"Yep."

"That's so cool. I want to be a writer one day too."

"What do you want to write?" Josie asked. "I write articles for magazines. All nonfiction."

"I write poems mostly," Maddie told her. "And I keep a journal that my mom gave me for my tenth birthday."

Tuck listened as the two of them talked like fast friends. Maddie had opened up to Josie more in five minutes than she had in several therapy sessions with him. It was fascinating, really, and he had to guess it was the young, beautiful female factor that drew Maddie in. He was a guy, which made him harder to relate to, and Beverly was older and sick. Maddie seemed to hunger for the interaction she currently found herself in.

Maddie laughed at whatever Josie had just said—he'd been too lost in thought to hear it—and then Josie started laughing too.

"Are you two laughing at me?" he asked with growing suspicion.

Josie gave a sheepish grin. "*With* you," she clarified.

"But I'm not laughing," he pointed out. This made the two females start giggling again. He couldn't help but smile. This was good medicine for Maddie. So was offering to take her to the dance.

"Okay, Maddie. If you want to be attending that dance on Thursday night, you still have more work to do. One more round of standing," he said.

Maddie groaned but her demeanor was considerably more upbeat now. "Stay and talk to me while I stand?" she asked Josie.

"Of course."

Tuck set his timer for ten minutes and kept his focus on his patient. He didn't want to let himself get distracted by watching Josie. No way was he letting Maddie fall and hit the ground.

No way was he letting himself fall either. Josie obviously had reservations about dating someone with his past, and now that he was ready to start dating again, he needed to find someone who shared his same values. Family topped that list. Josie clearly valued work and success. The other glaring reason he and Josie couldn't be together was that she wasn't staying in Sweetwater Springs and he was. He was ready to put himself out there in the dating world again but he didn't want to set himself up for another heartbreak.

So there it was in no uncertain terms. They were incompatible in every way that mattered.

* * *

On Wednesday morning, Josie rode her bike into town to work on all the ideas she'd come up with over the last week. For a change of scenery, she'd decided to work at Dawanda's Fudge Shop today. Dawanda was an eclectic character if Josie had ever known one. The tiny woman talked a mile a minute and was as bright and cheery as her spiky red hair.

"Can I interest you in a cappuccino this morning?" Dawanda asked with a Southern lilt to her hopeful voice.

Maybe it was finally time for Josie to indulge in one of

these infamous cappuccino readings. Perhaps Dawanda could even tell Josie the fate of her career.

"Sure," Josie said with an easy smile. "I'd love one."

"Oh, how exciting." Dawanda clapped her hands in front of her chest. "You get settled, and I'll be right back."

Josie watched the petite woman hurry back behind the counter. This would be fun. When Kaitlyn had her reading last year, Dawanda had predicted that she was heading into a long-lasting relationship. That had certainly come true with Mitch and in her business partnership with Mitch's mom, Gina. Tuck had told Josie to be careful in believing Dawanda's predictions. He hadn't said as much but she suspected the friend he'd spoken of had actually been his wife.

The wife he still wasn't quite over.

Dawanda returned with a tray and a small pitcher of steaming, white milk. She set a cup of coffee in front of Josie and sat down at the table. "You're not a believer. I can already see that in your eyes." She held up a manicured finger with sparkly pink polish. "But you will be."

"Are you a mind reader too?"

"No, and I don't want to be. I'd be scared to know what's going through some minds." Dawanda shuddered, making Josie laugh out loud.

"I would too." Minds like Bart's were especially scary.

Dawanda reached for the handle of the cup and turned it until it was pointing toward Josie's chest. "The cappuccino needs to know who it's reading."

"Oh. Okay." Josie frowned, suddenly intimidated by the cup's handle jutting at her breastbone. *Do I really want to know?*

Dawanda lifted the pitcher ceremoniously over the dark brew inside the cup and poured it in a straight line at the center. Afterward, the shop owner set the milk down and leaned forward over the cappuccino, a serious expression pinching her face.

Josie wasn't sure why but her heart was suddenly racing. "What do you see?"

"Well, this is very interesting," Dawanda murmured, leaning even farther in. "It seems you are entering into a period of new birth. Do you see the mother figure holding a child?" She pointed at a white foamy oval that curled around another.

Josie's breath hiccupped in her chest. "Oh, no, I'm not pregnant." And she never wanted to be again.

Dawanda glanced up and narrowed her bright-blue eyes as if alerted to the rise in Josie's voice. "Of course you're not, dear. New birth is similar to a self-awakening. The old becomes new. The caterpillar transforms into a beautiful butterfly." A wide smile spread along her lipstick-stained lips.

That kind of sounded intimidating too. "What if I don't want to be...transformed?"

"Don't worry. It's a good thing. The cappuccino would tell me if it wasn't." Dawanda continued to stare into Josie's drink. The white foam inside moved gradually, making small air bubbles that popped and thinned. "Oh, there. I also see a bird."

"A bird?" Josie squinted and strained her eyes to see the same. "What does a bird mean?" she asked, thinking of the raspberry-colored one she'd seen behind Kaitlyn's bed and breakfast the week before.

"Well, birds fly away for the winter months but return home in the springtime." Dawanda looked up with a satisfied glint in her eyes. "A homecoming and a self-awakening are in your future."

Josie frowned. "Well, I'll be returning home to New

York soon," she said, trying to make sense of Dawanda's reading.

"The cappuccino's message isn't always literal, dear. In fact, it usually isn't."

Josie shook her head. "What do you mean?"

"You're the writer, and you don't know what literal means?" Dawanda asked.

"Well, I do but I don't understand my reading. What's going to happen?" That's what Josie really wanted to know. Her life was suddenly up in the air these days.

Dawanda stood and moaned softly as she held a hand to her temple. "Doing those readings always takes the juice right out of me," she said, ignoring the question. "How about some fudge? Would you like a few pieces?" She dropped her hand back to her side.

Josie was still trying to make sense of caterpillars, beautiful butterflies, and a bird. "Umm."

"Of course you would. I'll be right back with it." Dawanda lifted the tray and pitcher of milk and hurried back behind the counter.

Well, that was just as strange as Josie had expected it would be. Maybe stranger. Keeping her eyes trained on the frothy substance—and still not seeing anything—she lifted her cup of cappuccino and took a sip.

* * *

It was Wednesday afternoon, which usually meant Tuck stopped by Little Shop of Flowers for a bouquet and took it to Sweetwater Cemetery on his way home. Luckily, Halona's store had been busy today so she'd just handed him something preprepared and signaled for him to call her later.

When was his younger sister going to learn that he didn't enjoy talking on the phone? Face-to-face was his preferred form of communication.

He parked in the cemetery parking lot, opened the gate, and followed the familiar path toward a shaded spot in the back. A gentle breeze rustled through the nearby oaks, standing tall and acting like their own sort of fence. His steps slowed as he neared the spot where Renee had been buried. Memories always rustled around in his mind in the same manner as the wind when he was here.

Two years ago, it had seemed impossible that life might go on without the woman who'd so completely stolen his heart. But it had. Breath by breath, step by step, day after day.

He dipped to place the flowers in front of the headstone, at a loss for words this afternoon. Sometimes he sat and droned on about all the things that were going on in his life but there was so much right now that he didn't even know where to start. What would Renee say if she knew he'd kissed another woman and had fantasized about doing more?

When she was sick, she'd made him promise that he'd find someone again one day. She was so unselfish. He wasn't sure he could've asked the same thing of her if he'd been the one dying.

As he thought, he stared at Renee's grave marker for a long moment and tried to remember her face. The details were starting to fade away just like people said sometimes happened. That was no doubt life's way of helping him move on but it was cruel, in his opinion. Couldn't he move on without losing her too?

"See you next week," he finally said, turning and walking back toward his Jeep. His cell phone buzzed in his pocket. He pulled it out, guessing it was Halona. Instead it was the other interfering and nosy woman in his life calling.

"Hey, Mom," he answered as he closed the cemetery gate behind him.

"Tucker James Locklear, I hear there's a lady friend living with you," his mother said.

He reflexively rolled his eyes the way Maddie sometimes did in their sessions. "She's staying in my garage apartment, yes. That's very different from living with me, Mom."

"That's good. I'm not a fan of living together out of wedlock. You know that." His mom was conservative and traditional. She also hadn't approved when Halona and her ex-husband, Ted, had filed for divorce.

He got inside his Jeep and pulled onto the road, doing his best to keep his voice even as he responded. "We're not dating. Josie is a renter, and she's only here for a couple of weeks."

"Have you met her parents?"

Tuck pulled the cell phone away and looked at it. Was she serious? "Why would I meet my renter's parents?" he asked when he put the phone back to his ear. "Do you do this to Halona too?"

"No, of course I don't. She's not ready for a relationship yet. She's got little Theo to take care of. But a man your age living all alone?" she asked with obvious disapproval.

"I have a dog," he said flatly. "And I'm considering getting horses."

She ignored this. "I've made some Three Sisters Stew. I'll bring you and your new lady friend some. It'll give me a chance to get to know her. Are you on your way home?" she asked.

Dread shot through him. "Yes, and I love you but you're not invited tonight."

"Oh, I won't stay—don't worry. I'll pack you up some right now."

He started to protest but she disconnected the call. Cursing, he laid his foot heavy on the gas pedal. It was a good thing he was best friends with two officers at the Sweetwater Springs police department. If Josie was going to be subjected to his mom, he needed to get home fast and give her fair warning.

* * *

Josie was usually nervous when meeting someone else's parents but Tuck's mom was delightful.

"I just love the article you wrote for *Loving Life* magazine," his mom said, sitting across from Josie at the outdoor table on Tuck's deck.

Josie glanced over at Tuck, who'd warned her that his mom was coming just half an hour earlier. "Oh, I won't bother you two, then," Josie had told him. "I'll just stay up in my apartment and work."

"She's coming to meet you." He'd worn an apologetic look in his eyes when he'd told her.

Josie wasn't sure what he'd been so worried about though. His mom had been nothing but nice since she'd arrived with a big pot full of stew. She'd told them both she wasn't staying long but had then sat down and proceeded to start up a lively conversation.

"I love that magazine. I've been subscribing to it for years," Tuck's mom said.

"That's so nice of you to say, Ms. Locklear."

"Please, call me Lula."

Josie smiled. "I love the name Lula."

"Thank you," the older woman said. "It's a family name. Also Cherokee."

"*Mom*," Tuck growled, "I thought you said you needed to get back to Dad."

"Nonsense." Lula waved her hand. "Your father can take care of himself. It's not often that I get to meet a celebrity."

Josie looked away briefly. "I wouldn't call being a journalist a celebrity."

"Well, your name is plastered on magazines across the country. What would you call it?" Lula asked. "I always say, 'Own who you are.' I used to tell Halona and Tuck that when they were picked on in school for being different. There are a lot of American Indians around here but we're still the minority, you know."

From the corner of her eye, Josie saw Tuck cover his face with one hand, apparently embarrassed by his mom.

"If I had it my way, they'd have been raised on the reservation like I was, but they have two very different parents. That's what makes them who they are."

They continued to talk for another ten minutes while Tuck kept his arms crossed at his chest and his forehead deeply wrinkled like this was the worst thing that had ever happened.

"So do you have anyone special back home?" Lula asked.

"No. The magazine keeps me very busy but I'm thinking about getting a cat."

"A cat is something you take care of. But who's going to take care of you?" Lula asked.

"Mom, that's old-fashioned. Josie can take care of herself."

"You know what I mean. Everyone needs somebody to care for them." His mom gave him a pointed look.

"I can take care of myself too, Mom. I'm doing just fine on my own."

By the tone of their voices, Josie gathered that this wasn't the first time Tuck and his mom had discussed this matter.

"But Dad, on the other hand, can't," he said, sitting up. "He's probably at home helpless right now and wondering where you are."

Lula silenced him with a look. "I know when I'm not wanted. You two probably need a little alone time anyway." Her face brightened as she turned back to Josie. "Josie, we need to set a time to chat again before you go back to New York." Lula pushed back from the table and stood. "I'm part of the Ladies' Day Out group in town. We get together and do all sorts of fun things. Your friend Kaitlyn has recently joined us. Maybe you can come out with us next time too. We'd love to have a famous writer in our midst."

"Thanks. Maybe I will."

Lula turned to Tuck, who also stood and leaned in to kiss her cheek. "And you," she said, jabbing her finger into his chest, "you need to call your mother more often." She looked at Josie. "I bet a nice girl like you calls her mother all the time."

Josie pulled her lower lip between her teeth and nibbled softly. She was guilty of not having called her mom since she'd come to Sweetwater Springs. Even though her mom had retired from her job since she'd remarried, she still kept very busy. It was hard for Josie to even get her on the phone sometimes. "I'll give her a call tomorrow," Josie promised Lula to avoid confessing that she hadn't done so in a couple of weeks.

"See? Such a nice girl. Tuck, you would do good to find a woman like that."

"*Mom.*"

Lula chuckled softly to herself and patted her hand to his chest before turning back to Josie. "Josie, the Cherokee never say goodbye. Instead, we tell each other *donadagohvi*, which means 'till we meet again,'"

"That's beautiful," Josie murmured.

"Yes. The entire Cherokee language is."

"But Josie doesn't need a lesson tonight," Tuck said, as he started to walk his mom to her car.

Lula held up her hand to stop him. "Stay, stay. You have a guest to attend to." She winked at Josie and then headed down the steps.

After she was out of earshot, Tuck sat back down and frowned. "Couldn't you have at least tried to be not so likable?"

Josie let out a startled laugh. "You didn't want your mom to like me?"

"No. Now she's going to be coming up here every day."

Josie shrugged. "That's fine by me. I like her."

Tuck shook his head but the smallest of smiles was settling on his mouth. He gestured toward the pot his mom had left. "Care for some of my mom's Three Sisters Stew?"

"Sure. I've never heard of that before."

"My mom is passionate about our heritage, as you can see. Three Sisters Stew is an American Indian dish and a specialty of hers. She makes it at least once a week but I never tire of it."

"Well, I'd love some."

"Great." He went inside the house and returned a moment later carrying a couple of bowls. After serving them both a generous helping from Lula's pot, he sat down.

Josie sampled the broth. The flavor was unlike anything

she'd ever tasted. She wasn't an expert or even an amateur in the kitchen but she guessed there was a special blend of spices involved. She could pick out the cumin and maybe some turmeric. "Mmm. This is delicious. I'd visit my mom more often if she made this on a weekly basis."

"It's a town favorite."

"I can see why," Josie said, taking another taste. They ate in silence for a moment and then Josie looked up. "So how was your day?"

"Fine, I guess." He blew into a spoonful of steaming stew. "I saw all my usual Wednesday patients. Two are on their way toward discharge but I got a new referral today for an older man who broke his hip."

"That's good news, I guess." She frowned and then laughed. "I'm not sure I'd be able to do your job. People in pain make me squeamish."

"It's different when you know that you can help relieve that pain," Tuck told her.

"Was your wife a physical therapist as well?" she asked, unable to resist her morbid need to know more. The only thing she needed to know about his late wife was that he still kept her things. Still missed and loved her, as he should.

"She was a recreational therapist," he told her.

Josie looked up as she dipped her spoon into her bowl, debating whether to admit that she had no idea what that was.

The corner of his mouth twitched as he met her gaze. "I had to ask her what that was too when she first told me that's what she was going to study. A recreational therapist works in different types of facilities: nursing homes, hospitals—places like that. They lead patients through leisure activities to help them stay in a good mind-set. Renee loved to do painting and craft projects with her patients. She said it helped distract them from their illness and injuries."

"She sounds like a saint. You must have loved her very much."

Tuck froze, holding his spoon in midair momentarily. "From the first moment I met her, I just knew we were supposed to be together."

It almost sounded like that line from *Sleepless in Seattle*, Josie thought. When Tom Hanks was on the phone with the radio host. *I knew it the very first time I touched her.*

Josie swallowed, wishing she hadn't brought up the subject. It was too sad, and somehow it made her feel jealous, which only worked to make her feel like a terrible person. Being jealous of a dead woman was ridiculous. Lusting after said dead woman's husband was even worse.

"Finished?" he asked, as she pushed back from the table a little while later.

"Yeah. If I eat another bite, I might explode."

"Mom's food has that effect," he said.

She turned and looked out at his yard for a moment. "It's so pretty here. I'm a little envious of your view. If I were you, I might never leave this back deck."

From the corner of her eye, she saw him look out as well. "The sunset out here is nothing short of spectacular. If you want to stay, we can watch it together."

Together. That was a loaded word. And the proper response was to regretfully excuse herself. Then again, she hadn't listened to the little voice in her head since she'd met Tuck.

"I'd love to."

They moved to a wooden swing in Tuck's backyard, and over the next half hour, they watched the sun marking time as it disappeared behind the tree line. Josie couldn't take her eyes off it. It was living art, available only for a short time to those who made a point of noticing.

"I'm so glad I didn't miss this," she whispered in awe. "Thank you."

Darkness settled in around them as the sun relinquished its spot in the sky. Then Josie turned to Tuck, finding him closer than she expected. She also found him watching her instead of the horizon.

"Thank *you*," he said in a low voice. "I must say, Mom isn't easy to win over. I suspect she came to make sure she approved of you before we got married."

Josie's mouth fell open. "Married? We're not even dating."

"That's just a technicality to my mom," he said on a soft chuckle. "And since she likes you, she'll start planning the wedding tomorrow. It'll be a traditional Cherokee ceremony, of course."

Josie laughed quietly too. "I'm sure she's well-meaning."

"She is. And for the record, Mom always finds fault with the women I've dated, ever since high school. Even Renee at first."

"Really?"

"You're the first one she genuinely seemed to like from the get-go. She'll be disappointed when she realizes that there's nothing going on between us."

Josie swallowed. "Aside from those two kisses." And a whole fleet of butterflies in her belly.

"I have a confession to make," he said, his voice dipping even lower.

She ran her tongue over her lips, wetting them just in case of an accidental collision of their mouths. "Oh?"

"That first kiss didn't get anything out of my system. The more I try to resist you, the more I want you, Josie." His gaze dropped to her mouth, and everything inside her seemed to buzz with intense awareness.

"I know the feeling," she said without thinking. That happened a lot when he was mere inches away.

He slid even closer, keeping his heated gaze locked with hers. There was something hungry in his eyes. She felt it too. Three Sisters Stew couldn't quench this hunger. The only thing that could was his mouth, his hands, his body.

He reached behind her head and pulled her hair tie out. "I've been dying to do that since the day we met."

She laughed, surprised to find his quick movements oddly erotic. Then, midlaugh, his mouth covered hers and they were kissing. His hands threaded through her hair as he tugged her to him. He was such a good kisser that she could only imagine how great he'd be at other things. Things she shouldn't be fantasizing about. Tuck was right. The harder they resisted, the more tension crackled between them, driving a need within her for more, more, more.

If they stayed on this swing though, there was no risk of going too far.

Shadow pressed her wet nose into Josie's thigh. She started to pull away but Tuck held her to him.

"Oh no you don't. You're mine right now," he whispered against her mouth.

And she was. All his, if only for this moment.

CHAPTER ELEVEN

The next evening, Tuck sat on the bottom step of the garage apartment's stairs. He'd been waiting for ten minutes beyond the time when he and Josie had agreed to meet outside for the Sweetwater Dance. They still had to pick up Maddie, and he didn't want his patient to think he was going AWOL on his promise.

He blew out a breath. Josie had been great with his mom last night, and that was no easy feat. Josie had sat and talked to his mom like they were two old friends. Even when his mom had interrogated her, she'd kept her cool.

Tuck smiled to himself. Josie had won his mom over, and him too. That kissing session on the swing had kept him restless in bed all night. Good thing they'd ended things early. She'd claimed to be tired, and he'd said the same. In reality, his body had been alive with need. He'd wanted her. *Still* wanted her. And if he went upstairs right now, they might not make it to this dance.

Good thing he'd installed a signal booster device earlier in the week so she had better cell reception and Wi-Fi access up there. He tapped his finger on his cell phone's screen. Coming?

He imagined her phone meowing upstairs. That ringtone had annoyed him when he first met her. Now he found it endearing in the same way she talked too much and too fast when she was nervous. How she used her hands to smooth the wrinkles in her clothes when the subject turned to her. How she held her index finger to her chin when she was thinking—no doubt about future article ideas.

Yep. Just one more minute, she responded.

What was it about the female population that they took every available second and then some to get ready?

True to her word, the door opened behind him a minute later, and he stood to face her. His heart slammed to a painful stop. He no longer cared how long it'd taken her to get ready. It was worth every second.

To some degree, Josie still stood out in Sweetwater Springs. At first it had been those expensive shoes she'd worn. People here just didn't wear shoes like that on a regular basis. But after she'd sprained her knee, she'd stuck to flats and sneakers. Then it was still that polished ponytail and those black movie star sunglasses she wore. Just something about her screamed city girl.

But now...Tuck swallowed past the grapefruit-size lump in his throat. Dressed in a pale blue sundress with a pair of gold-colored sandals, she looked as fresh as a spring morning. Her hair was down around her shoulders, making gentle waves that his fingers longed to run through. Her locks had been silky soft last night, he remembered. So had her skin. He could touch it all day.

"You're supposed to tell me I look pretty or something equally as charming," she said with a smile as she came down the steps. She wore just a faint glimmer of lip gloss that had him staring at her mouth.

"You look...well." He swallowed. If he thought last night was restless, tonight might be even worse. "That's a great dress," he finally said, letting his gaze roam down her body.

She stepped off the bottom step and stood right in front of him. "That'll do, I guess. You don't look half-bad yourself."

He glanced down at what he'd pulled together. Just a pair of jeans and a favorite T-shirt.

"Men have it so easy," she said on a grin. "I bet you didn't even have to make a special trip to Sophie's Boutique for that." Her eyes danced in the scattered sunlight below the trees.

"Not this time." Truthfully, he'd avoided thinking about the dance tonight. It wasn't his cup of tea, even if he was considering it a form of physical therapy for Maddie.

Josie's lips curved, and they stared at each other for a breathless moment. Today was also a chance to get to know the woman in front of him better, and that excited him more than it probably should. Why get to know someone who wasn't sticking around?

"Well, we better go." He led her to his Jeep and opened the passenger door for her, noticing the way her dress rose on her thigh as she stepped in. His fingers curled at his side, longing to touch her. Instead, he closed the door and walked around the front of the vehicle. Then he drove to pick up Maddie, who was on the porch waiting for them when they pulled up.

"Tell her she looks pretty," Josie said as he parked. "Girls like that."

Apparently, Josie and his sister thought he needed coaching in how he related to the female population. He'd have them know that, once upon a time, he'd done quite well.

He got out and headed toward the porch as Maddie struggled to stand with her cane.

"I was beginning to think you weren't coming," she said, grimacing in what looked like pain.

"Why would you think that?"

"I don't know. I have an absentee dad, my mom is dead, and my grandma is always hiding out in her bedroom lately. I wouldn't be surprised if you disappeared too."

Tuck moved quickly to her side as she wobbled. "Where's your wheelchair?"

"I'm not taking it."

"Yes, you are. The deal was you sit most of the night. The cane is just for a few minutes."

"And I will sit. In a regular chair," Maddie told him, jutting out her chin.

Josie was out of the Jeep now too, standing on the other side of the girl. "You look very *pretty* tonight, Maddie," Josie said, casting Tuck a pointed look.

"Right. Yeah, you do. But you won't look pretty if you're sprawled out on the floor."

Maddie and Josie groaned in unison as they headed toward the vehicle.

"I'm going inside to grab the wheelchair," he said, once Maddie was in the back seat of his Jeep.

"I'm not using it at the dance!" Maddie called after him.

"We'll see about that!" He headed to the door, knocked, and turned the knob when no one answered. The house was dark. "Beverly?" he called. No answer. "Bev?" He glanced around the disheveled mess in the living room, concern for Maddie's welfare growing. He understood that Beverly was sick but Maddie still needed to be cared for.

"Bev?" He turned down a hall that led to what appeared to be the bedrooms. Opening one, he peeked inside and saw a human-size lump burrowed under the covers. Maddie just told him Beverly was always in here. Was she too sick to even get up and see her granddaughter to the door for her first dance?

Tuck stepped inside the room, wondering momentarily if she was dead. Beverly's body shifted slightly though, and he saw the steady rise and fall of her chest. *Still breathing. Good.* He closed the bedroom door behind him and located the wheelchair in the living room. Grabbing it, he headed back out to his Jeep, where Josie and Maddie were giggling about something.

"Were your ears burning again?" Josie asked on a laugh after he loaded the wheelchair and then climbed behind the wheel.

He glanced at her and then over his shoulder at Maddie, who wasn't scowling anymore, thanks to Josie. He was so glad Josie was with them, even if it would be torture to keep his hands to himself tonight. "You were talking about me again, huh?"

"Can't help it. It's so much fun." Josie shifted in the seat to face forward as he pulled onto the road and headed to Sweetwater Springs High School for the town's dance.

"Glad to be your entertainment." After a few minutes of driving, Tuck glanced at Maddie in the rearview mirror. "Beverly was sleeping when I went in for the chair."

"She's not feeling well today," Maddie explained. "As always."

Tuck felt for Beverly's situation but he was also start-ing to wonder if she was fit to be Maddie's guardian. It appeared to be taking all the energy she had to take care of herself, much less a young girl. An uneasiness wrapped around him as he pulled into the parking lot of the school and cut the engine. He got out and grabbed the wheelchair from the back and set it up beside Maddie's door.

The girl sneered from the back seat, making her look like a full-blown teenager instead of an eleven-year-old. "I'll sit in that thing just until we're at the gym's entrance. Then I'm using the cane. I want to be normal tonight." There was a vulnerability in her voice, a sharp contrast from her usual snarkiness.

Normal. Isn't that what every kid wanted? He'd desperately wanted it when he was her age. Now the big difference between himself and others was that he was the only widower among his friends.

"Fine. But I'll walk you to an area to sit down inside where you'll stay seated for the entire night unless I'm right beside you."

He and Maddie stared at each other, having a battle of wills with their eyes. "Fine," she finally huffed, scooting to the end of the back seat and transferring herself to the wheelchair he'd just set up.

Then he, Josie, and Maddie approached the school in silence. What he'd learned from all his teenaged angst and desire to be "normal" was that this *was* normal. Angst and heartache, struggle and disappointment, feeling out of place and like an outcast sometimes. All of it was part of life. Everyone felt that way. Some were just better at hiding it.

* * *

Josie watched Tuck escort Maddie to her group of friends on the opposite side of the gym. Even though Maddie made a show of not wanting him crowding her, Josie thought the little girl also enjoyed having someone who cared enough to do so. Josie had heard somewhere that kids thrived with rules and boundaries. They thought they wanted freedom but in reality, they felt more loved and supported when they had structure.

"Do you think she'll listen to you?" Josie asked when Tuck was back at her side.

"If she knows what's good for her," he muttered, folding his arms in front of him. "But she's eleven so she has no idea what's good for her yet."

Josie laughed softly. "We'll both just have to keep our eyes on her."

Tuck nodded. "I'm glad you talked me into coming out tonight."

"See? It's not so bad."

"No, but I'd still rather be on my back deck with Shadow, looking out at the stars and hearing myself think."

"You can do that any night of the week. It's good to be among people." She reached for his hand and tugged, a mischievous glint flashing in her eyes. "It's also good to let yourself dance every now and then." She dragged him toward the middle of the dance floor, and then she pivoted and looped her arms around his neck. "There. This is much better," she said.

"Watch your feet. I'm not much of a dancer, remember?"

"If you step on my feet, I might need a PT when the night is over," she teased.

"I know a good one."

Josie's heart did a little jig of its own. With her arms

still looped around his neck, she slid a finger under the silver chain he always wore and then lifted it off his chest to look at the dangling pendant with an engraving of a bear. She'd seen the chain disappearing under his T-shirt before and had wondered about it. "What's this?" she asked, leaning in closer so he could hear her over the loud music.

"A bear."

Josie rolled her eyes. Then she put the charm down and clasped her hands back together. "*You* are a bear."

"And yet you keep poking me," he teased.

"Sorry," she lied. She loved joking with Tuck. Loved talking to him. Being in his arms felt right too. She'd thought maybe he was still too hung up on his late wife but now she wondered if that was true. He'd overcome a difficult past, and she admired him more for that. It made him the man he was, a guy who was kind, giving, and who looked at her with unprecedented desire.

"I feel like people are watching us," she said after a moment.

"I'm sure they are. I'm single, and I've come to a town event with the famous Josie Kellum, who shone a light on the town with her talented writing."

"Hmm. What if I kissed you right now?" she asked.

Humor danced in his dark eyes. "Then we'd be doing everyone a favor and giving them something to talk about for at least a week around here."

Heat swirled in her belly. They were already dancing so closely that all she'd have to do was lift slightly on her tiptoes and press her lips to his. Anticipation lingered between them, and it almost felt like a shame to cut it short by going in for a taste too fast. Desire was sexy.

* * *

Every sense that Tuck had was on overdrive. Josie looked and smelled amazing, and the feel of her curves underneath his hands was driving him out of his mind.

Being under a strobe light on a dance floor thrust him back to his high school days. Even back then, he'd avoided scenes like these. He'd met Renee during her sophomore year, and they'd preferred to skip these kinds of things. This wasn't torture though, especially in the company of Josie. *What is going on with me?* Somewhere in the last couple of weeks, he seemed to have lost his mind over a city girl who seemed to be fitting in just fine here in Sweetwater Springs.

"You're a pretty good dancer," she commented, pressing her body to his. "Almost as good as you are at kissing."

Reflexively, he gripped her more tightly. "Don't tell anyone, okay?" he said in her ear.

"Don't worry. I'll take your secrets back with me to New York."

That was a mood kill. The fact that she was temporary meant this new energy and lightness he felt were also temporary. "Any news on your apartment?" he asked, hoping the answer was no.

She shook her head. "But I haven't called to check on it either. I'm surprisingly not in such a hurry to get back. Maybe your quiet, easygoing ways are rubbing off on me just a little bit. I'm stopping to smell the roses and enjoy the moment. Especially this one."

"Me too." In fact, he wouldn't mind staying rooted in this one spot and holding Josie in his arms for the rest of the night.

A commotion arose from the corner of the room. They both turned to where Maddie was sitting. Keyword *was*. She wasn't there anymore. Now she was on the floor, just like he'd envisioned in his worst nightmares for tonight.

Tuck took off toward her, weaving around and through couples. "You okay?" he asked once he was crouched at her side.

Maddie's face was drawn up in pain as she clutched the side of her leg. "Yeah. I think so. Just...Ow!"

Tuck palpated the area she was holding, looking for any abnormal lumps. "I don't think you broke anything," he finally said.

"How do you know?" Maddie asked with a strained look on her face.

"For one, you'd be screaming if you had." He should've been keeping a closer eye on Maddie instead of lusting after Josie. This was his fault.

All the dancing in the room had ceased, and now a crowd was gathered around.

"Need me to call an ambulance?" Kaitlyn Russo asked, standing among the group.

"No." Tuck turned to Josie. "Can you get the wheel-chair?"

She nodded quickly and rushed to grab it from against the wall and unfold it.

Maddie looked resigned, almost forlorn, as he helped her stand and pivot into the chair's seat. It was either this chair or the cane, and Maddie had just proven to him that she wasn't ready for the latter.

"Let's go," he said to Josie.

The three of them weaved through the thick crowd, dodging concerns, questions, and well-wishes until they were through the double doors.

Maddie kept quiet with her head down the whole way.

"Looks like you had fun for a while," Josie said, once they were inside the Jeep.

Maddie huffed. "That was so embarrassing. My friends will probably never talk to me again. I can't even stand with a stupid cane."

"You will," Tuck encouraged. "We just got ahead of ourselves."

"We? There is no *we*. I'm in this on my own. I'm the one who looked like an idiot in there."

Where was his pocketful of chocolate when he needed it?

"You only think you look like an idiot. People fall. It happens all the time. Josie fell just a couple of weeks ago."

"Maybe older people fall for no reason. People my age only fall while doing cheerleading and playing sports. I can't even stand," Maddie said, her voice cracking with obvious frustration. "Everyone is probably laughing and talking about me now."

Tuck glanced at her in the rearview mirror. "I doubt that's true. By tomorrow, everyone will probably have forgotten."

"You're just saying that because you feel bad for not watching me like you were supposed to."

"I *was* watching you," Tuck said.

"No," she countered from the back seat, "you were kissing your girlfriend."

* * *

Beverly was awake and sitting on the living room couch when Tuck helped Maddie inside.

"Is everything okay?" Beverly asked, looking between Maddie and Tuck.

Maddie was still visibly upset with her arms tightly crossed over her chest as he wheeled her in.

"We had a little accident at the dance," Tuck explained. "But Maddie is fine." At least physically. It was her emotional well-being he was concerned about.

"I'm tired. I just want to go to bed." Maddie pushed her wheelchair toward the hallway that led to her room. Beverly offered an apologetic smile and then got up from the couch and followed her granddaughter.

"Good night," Tuck called after them. "I'll check in tomorrow!" He turned to let himself out. Josie was waiting for him in the Jeep, and despite Maddie's fall, he couldn't wait for some private time with her.

He took a few steps, once again thinking that Beverly's house needed straightening up. This was no place for a kid. Then he saw a photograph of a woman hanging on the wall beside the door. She looked like a younger version of Beverly with her pale skin and hair color. She had gray-blue eyes that he remembered. He knew her.

Crystal Sanders.

Why hadn't he made the connection between their last names before? He'd dated Crystal briefly in college when he was broken up with Renee. Crystal had told him she lived on the outer limits of Sweetwater Springs but they'd dated so briefly that he'd never visited her outside of her dorm. If he remembered correctly, they'd called things off just before winter break, and Crystal had never returned for the next spring semester. That had been a good thing because Tuck had reunited with Renee that Christmas, falling more deeply in love with her than he'd been before. Crystal was the one and only time he'd ever felt anything for a woman other than Renee—until Josie.

Crystal is Maddie's mother? Crystal is dead?

His knees felt weak with the realization, and he almost needed to sit down. Instead, he opened the front door and let himself out, gulping in the fresh mountain air. A million questions sprung into his mind as he descended the steps and got back inside the Jeep.

"Everything okay?" Josie asked.

"Yeah," he said numbly. "Maddie's upset but she'll be fine."

"Good." Josie reached out and rubbed her hand along his arm. Until now, her touch had only worked to fuel his desire. Now it comforted him, whether she knew it or not. He hadn't seen Crystal in at least eleven years, maybe twelve. She'd been a beautiful person inside and out, and she was far too young to die.

"Are you sure everything is okay? You look like you've seen a ghost or something," Josie said, pulling her hand back to her lap as he pulled out of the driveway and onto the road.

He glanced over. That's exactly how he felt but this new information was too raw to discuss right now. "Just worried about Maddie, I guess. And her grandmother. Beverly isn't looking too good."

"I wish I could help."

"Me too."

They drove back to Hope Cottage quietly. He'd considered that he might bring Josie inside his house after the dance tonight. Not necessarily to sleep with her. He wasn't sure his heart was ready for that, even if his body was long past. But now the news of Crystal's death was weighing too heavily on him. And the realization that she was Maddie's mom.

He parked, walked around the vehicle, and opened the passenger door.

Josie stepped into him, going on her toes to kiss him sweetly. "You have a lot on your mind. I understand," she said, even though he hadn't spelled it out for her. "Thank you for tonight. See you tomorrow."

"Thank *you*," he whispered against the chorus of crickets and bullfrogs, and the worry humming inside him as he watched her go.

Was it just a coincidence that he was treating the daughter of a woman he'd once dated? Or something more?

CHAPTER TWELVE

She was dreaming. Josie didn't have to be awake to know that. But she was at the edge where the dream felt real enough. Tuck's hands were running along her inner thighs, working their way up while he kissed her, slow and deep.

Teetering on the edge of being asleep and awake, she could opt in to the dream or opt out and get started with the day ahead.

Josie opted all in. Dreams were the playground of the subconscious after all, and she'd spent far too much of her life working.

She wriggled closer to his body as they kissed, willing those hands of his to move higher up on her thighs but they wouldn't. Tuck laughed softly against her mouth, teasing her the way he did.

She flicked open a button on his shirt, kissing the hard-muscled chest as she popped more buttons. Then she sank lower until her mouth reached his chiseled abs.

They clenched under her butterfly kisses so she stayed awhile, teasing him right back. That seemed to be their thing, both in real life and dreamland.

"I want you, Josie," he groaned.

Those four words increased her need one hundred–fold. She wanted him too. And she was going to have him. Right here, right now. No more games.

A cat jumped between them and meowed in Josie's face. She tried to push it off Tuck's washboard abs but the cat had ninja skills. It swatted a paw at her cheek, defending its territory.

Meow.

Josie's eyes fluttered open, and she sighed deeply.

Meow.

Couldn't they have at least gotten to second base in the dream? Her cell phone meowed again from the nightstand. Then after another moment, it began to ring. She had no issues with cell reception now, and yet some part of her wished she did.

She pulled her phone to her ear. "This better be good," she said, not caring who was on the other end of the line.

"Hi," Kaitlyn said. "Just calling to check on Maddie after last night."

Josie's heart tugged, remembering the commotion and the dull look in Maddie's eyes when they'd dropped her off.

Josie massaged the sleep out of her eyes. "She didn't injure anything, except her already fragile self-esteem."

"Self-esteem is so important when you're her age," Kaitlyn said. "Poor thing."

Josie sat up in bed. "Yeah. I wish there was something I could do to help her."

"Are you serious? You're the queen of ideas. When I need an idea, I always go to you."

Josie reached for a cardigan, pulled it on, and dragged her body toward the small coffee maker on the kitchen counter. "Well, ideas never come before caffeine. I'm not sure there's anything anyway—" Josie started to say when Kaitlyn cut her off.

"Wait. I have an idea."

Josie went through the motions of setting the coffee maker to run. "Okay, I'm listening."

"Let's have a girls' day out. I'm involved with the Ladies' Day Out group that gets together regularly. We do all sorts of fun stuff."

Josie remembered Lula talking about it when she brought over her Three Sisters Stew the other day.

"What if we did something similar? Just you, me, and Maddie. I can get Gina to watch the inn. There are all kinds of sales and specials going on downtown right now for tomorrow's Sweetwater Springs Festival. We can take Maddie shopping and give her a little makeover. We can get mani-pedis at Perfectly Pampered Salon too. It'll be a blast. Exactly what a girl who's low on the self-confidence barometer needs."

Josie stared at the dark liquid pouring into her coffee mug. Even without it, she could appreciate what a great idea this was. She wouldn't mind a girls' day out herself. Painted nails and some new clothes might also be just what a sexually frustrated woman needed. "That sounds like fun."

"Great. Can you set it up with Maddie?"

Josie grabbed her full mug and headed over to the kitchen table. "I'll ask Tuck for her number and make the call right after we hang up."

"Yay! This is so exciting. Text me the time, and I'll swing around to pick you and Maddie up."

"Sounds good."

They disconnected, and Josie sat for several minutes drinking her cup of coffee and slowly feeling herself return to the land of the living. Excitement began to rumble inside her at Kaitlyn's genius idea. Josie couldn't wait to tell Tuck about it. He seemed to really like Maddie and was protective of her. It was just one more thing she found attractive about him.

After showering and dressing, Josie walked over to Tuck's house to get Maddie's contact information but he'd already left. She tried calling his cell phone but he didn't answer. He was probably already working with a patient.

Josie dialed Kaitlyn's number. "Bad news. Tuck has already left, and he isn't answering his phone. I have no way of getting Maddie's number."

"No problem. Mitch can look it up for me at the police station. I'll call him right now."

"You are full of ideas today," Josie said, looking out on Blueberry Creek from Tuck's front porch. It really was beautiful. She couldn't imagine living here for the rest of her life. Or she could, and that was scary. She was a city girl, always had been. She and the simple mountain life weren't supposed to be a good match.

Her phone meowed from her pocket. She pulled it out and read a text with an attached phone number for Maddie.

Will you call her? Kaitlyn asked.

Sure.

Josie tapped the number into her phone and dialed. She was just about to hang up when Maddie answered.

"Hey, Maddie. It's Josie. How are you this morning, sweetheart?"

"Never better," the girl said in her usual sarcastic voice.

"Well, I wanted to see if you felt like coming out with me and my best friend for a girls' day today. We want to take you out for some shopping and time at the salon. Everything is better after a day of pampering. Trust me."

"Um," Maddie hummed into the receiver, "I don't know."

"Oh, come on. It's your spring break. It'll be fun—I promise," Josie said.

"It's not that." Maddie hesitated. "I just don't really have any money."

"Oh. Well, you don't need any. It's my treat today."

"Why?" Maddie asked with a note of suspicion in her voice.

"Because we're friends and you need a pick-me-up. Say yes. Pleeease?" Josie added.

"Okay," Maddie finally said. "But only if I don't have to bring my wheelchair."

"That's not a promise I can make, sweetheart. Tuck says you still need it to get around, and I can't overrule him. I hope that doesn't change your mind about going with us." Josie grew nervous as she waited for Maddie to answer.

"Whatever. I use the chair every day at school anyway."

"It's not forever. Just temporary," Josie reminded her. "Ask your grandma and make sure you don't have something else to do today."

"I don't, and she won't mind," Maddie said. "She'll probably be relieved that I'm someone else's responsibility for a while."

Josie doubted that was true. From what she'd gathered, Beverly was doing all she could for the little girl. Josie understood how Maddie might not feel that way though.

"Okay, we'll pick you up in an hour." Josie was almost glad that Tuck wasn't here this morning. Now they could swing by Hope Cottage and surprise him later with their glamorous transformations. Gooey warmness spread all through her body just thinking about it. "Wheelchair and cane," she reiterated.

"Fine," Maddie said but her voice was stronger, and Josie thought she could even hear the girl smiling.

This was going to be good for Maddie. And for Josie too.

* * *

"This is fun for you, isn't it?" Mr. Sajack huffed as he swung his good leg forward while leaning on his new prosthetic. "Torturing people is your sick entertainment."

Tuck had to laugh. "Working with you is fun, yeah. I don't consider it torture. We're getting you to a place where you can stroll down the street like you used to. That's a good thing, right? No pain, no gain."

"Now you sound like Jane Fonda. 'Feel the burn.' My wife still watches those old videos even if she doesn't do them anymore. I always used to like watching her exercise. It was a good workout for my own heart."

Tuck laughed again. He enjoyed working with Mr. Sajack and suspected, despite the old man's protests, that he enjoyed working with Tuck as well. "Okay, almost to the mailbox. Then we can get hold of all your fan mail."

Mr. Sajack shook with a deep laugh. "More like bills. They can all stay there, for all I care."

"Then you'd start getting mail from debt collectors. Nobody wants that."

They continued forward, one long, suffering step at a time, until Mr. Sajack had turned and pivoted to stand directly in front of his mailbox. He shifted his body weight over his good leg while he reached to open his mailbox. Then he carefully pulled out the mail and put it in a lightweight messenger bag that Tuck had gotten for him. Holding things in his hands while he walked was a challenge right now. He needed his hands free in case he started to fall. When Tuck wasn't with him, Mr. Sajack used a cane these days. Not as fancy as the one Tuck had provided for Maddie but it was durable, with four prongs at the bottom for extra stability.

Tuck's cell phone rang from where he'd placed it on the bumper of his Jeep. The call would have to wait. Right now his sole focus was on Mr. Sajack.

"Don't you need to get that?" his patient asked once the phone stopped and started on its third round of ringing. "Must be important if they keep calling back."

"Your safety is important. We're almost to your chair."

A couple minutes later, Mr. Sajack took a seat, and Tuck handed him a bottle of water.

"Drink and open those bills," Tuck advised. Then he walked over to his vehicle and grabbed his phone, seeing a missed call from Josie and two from Beverly. He was supposed to be treating Maddie after his session with Mr. Sajack. He'd also hoped he could talk to Beverly about Crystal. He had questions that needed answers.

He was about to call Beverly back when his phone started ringing with another incoming call from her. "Hello."

"Tuck. This is Beverly. I'm just calling to cancel Maddie's appointment with you this afternoon."

"What? Why is that? Everything okay?" While his curiosity about Crystal was piqued, his primary concern was for Maddie. He sure hoped last night's fall hadn't been a setback. She needed to stay focused and keep working hard.

"Oh, she's fine. She just hasn't returned from her girls' day out with Josie and Kaitlyn yet."

Tuck frowned. "Girls' day?" he repeated. Josie hadn't said a word about that to him.

"Yes. Maddie was so excited when Josie called this morning. I haven't seen my granddaughter that happy since, well, since last night when you two took her to the dance. I really appreciate all that you've done for her."

Tuck turned to look back at Mr. Sajack, who was still seated and drinking from the bottle of water. "It's really no problem. Maddie is an amazing little girl. I'm sorry to hear she'll miss therapy today but missing one appointment won't hurt anything. I don't want her making a habit of skipping though."

"Of course. She's doing much better with therapy this time around. I think that's thanks to you. You have a way with her."

Tuck wasn't so sure about that as he remembered Maddie blaming him for her fall last night at the dance. She was right; he should've been watching her more closely. Then he would've realized that she was standing without her chair or even the cane. He could've stopped her.

"Where did the girls go?" he asked. "Do you know?"

"Downtown, I think. Honestly, I thought they'd be back by now. But I'm glad Maddie is having a good time."

"Me too." And some part of him was jealous that they were doing it without him.

Tuck disconnected the call and walked over to Mr. Sajack. "How do you feel?"

"Tired," Mr. Sajack said as his shoulders rounded.

"Let me help you back inside."

"Nah. My wife will help me inside the house. I want to sit and enjoy the sun on my face awhile longer."

"You sure?"

"Positive. I'm betting you have other things that you can tend to."

As a matter of fact, he did. He had a girls' day out to crash.

* * *

Josie couldn't remember the last time she'd had so much fun shopping, and she hadn't bought a single thing for herself. Her arms were full of bags containing only items for Maddie. Josie and Kaitlyn had taken turns over the last couple of hours spoiling the girl. Material things wouldn't fix the fact that Maddie missed her mom or that she was in a wheelchair but it was a break from dwelling on her problems—at least for one day.

"This is so much fun," Maddie said with a large face-engulfing smile puffing up her cheeks.

Josie wished that Tuck could see it right now.

"Thank you for today," Maddie said.

"Well, it's not over yet," Kaitlyn told her.

They'd gone in all the clothing shops and had gotten their nails done too. Josie and Kaitlyn had chosen a soft rose color for their mani-pedis but Maddie had gotten a bright-purple polish that suited her perfectly.

"Unless, of course, you need to get home," Josie said. "What time did your grandmother say you had to return?"

Maddie averted her gaze, and her smile wilted just a touch. "She didn't say. She's not expecting me back anytime soon though. As long as I'm back by dark."

"Well, that's hours from now," Kaitlyn said. "Dawanda's Fudge?"

Maddie cheered. "Definitely!"

"Sounds good to me too," Josie said, wondering if she should call Beverly to check in first. Just to make sure. She would after the fudge, she decided. Beverly might be sleeping, and Josie didn't want to disturb her. Plus, Josie had given Maddie her phone number to leave with her grandmother. Beverly could call if she needed to.

Josie held the shop door open for Kaitlyn and Maddie and then stepped in behind them and breathed in the delicious smell of chocolate, peanut butter, and gooey caramel.

Dawanda peeked over the counter at them. "Well, hello there, Kaitlyn and my new friend, Josie. Looks like you brought a newcomer today."

Kaitlyn waved. "Hi, Dawanda. This is our friend Maddie Sanders. She lives on the town limits with her grandmother."

"We don't get out much these days," Maddie told Dawanda. "But my mom brought some of your peanut butter fudge home to me once." Maddie's gaze shifted for a moment but she continued to smile like she'd done all afternoon.

Dawanda looked between the three of them. "Well, a friend of Kaitlyn and Josie's is a friend of mine. Sit down, sit down. I'll bring you all a sampler plate on the house."

"No, Dawanda. You don't have to do that," Kaitlyn protested but it fell on deaf ears.

Dawanda put her hands on her tiny hips. "Of course I do. Josie is a legend here in Sweetwater Springs after writing the article that put us on the map. And Maddie is new New friends always eat for free."

The three sat down at a table against the wall where there was plenty of room for Maddie's wheelchair.

"I can't wait to be rid of this thing," Maddie huffed as she positioned herself.

Josie resisted the urge to help Maddie maneuver. The girl was tough and independent. "Keep working with Tuck, and I'm sure it'll be no time at all before you're dropping that wheelchair off at the Goodwill for someone else to use."

Maddie got settled and propped her elbows on the table in front of her. "I know. Next time we do this, I'll be walking with you two."

"Next time. I like the sound of that," Kaitlyn said with a bright smile.

"Me too." Josie pondered when that would be. She usually never broke from work long enough to leave New York. Being here was unusual for her, and soon she'd be booking her flight back home. She'd just have to make time to come back and visit, she decided. Kaitlyn was her best friend, and she wanted to continue her new friendship with Maddie. And with Tuck.

Dawanda reappeared with a plate full of samples of various fudges and laid it on the table in front of them.

When they were halfway through devouring the tiny squares, the bell at the front entrance chimed. Josie's back was facing the door but she turned when she saw recognition cross both Kaitlyn's and Maddie's faces.

Tuck stood there, staring at them, a mixture of emotion swirling on his handsome features. "You," he said, pointing at Maddie. At first Josie thought he was upset, until he broke into that grin of his that she loved so much. "You're missing physical therapy right now, young lady. I hope you have a good excuse."

* * *

Tuck looked between Josie, Kaitlyn, and Maddie, and then back to Josie. Something kicked inside his chest. That was happening more and more when he was with her.

"We can offer you fudge to make up for it." Josie gestured toward their plate.

"Well, I've never been able to pass on Dawanda's fudge," he said loud enough for the shop owner to overhear.

Dawanda poked her head out from where she was working in the kitchen. "Hi, Tuck. Are you in the mood for a cappuccino today?"

He laughed as he moved to the table where they were sitting. "Not today. Just fudge."

Dawanda's mouth pinched. "Sometime soon, then. You've been dodging me far too long."

And he'd continue to dodge having his fortune told if he could help it. Like a fool, he'd believed the fortune she'd given Renee. He'd reminded himself of it when Renee had fallen sick, and it'd been a source of hope to him. Renee was supposed to live a long, happy life because the foam in some stupid cappuccino had said so.

He looked at Josie, who offered up a fudge square.

"The dark chocolate fudge is to die for," she said.

He took the square, keeping his gaze locked on her. "It can't be that good."

"Oh, it can." She giggled as she pulled her hand away and licked her fingers, stirring a longing inside him.

Kaitlyn cleared her throat. "Do you two, um, need me to take Maddie back to her grandmother's place?"

Josie straightened and, if he wasn't mistaken, blushed a little. "No. Why would you do that?"

"Because everyone else disappears when you two are together," Maddie said with a laugh.

"Hey, that's not true," Tuck objected. "In fact, I'm heading in the direction of your grandmother's house right now. How about I give you a lift home?" he asked Maddie, unable to miss the fact that they had the same hair, eye, and skin color. Her chin was shaped like his, her nose like Halona's. Was he crazy for the questions popping up in his head? Was Maddie his daughter? Was that even possible?

He cleared his throat and his thoughts. "Your grandma was expecting you home an hour ago, you know," he told Maddie.

Josie turned to the girl. "You didn't tell us you had a curfew."

Maddie shrugged. "Just because of my PT appointment."

"Which is very important," Tuck said. "If you start slacking off now, I'm taking the cane back and keeping you in the wheelchair."

Maddie held up a hand. "Okay, okay."

"Good." He stood from the table. "You two finish your fudge," he told Josie and Kaitlyn. "Maddie and I will begin our makeup session by walking all the way to my Jeep. No cane."

Maddie's face lit up. "Really?"

He nodded. "I'll be sticking close by though, just in case. If that's okay with you. And I promise I won't let you fall this time."

CHAPTER THIRTEEN

"Did you have a good time today?" Tuck asked as he drove Maddie home. He glanced over and noticed her shiny purple nails. They must've gone to Perfectly Pampered. Claire Donovan had attempted to spend one of her therapy sessions at the salon, claiming that getting her roots touched up required walking to and fro.

"The best time. Josie is so cool. So is Kaitlyn."

Tuck grinned. "I think so too."

"But especially Josie, right?"

Tuck gave her a sideways glance. "What are you talking about?"

"You like her," Maddie said. "Are you dating her yet?"

"None of your business. How old are you again?" he asked, sliding his gaze sideward at her.

Maddie shook her head. "Old enough to see that you have a major thing for her. And she likes you too."

"You think so?"

"It's so obvious. She talked about you a lot today. It was a little disgusting actually," Maddie said with a giggle.

Tuck pulled onto her road and followed it to the cul-de-sac where she and Beverly lived. "Well, it didn't appear to ruin your day. Looks like you got a few things."

"Gifts from Josie and Kaitlyn. It won't even matter if the kids at school pick on me when school starts back up on Monday, because I'll be dressed better than them anyway."

"Clothes don't matter. It's what's on the inside that counts, you know."

"You sound just like a dad."

Tuck forgot to breathe for a moment as he parked the Jeep and walked around to help Maddie. He'd done the math. Maddie was eleven. That put her conception during the time that he and Crystal would've dated.

It can't be. Crystal would've told him if he had a child. She was a nice person. Always sweet and caring. From what he remembered, there wasn't a malicious bone in her body, and keeping a child hidden from her parent was cruel.

He opened the passenger door for Maddie and started to help her stand.

"Nope. I got this." She swung her legs around, planted them on the ground, and took the cane from his hand. Then she started walking, slow and steady, toward the front porch.

Pride rose through him. This wasn't all on him though. Maddie had worked hard. And Josie's outing with her had instilled new confidence in the little girl with long, dark locks, light-brown skin, and large mahogany eyes. Just like his.

Tuck stood frozen for a moment until Maddie glanced

over her shoulder and wobbled slightly. He quickly stepped to her and followed her inside.

Beverly was waiting for them on the couch. "There you are! Did you have a good time?"

"So much fun!" Maddie told her. "It was an awesome day!"

"Wow. You sound like you mean it too." Beverly nodded. "I can cook dinner for you in a little bit."

"No need. I ate fudge," Maddie said.

"Fudge is not a food group," Tuck pointed out, sounding just like his father when he was a kid. Tuck's breaths grew shallower. It simply wasn't true. But it was possible, and he needed to know.

"Beverly, can I see you outside?" He didn't wait for the older woman's response. Instead, he stepped back outside onto the porch and bounded down the steps.

"I saw the picture of your daughter, Maddie's mom. I knew her," he said once Beverly came out the front door. He scrutinized her reaction. Did she know that he and Crystal knew each other? That they'd dated?

Beverly came down the steps to meet him. "I know," she finally said. "Honestly, that's why I came looking for you, Tuck." She looked frail and vulnerable as she faced him. "Crystal told me about you. I knew you lived in Sweetwater Springs and that you were going to school to be a physical therapist when you dated. Crystal was the kind of daughter who told me everything." Beverly stared at him for a moment. "I also knew that you were Maddie's father."

Tuck swallowed hard, feeling like someone had body-slammed him to the ground. "Crystal would've told me. I was always good to her. She knew exactly what kind of man I was and that I would've stepped up and taken

responsibility. Crystal wouldn't have kept this a secret."
He was suddenly trying to argue against what deep down
he already knew was true.

"Maddie is yours, Tuck," Beverly said.

Tuck curled a hand behind his neck, feeling the silver
chain beneath his fingers, reminding him that he was strong.
He didn't feel strong right now though. He needed to sit
before the gravity of the situation pulled him down.

"I don't have any proof. All I know is what Crystal told
me in a crying hysteria one day after she told me she was
pregnant with Maddie. She said you were in love with
someone else and that you didn't want her," Beverly said.
"I knew how much she loved you. You guys only dated for
a brief amount of time but you were all she talked about
back then. Oh, she was so heartbroken and determined to
raise her child on her own. I tried to talk her out of it"—
Beverly shook her head—"but she wouldn't listen."

"I'm not sure what to say."

"You can look at Maddie and know that she's your
child, can't you? She looks just like you. Frankly, I
thought you might have figured things out as soon as you
saw her."

He blew out a breath. "I had no reason to think I had a
daughter. Why didn't you find me and tell me sooner?" he
asked, anger sparking against all his other emotions.

Beverly shrugged. "It wasn't mine to tell. Crystal was
an adult, and so were you. All I could do was advise her
and hope that she would listen. She never did."

"So why are you telling me now?" he asked.

Beverly frowned, the folds of her face growing deeper
with sorrow. "As you've probably guessed, I have cancer.
The prognosis is good, they caught it early, and I'm a
fighter. But Maddie has lost her mom, and I'm not in the

best condition to take care of her. She needs her father right now. She needs *you*."

* * *

When Tuck got back to Hope Cottage, he found Josie waiting for him on the back deck. She had her laptop laid out in front of her along with a mug of coffee. After the news he'd just been handed, he should probably be alone but having Josie here felt right somehow.

"Little late for caffeine, isn't it?" he asked, stepping out of the sliding glass door. Shadow barreled past him and into the yard.

Josie looked up. "Caffeine doesn't keep me up at night. When my head touches the pillow, I'm out like a light. Always."

"That's a sign that you squeezed every drop out of your day." He pulled up a chair and sat next to her, facing the backyard where Shadow was sniffing and yapping at butterflies.

"Everything okay?" she asked.

She'd asked him that last night too, after he'd seen the picture of Crystal in Beverly's home. The implications hadn't immediately dawned on him then. Instead, they'd slowly turned like pieces of a puzzle, rotating and shifting until the picture was complete.

"Not really," he said. "I found out that I knew Maddie's mom. I didn't know until last night. I saw Crystal's picture when I went inside with Maddie's chair."

"Wow. Small world, huh? Did you know her well?" Josie asked.

He looked over. "I guess you could say I knew her *very* well."

"Oh." Josie's brows lifted, letting him know she understood exactly what he meant.

"We dated about twelve years ago during a time when I was broken up with Renee. Maddie is eleven now," he pointed out. He saw the moment that Josie connected those dots as well. Her hand immediately flew over her mouth. "Are you sure?"

Tuck sighed, turning his attention to Shadow. "I don't have proof but Crystal told Beverly I was the father. That's partly why Beverly contacted me for therapy. She could've found a pediatric physical therapist but she wanted me. Maddie looks more like me than Crystal, so...maybe it's true." If he listened to his heart, he was 99.9 percent sure that it *was* true.

"That's crazy. You might be a dad."

He nodded. "And if so, I've been a dad for eleven years and didn't know. Maddie thinks her dad abandoned her and her mom. She hates that guy, and now I find out that it's me. Maybe."

Josie reached across the table and touched his forearm. "She hates the lie that she's been told. The truth is that you didn't know about her. If you did—"

"I would've been there for her. No question," he said quickly.

Something sad passed through Josie's eyes when he looked at her. Then, like a tide retreating into the sea, it disappeared. "Of course you would have. You're a good person, Tuck. And you'll make a great dad, if she's yours."

He reached for her hand. "Thanks. I'm glad you're here. And thanks for taking Maddie out today. That was a great idea. Why didn't you tell me you were doing it?"

Josie shrugged. "I tried but you didn't answer your

phone. Then I thought it'd be nice to surprise you this afternoon. After Maddie's makeover, we were going to swing by and show off our new looks. It's silly." Her cheeks flushed as she looked down at their hands.

Tuck sucked in a breath. He really wished there was something unlikable about this woman. She was thoughtful and caring and heart-stoppingly beautiful. His life was getting more and more complicated by the second, it seemed. Falling for Josie would only complicate things further. He was already well on his way though, and he couldn't seem to slam on the brakes.

* * *

One minute, Josie was holding Tuck's hand and consoling him on this dramatic turn-of-life event. The next, he'd pulled her up against him, and they were kissing like their lives depended on it. His tongue slid against hers, and her knees threatened to buckle. They kissed and did a clumsy dance in each other's arms until they'd moved back inside the house and were leaning against his kitchen counter.

Josie clutched the fabric of Tuck's shirt in her hands, holding him hostage as he trailed kisses down the curve of her neck, sprinkling them on the bare skin of her upper chest. She'd debated about wearing a top with a higher neckline this evening. Thank goodness she'd gone with the lower-cut V-neck.

He lifted his head just long enough to ask, "Am I moving too fast? Is this okay?"

"Trust me—you would know if it wasn't okay," she said with a tiny moan tumbling off her lips. "If anything, you're moving too slow." If he went any slower, her brain might catch up to her body, and she didn't want anyone or anything to interrupt this make-out session. She needed it.

They continued to kiss until Shadow came running back into the kitchen with a bark.

Josie felt a smile lift through her cheeks even as they continued to kiss for a few seconds more. "That was...fun," she said, finally pulling back.

Tuck reached for her hand. "Fun is an understatement. Half a second more and I'd have swept you off your feet and carried you down the hall to my bedroom."

Her chest lifted on an inhale. "I'm not sure I'd have resisted." In fact, she was quite sure of the opposite. It'd been a long time since she'd been to bed with a man, and this one was all too tempting. "But..." she said, shutting down her desire. Tuck had just been hit with the news that he was a father. Sex would just be a Band-Aid, and that's not what she wanted. "I did spend all day with Kaitlyn and Maddie, and I have something pressing to do. A prospective employer that I'm excited about asked me to send a couple of my past articles to them ASAP. It's time sensitive, and I can't afford to miss the opportunity."

Tuck groaned, looking hot, bothered, and disappointed. "And I need a cold shower."

She nibbled on her bottom lip. "Sorry."

"I'm not." He leaned forward and brushed his lips to hers.

"Well, if you want to spend more time together, I'm free tomorrow," she said. "I was hoping to go to the Sweetwater Springs Festival downtown."

Tuck hesitated. "You know that's not my kind of scene," he said. "But—"

"But?" she echoed in question.

"You seem to make going to these community events fun. I actually enjoyed the dance until Maddie got hurt."

"Me too." She grinned up at him. "So that's a yes?"

"Any chance to spend more time with you."

"Maybe we can take Maddie. I'm sure she'd love to go," Josie added. "It could be a little bit of bonding time for you two."

"That's a good idea. Maddie seems to like me better when you're around," he said. "I kind of like me better when you're around too."

They were just words but they turned her insides to mush. "So it's a date?"

"First a dance, now a festival. What are you doing to me, Josie Kellum?" He tugged the hand he was holding, pulling her against him, and kissed her softly. This was a sweet kiss, full of promise. "It's a date. See you tomorrow."

"Tomorrow." With a wave, she went out the back door and across the yard to her steps. Once upstairs, she closed the door behind her and closed her eyes. What was *he* doing to her?

* * *

A short while later, Josie had sent off sample material to *Heartfelt Media*, hoping they would like what they read. Just in case they didn't bite, she decided to do another search for job openings for journalists in and around New York City. Although she was open to relocating these days. She might even like a change of scenery.

Tapping her fingers along her keyboard, she did a search. Several homemaking magazines that catered toward motherhood popped up, giving her an almost visceral reaction.

What do I know about being a mother?

She'd given up her child. She didn't even have baby-sitting experience. Taking Maddie out today was the most she'd ever done with a child, and Maddie was halfway to adulthood. Refining her search, Josie excluded parenting magazines. That sliced the employment opportunities in half. And the pay potential in half too.

After applying for three uninspiring jobs, she closed her laptop and stared outside her window at the setting sun. She ventured to guess that Tuck was staring at it too, and she was tempted to go downstairs and join him. Without a doubt, that would lead to things she wasn't sure either of them were ready for though. It would be one thing if it were just physical between them. But it was more than that. Somewhere along the way, she'd developed feelings for Tuck, and she had no idea what to do with them.

* * *

Midmorning the next day, Josie headed down the steps and met Tuck at his truck. It was a beautiful day to go to a festival. The temperatures were in the midseventies, and the sky was clear, unobscured by clouds.

Josie slid her black-rimmed sunglasses over her eyes and allowed Tuck to open the passenger-side door for her.

"Your light stayed on pretty late last night," he observed as they drove.

"You spying on me, Mr. Locklear?" she teased.

"For some reason"—his gaze slid over her momentarily—"I couldn't sleep. I was up getting a glass of water and noticed you were still awake. I have to admit I considered going up and knocking on your door."

She was only thirty years old but a hot flash tore through her. "I ended up working until after midnight."

"I think I'll keep my nine-to-five hours, thank you very much," he joked.

"I sent off sample material for the company who requested it, and then I sent out more résumés. I won't fit into Bart's new vision for *The Vibe*, and that's okay."

"So, what you're telling me is that kissing me led to an epiphany." He continued to watch the road.

She laughed easily, enjoying their flirty banter. "I hate to bust your bubble but the epiphany came long before we kissed."

He pretended to stake a knife through his chest. "Did you apply for anything good?"

Josie shook her head. "Not really. Working for *Loving Life* magazine was my dream job. But the place I work for doesn't exist anymore." She shrugged. "Things change."

They pulled into Beverly's driveway, where Maddie was already waiting for them outside, dressed in one of her new outfits from their girls' day out yesterday. She had her cane but she was barely leaning on it.

"Josie," Maddie said, brown eyes narrowing as Josie approached, "I didn't realize you were coming too."

"It was her idea," Tuck said, grabbing Maddie's wheelchair.

Maddie looked between them, her demeanor notably subdued. "Thanks for inviting me. Grandma already said no when I asked a few days ago. She doesn't have the energy."

Maddie's gaze cut to Josie, her frown deepening. There was a definite vibe radiating off her. She'd acted like she and Josie were BFFs yesterday while downtown. Now she seemed disappointed that Josie was here.

"Well, Tuck and I have plenty of energy," Josie said, "and we'll all have lots of fun today."

Maddie smiled just a touch. "Is Shadow coming?"

Tuck gave his head a hard shake as he opened the Jeep's back door. "Too many sights and smells. I promised to give her a little extra love and a treat tonight."

Josie watched as Tuck helped Maddie into the back seat. Then Josie climbed into the front and they set off. Twenty minutes later, they headed into a crowd of people who'd all come out to enjoy the festivities.

"This must be every single person in Sweetwater Springs," Josie said, surprised at the turnout. She'd expected something smaller.

"And then some. The Sweetwater festival pulls in a lot of tourists. People from Shadow Ridge usually join in the fun too," Tuck said, pushing Maddie's chair. Even Maddie understood that trying to walk through this crowd would be crazy.

"You've really never come out to one of these?" Josie asked Tuck.

"Only once since I've been an adult. Halona had something to do and asked me to take my nephew, Theo. I can't say no to that little guy. Or to you, apparently."

"Gross, you guys," Maddie called back to them. "I can hear, you know?" She craned her neck and narrowed her eyes. "I hear *a lot* more than you think."

Josie noticed the sharpness in Maddie's tone. There was definitely something bothering the little girl. Maybe Maddie had just had a bad morning at home but Josie's journalistic gut told her there was more to the story.

* * *

"Win me a stuffed animal," Maddie begged, sounding more like a six-year-old than an eleven-year-old. She'd seemed a little sullen when Tuck had first picked her up but her mood had quickly lifted by the festival's mix of laughter and fun.

"It'll cost more to play the game to get that stuffed animal than it would to just go to the store and buy it for you," Tuck countered.

"That's not the point, Tuck," Josie teased, laying a hand lightly on his shoulder.

He tried to suppress his body's reaction to her. Every muscle stiffened under her touch. *Every* muscle.

"No one's ever won me a stuffed animal at a fair before," Maddie said. "It's on my wish list."

How could he say no to that? "Fine." Tuck dug into his jeans pocket for some cash and handed it over to a jolly guy behind the booth.

"Which one do you have your eye on, little miss?" the guy asked.

Maddie pointed to the biggest stuffed animal of the bunch, of course. "The huge purple unicorn would look nice in my room," she said.

Josie snickered beside Tuck as he massaged his forehead. Then he leveled the guy with a stare. "What exactly do I have to do to win that?"

"Pop the target four times in a row, three games in a row. That's all."

That sounded simple enough. He paid for three games and set to shooting the target, hitting every shot with precision.

"Whoa, man. You should be on the force with us," Alex said, coming around in his Sweetwater Springs police uniform. As the chief of police, Alex usually wore a nice button-down shirt and jeans. But on days like today, Tuck knew the uniform was so that people who didn't recognize Alex would easily identify him as law enforcement.

"Not a chance," Tuck said with an easy grin for his friend. They shook hands, and then Tuck collected the large purple unicorn for Maddie and started to hand it over.

"I can't carry that thing all over the festival. I won't be able to see where I'm going," she complained.

Tuck looked between Josie and Alex and then back at the little girl. *His* little girl? "So you made me win a purple unicorn, and now you expect me to carry it around for you too?"

Alex stifled a laugh.

"Not funny," Tuck growled, pointing a finger. Nothing could touch his mood today though or his growing affection for Maddie. "Fine. I'll carry the purple unicorn."

"What about Josie?" Alex said. "I'm sure she'd like you to win her a stuffed animal." There was a mischievous glint in Alex's eyes.

"Why, as a matter of fact, I would," Josie said, playing along. Then she pulled an index finger to her chin and tapped as she looked at the display of stuffed animals. "I want the little stuffed kitten over there."

Tuck turned to see the smallest prize available. A fluffy white kitten with bright-blue eyes and a pink collar. "To match the ringtone on your phone?"

She grinned. "Exactly."

The guy behind the booth propped his hands on his waist. "You can win that in one game if your aim is good."

Tuck sighed and then shoved the purple unicorn into Alex's arms for the moment. "Here. You hold this while I shoot. Lucky for you, it's not a real gun."

"I think that might count as threatening an officer of the law," Alex countered behind him. "Might have to lock you up in jail for that one."

Tuck pulled the trigger, hitting his target all three times.

"Winner, winner, chicken dinner!" the booth guy exclaimed before handing the small kitten over to Tuck.

Tuck collected it and turned to Josie. "Sorry, but you'll have to carry your own stuffed animal."

Josie's eyes lit up as she took the small kitten into her arms. He was fascinated by her reaction for a moment. She seemed genuinely thrilled over something he would've found suitable for the donation pile.

"No one's ever won you a prize either?" he asked.

Her gaze flitted up to meet his. "My mom was always working during these kinds of things. Better to feed me than entertain me, she used to say. I always wanted someone to win me something though. Thank you."

"You're welcome." He swallowed back some emotion he couldn't quite pinpoint. Then he groaned as a huge purple unicorn was shoved back into his arms.

"Duty calls. I have to continue making sure the town and its citizens are A-okay. Looks like you guys are doing just fine here." Alex looked between Josie and Maddie. "Good to see you both again."

"You too," Josie said.

"Keep this guy in line." He patted Tuck's back. "Hey, let's do the Tipsy Tavern again soon. We'll rope in Mitch too, for old times' sake."

Tuck nodded. "Sounds good."

With a wave at them all, Alex continued through the crowd while Tuck carried Maddie's stuffed unicorn under one arm and got behind her wheelchair to push. "Where to next? You ladies are leading the show today."

Josie looked down at Maddie. "I don't know. What do you think? We've tasted Dawanda's fudge, looked through the crafts, and we've gotten Tuck to win us a prize."

Maddie pointed up ahead. "There's live music down there. Let's go listen."

"A music lover, huh?" Tuck asked, weaving through clusters of people who'd stopped to chat, effectively clogging up the walkway. "My sister used to love to listen to the live music when she was young too. I'm willing to bet she's down there right now with my nephew."

If Maddie really was his daughter, she had an aunt and cousin somewhere out here that she hadn't met yet. And a second grandmother and grandfather. His mom was likely somewhere here too, teaching the community about the dances, games, and foods of the Cherokee people. His mom would go nuts over her first girl grandchild and likely insist on teaching Maddie all about her Cherokee heritage. It's important to know who you are and where you came from, his mom had always told him. *Cherokees are strong. You are strong.*

"I see some of my friends over there," Maddie said. "I can go hang out with them instead."

Friends? He thought Maddie said she didn't have any. This was great news.

"I'm guessing you and Josie don't need me getting in your way anyway," she added, a slight gloom falling over her again.

"That's not true," Josie objected. "But you'd probably rather be with them than us fuddy-duddies."

"You have to stay in your chair," Tuck told her, bracing for an argument. "There are too many people that could knock you down out here on your cane."

Maddie shrugged. "Whatever you say, *Dad.*"

It was just her typical sarcasm, of course. She didn't

mean it but it still knocked the breath out of him for a moment as he watched Maddie wheel herself toward the cluster of girls.

"How'd it feel?" Josie asked, leaning into him. "To hear her call you that."

"She was just being a smart-ass."

"Even so." Josie looped her arm through his. He liked the feel of that almost as much as hearing his daughter call him Dad.

"I don't need a DNA test. She's mine. I can feel it." He swallowed hard and then looked at Josie, who was smiling back at him.

"I think you're right."

People bumped against them as they passed, but for a moment, as he looked at Josie, they were the only ones here at this festival.

Josie looked away first. "Hey, what's that over there?" She pointed at a booth up ahead.

"Oh. That's probably Michelle Waters. She's the editor in chief of *Carolina Home* magazine. She sets something up every year. Come on. I'll introduce you to her."

They headed over, and sure enough, it was Michelle. Tuck had treated her once for lateral epicondylitis, otherwise known as tennis elbow.

"Hey, hey. My favorite physical therapist," Michelle said, offering him an easy smile. She moved her arm around for show. "Good as new, thanks to the best physical therapist in town."

"Glad to hear it. Michelle, I'd like you to meet a friend of mine. This is Josie Kellum." He realized his arm was still looped with Josie's.

From the look in Michelle's eyes, she'd made the obvious assumption. And surprisingly, he didn't mind.

"Josie Kellum of *Living Life* magazine?" Michelle asked. "I heard you were in town. It's so nice to meet you. Great article on Sweetwater Springs last year, by the way."

Tuck nudged Josie playfully. "Looks like my mom was right. You're a celebrity around here."

"Far from it." Josie turned back to Michelle. "Kaitlyn keeps a copy of *Carolina Home* at the inn. I flipped through it while I was there."

"Well, here. Take a complimentary copy." Michelle picked up a magazine and handed it over. "We focus on everything that goes on in the state. Vacation spots, events, well-known people, people who make a difference but don't get noticed the way they should. If it happens in North Carolina, we write about it."

"Thanks. I'll take a look tonight," Josie said.

Tuck held back his objection, because *he* was vying for Josie's undivided attention tonight.

CHAPTER FOURTEEN

The sun was on its descent behind the mountains, creating a neon-orange melting pot in the sky as Josie and Tuck pulled out of the Sanders's driveway and headed back to Blueberry Creek.

"Maddie seemed to have enjoyed herself today," Josie said, looking over at Tuck. "You too."

He gave a quick nod. "It was a great day. Thanks for dragging me out."

"You're welcome." She'd noticed how Tuck had catered to Maddie today. It was more than just a friendly gesture or because he was her physical therapist. He'd played the role of father today, and he'd been a natural at it. Any girl would be lucky to have him as her dad. And any woman would be lucky to have him in her arms.

Tuck's gaze slid to meet hers in the dim truck as if sensing her train of thought. "You're thinking how irresistible I am right now. Admit it."

She laughed. Tuck was joking around a lot more often, she'd noticed. "Getting more irresistible by the second. Thank you for winning me my first festival stuffed animal."

"You'll have to keep it forever," he said.

She hugged it against her. "Wouldn't dream of getting rid of it." She didn't let herself consider why she adored the little kitten so much. It was more than just because it was soft and cute and the first thing a guy had ever won for her.

Swallowing, she looked outside the window, watching the sky transform by the second. "It really is beautiful here."

"No place on earth like this one." He scratched his chin. "I have to confess I was miffed when a journalist named Josie Kellum wrote about my town, inviting more tourists here. Sweetwater Springs is one of the nation's best-kept secrets in my opinion, and you outed us."

"Sorry."

He tipped his head. "Liar."

"You're right. I'm not sorry. It's been good for the town though, right?"

He nodded. "Very. And that benefits me and my sister Halona's business, your friend Kaitlyn's—everyone's. I'm glad you wrote it. And I'm glad you came here to see how great a place this is yourself."

"Me too." She'd been in town for only three weeks now but already she felt at home.

"How was your knee today? It was a lot of walking. You okay?" he asked, looking over with concern deepening the lines on his forehead.

He was protective of Maddie for good reason. But he also looked out for Josie's well-being. Like his mom had said the night she'd brought them stew, people needed someone to take care of them. Or maybe they didn't need it but it sure did feel good. "My knee hasn't given me any trouble in over a week."

"Great."

They pulled into the driveway of Tuck's home, and he cut the engine. Josie didn't move for a moment, unsure of where her next steps would take her. Up the stairs to her garage apartment? That's where she probably needed to go. Inside with Tuck for a nightcap? That's where she knew she was heading. She'd made enough excuses to distance herself from this man. She was done.

"I need to let Shadow out," he said.

"She's probably chomping at the bit to go."

"Probably." He looked at her for a long moment. His eyes on her weren't enough though. She wanted more. "The sunset is long past, but if you're not tired, I can pour you a drink, and we can sit on the back deck for a little while."

"I'm not tired," she answered quickly. Which was true. Even though she probably should've been exhausted after their eventful day, her body was restless.

Tuck pushed out of his Jeep and led her inside. Shadow barked in greeting and then propped her paws on Josie's thigh.

"She says she missed you."

"You speak dog?" Josie asked.

"Of course." He walked through and opened the back door. "Go ahead, Shadow. We'll be out in a minute." He headed to the kitchen and retrieved a bottle of wine and some glasses. After he poured them both a generous helping, they stepped outside.

The night had gotten cooler as the sun disappeared. Josie pressed her hips against the railing of the deck while holding her glass. Then Tuck came up behind her and bent to kiss the exposed skin of her neck. She closed her eyes, barring the beauty outside so that she could focus entirely on the feel of his mouth scraping his delicious five o'clock shadow over her skin. His hands anchored low on her waist as the weight of his body pinned her in place.

Josie wriggled just enough to turn in his embrace and lifted her mouth to his, tasting the bittersweet trace of red wine on his lips. The kiss went on until she reached for his hand. Her heart raced with the proposition she was about to make. "I'm ready for bed now."

His eyes darkened as he seemed to understand exactly what she meant. She wasn't tired, and she didn't want to retreat to her apartment above the garage. Not this time. Tonight, she wanted to go to his bed and continue what they'd started.

"Are you sure?" he asked, trailing a finger down the line of her jaw.

"Very."

The consent was barely out of her mouth before they were kissing, hands roaming, and chasing each other into the house with Shadow following behind. Tuck closed the back door, grabbed a treat from a jar on the kitchen counter, and tossed it toward Shadow. "As promised," he told the Lab. Then he reached for Josie and tugged her toward the hall that led to his bedroom.

She'd already waded into deep waters with Tuck. Going any further would put her in over her head. She knew that, even as her feet continued forward. Even as she lifted her shirt over her head and moaned when he touched her body. As she traced her own fingers down the muscled contours of his chest and abs.

She knew it, and yet, she didn't care.

* * *

Birds tweeted outside the window, pulling Josie from the most amazing dream. A purple-colored bird like the one she'd seen on her hike behind the Sweetwater Bed and Breakfast fluttered ahead of her, seeming to lead her toward something wonderful.

Curious about the little bird, Josie followed. The air was cool and fresh on her skin as she walked briskly along the yellow-brick path. She was apparently Dorothy in this dreamland, and instead of Toto as her sidekick, she had a magical purplish-pink bird. A castle appeared in the distance as she walked. The Wizard of Oz would know how to send her home.

Josie stopped walking. "I don't want to go home though," she said as she looked down at her ruby-red stilettos. She had a closet full of heels in her New York apartment but none were as eye-catching as these.

She bent her ankle to admire one and accidentally clicked the side of her left heel to her right. On a gasp, she started shaking her head. "No, no, no. I don't want to go home. Not yet."

The call of birds tweeting in the distance grew louder as the purple bird zipped all around her. Looking up, she realized the castle and its wizard were disappearing. She didn't want to go home so soon.

"Not yet," she moaned, curling into the pillow.

"Josie?"

Tuck's voice was her final pull into reality.

She cracked one eye, then both, blinking him into focus.

"Good morning, beautiful," he said with a smile.

"I was having the weirdest dream." Her voice was coated with sleep. She wasn't a morning person, not until her first cup of coffee.

"Yeah? Was I in it?" he asked, dipping to sprinkle kisses along her bare skin. She could get used to waking up like this.

"No." She rolled to her side and propped her body up on one elbow. "But you should've been...Is that coffee I smell?"

"Yep. You were sleeping pretty good so I got up and made us breakfast."

Her eyes widened. "Really?"

"Figured you'd be hungry after last night," he said.

"You'd be right. Let me get dressed"—brush her hair and teeth too so she didn't scare him off—"and I'll join you."

"Or..." He nipped her lower lip.

"Or?" she asked, her body humming with a sudden need that the cooked breakfast in the kitchen couldn't satisfy.

"Or breakfast could wait a few more minutes," he suggested.

"Yes, it can." Josie let herself fall back on the pillow. Food and coffee could definitely wait.

* * *

Sunday was Tuck's favorite day of the week for so many reasons. Today it was because he had a beautiful woman in his bed and he didn't have to rush off for anyone or anything.

"Are we ever going to get out of bed?" Josie asked, lying across his outstretched arm. They'd had breakfast and then dove right back under the sheets.

"Not today," Tuck said, half teasing. "I suppose I'll have to let Shadow out again at some point but not for a few hours."

Josie burrowed into the crook of his arm. "I never lie in bed all day."

"Too much of a workaholic?" he asked, already knowing that about her. He wanted to know more though. He wanted to find out everything there was to learn about this woman in his bed.

"Guilty as charged," she said.

"Well, it's my mission while you're here to help you slow down," he said, kissing her shoulder.

"Oh, is it?"

"Payback for dragging me out of the cozy confines of Hope Cottage for a dance and a festival."

Josie laughed. "Seems like we complement each other nicely."

"It does. So tell me about your family."

She turned her body to look up at him. "I've already told you. My mom was a single parent."

"Brothers or sisters?" he asked.

"Just me."

"Your dad?" Tuck asked. "Or is that too personal?"

She shook her head. "No. Dad was a financial guru in the city. He paid child support, and that was all. Mom got remarried to my stepdad when I was in college."

"Do you like him?"

"My stepdad? Yeah, he's nice. She deserves a guy who pampers her for once."

"So do you. I can't believe I thought you were spoiled at first impression," he admitted while stroking his finger along the side of her bare arm.

"Not anymore?" she asked.

"No."

She seemed to wait for him to say more. "Well, what changed your mind?"

"You did. You're not at all what I expected, Josie Kellum. You're a pleasant surprise."

"Hmm," she hummed, looking at him again.

"What?"

"I like your version of pillow talk. Makes a girl feel all mushy inside." She sat up, revealing a bare back.

Without thinking, he reached out and touched her. "Hey, where are you going?"

"As my grandmother used to say, the day is wasting."

"Lying in bed with the guy you spent the night with is a waste of time?" he asked, trying not to take offense.

She glanced over her shoulder. "No, that's not at all what I meant." Closing her eyes, she shook her head softly. "See, this is why I don't have a boyfriend back home."

"Because you're always running?"

She opened her eyes and narrowed them at him. "I'm not running."

He kept his gaze steady. "Sure you are. We're all running from something. Only a person who doesn't want to live their life spends all their time with their head down working."

A muscle twitched along her cheek. He'd hit a nerve.

"The hole in that theory is that I haven't worked enough since I've been here with you."

Tuck grinned. "Every outing we've had has been research for you in some way. I've seen you pull that little notebook of yours out of your purse. Your brain has been on overdrive every moment."

"Not *every* moment," she said, one corner of her mouth lifting softly.

He gently traced a finger along the soft skin of her back, loving every curve. This was the danger of him getting involved with someone. He invested too much, wanted too much, even if he wasn't willing to admit it. "Spend the day with me," he said. "Just you and me."

"What?"

"And not for research or any other pretense but because you want to. I promise it won't be a waste of your time."

A full smile upturned her lips. "It's a good thing I don't have someone like you in New York, because I'd be at the unemployment office."

"Don't worry. I'm one of a kind." He tugged her body toward him, pulling her until she was lying on top of him. Eyes to eyes, lips to lips, chest to chest, heartbeat to heartbeat. It was lucky he didn't have someone like her who was staying, because he could fall way too easily. He'd been down this road before, and it had led somewhere wonderful. Then somewhere awful. He wasn't ready to travel it again.

"What will we do if I say yes?" she asked, kissing his jawline toward his ear.

"If?" He raised a brow.

"Fine. My answer is yes but I still want to know what I'm saying yes to."

"I need to see a man about a horse."

She pulled back and giggled. "Seriously? I've gone from the *Wizard of Oz* to a John Wayne movie in one morning?"

Tuck swiped a lock of hair out of her face. "I'm not even sure what that means," he said on a laugh. "But I've been making plans to put a few horses in the field beside the garage. For therapy purposes. A man has a couple for sale. I told him I'd take them for a ride."

"I've never ridden a horse before," Josie admitted.

"Well, there's a first time for everything, right?"

She rolled off him. "I can't believe I'm about to say so but this sounds like fun."

"Fun is good. No work allowed today," he added. And no falling any harder for the woman he was with either.

* * *

Josie held on to the horse for dear life. "If I fall off this thing, you will pay."

Tuck was on another horse beside her, looking calm, cool, collected, and completely gorgeous. There was an ease about him in the saddle that made her jealous and wildly attracted to him at the same time.

"If you fall off, I promise to give you unlimited physical therapy."

She narrowed her gaze, hearing something naughty in his tone. Maybe she *should* fall off and take him up on that offer. Before she could contemplate doing so or say anything more, her horse took a step forward, and she let out a startled squeak.

"Relax. You'll be fine—I promise. The horse can sense your fear so you want to radiate well-being."

"Easy for you to say." Josie sucked in a cleansing breath and then another, feeling more like she was hyperventilating than relaxing. Then she listened as Tuck coaxed her on how to lead the horse, moving the reins one way and the other. After ten minutes, she felt more at home on her horse and could enjoy the soft breeze in her hair, the sounds of nature nearby, and the smell of horse, hay, and fresh mountain air. The combination aroused her senses, putting them in overdrive.

"Looking good over there," Tuck called from a few feet away.

"Could say the same about you. So, you want to use the horses for therapy?" she asked.

"That's the plan. It's called equine-assisted therapy. Shadow is so good with some of my patients. Animals have a way of getting through to people in a way that we can't. Horses are great because they also help with your core muscles." He patted his firm six-pack that she'd been up close and personal with only a few hours before. Then he patted a hip. "These muscles right here. The subtle movement of the horse keeps your body shifting and adjusting. It's more of a workout than you might think."

"What if your patients don't want to do it?" she asked, moving the reins and walking her mare closer to Tuck's.

"Then they don't have to. Some of my patients fear dogs or are allergic. I don't bring Shadow with me to treat those patients." He shrugged. "There's no 'one size fits all.' That's why I like my practice. In the rehab center where I used to work, we tried to fit patients into a therapy mold that matched everyone else's. It worked for some but not for others."

"Your patients are lucky to have you."

He slid his gaze to meet hers. "I work hard, but when the day is done, I stop. There has to be balance."

Josie swallowed, seeing immediately where he was going with the conversation. He'd accused her of running earlier. He was like a dog on a scent, sniffing out her weaknesses and wanting to explore them. She wasn't exactly running from anything but he was right about her avoiding certain areas in her life. She'd given up the idea of a family in college. She'd had her chance and hadn't taken it.

"After my wife died, I buried myself in work. It was easier that way."

"People have different ways of coping, I guess," she offered. "I did an article on coping skills once."

Tuck shook his head. "That's just it. I wasn't coping. I was shoving everything under the bed. Then I finally started dealing with her death in my own way. Not on some counselor's couch like others had suggested."

"What did you do?"

Tuck glanced over. "I started nature walking. Renee loved to take long nature walks. It was her personal time to think about life or cool off after I'd made her mad. She usually took her painting supplies with her and scoped out a place to paint." A slight smile pulled on the corners of his mouth as he talked about his late wife, making Josie feel a little uneasy. "So my eventual grief therapy was doing the same. It helped. During those walks, I eventually came up with the idea for my physical therapy practice."

"That's a good story."

He looked over with a wry expression. "No working, remember?"

She went to hold up her hands but then tightened her grip on the horse's reins as the mare continued to stroll along the path. "I'm not. Although that would make a nice piece in a magazine."

Tuck gave a soft command to his horse and moved the reins, turning left on the path. Josie followed, falling slightly behind. After a few steps, he stopped his horse, causing her to do the same. He pointed at a bright-purple bird.

"Oh, wow. That's just like the one I saw behind the bed and breakfast. I saw it in my dream this morning too."

He looked at her with interest piquing on his brow. "American Indian culture believes in something called your animal spirit guide."

Josie took her eyes off the bird only briefly to give him a curious look. "So do you think that bird is my animal spirit guide?"

He let out a soft laugh, careful not to spook the bird, which had landed on the ground and seemed to be watching them as well. "Well, a purple finch isn't a traditional animal spirit guide. Eagles, falcons, and ravens are more common. A spirit guide can be anything in creation though. It speaks to you through dreams, physical appearance, signs, and symbols."

"You think that little bird is trying to tell me something?" she asked with just a hint of wariness in her voice.

He shrugged his broad shoulders. "Maybe."

"Well, you might be able to speak dog but I don't speak bird."

Tuck smiled. "Just slow down and listen to the voice inside you. That's usually how you get any messages that life is trying to send."

Josie had never been one to make time for yoga or meditation. "Do you have a spirit animal?"

He nodded. "A bear. I've been seeing them since I was young. Never in a threatening way. They're always just there, watching me in the same way that I study them. Sometimes I look up at the sky and the Great Bear, or Ursa Major, stands out to me."

"And what do they mean?" she asked, fascinated as Tuck explained some of his beliefs.

"Well, bears represent strength and introspection. They protect their cubs, or those they love." He looked over.

"Some guides come and go; they have different purposes. The bear is my life guide."

He pulled the necklace from around his neck, holding the pendant with the bear between his fingers. "I wear my totem around my neck to remind me of who I am. I needed this more than ever after Renee died."

Josie looked back at the path. "I never saw a bird like that one until I came to Sweetwater Springs."

"A journey animal guide appears at a fork in the road of your life. When you're faced with a decision. Maybe that's what this is for you."

Josie watched the creature for a second longer, and then it fluttered and took flight, disappearing down the trail. What did it mean? She wasn't sure but excitement stirred inside her. She really was at a proverbial fork in her road. Everything felt like it was changing somehow. Maybe that beautiful little bird really was trying to tell her something. But she had no clue what it was.

They continued riding for another half hour, and then Josie and Tuck returned the horses to the barn and Tuck chatted with the owner.

"Yours if you want 'em," the man in a cowboy hat said. "I'm retiring and moving out west where my daughter and grandchildren are. I'll miss the mountains but family is everything."

"Can't blame you there," Tuck said, reminding Josie that he wasn't her type at all. He was a family man at heart. That was who he was before Maddie, and now it was even truer.

"These horses need a good home. Looks like they bonded well with you two," the cowboy said.

Josie shook her head. "Oh, I won't be part of their home. I live in New York."

The cowboy frowned. "That's a shame."

"Well, maybe she'll come back to visit them every now and then," Tuck offered, not looking at her when he said it.

Would Tuck want her to come see him when she visited? Could this little fling of theirs continue after she returned to New York? Maybe she could return and visit Sweetwater Springs more often. A home away from home of sorts. Then she wouldn't have to say goodbye to Tuck, at least not just yet.

CHAPTER FIFTEEN

It'd been a long time since Tuck had a day like the one he'd just shared with Josie. Horseback riding, laughing, and now they were sitting on his back deck with a glass of iced green tea in hand. The perfect day.

"Sore yet?" he asked, admiring Josie in the quickly fading sunlight.

"You're right. I can feel muscles I didn't know I had." She ran a hand along her outer thigh as if to prove a point.

The only point she proved, though, was that he could want her no matter how tired he was.

"I might not be able to move tomorrow."

"I can help with that."

She narrowed her eyes. "What do you have in mind?"

"There's a natural hot spring right down from the creek. It does wonders on sore muscles. Best-kept secret in town."

"And you're sharing your secrets with me?" she asked with a growing smile.

"Not all of them just yet. I have to have a reason for you to keep coming back for more. Want me to take you there?" he asked.

"Where?"

"The hot spring. It's just a short walk through the woods. Do you have a swimsuit?"

Josie set her glass down. "Matter of fact, I do. I never travel without one because you never know where you'll get an opportunity to take a dip. I can't say I've ever been given an opportunity to relax in a natural hot spring. That sounds like a once-in-a-lifetime experience."

"Unless you live here. I find the mineral spring to be just as good for the soul as they are for the body."

Josie stood. "You've sold me on the idea. I'll be right back in my suit."

He pushed back from the table as well, making Shadow lift her head. "I'll grab mine too."

Ten minutes later, Tuck left Shadow in the house, and he and Josie started walking down the path he traveled with a lot of his patients. The sun had continued its descent and could barely be seen behind the pines and distant mountains. He estimated that they still had an hour and a half of daylight, and even if the sun went down, walking out here after dark wasn't a major concern. He'd seen a bear a time or two, but as he'd told Josie, he had a kinship with the burly creatures.

"You okay?" he asked as they walked.

She shivered in the sweater she wore over her bathing suit along with a pair of shorts. "It's a little chilly out here."

"Not for long. The water runs about one hundred

degrees Fahrenheit. We're almost there." He led the way through the woods. There were orange ribbons that he'd tied on the pines several months ago to ensure none of his patients ever lost their way. "Be careful. The ground is a little uneven in here." Tuck reached back for her hand to make sure she didn't fall but he didn't let it go once they hit easier terrain. The feel of her skin along his palm felt intimate and right.

"I think I hear the water," Josie said excitedly a few minutes later.

Tuck tugged her a few more steps and then the pines opened to a small clearing.

"Oh, wow." She stopped and stared for a long moment. It wasn't a large hot spring but it was big enough for a handful of people. Or just two who couldn't keep their hands off each other. "It's gorgeous," she said almost breathlessly.

Tuck was watching her as she took in the surrounding area of the water and the trees making a natural fence to outsiders. The hot spring was nice but *she* was the gorgeous one.

She turned back to look at him, her lips slightly parted. "Do you come up here often?"

He shrugged. "Often enough. Maybe once or twice a week unless I'm busy. I use it with my patients sometimes." Tuck led her closer to the spring, the sound of rippling water growing louder with each step. Somewhere in the distance, a coyote howled.

"You have a lot to offer here, don't you? Horses, a therapy dog, a hot spring. If you don't watch out, you'll be the most sought-after physical therapist in town. You won't be able to keep up with business."

He laughed and shook his head. "Most patients still

prefer to go to the hospital rehab center, and that's fine by me. I'm only one person, and there are limits to how many patients I can see in a week."

Josie turned back to the spring and then, before he knew it, she'd pulled her cardigan off and shimmied out of her shorts. She was wearing a modest two-piece bathing suit that showed off just a few inches of her toned stomach. Even though they'd spent last night together, her cheeks blushed just a little as she looked over her shoulder at him. "Aren't you going to take off your T-shirt and get in with me?"

"Oh yeah." He pulled his T-shirt over his head and discarded it on a nearby rock. "Let me go in first," he said, "just to make sure there aren't any loose rocks down there that might slide away under your feet. I don't want you reinjuring your knee...Try to follow in my footsteps." He lowered himself to the edge of the hot spring and put his right foot in first. The water was hot, and it awakened every nerve in his skin. He slid the rest of his body into the pool of water and then turned to help Josie.

"*Ohhhh!*" she moaned as she got in, awakening all of Tuck's other senses. "You were right. This is heaven. I doubt I'll have any soreness once I get out of this pool." She beamed at him. "But I still might need that massage once we get back home." Her smile faltered just a little when she realized what she'd said.

He'd noticed too. Even though she'd been at Hope Cottage for only two weeks, she'd called it home. He knew it was just a slip of the tongue but it also felt true. He'd tossed out the idea earlier that they could continue to see each other after she returned to New York but they hadn't discussed it. He just wasn't ready to let her go, and some part of him wondered if he ever would be.

* * *

Josie set out early the next day on her bike, heading downtown. She'd become quite fond of the Sweetwater Café, which had the best coffee she'd ever tasted. She didn't mind working in solitude sometimes but she found people-watching often conjured up lots of fresh ideas for articles. Some didn't go anywhere but some were keepers.

Her mind wandered as the gentle breeze ran its fingers through her hair. She was still processing the fact that Tuck was Maddie's father, not that she was surprised. In addition to Tuck's looks, she had his same temperament. They were both stubborn and determined. Both quiet and contemplative. Even on their girls' day out, when Maddie had been much more talkative than usual, she'd still been more of an observer, grinning ear to ear as she went along with Josie and Kaitlyn.

Josie slowed her bike and parked it in the bike rack downtown. Draping her laptop bag over her shoulder, she took her time strolling down the sidewalk. Now that the Sweetwater Springs Festival had ended, there were less people populating the quaint street. Josie still saw a few faces she recognized. She waved and said hello.

When she reached the Sweetwater Café, she stepped inside and breathed in the delicious aroma of freshly brewed coffee. There was no better smell.

"Josie!" Emma, the shop owner, said when Josie reached the counter. "Tall caffe latte with almond milk and three raw sugars, correct?"

"Impressive," Josie said, trying to remember any place she'd ever been that had remembered her order. Just one more of the many charms of being in a small town. "That's exactly what I want."

With a nod, Emma started to pour the coffee while talking over the steady grind of machinery on her countertop. "I saw you at the festival over the weekend. You were with Tuck and a little girl." One of Emma's brows poked up on her forehead as she glanced over her shoulder.

"Since I'm renting Tuck's garage apartment, he was nice enough to invite me along." Josie pulled her debit card from her wallet.

Emma's eyes told Josie she wasn't buying it but the line behind Josie was growing and there wasn't time to talk more. "Here you go! Come back up when you're ready for a refill."

"I will. Thanks." Josie paid and headed to an empty table in the corner. As she was walking, someone called her name.

"Josie!"

Josie stopped in her tracks and turned to the woman. What was her name again?

"We met over the weekend. I'm Michelle."

"Right. From *Carolina Home* magazine."

Michelle had her laptop open on the table in front of her. "Looks like you and I both have similar writing habits."

Josie patted the laptop bag she'd been using since college. "Sometimes the noise and commotion silence what's going on in my head."

Michelle gestured to the chair across from her. "Do you have time to sit and share a coffee? Before you get started on whatever you're working on?"

Josie's gaze wavered momentarily to the empty table behind Michelle. She'd been biting at the bit to work but it would be nice to get to know Michelle a little better. "I have all day to write so that would be nice." Josie pulled out the chair and sat down.

"Did you enjoy the festival?" Michelle asked, taking a sip of her beverage.

"I did. It was a lot of fun. I was so tired I slept like a baby on Saturday night though." After she and Tuck had their own festivities under the sheets, that is. "Did you get a lot of subscriptions for *Carolina Home* magazine?" Josie asked.

Michelle leaned back comfortably in her chair and crossed her legs. "Quite a few, actually, but nothing compared to the reach that *Loving Life* has." She gave Josie a meaningful look. "But it's also nothing to sneeze at. When I first started the magazine, I think I had twenty subscribers. Progress is progress, and I'll take it."

"That's great."

"So, what are you writing today?" Michelle asked, gesturing to Josie's laptop bag on the floor beside her chair.

"Oh"—Josie shrugged—"honestly, I have no idea. I finished my follow-up article on Sweetwater Springs and sent it off. I've jotted down a few ideas but nothing solid just yet. All the ideas I ran by my new boss the other day were shot down with military accuracy." She resisted the need to roll her eyes.

Michelle sipped her coffee. "I'd love to hear your ideas."

Josie was surprised. "Really? Okay, let's see. In the last week, I've suggested an article on dating among the elderly. But my editor told me that no one wants to read about old people having sex."

Michelle choked on a sip of coffee.

"I also suggested something on the wineries here. I was hoping to take a tour and do a write-up." Josie fiddled with the cardboard wrap on her cup. "I also thought about doing a piece on supporting local businesses versus buying from big chain stores. I was thinking of calling it 'Break the Chain and Buy Local.'"

"Such as getting your coffee here at the Sweetwater Café rather than going to the big chain coffee shops up the mountain," Michelle said with a nod. "I like it."

"Well, Bart didn't." Josie laughed softly. "His idea of an attractive headline is 'Sex in the Sticks.'" Josie made air quotes around the suggested title from Bart.

Michelle frowned and set her cup of coffee down. "With Sweetwater Springs being the sticks, I presume?"

Josie nodded. "Here's another suggestion from him." She made air quotes once more. "'Why Marriage Is for Those Living in the Dark Ages.'"

"Oh my."

"I mean, I'm not married and I probably never will be, but I believe in marriage."

Michelle tilted her head to one side, a thoughtful look in her eyes. "Hmm. Well, *Carolina Home* magazine is going to start a monthly section on interesting couples and singles across the state. Some will have a romantic appeal, some not, but they'll all give readers a chance to get to know some of their neighbors."

"I love that idea," Josie said.

Michelle grinned. "Me too. The only problem is that I don't have anyone to get it started yet." She narrowed her eyes at Josie. "Just a thought, but since you're here and you're not currently writing anything right now..."

Josie sat back in her chair. Was Michelle offering her a job?

"I know you work for *Loving Life* so this would be freelance work, of course. Just think about it."

Josie's heart was beating fast and it had nothing to do

with the jolt of caffeine she'd just gotten from her drink. "No need. I'd love to write an article for you."

* * *

Maddie had been up on her feet for at least fifteen minutes and there was no sign of fatigue. Tuck wasn't even worried that she might fall. Over the last week, with daily physical therapy and a good dose of motivation on her part, her strength and endurance had improved drastically. She'd achieved in a few weeks' time what it would take his older patients a year or more to achieve in some cases.

"Do you want to sit?" he asked.

Maddie shook her head, keeping her gaze straight and shifting her weight from leg to leg slowly like she'd been doing since this session had started. "No, I'm fine."

"You don't want to wear yourself out. Taking a break is good. Then after a minute or two, you can stand up, and we can go again."

Maddie's stubborn chin lifted toward her mouth. "I'm a kid," she told him, as if that wasn't already obvious. "Kids have unlimited energy."

That was one thing that Tuck missed about being younger. That unlimited energy that never seemed to run out until your head hit the pillow. Since Josie had come into his life, however, there'd been a new energy about him. Seeing someone romantically was like a shot of adrenaline into his system. It sounded cliché but he had a skip in his step these days.

"All right," he conceded, "but you tell me when you need a break. If you push yourself too hard, it could cause a setback, and neither one of us wants that."

"Deal." Maddie shifted on her cane and swung her

other leg forward. She repeated the action for twenty more steps before looking at him. "I could use that chair now," she finally said.

Tuck went to retrieve it and helped her sit down. "Wow. You're really making quick progress these days."

"Thanks. I'm just tired of being a burden on my grandma." She looked up at him, a strand of dark hair dangling in her eyes before she batted it away.

"You're not," Tuck said.

Maddie shrugged. "It'll be better for people when I don't need to drag around any equipment though. When I can take care of myself and no one needs to worry about me all the time."

"You're still a kid," he reminded her. "You don't need to take care of yourself, and worrying is what adults do. It can't be helped." He nudged Maddie's shoulder. "But I was going to tell you that I don't think you need to drag that wheelchair anywhere anymore. You're good with the cane."

Maddie's expression brightened.

"As long as I can trust you to know when to take a break."

Maddie nodded vigorously. "You can. You can," she insisted.

"Good. Then it's a deal."

Maddie stared at him for a long moment, and he could see the wheels in her mind turning. "I get why my grandmother cares," she said with hesitation, "but why do you care so much?"

"Well, because you're my patient. Of course I care about you."

He could tell by the way Maddie was looking at him that she wasn't completely buying that answer.

"I've had a physical therapist before and he didn't do all the things that you do. I mean, you're seeing me every day, and you're not even charging my grandma. You care about where I go and what I do and who I'm with. You've taken me to the dance and the festival." She shrugged while continuing to pin him with her stare.

Tuck was having a hard time taking in a full breath at the moment. Was it time to tell her the truth? He needed to discuss it with Beverly first. When the time came, they needed to do it together. Maddie would demand answers, some of which he didn't have.

"I mean, my own dad didn't even stick around," Maddie said.

That statement felt like a poisoned arrow through his heart. "How do you know that's true? Maybe your dad didn't know about you. Or maybe he wanted to be part of your life but couldn't."

Maddie looked at him, long and hard. "Do you think that's true?" she finally asked.

"Where are all these questions coming from anyway?" Tuck asked.

"I don't know. It just doesn't make sense why you're so nice to me—that's all."

"Maybe it's because I like you," he said. "I think you're a really cool kid, and I want the best for you. I can also see how much potential you have, and I don't want you to throw it away. You've got a long, full life ahead of you, Maddie, and those legs of yours are going to take you places you can't even imagine yet."

A soft smile curved her lips. "Okay," she said after a moment. "Break's over. I'm going to walk one more time before we finish our session."

"Okay," he agreed, glancing at his watch. Maddie was

his last patient of the day. After she was gone, he'd head back inside the house for a drink. And hopefully by then, Josie would be back from wherever she'd spent the day. She'd said something last night about going downtown to work. Considering that she was still gone, he guessed she'd probably met up with Kaitlyn and they'd run a few errands together or Josie had gone back to the bed and breakfast to help with any number of things. It was great that her schedule was full during the day. He just hoped her nights would remain free for him.

CHAPTER SIXTEEN

Josie still wasn't sure where her day had gone. She was supposed to be coming up with new, exciting ideas that would make Bart happy. Instead, when Kaitlyn had called around noon asking to meet up for lunch, Josie had asked how many married couples were currently staying at the Sweetwater Bed and Breakfast.

"Oh, I don't know," Kaitlyn had responded. "Let's see. Mr. and Mrs. Jacobs. Mr. and Mrs. Robinson. And the Browns. There's another couple occupying the *Dirty Dancing* room but they aren't married. They're college students here on spring break. The young man is preparing to propose to his girlfriend this summer though," Kaitlyn confided. "He told me that and made me promise not to tip his girlfriend off."

Excitement had swelled in Josie's chest as she'd listened. "Do you mind picking me up downtown and taking me to the inn for the rest of the day?" she asked. "If you can't, I can call a cab and find my way there."

"Sure," Kaitlyn said. "But why? What's going on?"

"I'm writing a new article," Josie told her. "At least I might be. Are any of your guests from North Carolina?"

"I know at least one couple is," Kaitlyn said.

"Great! Do you think they'll mind if I interview them?"

"I don't see why they would. Gina is here with me today. She can watch the inn while I run over to get you."

Twenty minutes later, Josie was sitting at the dining room table at the Sweetwater Bed and Breakfast with Mr. and Mrs. Robinson. She had her laptop set up in front of her, and she was recording everything they said.

"We met at a family reunion," Mrs. Robinson told her.

Josie lifted her fingers off the keyboard. "Oh?" Meeting the love of your life at your own family reunion didn't sound romantic, or even legal.

The couple shared a knowing look as they laughed.

"Mary was spending the day with my great-aunt," Mr. Robinson explained, "while Mary's mom was in labor with her sister."

"So I wasn't supposed to be there. It was an emergency-type situation. I wasn't part of the Robinson family," Mary clarified.

"Not yet." Mr. Robinson reached for her hand and gave it a loving squeeze.

"How old were you two?" Josie asked.

"I was fourteen," Mrs. Robinson said.

"And I was sixteen. I recognized her from school. We exchanged phone numbers after a while. Even though I liked her, she was too young for me at the time."

"I had such a huge crush on Danny," Mary said, looking over at her husband. "When I turned sixteen, he asked me on our first date," she said. "I scared him when I nearly screamed yes."

"Where did you two go?" Josie asked, so immersed in the story that she nearly forgot to type.

"I invited her to the Robinson family reunion again," Danny said.

"He told me that evening that I would be a Robinson one day when he made me his wife." Mrs. Robinson chuckled at the memory. "I haven't missed a single Robinson family reunion since I was sixteen years old."

"That is so romantic." Josie sighed.

The couple shared a look with one another that spoke volumes. They told her about their wedding and honeymoon then. Their years of trying to have children but never being able to conceive.

"It was hard," Mrs. Robinson said. "For a while, I felt like less of a wife for not being able to give Danny children. I was so depressed that I even considered leaving him. Why would he want me? I was a failure."

Danny took her hand and then brought it to his mouth for a kiss. "It never changed my love for you." He looked at Josie. "We adopted two kids when we were in our thirties. Dustin and Diana. They live here in town. They're about your age, I'd say."

"That's wonderful." Josie's eyes burned as her fingers flew across the keyboard. Danny and Mary wouldn't have been able to have children if someone else hadn't given them the chance to adopt. They were a loving couple, and Josie had no doubt that they'd given Dustin and Diana a good home.

The interview took about an hour. When it was over, the couple stood.

"If you live in town, why are you staying here at the bed and breakfast right now?" Josie asked.

"It's our anniversary week," Danny said. "I felt like we needed to go somewhere romantic to celebrate."

"And the Sweetwater Bed and Breakfast was named as one of the most romantic retreats last year."

Josie nodded, realizing they didn't know she was the one who'd penned the article.

"Why drive hundreds of miles or more when you can travel a couple of miles and have the same experience?" Mary asked.

"Well, thank you for taking the time to talk to me during your anniversary celebration."

"It was fun to reflect on it all. It's been such a wild ride," the older woman said. "And it's nowhere near finished yet."

"Let us know when our story comes out. We'll be famous," Danny said.

Josie laughed. "I will." She watched them grab cookies from the plate that Kaitlyn had laid out for them and then stroll hand in hand out of the dining room.

Kaitlyn peeked into the room. "Done?"

"Yes. They had an amazing story." Josie sighed.

Kaitlyn stood there watching her. "I can't wait to read it. Will it be in an upcoming issue of *Loving Life*? Or, I'm sorry, what's the magazine's new name?"

"*The Vibe*," Josie said. "And no. Bart would never approve of an article like that. This is for Michelle at *Carolina Home* magazine."

"What? Really?" Kaitlyn slid into the chair across from Josie and grabbed a cookie for herself. "This is new."

Josie shrugged. "The opportunity arose, so . . ."

"Did you get what you need? Want to interview someone else?"

"Not right now," Josie said. "But maybe another time."

"Well then maybe, you can help me get started on my grandma's made-from-scratch biscuits for tomorrow's breakfast."

"Haven't you learned that I'm an awful cook by now?" Josie asked on a laugh.

"Yes, but I haven't given up on teaching you. Unless you're in a hurry to get started on writing your new article," Kaitlyn said, patting Mr. Darcy's head as he padded over and pressed against her thigh.

Josie wasn't in a hurry to get started on the article though. She was in a hurry to get back to Tuck.

* * *

The next day, Tuck walked into a little diner on the edge of town and looked around. Maddie was back to school this week so he'd arranged to meet with Beverly. There were important things that had yet to be discussed. Beverly was already seated in a corner booth, her hands folded on the table in front of her. She waved when he looked in her direction. With a nod, he headed over and sat down.

"Good morning," he said. He noted that Beverly was fresh faced this morning, and the dark circles under her eyes weren't as pronounced. Maybe she'd put on a little makeup or maybe she was feeling better. He hoped it was the latter. "How are you feeling?"

"Oh, each day seems to be a different story. Today I'm feeling good. My chemotherapy ended last week so my energy levels are up. I'll see my doctor again next month, and he'll determine if I need to go back for more."

Tuck didn't want to pry—Beverly had told him before that she expected to recover—but he needed to make sure for Maddie's sake. "What's your prognosis?"

Beverly smiled at him. "The same as yours, I guess. Nobody knows how many days they have left on earth. I could die tomorrow or live to be one hundred."

"True enough." He and Renee had tried to stay positive too, focusing on the best-case scenario instead of the worst. But then the worst had happened. He swallowed past the emotions that always surfaced when he thought about that time in his life and how things might have worked out differently.

A waitress came to their table and placed two vinyl menus in front of them. "Hi, guys. Just wave your hand at me when you're ready to order."

"Thanks," Tuck said. When the waitress had gone, he didn't reach for his menu though. "I asked to meet you today because I want to talk about Maddie."

"I guessed as much."

"I don't need proof to know she's mine," he said.

Beverly didn't look surprised by that either.

"I understand we probably need to have a DNA test to appease the courts though. That way I can take over custody of Maddie."

Beverly's eyes shined. "I love my granddaughter, Tuck. I want what's best for her. I don't know why Crystal was so adamant about keeping you out of Maddie's life. I suppose she thought it would be easier that way."

"Easier for who?" Tuck asked, unable to tame his anger. "Certainly not for me or Maddie. We had a right to know."

"I don't disagree."

"If we're going to do a DNA test, we'll have to tell Maddie what's going on," he said. "I think we should do that sooner rather than later." Maddie's questions had left him unsettled the other day. It was time to tell her that she was his daughter.

"I think we should wait," Beverly argued. "I contacted you because I needed to see if you would be a suitable guardian for Maddie. And I think you are."

"Of course I am. I'm her father."

Beverly met his gaze and continued, keeping her voice slow and calm in contrast to his. "But Maddie is just starting to get her feet back under her—literally. She's hanging out with her friends again. She's smiling and laughing. She hasn't done that since Crystal died. If we tell her that her mother lied to her all this time and kept her father a secret, it might put her back in a dark place, Tuck. Let's wait awhile longer."

Enough time had already slipped unknowingly through his fingers. He didn't want to lose any more. "I don't like her thinking that her father just walked out on her. She needs to know that she's loved. That she's wanted. I don't see how that can be a bad thing for her."

Beverly's hand was shaking as she reached for her glass of iced water. She took a sip as she seemed to be pondering the decision. In his mind, there was no question. This was what needed to be done, for Maddie's sake.

"She's taking her end-of-year test at school next week. The test will determine if she continues in her honors classes. Can we at least wait to tell her until after she's completed the assessment?"

Tuck thought about it for a moment. "That's a good idea," he finally said. "Then we'll make a plan to get the DNA testing done. In the meantime, I'll contact my lawyer and see what I need to do to start working on taking over guardianship of Maddie."

Beverly reached a hand across the table toward him, clasping cold fingers over his. "Please, Tuck, tell me you won't keep her from me. I need her, and she needs me. I know what Crystal did was wrong but don't hold that against us."

He shook his head. "I would never do that to you or Maddie, Beverly. You have my word. When Maddie comes to live with me, my door will always be open to you. Maddie needs all the people she loves around her while she's growing up. She deserves that."

He only wished Crystal had understood that as well.

* * *

Josie stared at the email she was typing to Michelle.

Hi, Michelle,

I found a little extra time in my schedule, and the opportunity arose to work on the article you suggested. I know we didn't formally agree on anything but I thought I'd send this your way in case you have room for it in an upcoming issue. It was so nice to chat over coffee the other day. I look forward to hearing from you!

Josie

Josie's finger hovered over the send button as nervous butterflies fluttered around in her chest. What if Michelle didn't like it? What if she decided another writer should do it?

Josie clicked the button and blew out a breath. Needing to blow off her nervous energy, she slipped her feet into a pair of sneakers and headed outside to see if Tuck was back yet. She knew he'd only scheduled patients for the first half of the day today because he was going to pick up the horses he'd purchased and bring them back to Hope Cottage.

She spotted his horse trailer behind the stables and headed in that direction.

"Hey," he called, when she was halfway to him. "Just acquainting Sugar and Chestnut with their new home."

Josie reached the horse she'd ridden a few days ago and petted her muzzle. "Hey, girl, I missed you. Did you miss me?"

The horse nudged her nose into Josie's palm.

"I'll take that as a yes. You're going to love it here—I promise. This is a wonderful place."

"You really think so?" Tuck asked.

She looked over. "Of course I do. I'm actually glad my apartment in New York got fire damage. Not because my clothes will smell like smoke for the next year but because things have worked out nicely. Springtime at Hope Cottage has been exactly what I didn't even know I needed."

She watched Tuck brushing the other mare for a long moment. "That looks oddly therapeutic," she said.

"It is. Want to try?" He offered her the brush.

Once she took it, he positioned himself behind her and took hold of her hands. She probably didn't need him to guide her on how to brush a horse but she wasn't complaining. She liked the feel of his arms wrapped around her. That was therapeutic too.

"Long, even strokes. Just like that," he whispered in her ear.

"I think she likes it," Josie said.

"Of course she does. This is something my patients can do too. Equine-assisted therapy is more than riding the horses. It's caring for them, feeding them, leading them through the field."

They continued to brush the horse in silence, and then Tuck pulled away and watched Josie work.

"I admit I've never been an animal person before but I

love Sugar." She reached over to pat the horse's shoulder. "There's something in her eyes that makes me believe she loves me too."

Shadow got up and moved to stand beside Josie.

"Uh-oh," Tuck said. "I think someone is jealous."

Josie laughed and petted Shadow as well. "Yes, I love you too, girl."

"Maybe you're more of an animal lover than you thought. I've always loved animals. Kids too."

Josie turned her attention to him. "How did your talk with Beverly go this morning?"

"Good. We're going to tell Maddie next week. We'll schedule DNA testing and go from there. Beverly will continue to be a big part of Maddie's life. That won't change."

Josie nodded. "Maddie is a lucky girl to have a grandmother and a father who love her so much."

"It just makes me sick that she believes her dad didn't want her."

Without thinking, Josie started brushing Sugar again, needing the distraction. *Is that what the child I gave up thinks? Does she even know about me?*

"I would never give up my own child. Never," Tuck continued. "A child needs to know they're loved. Wanted. To make them feel otherwise is despicable." There was a hardness in his tone of voice as he talked, more to himself than to her.

Josie continued to brush Sugar's coat, keeping her gaze pinned to the rich mahogany color. She didn't want to compare her situation with Tuck's. She'd made a choice that Tuck hadn't been given. By listening to him though, it sounded like he wouldn't approve of her decision.

"Are you okay?" Tuck asked once the conversation had lulled.

Josie's hand paused in midstroke. And crap, her eyes were stinging. "Yeah," she lied. "I'm fine."

"I don't think you are." He turned her shoulders and angled her to face him. "Did I say something?"

"No." She laughed lightly, averting her eyes from his. "Maybe I'm just allergic to Sugar. My eyes are suddenly watering." She wasn't sure her story was believable. For the most part, she never lied. As a journalist, she valued the truth. But right now, she didn't want to admit that she was upset. Tuck would want a reason, which she wasn't ready to disclose. "I'm fine." She handed him the brush. "And I'm happy for you. Having Maddie come to live with you will be an adjustment but it'll be great."

His gaze on her was heavy. "I think so too...How about dinner tonight? I got a couple of steaks at the grocery store the other day. One with your name on it. A bottle of wine too."

"Does the wine also have my name on it?" she asked. Because she could really use a glass of it right now.

"Matter of fact, it does," he said with a sexy smile.

"Sounds good. Can I at least help you cook this time? I feel like I'm taking advantage of you if you do all the work."

"You can make a salad. I have the vegetables in my fridge."

"Deal. I'll just freshen up and meet you back at the house in about an hour."

He bent to kiss her lips, and everything within her responded before her brain took over and reminded her of what Tuck had just said. In not so many words, he'd told her that walking away from a child was despicable. Right now, he was looking at her like she'd put the sun in the sky. Would he see her differently if he knew her secret?

CHAPTER SEVENTEEN

$\mathcal{S}$omething was bothering Josie but Tuck couldn't figure out what it was. She'd smiled enough over dinner. She'd laughed at his jokes as usual. She'd kissed him when he leaned down to brush his lips against hers. Nothing obvious was off but Tuck could feel the tension radiating off her.

"Penny for your thoughts," he said, setting his fork down and reaching for his glass of red wine as they sat outside on the deck.

She blinked him into focus, another clue that her mind wasn't completely with him tonight. "What?"

"You're thinking about something. Can I ask what?"

Josie reached down to pet Shadow, who was nuzzled at her knee. "The comment you made earlier, about being despicable if you walk away from your child. Did you mean that?"

Tuck shifted, noticing something vulnerable in her gaze. *What is that about?* "Yeah. I never would've turned my back on Maddie. That's not something I'm even capable of doing."

With her other hand, Josie reached for her glass of wine and took a generous sip.

"Josie?"

She looked up. "It's just... some people give up a child because it's the right thing to do. It doesn't make them a bad person, you know."

He narrowed his eyes, hearing the tremble in her voice. "Are we talking about someone specific?"

"Yes... me," she said quietly.

He took a second to process that, trying to make sense of what she was telling him. Josie was thoughtful and giving. He'd come to admire her so much since he'd first met her. She didn't seem like a person who would act selfishly. The Josie he knew was just the opposite.

"I gave up a child in college," she explained. "I was young, unemployed, and the father wasn't interested in sticking around. I didn't feel like I had a choice at the time." She tucked an imaginary strand of hair behind her ear, sucking in a breath and making her chest rise and fall shakily. "I did it for her. So she would have a better life than I could offer," she said, looking up at him.

Tuck swallowed. "I'm sorry if what I said earlier offended you."

"Do you think I'm a despicable person?" she asked, her voice cracking.

"No, Josie, I was talking about my situation with Maddie. My family would've helped me finish college and provide for my daughter. We could've made it work, and I would have... I think you are one of the best people I've ever met. You wouldn't have given up your baby if it wasn't the absolute best decision. I know that because I know you."

Her expression softened. "It was the hardest decision of my life. Part of me wanted to hold on to my baby forever. But I knew I wasn't ready to be a mother." She blew out a breath and turned to look out on the backyard. "I found a nice couple who'd been trying to conceive for years. They were employed, well-off, and they loved each other. That was so easy to see when I interviewed them."

"That must have been tough." Tuck reached across the table and took her hand. "Did you talk to anyone about this?"

She looked at him and nodded. "I saw the university counselor. After that, I focused on my studies and reminded myself it was what was best for Elizabeth. That's what the adoptive parents named her."

"It's a beautiful name," Tuck said.

"It is. It was an open adoption. I can go see her if I ever want to, but"—Josie shrugged—"I don't want to confuse her. Her parents post pictures on social media all the time. She's happy and healthy, and that's all I ever wanted for her." Josie's eyes were shining in the moonlight.

"You are the most selfless person I've ever met, Josie Kellum."

A startled expression overtook her face. "I thought you would think the opposite after hearing my story."

"You sacrificed your needs for those of your little girl. Even now, you're doing what's right for her. *You* amaze me."

Josie's hair fell in her eyes as she looked down at the table.

He knew she was doing her best to keep her composure. He longed to tuck that strand of golden hair behind her ear himself and show her exactly how amazing he thought she was. "Let's go inside. It's time for someone to take care of your needs for a change."

Her mouth fell open.

"Not necessarily *those* needs," he said with a grin. "If you need me to just hold you, then that's all I'll do. Whatever you want. The night is yours."

And *he* was hers. This was dangerous ground he was treading. He was a new father; he had to make up for a lot of missed time with Maddie. And some part of his heart still belonged to Renee, and always would.

But Josie had somehow captured another part of his heart. And if he wasn't careful, she'd be taking it with her when she left.

* * *

The rain had just started when Josie had rolled out of Tuck's bed and headed up to her apartment. Now it was a full downpour outside. Somehow her fingers typed faster and her brain circulated words and ideas more efficiently when the rain was coming down. She'd finished up an article proposal for Bart that she wasn't at all excited to write— in fact, she almost hoped he turned it down. Now she opened her email to peruse any new messages. Topping the list was one from Michelle at *Carolina Home* magazine.

Josie clicked on the email and started to read, her heart skipping around in her chest.

Good morning, Josie,

I just wanted you to know that I absolutely loved reading Mary and Danny's story. I'd like to publish the article in an

upcoming issue of *Carolina Home*. Maybe we can talk
more in depth about this later today? Let me know. If I may
be so bold, maybe we can discuss your next article for us
as well.

Talk to you soon,

Michelle

Josie laughed out loud. Why was she so happy about
getting Michelle's approval? She wasn't sure but it felt
good.

She typed a quick response telling Michelle she would
love to meet over coffee today if she was available. That
would mean riding her bike through the rain, however.
Josie frowned. Maybe Tuck could drop her off before one
of his appointments downtown. Added bonus was that
she'd get a little extra time with him.

It was seven a.m. now. Tuck would be awake and
probably getting ready for the day ahead. She pulled on a
raincoat and headed out the door and across the lawn. She
knocked lightly on Tuck's back door, hearing Shadow's
answering bark inside.

Tuck opened the door. "You're getting wet out there,"
he said, gesturing her inside.

She stepped over the threshold and pulled off the hood
of her raincoat. "Thanks." Then she went up on her toes
to give him a good-morning kiss.

"Now that's how I should've started my morning."

"Sorry. When the inspiration hits, I have to work."
At least that was the old Josie's way of thinking.
Something had shifted slightly since she'd been in
Sweetwater Springs though. She still had a strong work

ethic but her one-track mind had two tracks now. Work and Tuck.

"Did you just come over for my coffee?" he asked.

"I'd love a cup. I also came to ask for a favor," she said, pulling her lower lip between her teeth and biting down.

"Oh yeah? What kind of favor?" he asked as he walked across the kitchen and grabbed a mug from the cabinet.

Josie slid into a chair at the table. "Michelle just emailed, and she wants to talk about my article."

He placed a full cup of coffee in front of her. Josie took the cup between her hands, lifting it to her mouth for a sip. "This is so much better than the stuff I have in my apartment."

Tuck sat down beside her with his own full mug. "Did Michelle like the article?" he asked.

Josie shrugged. "She said she loved it."

"That's great."

"She wants to meet. The problem is it's supposed to rain all day, which would mean riding my bike for a mile and getting soaked."

"I don't mind dropping you off," Tuck said. "It's only a mile or two down the road so it's not much trouble. Plus, any chance I get to spend with you is worth it. I'm seeing Claire Donovan again at twelve thirty. Is that a good time for you?"

"Perfect, actually." Josie leaned over and planted a quick kiss on his mouth. "Thank you."

"Anything else I can do for you?" he asked. "Anything at all," he added with a gravelly tone to his voice.

Oh, I'm in so much trouble. And she didn't mind a bit. "Maybe later. I'm a little nervous to meet with Michelle again, and I'm not sure why." She took another sip from her coffee.

"You probably have as much journalistic experience as she does, if not more. There's nothing to worry about, especially if she told you she loves what you wrote."

"And there's no real job potential at *Carolina Home* magazine. I'm not even sure Michelle is hiring right now, so…"

"It's always flattering to have someone enjoy your work. Congratulations. Do you want me to pick you up after I'm done with my appointment with Claire?"

Josie shook her head. "No, I'll find my way back. I can call a cab or get Kaitlyn to take me home. I don't know how long Michelle and I will talk."

"Well, you have my cell phone number, and you can call me if you change your mind. You're not an inconvenience. You mean a lot to me, Josie," he said, reminding her of something similar he'd said last night.

He was always saying exactly the right thing, and they didn't feel like empty words. They felt rich and full, and they warmed her up as she dried from her sprint through the rain.

* * *

After dropping Josie off at the Sweetwater Café for her lunch meeting, Tuck continued toward the downtown parking lot. Once he came to a stop, he checked his phone and noted that Claire Donovan had canceled her appointment.

He sighed. The appointment he'd scheduled with Mr. Garrison, his lawyer, wasn't for another two hours, and since he was right at Little Shop of Flowers, he decided to go see Halona. Pulling the hood of his rain jacket over his head, he stepped out into the downpour and ran for the cover of the awning.

"Hey, stranger," she said as he walked in. "You here for flowers?" she asked. "I think you should hold off. The rain isn't expected to stop until tomorrow."

She was referring to his weekly habit of placing arrangements on Renee's grave site.

"No flowers today. I just got a cancellation with Claire and thought I'd stop in."

Halona tipped her head toward the back room. "I have coffee, and business is slow."

"Sounds perfect." Tuck followed Halona into the back room and watched as she poured him his third cup of the day. At this rate, he might not sleep for the rest of the week. That might have more to do with Josie, though, than how much caffeine he consumed.

"You're going to tell me eventually so go ahead," she finally said.

He looked up. "What do you mean?"

"You know exactly what I mean. Something's up. It's written all over your face. I noticed as soon as you walked in. I just can't decide if it's good news or bad."

He nodded, chewing on his thoughts. He'd have to tell his family eventually. "I do have news," he admitted. "Good news, I think. It turns out I'm related to one of my patients."

Halona's eyes widened. "What? Who? If you're related, then so am I. You can't keep that a secret."

He looked at her. "The little girl I've been seeing for physical therapy. Maddie Sanders."

Halona seemed to process this. "I remember her. She was with Josie and Kaitlyn when they stopped in the store the other day."

"For their girls' day out," he said with a knowing nod. "I wasn't invited."

"Why would you be? You're her physical therapist."

"It turns out she's the daughter of a woman I dated in college. Crystal Sanders."

Halona's forehead wrinkled as she thought. "When you were broken up with Renee, right? I remember her."

He swallowed, knowing that Halona would put two and two together in a quick second.

"Oh," she finally said, straightening as she reached the natural conclusion. "Are you sure that she's your daughter? That is what you're trying to tell me, isn't it?"

"Yeah."

"Have you been tested?"

He blew out a breath. "Not yet. But I know."

Halona placed a hand to her chest. "Oh, wow. I have so many questions. Mom is going to flip."

"She can't know right now. Maddie doesn't even know yet."

"What?" Halona reached for her coffee cup. "Okay, start from the beginning. Tell me everything."

Fifteen minutes later, Tuck had drained half the coffee in his mug and all the energy in his body's reserve.

"That is some surprise. I'm an aunt," Halona said with a smile. "And my niece is pretty cool. I loved her when she stopped in the other day. She's so beautiful and smart. Theo was here. She played with him, and he took to her just like a sister . . . Oh, Tuck, this is amazing news! What does Josie think?"

He lowered his brow. "What does Josie have to do with this?"

Halona tilted her head. "Oh, come on. You're spilling secrets so you might as well fess up on that one too. You like her. I'd say you likc her a lot."

Tuck looked down at his mug.

"I think it's great," his sister added. "It's time. I've been telling you that for a while now."

"But it's complicated. Everything is complicated right now." He massaged his forehead. "I have a daughter. She needs me...It's not the right time to be falling in love."

When he looked up, Halona's eyes were wide. "I didn't say anything about falling in love. I said *like*." Her eyes sparkled as she grinned. "This is incredible, Tuck!"

"No. Don't even go there. Josie is temporary. What she and I have is a casual fling."

He started to rattle off an excuse about his new responsibilities but Halona held up a hand. "Stop right there. Just because you're a parent doesn't mean you can't have a life."

"Look who's talking," he said, turning that statement right back at her.

She frowned. "Theo is younger than Maddie. He just lost his dad." Halona lifted her mug to her mouth, seeming to use it as a shield. Tuck was the widower but Halona guarded her heart even more than he did.

"It's not that I don't want to date but Theo needs me," she continued. "He's lost a lot."

"And Maddie just lost her mom," Tuck reminded her.

Halona's smile drifted, and sadness colored her brown eyes. He guessed she was realizing that, in some ways, they were now in the same boat.

"All I want is for my big brother to be happy again," she said.

Yeah, he and Renee had been happier than any couple deserved to be. A guy didn't get that lucky twice. Did he?

"So, what's the next step?" Halona asked. "With Maddie."

Tuck checked his watch. "I'm meeting with Mr. Garrison at two thirty."

"A lawyer? Why?" Halona asked.

"Because the plan is for Maddie to come live with me this summer."

Halona reached for his hand.

"It was supposed to be me and Renee. If she were still alive, what would she have thought of this news? I never told her about Crystal."

"You two were broken up. It's not like you lied to her."

"A child came out of it. What would she have thought?" he wondered aloud.

"The same thing that I think. That you'll be an amazing dad and Maddie is one lucky little girl. You for a dad and me for an aunt. She can't go wrong."

Tuck laughed, which worked to loosen up the tightness in his chest. His late wife had been a gentle spirit. Halona was right. Renee would have embraced Maddie with open arms if she were alive now.

Josie had that same quality. She'd already bonded with Maddie when she didn't have to. She was incredible, and his slip in conversation with his sister just now was true. He was falling in love with Josie. He hadn't intended it but he was.

If Renee was looking down on him from somewhere, he didn't even have to wonder at her response. She'd tell him it was okay because that's the kind of woman she was. Giving and loving. She wasn't perfect by any means. Renee had her flaws that had driven him insane when she was alive. But he'd loved her. The same way he was beginning to love Josie.

CHAPTER EIGHTEEN

The last hour with Michelle was not what Josie was expecting. They hadn't talked about work at all. Instead, like two old friends, they'd talked about everything, to include local gossip, diets, fashion, and their favorite late-night TV shows.

Michelle looked out the storefront window. "It's really coming down out there. I might have to get another coffee and hang out here until the rain stops."

Josie studied the downpour outside as well. "Same."

"Thanks for meeting me today, Josie. This has been nice."

"It really has but I have to admit I thought we were meeting to discuss my article."

Michelle smiled back at her. "What's there to discuss? I love it, I want it. I can only pay so much though."

"Don't worry about that," Josie said. "I'm just honored to have my work featured in your magazine."

"Well, I'm honored that you would even consider writing something for us. I'm quite a fan of yours. I read *Loving Life* magazine, and I always love your pieces."

"That's nice of you to say," Josie said. "And it means a lot. I told you the kind of articles my boss wants me to start writing though."

" 'Sex in the Sticks.' " Michelle nodded. "I remember. One thing I love about your writing, Josie, is that your passion shines through. If you don't love what you're doing, it'll show."

"I know." Josie molded her hands around her cup of coffee.

"If you decide to follow your heart and write the topics you choose, send them my way," Michelle added.

"Thank you."

They sat for a little while longer, and then Michelle gathered her things and stood. "I have to get back to work but thanks for today. Let's do this again sometime."

Josie didn't bother to mention that she'd be gone soon. Michelle already knew. Instead, she nodded. "Definitely." It was just what people said but Josie wished that she and Michelle could be friends. It was refreshing to have a fellow writer to chat with.

That would never happen with Bart.

Speaking of . . . Josie pulled her laptop out of its bag and opened it. Waiting for her was an email from him.

Received your latest article. Your update on Sweetwater Springs is now up on the e-zine.

Catch *The Vibe*!

Bart

The e-zine? Had she been demoted to writing for the e-zine now? After ten years working at the magazine?

Josie went to the website and pulled open the follow-up piece, the one that Bart had edited on his own. Her heart sank lower in her belly with each word, sentence, and paragraph.

"This isn't what I wrote," she mumbled under her breath, feeling her face turn hot. "I didn't say that," she nearly shouted at the computer screen.

"Everything okay?" Emma asked, walking over with a coffee pitcher in hand.

Luckily the shop was slow right now. The rain was keeping current customers inside and prospective customers away.

Josie looked up and gestured to her laptop. "No. This is not okay at all... but the coffee is great."

A little V of concern formed between Emma's eyes. "I'm not sure what's going on but would another cup help?"

Josie seriously doubted it. "That'd be great. Thank you."

Emma turned back toward the counter, and Josie continued reading the train wreck of what had been a very sweet, uplifting piece on the town. She'd spoken so nicely of the people here, telling how welcoming everyone had been to an outsider. She'd talked about the Sweetwater Springs Festival and all the great events leading up to it.

Her stomach soured. Bart's editing had made it sound like she was stuck here twiddling her thumbs and that she was miserable.

The one time of year that tourists come to Sweetwater Springs is for the small-town festival that offers little more than what you'd get at any local fair. If you're looking to buy crafts from old women or to hear a no-name band in an open field, it might be worth the drive into the valley.

Josie kept reading. It felt like she was trapped in a nightmare right now. She was so going to let Bart have a piece of her mind when she called him this afternoon. Then she'd demand that he take his hack job on her article down. Until then, she hoped no one read *The Vibe*'s e-zine. Especially nobody in this small town that she had fallen for so completely.

* * *

Tuck had met with Mr. Garrison several times over the years. The last time he'd been in this office had been with Renee because she'd wanted to make a will.

"I knew Crystal Sanders," Mr. Garrison said now, sitting across the table from Tuck. "She was a lovely woman. I always wondered who the child's father was but I never suspected that the girl's own father didn't even know about his paternity."

Tuck's stomach clenched as it did every time he thought of being shut out from Maddie's childhood.

"If Crystal were alive, this would be cause for legal action."

"If she were alive, I suspect I still wouldn't know the truth," Tuck pointed out. "Will it be hard to get custody of Maddie?"

"Shouldn't be. Once you have proof of paternity, the courts will look at your ability to take care of Maddie. Your record is clean. You have a good job and the means to provide for her. If Beverly isn't planning to fight you on this, then there are no obstacles in your way. Even if Beverly put up a fight, I think you'd win."

Tuck's shoulders relaxed as he exhaled softly. "Thank you."

"You're welcome. After you've gotten the test completed, come back to my office and we'll get started on the paperwork."

Tuck stood and shook Mr. Garrison's hand, and then they walked to the door, making small talk about Mr. Garrison's grandchildren and the weather.

"Still raining out there, I see." Mr. Garrison chuckled. "Well, that'll be good for the budding flowers."

Tuck pulled his hood over his head, said a final goodbye, and dashed out toward his Jeep in the parking lot, water splashing over his ankles from the puddles on the pavement. Once inside his vehicle, he caught his breath and cranked the engine.

He was in good spirits as he drove back to Hope Cottage. Part of him had dreaded meeting with Mr. Garrison today. He was a single man with no experience with children other than his nephew. He'd been worried that might not look good to the courts. Mr. Garrison had assured him that there was nothing standing in his way though. Tuck had missed the first eleven years of Maddie's life but he wouldn't miss the next.

When he pulled into his driveway, he noticed Maddie under the covered awning of his porch alongside Josie. Maddie's appointment was usually the last one of the day. That way he could spend as much time with her as he needed. She was standing with her cane, although barely using it for support. Josie stood close to Maddie, ready to catch her if she stumbled, and he trusted that she would.

He got out of the Jeep and darted up the steps. The ground was too soft and wet from a full day of rain to have a therapy session in the yard.

"Sorry I was running a little late," he said. "I had something to handle in town."

"Did it go okay?" Josie asked with knowing eyes.

"Better than okay."

"Great. I'll let you two work. I have something to handle myself," she said, her smile wobbling as she stepped away from Maddie.

"Everything all right?" he asked.

"No, but I'm going to do my best to fix it."

"Feel free to go inside the house if you want. There are tea and snacks in the fridge."

"Thanks." She turned to Maddie. "Work hard."

"I always do." Tuck didn't miss the slight roll of Maddie's eyes. While Maddie had liked Josie at first, she seemed put off by her lately. *What in the world is that about?*

Tuck watched Josie go inside and then turned his attention to his daughter. He couldn't wait to tell her the truth. The sooner she knew, the sooner they could become a family.

"Everything okay?" he asked.

"Yeah, why wouldn't it be?"

"I don't know. You just seem upset with Josie lately. Is there a reason?"

"No, she's nice enough," Maddie said with a shrug.

"But..."

"But nothing. I can see why you like her so much." Maddie averted her gaze.

Tuck debated pressing further, because he wasn't completely buying that response. Before he could say anything more, though, Maddie headed for the steps.

"Hold on there," he said. "Today, let's just work on the porch where it's dry. Afterward I'll take you to the stables. I want to introduce you to Sugar and Chestnut."

Maddie gave him a wide grin. "Horses? Can I ride them?"

"Probably not today. It's too wet. But you can say hello and offer up an apple slice."

"Yes!" Maddie slowly turned her body and walked the length of the porch, then pivoted quickly and headed back.

"Easy now. If you fall, we might not make it to the stables."

"I won't fall," Maddie said with renewed determination.

* * *

"Take the article down now, Bart. It's not the story that I wrote."

"It *is* the story," Bart insisted, "with just a little extra pizzazz. Readers need a little sensationalism to pique their interests."

"They don't need lies." Josie was pacing Tuck's kitchen with her cell on speakerphone.

"Name one thing I lied about."

"You told readers to find somewhere else to have their fun," she said through gritted teeth.

"That's not a lie, Josie. Admit it—Sweetwater Springs is not a tourist hot spot. There's nothing to do there."

"There are mountains, hot springs, and quaint little shops. There are wonderful people who call this place home." Tuck and Maddie came to mind. Even Kaitlyn considered Sweetwater Springs home now.

He yawned loudly into the receiver. "Sorry, but you're putting me to sleep."

"Take it down," she commanded, fisting her left hand at her side. It was a good thing there were several states separating them right now, because she might have been tempted to attack.

"Not happening. It's already had a thousand views, which is terrific for our e-zine articles. It's good for the magazine and for your career."

"The people of Sweetwater Springs are going to be livid."

"And why do I care?" Bart asked.

Josie stopped pacing and stared out the back window, realizing he was right for once. "You don't."

"Exactly, and neither should you."

Bart was nothing like his predecessor. *The Vibe* was nothing like *Loving Life* magazine and never would be. She'd known that for weeks, and this was one more example.

"I quit," Josie said, her voice oddly calm.

"Excuse me?"

"I quit. I'm not coming back to work for you. I can't write stuff I don't believe in."

"Great," Bart said, not even feigning disappointment. "I wasn't looking forward to rewriting all your stuff to make it work for *The Vibe*'s e-zine anyway."

Josie shook her head, anger flaring inside her. "And that's a stupid name for a magazine. The direction you're pointing your father's magazine in is stupid too. And to be quite honest, Bart, you're not too bright either." A smile spread through her cheeks, sore from clenching her jaw over the last ten minutes. "Goodbye and good riddance."

She didn't wait for his reply. She disconnected the call and put her phone down on the counter. Her body was trembling so hard she might have dropped the device if she hadn't.

"Wow."

She turned toward Tuck. "You heard?"

"I did. I haven't seen the feisty side of you since I found you on the hiking trail behind the B and B. I like it."

"Should I call him back and say just kidding? Because I kind of need that job until I find something else," she said.

"No you don't. And no. Don't call him back unless you want to hand the phone to me and let me give him a piece of my mind too."

She laughed weakly. "I've never been unemployed in my adult life. I think I might puke right now."

He stepped toward her, bracing his hands on her shoulders and looking deep into her eyes. "I'd hold your hair if you did."

She smiled up at him. "Why are you such a nice guy, Tuck Locklear?"

"Anyone who'd be anything other than nice to you is a fool. And I'm no fool."

Her frazzled nerves startled to settle. Tuck seemed to have a way of calming her. He'd done the same the other night when she'd told him about the child she'd given up in college.

"Why don't you get dressed?" he said.

"Are you sure you don't mean undressed?" she teased.

"That's for later. Right now, I want to take you out and celebrate."

"Celebrate quitting my job?" she asked.

His smile made him even more irresistible. "No, we're going to celebrate your newfound freedom."

CHAPTER NINETEEN

$\mathcal{T}$uck couldn't take his eyes off Josie.

"This restaurant is beautiful," she said, looking around.

"I'm glad you're enjoying yourself. That was the plan." He'd ordered a steak while she'd ordered eggplant Parmesan, and judging by her nearly clean plate, she'd loved her choice.

"This is our first public outing without Maddie," Josie pointed out. "So, in a way, that makes this our first real date."

"I have to admit that I'm shocked at how much I enjoy hanging out with a city princess," Tuck said.

His words seemed to pull her mind to exactly what he was trying to help her forget tonight. "Speaking of, I spoke to my landlady this afternoon, and my apartment is almost ready. It might be livable again starting this week-end." She shook her head. "Without a job, I can't afford to live there though. When I get back, I'll have to find a roommate or put in my notice."

"Where will you go?" he asked.

"I have no idea. I have money saved so I can stay there long enough to continue searching for jobs. Hopefully I'll find a good fit and figure things out from there."

"You know you're always welcome at Hope Cottage." And wanted, too, but he didn't tell her that.

She tilted her head. "I think that might complicate things."

"Seems to me things get easier when you're around," he offered. "It's even easier to breathe somehow."

He watched her throat constrict as she swallowed. *Slow down*, he told himself. "I guess both of our lives are complicated right now," he added. "If the timing were different and you could stay in Sweetwater Springs, though, we'd share a lot more dinners like this."

"That would be nice." She looked up and then away. "Let's talk about something other than my leaving, shall we? And anything other than work."

"Which used to be your topic of choice," he pointed out.

Her gaze slid back to his. "I guess things have changed."

She was right about that. Everything in his life had changed in the last month. *He'd* changed, and it had a lot to do with the woman sitting across from him. "How about we order a dessert to share?"

Her blue eyes sparkled in the restaurant's dim lighting. "I love it when you sweet-talk me."

* * *

Josie reached for the menu and looked over the list of delectable choices. A woman in her state needed chocolate and lots of it. The triple-decker chocolate lover's delight looked like a good choice. She was about to say so when an older man wearing glasses approached the table.

"What are you doing here?" he asked, an angry tone in his voice. "Are you here to tear down this restaurant too?"

"Excuse me?" Josie looked up.

"I know who you are. You're Josie Kellum, the lady who wrote that article on our town last year."

"That's right." She glanced at Tuck, who had straightened and seemed ready to take the guy out if need be. She also had her pepper spray in her purse if the guy became aggressive.

"You just did a piece online about Sweetwater Springs too. 'Beautiful but boring,'" he said, quoting her least favorite line. A line she hadn't written.

Josie's heart jumped into her throat. "I didn't write that," she said, looking around at the nearby patrons who were dining. A few had turned to witness the budding conflict. "You see, my boss edited my article without my permission. I tried to get him to take it down."

The older man held up a hand only a few inches from her face. "You're just some big-shot journalist on a power trip using your fancy words to bring tourists into our town and then using some more words to run them off."

"Mr. Jenson, this is not the time or place," Tuck said, cutting the man off.

Mr. Jenson? Wasn't that the old man that Halona claimed had a temper?

Mr. Jenson didn't even look in Tuck's direction. "You think you're special," he barked at Josie as his voice grew increasingly louder.

"No. No, I don't. I didn't write that, sir." She looked around again. Everyone was staring at the spectacle the man was causing now.

"Your name is on the article, isn't it?"

"Y-yes, but . . ."

"Why don't you just go back to wherever you came from? We were fine before you found us, and we'll be better than fine once you're gone." He finally turned to Tuck. "Enjoy the rest of your night." He gave her one last disapproving glare before walking away.

Josie's eyes stung. "I'm so sorry, Tuck."

"I didn't realize Bart changed what you wrote," he said.

She nodded, keeping her head down. Gradually the restaurant's patrons returned to their own meals. "It's an awful article, and I was hoping no one else would see it. Guess that was naive of me to think. Everyone in town is going to hate me once they read what I wrote," Josie said, wishing she could curl herself into a ball right now and have a good cry.

"But you didn't write it." He reached for her hand. "We'll fix this."

There was no *we* though. "You have enough to deal with right now. You don't need the town's new outcast on your plate too."

"You've been in Sweetwater Springs for a month. You know the kind of people we are. Good people. Understanding people." He pulled out his cell phone.

"What are you doing?" she asked.

"I'm contacting Mr. Garrison, my lawyer, on your behalf. We'll go see him tomorrow morning, and he'll write a cease-and-desist letter. I'd guess your ex-boss will back down at the first hint of a lawsuit, and the article will be down by lunchtime tomorrow."

Josie sucked in a breath. "You really think so?"

His finger tapped along the screen of his phone. "I know so." He grinned as his phone buzzed in his palm.

"Mr. Garrison says to tell you to be at his office at nine a.m. He'd love to help you."

"Thank you," she said. "You keep coming to my rescue."

"Just helping you out—the same way you've helped me."

Josie sighed as her gaze fell on the menu. "I hate to be a spoiler but I'm not really in the mood for dessert anymore. I just want to get out of here, if that's okay."

He took the menu and set it at the end of the table. Then he laid down the payment for the bill in cash and slid out of his chair.

"You don't have to pay," she protested.

"Yes, I do. Like you said, this is a date, and I want to treat you right." He reached for her hand. "And the date isn't over yet."

* * *

Josie stirred in the warmth of Tuck's bed. She didn't want to open her eyes but his phone was ringing. *What time is it?* The last thing she remembered, Tuck had been kissing her as her clothes somehow fell into a puddle on his floor.

She blinked the clock on his nightstand into focus: 12:13 a.m.

"Who's calling at this hour?" Tuck groaned. There was a sexy, sleepy quality to his voice that she liked. It made her want to wrap her arms around him and pull him to her again. Who needed sleep? She could just have an extra cup of coffee in the morning.

Tuck rolled over and grabbed the phone. "Hello?"

Josie alerted to the shift in his posture as he spoke to whoever was on the other end of the line.

He sat up. "What happened? What room are you in?

I'll be there as soon as I can." He disconnected the call and turned to Josie.

"Who was that?" she asked.

"Beverly. She's in the hospital. She was having shortness of breath, and Maddie called 911."

Josie gasped, suddenly wide awake too. "Oh no!"

"I'm going to the hospital to pick up Maddie. Beverly asked if she could stay here." He talked as he stood and started collecting his clothes—the ones she'd peeled off him just a few hours before.

"Want me to go with you?" she asked.

He hesitated as he stepped into his jeans. "I hate to ask you but can you do me a favor?"

"Sure. What do you need?"

"She'll be staying in the guest room. Can you prepare her bed? There are clean linens in the dresser drawer. She'll be tired when she gets back, and I want her to be able to lie down immediately."

"Of course—I can do that. Do you want me to be gone when you get back? Maddie might wonder why I'm here and not in my apartment."

"She might. But I'd appreciate the help. I'm not sure what to do with a preteen girl in the house. I can sleep on the couch. You take the bed," he suggested.

"Sure. Whatever you need. I'll be here."

He stared at her a moment, an unreadable expression in his eyes. "Thank you." Fully dressed, he bent and kissed her mouth. "I'll be back soon."

Josie watched him leave and then collected her own clothes and dressed. She headed down the hall to the guest room. Just like Tuck had said, she located clean sheets in the top drawer of an antique dresser.

Poor Maddie. She'd been through so much, and there

were still more storm clouds on the horizon. Maddie didn't realize Tuck was her father. In a short time, her life would be uprooted once more when she came to live here at Hope Cottage. Little did she know that the room that Josie was preparing might be Maddie's new permanent bedroom.

Josie looked around. The space was bright and cheerful. It would make a great room for an eleven-year-old girl. It might need a few special touches though. She could help with that. Maybe after she met with Tuck's lawyer tomorrow and put Bart in his place, she'd go shopping.

* * *

"I'm not going to school," Maddie said the next morning over breakfast. Josie had gotten up early to cook while Tuck tended to the horses. She'd learned a thing or two during the week that she'd stayed at the bed and breakfast with Kaitlyn. "I want to go to the hospital to see my grandma."

"You have an end-of-year test to prepare for, don't you?" Josie asked. "There's no need to miss class. You can see your grandma when you get home."

Maddie stabbed her fork into a fluffy mound of egg. "You're not my mom, you know."

"I know that, sweetheart."

"Then why are you trying to act like her, making me breakfast and talking to me about school? My mom is dead. And my grandma might die too."

Josie walked over to the table and sat down. She reached for Maddie's hand but Maddie yanked it away.

"See?" Maddie said, as if that was proof that Josie was trying to mother her.

"I'm just trying to be here for you. I am, you know. You can talk to me."

"Maybe I don't want to talk to you," Maddie huffed.

"Did I do something to upset you, Maddie? I thought we were friends but you've seemed angry at me over the last week."

"We're not friends. The only reason you're around is because of Tuck. I know that so you can stop pretending."

"But that's not true. He's not even here right now, and I haven't vanished, have I?"

Maddie frowned and looked away. "Whatever. I have to eat my breakfast so I can pay attention in class."

"Right. The bus will be here soon. Unless you want me to drive you to school," Josie offered. "I'm sure Tuck would let me use his Jeep." She was trying too hard; she could feel it. And the harder she tried, the more Maddie pushed her away.

"No. I'd rather take the bus," Maddie said, picking at her food again.

"Okay. Well, eat up, and I'll walk you to the bus stop."

Maddie narrowed her eyes. "I'm not an invalid. I can go on my own."

"I know that." Josie swallowed. "Of course you can. Tuck said you were ready for more independence."

"Perfect." Maddie pushed away from the table.

"Aren't you going to finish your breakfast?" Josie asked.

"I lost my appetite." Maddie stood and grabbed her cane. Then she headed to the front door and slammed it behind her.

"Was that Maddie?" Tuck asked, coming through the back entrance.

Josie nodded. "She wanted to go to the bus stop on her own. I don't think she's happy about me being here." Josie hadn't been around last night when Tuck brought Maddie to Hope Cottage. She'd purposely kept her distance. Then this morning, when Maddie had hobbled down the hall, Josie had been in the kitchen. Maddie's groggy smile had fallen fast, and then she'd practically snarled as she asked, "*What are you doing here?*"

Tuck put a hand on Josie's shoulder. "She's unhappy with everything right now. She's been through more than a girl her age should."

Josie nodded. "She's strong. She'll get through it. And you'll help her." Josie wished that she could stay and help as well. She was actually even considering the idea, which was just crazy. Insane. "Well, I better go get ready for my appointment with Mr. Garrison. Are you sure you can drop me off?"

"Not a problem. I'll meet you at your place in a bit."

"Thanks." Josie stood and leaned in to kiss his mouth. Then she retreated to her apartment to shower and get dressed. She really hoped he could scare Bart into backing off. Josie couldn't bear the thought of any other Sweetwater Springs residents reading that awful e-zine article with her name on it.

Twenty minutes later, she turned to a knock on her door. With one final look in the mirror, she grabbed her purse and headed out.

They drove downtown to Mr. Garrison's office, and Tuck dropped her off. She wished Tuck had been able to come inside with her but he had patients to see.

Up until a few weeks ago, she'd prided herself on being Miss Independent. Miss I-Can-Do-It-on-My-Own.

Since when do I need someone else?

The answer popped into her mind immediately. Since Tuck. She didn't need him beside her but she wanted him there.

CHAPTER TWENTY

*E*ven though Tuck had just spent an hour-long therapy session looking at outdoor decorations for a college graduation party, he was in a great mood. It had nothing to do with his patient Claire Donovan and everything to do with Josie. Whatever Maddie's problem was, he was sure it had nothing to do with Josie. She was good with his daughter. A natural. And watching them together only made his feelings grow deeper.

"What do you think, Tuck?" Claire asked, gaining his attention. "Am I ready to be rid of you yet? Not that I don't enjoy therapy with you but it's the start of my busy season. Weddings, grad parties, retirement functions. And I have my ten-year class reunion to plan. I think my leg is better, don't you?"

He wobbled his head back and forth as if weighing the decision. The truth was he'd already considered that it was time to discharge Claire from his caseload. "Are you going to keep up with your exercises at home?"

She raised a hand solemnly. "I promise."

"Okay, then."

She cheered and remarkably kept her balance at the same time. "You didn't graduate with us but you can come to the reunion I'm planning if you let me set you up with one of the single ladies there." She raised a brow. "What about Serena Gibbs? She's lovely and such a sweetheart."

"No, thanks," he said.

Claire narrowed her gaze. "Ah. I thought I saw sparks between you and Josie the other day." She grinned. "Well, I'll save Serena for another of my single friends, then."

"He'll be a lucky guy, I'm sure. Okay," Tuck said, quickly turning the subject from his dating life back to her leg, "if I'm going to dismiss you from PT, I need to see you walk back to your car without so much as a limp."

"Yes, sir," Claire said with a smile.

When Tuck returned home later that afternoon, Josie was already on the porch, her computer open on her lap.

"Maddie's bus should be here soon," she said as he climbed the steps. "I called the school to make sure I knew what time I needed to be back."

Tuck sat beside her on the porch swing. "Thanks. You didn't have to do that. I planned on being here."

"I know. I just thought it might help."

"Help who? Me or Maddie?" he asked.

She shrugged and then closed her laptop and slid it into a bag against the railing. "Both."

As she straightened, he leaned in to kiss her. "How'd things go with Mr. Garrison?"

"Great. He already had the cease-and-desist letter prepared when I got there. He called the magazine and spoke to Bart briefly to let him know that he was faxing a letter on my behalf." Josie flashed a big smile. "I checked the e-zine an hour ago, and the article is already down."

"That's terrific news," Tuck said.

"It is. And Mr. Garrison told Bart that we wanted my follow-up article on Sweetwater Springs back. I now have full rights to do whatever I want with it. I'm going to tweak it and see if Michelle wants to publish it in *Carolina Home*."

"Wow. That's incredible."

Josie laughed softly. "I was thinking I might beg Kaitlyn to help me bake something delicious to bring over to Mr. Garrison's office. He really did me a huge service."

"Food is said to be the way to a man's heart," Tuck agreed. "Although you haven't fed me yet, and somehow you still made it into mine."

When had that happened? he wondered to himself. Maybe when he'd told her about Renee. Or when she'd helped him with Maddie at the dance, festival, and again last night. When she'd disclosed the story about the baby she'd given up in college, or when they'd made love. Maybe it had happened all along the way, one little moment at a time.

"So what about the rest of your day?" he asked, quickly reaching for a neutral subject.

"Well, after I left Mr. Garrison's office, I strolled downtown a bit before working at the coffee shop. I got Maddie a present." She reached into a bag at her feet and pulled out a quilt with all the colors of the rainbow. "It was just so pretty. I thought it would really brighten up her room. Do you think she'll like it?"

"How could she not?" He watched Josie's face light up as she continued to tell him about her day and show him a few other little items she'd purchased for Maddie's room. Whether she knew it or not, she had the heart of a mother, which he found all kinds of attractive. He didn't dare say that though. She'd given him a glimpse into her past pain of giving her child up for adoption. It was a long time ago, and she'd said it was the best decision for the child. Even so, he wondered if that was driving her need to always be working. Did she think she wouldn't get a second chance to have a family?

"There's the bus!" Josie said excitedly. "I can't wait to help Maddie decorate her room."

Tuck grinned. "I'll go get her. She's still struggling with stairs, and I'm still her PT."

"And her dad." Josie stood with her bags in hand. "I'll go inside and make her a snack. Is it okay if I rummage through your fridge?"

"What's mine is yours."

She gave him a wide-eyed look before heading inside.

Tuck walked in the opposite direction toward the bus. *What's mine is yours?* This is exactly how he'd been with Renee when they'd first met. He'd fallen hard and fast, and when he'd started talking about marriage, everyone had warned him to take things slow. They were too young. That's why he'd broken up with her briefly when he was in college. He'd listened to everyone's advice that he didn't need to settle down too quickly. If he'd listened to his heart, though, he never would've broken up with Renee.

Here he went again, diving in heart first with Josie. The only naysayer this time was the little voice in his head reminding him that she was leaving soon, and they hadn't discussed continuing their relationship. What if she didn't want to continue it? She was looking for new jobs, none of them here, and soon she'd be out of his apartment and life, possibly for good.

* * *

Josie pulled Tuck's refrigerator door open and peeled inside. What did little girls like to eat? It shouldn't be too hard to figure it out; feeding an eleven-year-old girl wasn't rocket science.

Spotting some Gala apples in the bottom drawer, she grabbed one and took it to the sink to wash. Then she found an apple slicer in the drawer below the silverware and divided the apple into smaller pieces. With just a little more searching, she found a jar of creamy peanut butter in the cabinet.

She also poured a glass of chilled green tea that Tuck apparently always kept ready in the fridge. Josie hadn't had that growing up, or even in her adult life, but she would from now on. And she supposed she'd always think of Tuck when she did.

The front door opened, and Maddie's giggles filled the room.

Josie's heart squeezed hard. Maddie had been through so much. She deserved to be happy, and Josie had no doubt that Tuck would ensure she was. "How was school?" Josie asked as Maddie walked carefully into the room using her cane.

Maddie looked up, disappointment shading her eyes just like it had this morning when she'd seen Josie. "It was okay."

"Did you get compliments on your new outfit?"

"A few."

"See! I told you it was pretty," Josie said, knowing that she was trying too hard again. Josie couldn't help it though. She wanted Maddie to like her again.

"Almost as pretty as you," Tuck said, walking up behind Maddie and rustling her hair.

"Hey!" Maddie complained, swatting him away.

Josie laughed. "You never touch a girl's hair. Don't you know that?"

Tuck stepped over and did the same to her and then yanked out the hair tie holding her ponytail in place.

"Hey!" Josie squealed. She whipped around to smack Tuck playfully before realizing that Maddie was watching, and she didn't look the least bit entertained.

Josie reached for the plate of apple slices and peanut butter and shoved it into Tuck's hands. "These are for Maddie." She pointed at the table.

"None for me?" he asked, teasing.

"Not after messing up our hair." Josie watched him get Maddie settled at the table with the snack. "Well, I should probably go back to my apartment. To, um, work." Not that she had anything specific to do. She just didn't want to intrude. She wasn't part of Tuck and Maddie's new family, and Maddie obviously didn't want her around.

"What? So soon? I thought you had something special to do with Maddie." Tuck slid his gaze to the bags she'd brought back from her shopping excursion this morning.

"Oh. Right. Well, that can wait. I'm sure you two have things to do," she said, making more excuses.

"All I have to do this afternoon is hang out with two of my favorite people," Tuck said.

Shadow barked from where she was lying at Maddie's feet.

Tuck dipped his head to level his gaze at the dog. "Yeah, yeah. And you too."

"Stay?" Tuck asked, looking at her with hopeful eyes. "I might even cook dinner and put on a movie later. You wouldn't want to miss that, would you?"

She swallowed as her throat grew tighter. No, she wouldn't want to miss that.

"You want her to stay too, don't you, Maddie?" Tuck prodded.

Maddie looked up from her snack and frowned.

* * *

After dinner, Maddie had called and spoken to her grandmother in the hospital and reported that Beverly was doing much better. She'd probably stay through the weekend and go home on Monday. Then they all settled in on the couch, and Tuck begrudgingly put on *You've Got Mail*.

"Are you sure you two don't want to watch *Die Hard*? Or *Mission: Impossible*?"

Josie and Maddie laughed, which was his goal tonight. Whatever was going on between the two of them, he wanted to smooth it over.

"Fine. Two against one." He draped his arm around Josie on the couch and tugged her in close while Maddie lay with her head on the opposite armrest.

Halfway through the movie, Josie nudged Tuck in the ribs. "Maddie is sleeping."

He leaned forward to check for himself. "So she is. I'll get a blanket. She can sleep on the couch tonight."

He walked into Maddie's temporary bedroom, where he kept spare blankets and sheets in the dresser. For a moment, he stopped and stared. Josie had really transformed this room into something special tonight. She'd changed the bedding and hung some posters of boy bands. Josie had purchased a large stuffed horse for Maddie, too, that looked a lot like Sugar.

It actually looked like a little girl's room in here. The justification to Maddie had been that Beverly might need some time to herself over the next few months while she continued to get better. Maddie could come to Hope Cottage and stay whenever Beverly needed her to.

Once Beverly returned home, though, they'd sit down with Maddie and tell her the real story together.

It was time to tell Josie the truth too. He was falling in love with her. Yeah, it'd only been a month but he didn't see things slowing down between them. They had the potential to make this work if they wanted to. That's what he wanted. But what did she want?

CHAPTER TWENTY-ONE

*H*ere," Kaitlyn said, handing a large pot of water to Josie in the kitchen of the Sweetwater Bed and Breakfast the following week.

Josie held on to it and gave her friend a blank stare.

"Mind getting it boiling for me?" Kaitlyn asked. "I'll grab the noodles from the pantry."

Josie had agreed to come over this afternoon and help Kaitlyn cook for charity this evening. Townsfolk were participating in a clothing drive for the local women's shelter in exchange for a spaghetti dinner at the community center tonight.

Carrying the pot to the stove, Josie set it down on one of the burners. She turned the dial to high, and then turned back to Kaitlyn. "I'm getting the hang of this cooking thing."

Kaitlyn headed over with several boxes of noodles. "It's a big pot so we need the big burner, not the small one."

"Right." Josie nodded. "I still have a lot to learn."

Kaitlyn shifted the pot to the larger burner and turned the corresponding dial to heat the water. "You're doing great. Thanks for helping me today, by the way."

"I'm not sure I'll be much help." Josie plopped down on a stool at the kitchen island.

"You are, and it's nice to have someone to talk to. So, are you coming tonight? From what I'm told, you won't find better spaghetti anywhere. I can attest for the pot we're making at least."

"Not sure yet," Josie said with a shrug. "I don't have anything to get rid of."

"You're donating your time right now. That counts. Mitch is working at the police department tonight so you can be my date. It'll be fun. We can eat until we burst, and maybe you can find inspiration for a new article."

They made more small talk and then Kaitlyn remembered the stove. "Oh, the water's boiling. Want to do the honors?"

"Of adding the noodles?" Josie asked.

"Yes. Then you can tell people you made the spaghetti. It'll get you brownie points with the locals."

Josie laughed as she walked over to the stove and dumped the dry noodles in. Kaitlyn handed her a wooden spoon, and she stirred the contents around. "Good enough?" she asked.

Kaitlyn leaned in to take a glance. "See? I told you there was a chef waiting to be unlocked in you. Your future husband won't starve after all."

Josie swallowed as she stared into the bubbling water. Her future husband wouldn't starve, because he didn't exist. Even if she'd entertained a few fantasies of spending forever at Hope Cottage with Tuck. It was foolish thinking. He'd been married once already, and she wasn't even the marrying type. "Or at least I won't starve. Maybe I can even cut my take-out budget in half after this."

"And create a Sweetwater Springs travel fund so you can come back to visit more often," Kaitlyn suggested.

"There's an idea," Josie said. "This town of yours is really growing on me."

"And Tuck too. I saw the sparks between you guys when he crashed our girls' day with Maddie. They were off the charts. I might even venture to say it's more than just physical chemistry between you two."

Josie stirred the softening noodles around the pot again, needing something to do with her hands. "I'll admit I like him. A lot. But at some point, I have to return to real life where I go to an office every day and pay the bills."

"Can't you have both? The career and a love life? It doesn't have to be one or the other. I have Mitch *and* the job of my dreams."

"That's different."

"Not really," Kaitlyn said.

Josie didn't respond. She didn't know what to say. She'd been entertaining crazy, ridiculous thoughts over the last couple of days. Like maybe she could stay longer now that she was out of a job. She could write more articles for *Carolina Home* magazine. Summer was coming, and she could ride horses, walk along Blueberry Creek, write at the Sweetwater Café, and sleep with Tuck at night. It sounded like the perfect summer. Then she could stay here for the perfect fall, hiking through the mountains and picking apples at the local orchard.

What was happening to her?

A timer went off, breaking Josie's thoughts.

"That means the noodles are ready and need to be

drained." Kaitlyn grabbed the pot and brought it over to the sink where she'd set up a straining bowl.

"You're a natural at this stuff," Josie commented. Homemaking and being in love looked good on Kaitlyn, despite her city roots. But that didn't mean the same was true for Josie.

* * *

After seeing a few patients, Tuck picked up Maddie from school and took her straight to Beverly's house. Beverly had returned home from the hospital this morning and wanted Maddie with her. Tuck wasn't exactly thrilled about that but he didn't have custody yet. Plus, Maddie was homesick and eager to see her grandmother.

"Call me if you need to. It doesn't matter what time it is," he told them both, standing in their living room.

"Of course," Beverly said. "Thank you, Tuck. For everything."

He nodded and looked at Maddie. "Take care of your grandmother."

"I will. Maybe I can come stay with you again soon. In the room you prepared for me at Hope Cottage."

Tuck slid his gaze over to meet Beverly's just in time to see her eyes cloud over with a hint of sadness. "Maybe so," he said. "But right now, your grandma needs you."

Beverly offered an appreciative smile.

On his way out, Tuck glanced at Crystal's picture on the wall. His belly knotted with anger that only served to make him feel guilty.

He got back into his Jeep and drove home, disappointed to find Josie still not back from her day of cooking with Kaitlyn. The clothing drive and spaghetti dinner benefited the local women's shelter. Maybe Tuck needed to do a little spring cleaning himself, he thought. He could work off some of his frustration and donate to a local charity.

He opened the back door for Shadow to go out in the yard, and his gaze landed on the shed near the stables. It was full of Renee's belongings. There were boxes of clothes and shoes that were going to waste out there. He'd given Renee's cane to Maddie. Maybe it was time to give away more of his late wife's things. He couldn't use them, and holding on to the items felt like holding on to the past when he needed to be looking forward to the future.

He grabbed a hat off the kitchen counter to shield his face from the sun and headed in the direction of the shed. Swinging open the door, he peered inside. He'd been avoiding doing anything with these things because it was just too painful. Losing Renee had left a wound he didn't think he'd ever recover from. But in the last month, things had turned around for him. His heart felt full again, overflowing even. As with spring, where nature came back with a vengeance after winter, bringing with it new life, so it was with his heart. He had a daughter, and he was falling in love.

He reached for the first box labeled RENEE'S WINTER CLOTHES and carried it outside to the grass. Then he went back and found his late wife's fall, summer, and spring clothes. When he'd put them here in storage, he'd decided it might be hard to run into some stranger in town who was wearing Renee's things. Now he thought it would feel good. Renee had been such a giving woman. She'd want her clothes to go to someone in need.

One after another, he loaded five large tubs of items into the back of his Jeep. It was a start, and it'd freed up a lot of space in the shed for other things. Maddie's things. Or Josie's.

He headed inside the house to shower and then dress, feeling a little excited. He was in the mood for spaghetti tonight. And for Josie's company—if he could find her.

An hour later, he walked into a crowded community center full of lively conversation and the smell of Italian spices.

"Tuck! What are you doing here?" Halona asked as soon as he'd walked in the door. She was standing with his mom and nephew. Theo barreled into the lower half of his body and hugged his legs in lieu of hello.

"I brought some donations. Renee's things."

His mom's and Halona's smiles wilted.

"Really? That's a big step," his mom said.

Tuck shrugged as if it wasn't but they were right. "It was time."

"And I've never known you to come to a big community event on your own volition either," his mom pointed out.

Tuck didn't have an answer to that. Josie and her love for group events had rubbed off on him. He looked down at his nephew and rustled Theo's hair. "What are you feeding this kid?" he teased, changing the subject. "He's almost as big as I am."

"Well, tonight he's eating spaghetti." Halona shook her head as Theo smoothed his disheveled hair back down along his forehead.

"Your dad's over there in the corner," Tuck's mom said with a gesture.

"Oh. Thought I was attending a charity spaghetti dinner, not a family reunion."

Both his mom and sister laughed but it was a sweeter sound across the room that got his attention. Josie was seated at a table and laughing about something with Kaitlyn.

"Yep. Your new houseguest is here too," Halona said, following his gaze.

Tuck's mom raised her dark brows. "I hope you've been a good host to the town's celebrity."

"I'm just renting the garage apartment to her," Tuck reminded his mother. But it'd turned into so much more than that, and he didn't think for a minute that he was fooling his mom. In fact, his mom and Halona had probably already put two and two together and discovered that Josie was the reason he was taking more steps to move on with his life. He didn't want to forget about what he'd had with Renee but it wasn't healthy to assume he'd be alone forever.

Theo tugged on Halona's shirt, and she looked down, the corners of her eyes crinkling as she smiled at him. "I'm guessing you're pretty hungry, huh? Better get in that line before we miss out on all the good stuff." Halona took his hand and looked at Tuck. "Are you joining us for tonight's meal? Or maybe you want to sit with Josie and Kaitlyn instead?" she asked with a knowing look in her eyes.

Yep, they knew. "I'll be sitting with you guys, of course." He directed his attention to his only nephew. "I have to try and see if I can out eat Theo here."

Theo's smile lit up his entire face.

Tuck and his mom followed Halona and Theo toward the spaghetti line. As they did, he couldn't help glancing back to where Josie was. She looked beautiful tonight. He longed to get out of line, walk over to her, and kiss her silly. He was hungry, all right, but his appetite was for her.

When he turned back to the food, Halona was watching him.

"Your eyes are bigger than your stomach, buddy," Tuck told Theo as his nephew pointed at one pot after another and Halona dutifully scooped a sample from each. "Just don't bite off more than you can chew."

It was the same advice he'd been giving himself for weeks regarding Josie. But now it was too late.

* * *

Here was an article idea. Everyone in town had come together for a good cause. It was incredible, really. Several dozen families sat together at long rectangular tables, laughing and eating after donating their gently used things. This was the kind of story that her old boss, Gary, would've eaten up with a spoon.

Family. Friends. Community. Life. These were great leads for a freelance article, possibly for *Carolina Home*. Maybe she'd shoot Michelle an email later.

"Hey, you two." Mitch walked up to the table where they were sitting. He was still dressed in uniform, and Josie noticed that half a dozen ladies were craning their necks to check him out.

There. *"Why Women Love Men in Uniforms." Yes!*

Josie got a little jolt of excitement and pulled out her phone while Mitch and Kaitlyn kissed. She'd never been a huge fan of public displays of affection. The *p* in PDA should've been *private* instead of *public* in her opinion.

There! Another article. She was feeling all kinds of inspiration suddenly. She attended a lot of events in New York but there was something different about taking part in these small-town, feel-good community activities; they were good for her writing mojo.

"I'm just going to grab a plate and come join you two,

if that's okay," Mitch said, lifting his gaze from Kaitlyn to Josie.

"Of course it's okay," Josie said, even though she really wanted Kaitlyn all to herself. There was another lead for an article: *"How to Ration Time Between Your Best Guy and Best Girl."*

Josie started typing in her notepad app on her phone.

"Here you go, Mitch," a sweet older woman said, handing him a plate. "I saw you walk in and fixed this up for you."

Mitch accepted it and kissed the woman on the cheek. "That's nice of you, Ms. Shelby. By the looks of this, you must think I'm starving to death."

The older woman appeared to blush at his attention. "I've always loved a man in uniform. And you fill yours out beautifully." She winked at him, blushing even darker.

"Dating Among the Senior Population." Another idea!

"Are you working?" Kaitlyn asked, looking over Josie's shoulder at her cell phone.

"The ideas are pouring in. This place is gold."

Kaitlyn shook her head with a laugh and then turned her attention back to Mitch. Josie placed her phone back in her purse, finished her plate of food, and finally got up to say hello to Tuck, whom she'd spotted sitting near his sister, Halona, and her son, his mom, and a man who Josie guessed was his father.

"Josie!" Lula said as she approached their table. "Hello, dear. Are you having a good time?"

"Yes. This is a wonderful thing. I'm afraid I only had a few items to donate but I helped Kaitlyn cook a pot of spaghetti and some of the bread."

"Oh. Do you hear that, Tuck? Josie cooks. I'll have to

invite you over one day so I can teach you some of my American Indian specialty dishes."

Josie nodded. "That sounds fun. The Three Sisters Stew you made the other night was delicious."

Lula looked pleased. "Thank you. This is Tuck's father, Don."

Like Tuck had told her before, Don was Caucasian and balding. Tuck didn't seem to have inherited any of his genes from him.

"Nice to meet you, Josie," he said with a nod.

There was a familiarity to his smile that did remind her of Tuck, however. "So nice to meet you." She waved at Halona and Theo sitting across from them.

"Why don't you join us?" Lula asked.

"Actually, Mom," Tuck said, scooting back from the table, "I'm done eating. I was thinking of heading home." He looked at Josie. "Would you like a ride?"

Josie felt her cheeks heat and hoped his family didn't notice. Maddie was back at Beverly's tonight, and she wouldn't mind having Tuck all to herself. "Yes, that'd be great. I rode with Kaitlyn but now that Mitch is here I feel like a third wheel."

"I'll call you about doing some cooking together," Lula said. "I hope you're not leaving town in the next week."

"I'm not sure." Josie had thought her apartment building would've reopened already, not that she was complaining. She hadn't figured out what she was going to do about Tuck when she left. A clean break was probably best but she didn't like to think about that.

Tuck stepped up beside her. "Ready?" he asked.

"Yeah. Let me just tell Kaitlyn so she doesn't wonder where I've run off to." Josie weaved through the crowd, spotting Mr. Jenson, who'd made a scene at the restaurant the other day, and veered in the other direction. She didn't need a repeat of that incident. Thank goodness Mr. Garrison had gotten the article taken down.

Speaking of Mr. Garrison, she spotted him sitting with his family at one of the tables and waved. She also waved at Dawanda from the fudge shop and Sophie from her new favorite boutique. So this is what small-town living felt like. It was warm and cozy, like a pair of wool-lined slippers on a chilly night.

Josie reached Kaitlyn and dipped down to whisper in her ear. "Tuck is taking me home."

Kaitlyn gave her a playful grin. "Since when have you started thinking of Hope Cottage as home?"

* * *

Tuck pulled into his driveway and cut the engine. "We could stay here and make out like teenagers," he suggested, gaining a laugh out of Josie. He loved her laugh. Loved pretty much everything about her.

"Were you guilty of back seat make-out sessions when you were younger?" she asked.

"I was a hot-blooded male after all. I still am," he said in a deep, raspy voice.

Josie leaned across the seat and pressed her mouth to his. Her tongue traced the edge of his outer lip before he opened to her and deepened the kiss.

"I missed you last night," he groaned, letting his hands roam over the curves of her body. When Maddie was sleeping under his roof, they'd reverted to no touching. He had no intention of keeping his hands to himself tonight though.

"Me too," she said as she slid her fingers through his hair and her tongue stroked his.

They kissed for ages, his desire for her mounting. Also gaining momentum was his need to tell her exactly how he felt. There was no time like the present; nobody was promised tomorrow. He'd learned that hard lesson already. He'd told Renee he loved her every day but had she really heard him? Had she known?

"Josie," he said, pulling back and looking at her in the dimly lit Jeep. "I don't know what it is about you but you drive me crazy in the best possible way. I'm whistling as I work and going to community events that I would never enjoy. A month ago, you couldn't have paid me to go to something like one of those dances or that festival. You make everything fun. You make waking up every morning seem easy, when for the last couple of years, it's been a small feat. I feel like I've been given a second chance at life because of you."

Her lips, swollen from kissing him, parted as she sucked in a breath. "Tuck," she whispered.

Like a boulder rolling down the mountainside, his path was set, and he couldn't stop now. He took her hands in his. "You don't have to go. You could stay here at Hope Cottage."

Traces of something wild flickered in the depths of her blue eyes. "What?" she asked, drawing back just slightly.

"There's no reason you have to leave so soon. You could stay and give us a shot."

"Us," she repeated.

"Yeah. Us. You don't have to say anything right now. I just wanted to tell you how I felt. Then I wanted to take you inside and show you."

A slow grin emerged on her lips. "I've always loved show-and-tell," she whispered.

This thing between them wasn't one-sided. He could see that much in Josie's sparkling eyes. He brought one of her hands to his lips, kissing the delicate skin. Then he got out of the Jeep and walked around to open her door and lead her inside. Maybe if he gave her a good enough reason, she'd change her plans and choose to stay in Sweetwater Springs. She'd choose him.

CHAPTER TWENTY-TWO

*T*uck waited at the bus stop the next afternoon. Beverly had a follow-up appointment so he'd agreed to meet Maddie after school. He'd seen her last night at the spaghetti dinner but he'd barely gotten to talk to her. He'd been too busy with Halona and Theo, his mom, and then Josie.

Had he even said goodbye to Maddie? Guilt socked him in the gut. He'd make it up to her this afternoon. Maybe he could take her out for ice cream or something.

Thunder rolled overhead. Another storm was brewing. Hopefully, it would hold off until Maddie was off the bus. She was getting around much better these days but muddy ground would make it more difficult.

The bus rumbled around the bend with its noisy engine and stopped to let several students off. Tuck stood, his heart lifting in anticipation. The angry little girl he'd met a month earlier had turned into a feisty, witty clone of Halona at that age. She had a lot of his own qualities too. She was quiet, reflective, and loved animals. And he loved her more than he ever thought he could.

He also loved Josie. He'd wanted to tell her last night when he'd asked her to stay at Hope Cottage but he'd held back. It was enough that she knew that he thought they had something worth pursuing. And they did. Two females had completely stolen a heart that he was beginning to wonder would ever be whole again.

A boy Maddie's age stepped off the bus and gave Tuck a curious look before turning to walk down the road. Tuck watched the steps. When no one else came down, he drew closer to talk to the bus driver.

"Maddie Locklear?" he asked.

The driver shook his head. "She didn't get on this morning."

"Of course she did. I spoke to her grandmother."

The boy turned back. "Maddie was absent today," he called. "She didn't come to class."

Tuck looked at the bus driver again and then stepped away so the bus could continue on its route. "Are you sure?" he asked the boy.

"Positive. We have the same homeroom."

"I see. Thanks." Tuck watched the boy walk away. Maybe Maddie had stayed home, and Beverly had failed to mention it. Beverly had an appointment though. Would Maddie have stayed at the house alone? Was she old enough for that? he wondered, pulling his phone out and dialing Beverly.

"Hello?" she said, answering on the third ring. "Tuck? I'm at my doctor's appointment. Is everything all right?"

"Yeah. Just making sure Maddie is with you," he said easily. Beverly had a lot on her plate. He couldn't fault her for forgetting to mention Maddie's absence from school.

"No, you're picking her up at the bus stop near my home, remember?" Beverly said. "Oh, Dr. Metts just came in. You are at the bus stop, aren't you? I don't want Maddie to be alone."

Tuck looked around. Yeah, he was at the bus stop but where was Maddie? "Don't worry. I'm here." He didn't elaborate on the situation. Beverly needed to focus on her health right now. And hopefully, by the time she was done with her follow-up, he'd have figured out what was going on. And whatever it was, Maddie better have a good excuse.

"All right. I'll see you in a couple of hours," Beverly said.

"Yep." He disconnected the call and dialed Josie. Maybe Maddie had skipped school to go on another shopping trip. Josie wasn't that irresponsible but she really wanted Maddie to like her again. It was possible.

"Hi," she said cheerfully.

Tuck swallowed the bitter taste in his mouth. "Where are you?"

"The Sweetwater B and B with Kaitlyn. I was thinking about doing another interview for *Carolina Home*."

"Just you and Kaitlyn?" he asked. *Please say no.*

"That's right. Why? Is everything okay? Did you remember to pick up Maddie at the bus stop?"

He started walking fast to Beverly's driveway, a bad feeling settling in his gut. "I showed up but Maddie apparently didn't make it to school today."

"What? Where is she?"

"Good question," he said, pulling his keys out of his pocket. He got inside the Jeep and cranked the engine. As he did, he heard another rumble of thunder overhead. The skies had turned darker in the last fifteen minutes. "I was hoping she was with you."

"No. I haven't seen her since the spaghetti dinner last night."

Tuck pressed the gas and took off down the street. "Did you get to talk to her there?" he asked.

"I tried," Josie said, her tone of voice telling him that the conversation hadn't gone well.

"I see. I'm going to look for Maddie now. Any idea where she might have gone?"

"On foot?" Josie asked. "Not a clue. Maybe downtown if she got a ride."

And that was something else he didn't want to contemplate. Any stranger could've picked Maddie up and taken her who knew where. "I'll let you know when I find her," he said, ignoring the next question that popped into his mind. *What if I don't find her?*

* * *

"I need a favor," Josie said, turning to Kaitlyn. "I need to borrow your car."

"What? Why?" Kaitlyn glanced over her shoulder as she stood over a pot of boiling water on the stove.

"Maddie didn't show up for school today, and Tuck is searching for her." Josie felt breathless as she spoke. Josie had skipped school many times as a student but so many things could happen to a young girl. Especially one who couldn't move fast enough to get away. "Please," Josie added.

"Yeah, of course. My keys are in my purse. I don't need them; I'm watching the inn for the rest of the night."

"Hopefully it won't take that long to find her." Josie grabbed Kaitlyn's purse and dug inside.

"Where will you go?" Kaitlyn asked.

"I don't know. The mall maybe?"

Kaitlyn turned to face her. "That's a good start. Little girls love the mall, right? Let me know what happens. I'm sure she's fine."

"I hope so." Josie located the keys and jingled them in the air. "Found 'em. Thanks." She hurried out the front door of the B&B as a light sprinkle began to fall. Maddie would definitely want to take shelter somewhere. But what if she couldn't?

Fear gripped Josie's heart. Tuck must be out of his mind with worry. She headed to the mall a few miles away and walked around, searching every corner. She flashed a picture that she'd taken of Maddie on her phone to a few store clerks, who just shook their heads. After the mall, Josie wrapped her raincoat around herself more tightly and walked downtown.

"Oh, I do hope you find her soon," Dawanda said when Josie stopped in to ask if she'd seen her. "The storm is supposed to be another nasty one. I heard Serena Gibbs saying so on the news this morning."

Josie was already cold and shivering herself. "Any suggestions for where I can go? A place that young people like to hang out?"

"The movie theater was always my hideout," Dawanda offered. "Or maybe a friend's house."

Josie shook her head. Maddie always said she didn't have friends but she'd hung out with a few girls her age at the festival. Josie had been too absorbed in Tuck to find out who they were. She should've asked. "Thanks. I'll keep looking."

"Good luck!" Dawanda called.

Josie stepped back onto the sidewalk, and a gust of wind hit her with enough force to make her take a step backward. Maybe Maddie was at the salon. Or maybe the Sweetwater Café. Perhaps Sophie's Boutique. There was a rack of teen clothes in the back that Maddie had enjoyed looking through on their day out together.

As Josie continued walking, her cell phone buzzed in her pocket. She looked at the caller ID and tapped the screen before holding it to her ear. "Please tell me you found her."

"No," Tuck said. "I was hoping you had."

"I would have called you," Josie told him.

"I know. I'm about to dial up Alex at the police department. It's time to call in reinforcements. I need to call Beverly too."

"She doesn't know?" Josie asked.

"I didn't want to worry her unless it was necessary," Tuck said. "And now it's necessary."

* * *

Tuck pulled into the parking lot of the Sweetwater Police Station and nearly ran inside.

Tammy, the secretary, looked up as she sucked on a straw in her Coke bottle. "Can I help you, Tuck?"

"Yeah. I need to see Alex. Is he back there?"

"He is. Want me to call him and ask—?"

"No," Tuck said, turning down the hall toward his friend's office. This was an emergency, and he knew Alex wouldn't mind.

"Maddie is missing," Tuck said, flinging open the door.

Alex looked up from a file on his desk. "What?"

"Maddie, the little girl I was with at the festival. She's missing. She didn't come home from school today. Actually, she didn't show up at school today either."

Alex stood and grabbed his jacket from the back of his chair as they talked. "You'll fill me in on the way out. Let's go. Any idea where to look?" Alex asked.

"I should know where she likes to hang out but I don't."

"You're her PT. Why should you know where she'd be?"

Tuck glanced at Alex as they hurried past Tammy's desk and out the front door, realizing he hadn't told any of his buddies the truth yet. "Because I'm her father."

Alex narrowed his eyes. "You'll also explain that on the ride. I'll drive, you look."

A moment later, they climbed into Alex's SUV and tore out of the parking lot.

"She's not Renee's?" Alex asked once they were on the road.

"Of course not. If she were, she'd have been with me the entire time. It happened when Renee and I were broken up in college. I didn't know about Maddie until a couple of weeks ago."

"Why not?"

Tuck shrugged, his gaze glued out the window, looking in places that didn't make sense for Maddie to be. In trees, ditches, the neighbors' yards. "I'd ask Maddie's mom but Crystal died six months ago in the accident that injured Maddie's leg."

Alex shook his head. "That's tough, man. But congratulations on having a kid."

"Thanks. She doesn't know I'm her dad yet. I'm planning to tell her this week." Assuming they found her. Where was she?

They came to a stop sign, and Tuck pointed straight ahead toward the downtown area. "Let's try looking in that direction."

"Good idea." Alex pressed the gas.

"Do you think someone might have taken her?" Tuck asked.

"You mean like a kidnapping?" Alex looked over. "It's possible but I doubt it. She's a little girl, and it sounds like she's been through a world of change. This is likely just a cry for attention."

"She's walking with a cane. Wherever she is, she won't make it far," Tuck said. He saw a group of girls that he remembered seeing Maddie with at the Sweetwater Springs Festival. "Pull over. I want to talk to them." He gestured at the threesome standing on the sidewalk.

"I'll come with you."

They parked and got out. When the girls saw them approaching, they stiffened, no doubt the effect of Alex's badge and status as chief of the Sweetwater police.

Alex held up a hand. "You're not in trouble. We just need help. Do you know Maddie Sanders?"

A petite girl with long blond hair nodded. "She's in my class."

"When was the last time you saw her?" Alex asked.

The girl fidgeted slightly as she looked around at her friends and then up at him. "At dismissal yesterday, I guess. She was carrying her book bag and lost her balance a little bit. I asked if she needed help but she said no. Maddie never asks for help, because kids make fun of her if she does."

The muscles along Tuck's jaw tightened. Didn't Maddie have enough difficulty in her young life right now without her classmates adding to it? "None of you have seen her down here?" he asked. "Are you sure?"

"She's hard to miss with that cane," the brunette in the group said with a slight eye roll.

The third girl giggled at her side.

It was all Tuck could do to keep his mouth shut. He didn't want to be hauled off to jail tonight for yelling at a couple of little girls with bad attitudes. What he wanted was to find Maddie.

"Thanks." Alex turned away from the girls and gave Tuck a steady look that said they needed to keep walking. They continued down the sidewalk, looking in storefront windows. Thunder rumbled beyond the mountains. The local news had been warning about the storm for the last few days. There were supposed to be heavy downpours over the next forty-eight hours. After the rainstorm last week, townsfolk had already been prepping for possible flooding from the river.

"Let's get back to the vehicle. We can try the mall," Alex suggested, turning back.

"Yeah."

They returned to his SUV and started driving. When they came to another police car going in the opposite direction, both vehicles slowed and Mitch rolled down his window. "Kaitlyn told me about Maddie. Any luck locating her yet?" he asked.

Alex shook his head grimly.

A soft rain started to splatter on their front windshield, ratcheting up Tuck's anxiety level. Hopefully Maddie was safe and warm wherever she was. He hoped she was also coming to her senses.

"We're going to the mall," Alex told Mitch between the vehicles. Luckily there were no other cars on Main Street right now.

Mitch shook his head. "Josie has already searched the mall. She isn't there."

A warmness spread through Tuck from his toes right up to his heart. Even though Maddie was resisting Josie's efforts, Josie was trying hard to be there for his daughter. That meant everything to him.

The rain began to fall harder, forcing them to roll up their windows and press on.

After another hour circling the town, Alex drove Tuck back to his truck at the police station. "Go back to Hope Cottage in case she shows up there," he suggested. "I'll put a few more officers on the case, and we'll continue searching until we find her. She's a smart girl. I'm sure she's found shelter somewhere. Maybe at your place."

"I hope that's true." Tuck knew Maddie was smart but he couldn't help imagining that she'd fallen and was hurt somehow. That she couldn't get to a dry place. He hadn't been there for her all these years but he wanted to be there for her from now on.

CHAPTER TWENTY-THREE

If I were an eleven-year-old girl, where would I go?

Josie tried to put herself in a hurt, angry, grief-stricken girl's shoes as she drove Kaitlyn's car. Maddie couldn't have gone far on foot. But maybe she'd gotten a ride from someone. Maybe she'd gone to a boy's house... No, Maddie wouldn't want to be at a boy's house when she was feeling so low. She would probably want to avoid all human interaction.

A gasp caught in Josie's throat. It was just a hunch but something about the idea resonated with her. Maddie was like Tuck in so many ways, one of which was her bond with animals. They were therapeutic. If Maddie wanted to be away from the people in her life, it didn't necessarily mean she wanted to be alone.

Josie turned Kaitlyn's car in the direction of Hope Cottage and sent up a little prayer that she was right.

She parked in Tuck's driveway, seeing his Jeep, but

didn't bother going toward the house. She didn't want to get his hopes up if she was wrong. Instead, she pulled the hood of her raincoat over her head and sprinted through the field toward the stables.

The rain was coming down harder now, beating against her skin in angry pellets. Her pants were stuck to her like a second skin by the time she reached the stable door. Throwing it open, she dashed inside the darkened barn. For a moment, it was illuminated by a flash of lightning, and then it fell dark again.

"Maddie?...Maddie, are you in here?" Josie breathed in the scent of hay and horses. There was a rustling inside the barn from Chestnut and Sugar but that was all.

Her heart sank with a thud into her belly. She stepped farther inside and peeked into Sugar's stall. "Hey, girl," she said to the horse that she had bonded with during her rides with Tuck. "I'm looking for someone. Have you seen her?"

Josie was soaking wet, exhausted, and she had no idea where to search next.

"I'm right here," a small voice answered.

Josie turned toward an empty stall next to Sugar's and stepped over to peer inside. There in the corner sat Maddie with Shadow's head resting in her lap. "How'd you find me?" she asked, lifting her chin in the dark.

Josie opened the stall and moved to sit beside her. "I imagined where I'd go if I were you."

Maddie looked down at her hands resting on Shadow's back. "Is my dad looking for me too?"

"Of course he is..." Josie gasped as she realized what Maddie had just asked. "You know?"

Maddie looked up. "I overheard him and Grandma talking about it outside the other week. She told him the truth."

Everything started clicking into place in Josie's mind. That was when Maddie started acting like she didn't want Josie around. *But why?*

"It makes sense," Maddie said. "We look alike, don't you think?"

Josie nodded. "I do. Why didn't you say anything?"

Maddie ran her fingers through Shadow's coat. "Because *he* didn't say anything. I've been waiting for him to tell me the truth but he never did. I was beginning to think that maybe he didn't want me to know, because he didn't actually want me."

"Oh, Maddie, of course he wants you. Why would you think otherwise?"

Maddie looked at Josie and narrowed her dark eyes. "Because I'm invisible when you're around," she said, chin quivering. "I don't mean to be mean to you but I don't have a mom and my grandma is sick all the time. I need Tuck. I've always wanted a dad, and now that I have one, I just want him to notice me." Tears slipped off her eyelashes and streamed down her cheeks. "I've been in this stupid barn all day, and no one even realized that I was gone. I listened for someone to call my name, and no one ever did." She hiccupped as she started to cry.

"Oh, honey. You have so many people who love you and want to be here for you. I know it feels like you're all alone sometimes but it's not true."

"What do you know about feeling alone?"

"A whole lot, believe it or not," Josie said. "I get it, and I'm sorry if I'm partly to blame for how you feel. I don't want to steal your dad's attention away from you. And trust me when I say you are the most important person in his life. He wants you with him more than anything."

More tears welled in Maddie's eyes. "I want him too,"

she said in a shaky voice. She sniffed and continued to pet Shadow, who was watching them intently.

A draft blew through the barn, and Josie shivered, less because she was cold and more because she hadn't realized just how much Maddie was dealing with on her own. "Your grandma and Tuck are just trying to do what's best for you, sweetheart. And they were planning on telling you the truth this week."

"They were?"

Josie nodded. "Yep."

"I keep thinking that if my mom had told me the truth in the first place, I could've had a dad all along. Why did she keep something so important from me?"

"Parents make the best decisions they can in the moment. They're not perfect, you know." Josie couldn't help it. She lifted her arm and wrapped it around the girl tightly. "I know that everything seems out of place right now but it's going to get better."

The girl sniffled softly. "Promise?"

"I promise. But right now, we need to go inside. People are out there in the storm looking for you. They're all worried sick. Tuck is in the house, probably pacing a hole in the floor."

"Do you think he'll be mad at me?" Maddie asked.

Josie laughed. "Truthfully? Oh yeah. But first he's going to want to hug you and never let go."

"That doesn't sound so bad," Maddie said as she wiped at her tears.

"Here." Josie took off her raincoat and helped Maddie slip it on. She pulled the hood over the girl's head. "I don't want you running, okay?"

"I just started walking again. I can't run even if I wanted to." Maddie offered a sheepish smile. That was progress.

"Just lean on me, and we'll make it together."

"But without your coat, you'll get all wet," Maddie objected.

"It's okay," Josie assured her. "Better me than you."

They headed to the stable doors and opened them to the driving rain. The cottage was barely visible in the downpour.

"On the count of three. Remember, go slow. I don't want you to fall."

"Okay." Maddie nodded. Josie's rain jacket was large on her, which would give Maddie extra protection.

"One, two, three!" They walked slowly, one step at a time. The journey seemed to take forever. Shadow stayed right beside them though. She could've run ahead but like the loyal dog she was, she didn't. When they got to the front porch steps, the door was flung open, and Tuck appeared. He ran down the steps and lifted Maddie up, taking her inside. Josie and Shadow followed.

Josie didn't go past the welcome mat. She didn't want to leave a pond in her wake.

Tuck peeled the jacket off Maddie. "Stay there. I'll get you two some dry towels. Then you'll tell me where you've been," he told Maddie.

A minute later, he returned with a stack of towels. He wrapped one around Maddie's shoulders and then took several to Josie. "You must be freezing," he said, looking deep into her eyes.

"I'm okay. Maddie's the one who needs you right now."

And Maddie needed him from now on. Tuck needed to shower his attention on his emotionally fragile daughter. Staying in Sweetwater Springs and at Hope Cottage would be selfish, and Josie cared too much for Tuck and

Maddie to do that to them, no matter how much she wished things were different.

Josie watched Tuck kneel in front of Maddie, talking softly to her. "Where were you? We were all worried sick."

Maddie trembled under his touch. "I'm sorry," she cried. "I didn't mean to worry anyone," she said. "I'm so sorry."

Tuck touched her cheek. "The important thing is that you're safe. We need to let your grandma know." He pulled out his cell phone, dialed Beverly's number, and then offered the phone to Maddie. "She'll be relieved to hear from you."

As Maddie held the phone to her ear, Tuck stood and turned his attention to Josie. "I need to call Alex and call off the search," he said. "But after that, I want to thank you properly. Can you stay awhile longer?"

Her heart rate picked up in her chest. She loved this man so much. How in the world was she going to do what she knew she had to? "Yeah. Of course."

"Good. I'll get you some dry clothes from my dresser. I don't want you catching a cold after all your work as Superwoman today."

Josie laughed quietly. "I'm not Superwoman. Far from it."

"You're an amazing woman, Josie Kellum. I hope you know that."

She swallowed as he turned and led her down the hall to his bedroom. They'd had a lot of fun in this bedroom over the last couple of weeks but that was over now. Done.

He pulled out some clothes and laid them on the bed. "They'll be way too big for you but they're dry and they're warm. You can shower in the guest bath, and I'll make you a hot cup of tea when you're out."

"Thank you."

He turned and pinned her with his dark eyes. "Thank *you*," he said before shutting the door behind him and leaving her alone.

A lump lodged in her throat. There would be no more kissing Tuck or losing herself in his arms…No, she hadn't lost herself. She'd found herself here at Hope Cottage, and she'd realized that she could have more.

But she couldn't have Tuck.

* * *

After calling Alex and letting him know they had found Maddie, Tuck returned to find his daughter still sitting on the couch where he left her. His daughter.

"Grandma says she misses me," Maddie told him.

"I'm sure she does." Shadow leaned against Maddie's leg, offering her support as Tuck sat down to talk to her. "Do you want me to take you back to her house?"

Maddie shook her head. "I told Grandma that I'd stay here tonight, if it's okay."

"Of course it is," he said.

"I'll go back tomorrow"—she looked at him shyly— "Dad."

Tuck swallowed. Did he just hear Maddie correctly? "How long have you known?"

"As long as you have," she confessed. "I heard you talking outside my house. It was my leg that was broken in the accident, not my ears," she said sarcastically. "You guys weren't even whispering."

This made him laugh, which felt kind of good after the hours of worrying about the girl sitting beside him. "I see. Is that okay? Do you mind being stuck with me for a dad?"

Maddie offered a small smile. "Could be worse, I

guess. You're pretty fun to be around, and I like animals, so . . . Besides, all my classmates thought you were pretty cool at the Sweetwater Springs Festival."

"Yeah?"

"Don't let it go to your head though, Dad," Maddie said, holding up a hand. "And don't think I'm going to let you chaperone all my activities from now on."

Dad. He liked hearing that name coming from Maddie, and he looked forward to hearing it a lot more.

"So am I going to come live with you now?" Maddie asked.

Tuck blew out a breath. "Beverly and I are working on a plan so you can spend time with both of us."

"Maybe I can have a home here and at my grandma's house."

Home. He liked the sound of that word on Maddie's lips as well. "That sounds good." He patted her thigh and stood. "All right, *usdi*," he said, using the nickname his mom had always used for him growing up, meaning "little" in the Cherokee language. He'd only been a dad for a short time but he was already infusing elements of his childhood into Maddie's. He was certain his mom would start coming by as soon as she could to do the same. "Are you hungry?"

"Starving. Running away is hard work," Maddie said.

He pinned her with a look. "How about you do your dad a favor and don't do it again? Deal?"

She giggled. "Deal."

* * *

An hour later, Maddie was tucked into her bed and reading quietly. As Tuck walked into the kitchen, he noticed

Josie sitting on the back deck. The rain had stopped, and she was holding a steaming mug of something hot and looking out on the view with Shadow curled at her feet.

She turned when he opened the door and stepped out.

"Hey," she said.

"Hey, yourself." He took a seat beside her and looked out on the backyard.

"Is she asleep?" Josie asked quietly.

"I'm pretty sure. It's been quite the day for her. For you too." He glanced over and caught her eye. "Thanks for finding her and bringing her home."

"It was no big deal."

"It was to me. Who knows what could've happened to her?"

"Maybe if she had gone somewhere else," Josie said. "She was in your barn, right under your nose all day though."

"Quiet as a mouse," he added. "I guess Shadow here sniffed her out. I can't believe I didn't realize my dog was missing too."

Shadow lifted her head at the mention.

"How'd you know where to go?" Tuck asked then.

He watched Josie suck in a breath, keeping her gaze outward. She seemed distant somehow.

"Instinct, I guess."

"The mother's instinct."

Now Josie whipped her head to face him. "I'm not her mother, Tuck."

"I know that. You're good with her though. That's all I meant. I know she gives you a lot of pushback. A lot of women wouldn't take it with so much grace."

"She's just hurting. I get it." Josie tucked a loose strand of wet hair behind her ear.

He reached for her hand as it fell back into her lap but she pulled it away.

"You okay?" he asked.

"Yeah. I, um, just wanted to tell you that I'm leaving." She quickly stood from the chair, making Shadow rise as well.

"To return Kaitlyn's car? How will you get back? I don't want to leave Maddie alone right now."

"No, I'm not coming back, Tuck. I'm about to pack up my stuff. The B and B has a room available, and I'm taking it." She smiled stiffly. "I got an interview for the job I wanted so I'm heading back to New York. I spoke to my landlady a few minutes ago. My apartment is free and clear."

"Just like that?" he asked, feeling like he'd been sucker punched in the gut. He thought he'd lost Maddie this afternoon but apparently it was Josie that he was losing.

"We both knew it was just a matter of time," she said, still holding that smile.

"What about us?" he asked.

"Us?" She met his eyes, a coolness to her expression. "What about us? This was fun, and I appreciate you allowing me to stay here. I think I'm paid in full on my rent so everything is tied up nice and neatly."

Was she serious right now? Because she sure as hell looked it. "Fun," he repeated. It'd been more than just a good time to him.

"Well, you've been a great friend as well. Thank you for fixing my knee. And for helping me with the issue with Bart. Will you tell Maddie that I'm glad she's okay? Tell her that I'll FaceTime her from the city. I'll show her some of the skyscrapers she wanted to see." Josie nodded but didn't wait for him to respond to anything she'd just rattled off. He wasn't even sure he knew how to respond. "Okay, well, I'll see you around." She offered a weak smile that didn't touch her beautiful blue eyes.

His heart screamed for him to do something, change her mind, beg her to choose him over some job that would never make her happy. He knew it wouldn't. Instead, he clamped his jaw tightly shut. If this was what she wanted, he wouldn't stop her. Maybe he was the fool for thinking there was something longer lasting between them.

"Goodbye, Tuck." She waved and then hurried down the steps, disappearing to the garage apartment next door.

He didn't return the sentiment. The Cherokee didn't say goodbye. They said *donadagohvi*. Till we meet again. But some part of him wondered, when Josie left to go back to New York, if she would ever return to Hope Cottage.

CHAPTER TWENTY-FOUR

$\mathcal{T}$wo hours later, at nearly nine p.m., Josie was back where she started in the *Pride and Prejudice* room at the Sweetwater Bed and Breakfast. The room had come available this afternoon when someone had canceled their reservation. Things had fallen into place like they were meant to be but she didn't feel like anything was right at all.

"I come offering chocolate," Kaitlyn said, peeking her head inside the room. "You okay?"

"If you indeed have chocolate, then you can come in," Josie said, sitting up in bed. She set her laptop on the nightstand. Her plane ticket was booked for late tomorrow afternoon.

Kaitlyn climbed onto the other side of the bed to sit beside her and placed a bag of dark chocolate between them. "Want to tell me what happened and why you suddenly needed to come here? Why are you in such a hurry to leave?"

"I was supposed to leave last month, remember?" Josie asked as she unwrapped a piece of candy. "And I already told you my apartment is available, and I have a job interview. It's time."

Kaitlyn reached for a chocolate as well. "I still can't believe you quit *Loving Life* magazine. You loved working there."

"It's called *The Vibe* now," Josie corrected. "And *loved* is the key word."

Kaitlyn was staring at her. "So what happened with Tuck?"

Josie swallowed and gave her head a quick shake. "You were right. We got in over our heads."

"I never said that. I said you liked him, and I think that's great."

"No, it isn't. He's a dad, and I'm just Josie." She held up her hand. "Don't get me wrong. I'm not having a pity party. I have great self-esteem. I just know my strengths and weaknesses. I'm not good with kids, and I'm getting in the way there."

"I doubt that."

Josie leveled her with a look. "Maddie ran away, Kaitlyn."

"And *you* found her! Doesn't that count for something?"

Josie frowned. "Not if the reason she ran away was because of me." Josie had already told Kaitlyn the full story of what happened, swearing her to secrecy. If Tuck knew, he'd be torn on what to do. Josie wasn't torn. Maddie needed him and that was all there was to know. Josie was a grown woman. She could take care of herself just like she always had.

Kaitlyn smiled weakly. "I really thought you two had a chance. I wish things were different for you."

Josie reached for another chocolate and popped it into her mouth. "Me too."

* * *

"Looking good, Mr. Sajack," Tuck said, walking beside his patient the next day.

Mr. Sajack looked over and laughed. "Well, you're looking plumb awful. What's wrong with you? You sick? If you are, my wife makes the best chicken soup. It'll knock whatever's ailing you right out."

Tuck shook his head. "I'm not sick. I'm fine."

"Well, you look crummy." Mr. Sajack put one foot in front of the other, going faster than he had even a week ago as he walked toward his mailbox.

"You know, you're great for my self-esteem," Tuck said sarcastically, sounding like Maddie.

Mr. Sajack laughed so hard it threatened to throw him off balance.

"Easy there. You're doing too good these days to fall and have a setback," Tuck said.

"Don't worry about me." Mr. Sajack reached his mailbox, pivoted the way Tuck had taught him, and reached to pull down the lid. "What do you know? I have mail. Probably bills and whatnot."

"That's what you say every time," Tuck said on a humorless laugh. He didn't feel like exchanging jovial banter.

"That's because it's true." Mr. Sajack placed the stack of letters in his fanny pack and turned to face his house. "Now I'm going to leave you in my dust while I make my way back to my TV for the news at noon. That broadcaster Serena Gibbs is a looker."

"Don't let Mrs. Sajack hear you say that. She might cancel your cable."

Mr. Sajack wobbled slightly as he chuckled again. "She just might."

After leaving Mr. Sajack's place, Tuck drove downtown. The spot in his schedule that Claire Donovan had held wasn't filled yet so he stopped into Halona's flower shop for a bouquet.

Halona had several customers when he walked in. He browsed around the displays as he waited for her to finish up.

"Hey," she finally said, walking over. "Flowers today?"

He nodded.

"For?"

She'd never had to ask before. There'd only been one woman in his life. Now there were three. His late wife. His daughter. And the woman he was in love with. Except the third option was no longer his, and these flowers were for none of the above.

"Nosy much?" he asked, dodging the question.

Halona put her hands on her waist. "I'm going to pretend you didn't just ask that."

He grinned.

"Just give me a few minutes." She started collecting flowers from her freezer and set to binding them together as Tuck watched.

"How is Josie anyway?" she asked, leading him to believe that's who she thought the arrangement was for.

He swallowed thickly. "She's great. Her apartment in New York is open again, and she has a job interview up there that she's excited about. Life is apparently working out perfectly for her."

Halona stopped working and looked at him sadly. "Oh, Tuck."

He looked away. "I don't want to talk about it, okay? I just want the flowers."

She hesitated and then returned to working. She tied a

lavender ribbon around the bunch and handed them over. "Here you go. Tell Renee I said hello."

"Thanks, but I'm not stopping by Renee's grave today." He winked playfully even though his mood was anything but. He didn't bother trying to pay Halona. She never took his money anyway.

"Bring Maddie over here one day, okay?" Halona said, still fishing to see if that's who they were for as he headed for the door. "I'm ready to say hello to my niece."

He had to smile. "I'm picking her up after school. Maybe we'll go grab ice cream together."

Halona grinned. "Sounds like fun, big brother. How about I invite you two over for dinner next week?"

"That'd be great," he said. "And the flowers aren't for Maddie either," he called over his shoulder before slipping out the door, satisfied that Halona would likely be going nuts for the rest of the day, trying to guess who the arrangement was for. Then he got into his Jeep and drove to the edge of town, parking in Forest Grove Cemetery.

Renee was buried in Sweetwater Cemetery near the river. He visited often and was used to walking among the graves there. This burial place was shadier. There were flowers lying at the various sites.

He headed all the way down the path, just as the cemetery caretaker had instructed him a moment earlier, until he came to a headstone that read CRYSTAL BETHANY SANDERS. BELOVED MOTHER AND DAUGHTER.

Tuck stared at the granite headstone with a statue of an angel adorning the top.

He stepped closer until he was standing right in front of the place where she was buried. There were so many questions he wanted to ask and things he wanted to say. They all caught in his throat. As it was with his late wife,

Crystal wasn't here anymore. He believed that her spirit was free. Visiting headstones was for the visitor—him—and there was only one thing he needed to get off his chest right now.

"I forgive you."

He wasn't sure what Crystal's reasons were for hiding Maddie from him. Facing parenthood was terrifying. When Crystal had discovered that she was pregnant, they'd been broken up. Maybe she was mad at him. Maybe she thought he wouldn't step up to the fatherhood plate so why bother telling him?

"I'll be a good dad to our daughter," he promised, voice cracking. "Beverly will always be in our lives. I'll make sure our daughter remembers you and knows that you loved her, because I know that's true." A mother's heart was selfless. They made choices in the best interests of their children. Whatever Crystal's reasons, wrong as they were, he had to believe she'd made them out of love.

He placed the flowers on her grave site and then turned, retracing his steps back to his Jeep. He felt lighter somehow as he got behind the steering wheel. Carrying around blame for someone who'd robbed you of something was tiresome—almost as tiresome as loving someone who didn't love you back—and he needed all his energy for Maddie.

* * *

The spring air was cool and crisp as Josie walked the hiking trail behind the bed and breakfast. There was a sign that told her to stay on the trail.

Don't worry about that, she thought, remembering when Tuck had come to her rescue a month ago. So much had changed since then, and yet she was still the same old Josie.

Dogwoods bloomed from where they bordered the path. She admired them as she processed all her many feelings and thoughts. She was already packed. In an hour, Kaitlyn would be driving her to the airport.

The walking trail looped and headed back to the inn at the one-mile marker. As she rounded the bend in the path, there was a flash of color in front of her. She stilled and located the purple finch on the limb of a bordering pine. Tuck had suggested that the creature was her spirit animal.

"What are you trying to tell me, little bird?" she whispered.

Its wings fluttered like it might take off at the sound of her voice but it didn't. Instead, it stayed awhile, watching her just like she was watching it. When it finally did take off, Josie didn't chase after it this time. She was done following colorful birds, and her heart. At least where Tuck was concerned.

"Nice walk?" Kaitlyn asked when Josie entered through the back door. Mr. Darcy left Kaitlyn's side and beelined toward Josie's leg.

Josie patted the pup's head. "Very. I wish I had a trail behind my New York apartment to do that every day."

"You have Central Park," Kaitlyn said on a laugh.

"Not the same. Nature-watching is very different from people-watching. Both have their advantages though."

Josie retrieved her luggage from where she'd set them beside the door.

"Ready?" Kaitlyn asked, pulling her purse on her shoulder.

That was a loaded question. Was anyone ever ready to

say goodbye to the people they loved? Kaitlyn was her best friend, and she loved her.

And she loved Tuck in a whole different way. A way that made it hard to breathe.

"Ready," she lied.

On the ride to the airport, Kaitlyn carried the conversation, talking about guests and upcoming plans for the inn.

"I wish you could be here for that," she said wistfully, keeping her eyes on the road ahead.

Josie blinked, realizing she hadn't heard a word that Kaitlyn had said. "For what?"

"For the concert series in Evergreen Park this summer. If you were staying, Tuck could take you. I hear that couples get up and dance barefoot on the lawn. It sounds so romantic. It might make a great article too," Kaitlyn suggested. "Just saying."

Josie looked at Kaitlyn. "Michelle at *Carolina Home* will probably write about it. But Tuck and I are over. I can't use him for a story."

"Of course not. I just thought you might want to come back and see him—that's all. The story angle was just my way of trying to convince you. Food is the way to a man's heart, and work is the way to yours."

"That makes me sound so cold," Josie mumbled as she white-knuckled the door handle and tried not to look out the window.

"Stop that. You're being a Debbie Downer. I get it. You just broke up with a guy but that was all on you. It was your choice, not his, so you don't get to sulk."

"Yes, I do," Josie protested. "I had no choice."

"You always have a choice, Jo. There's the right one and the wrong one."

Josie turned to her. "You think I'm making the wrong choice?"

"Of course I do. You and Tuck are great together." Kaitlyn looked over at her.

"Eyes on the road! We're on a very tall mountain," Josie exclaimed, reflexively reaching for the sides of her seat to brace herself in case Kaitlyn's car plunged off a cliff.

Kaitlyn giggled, returning her gaze forward. "Don't worry. I'm a pro at mountain driving these days. You're in safe hands with me."

Josie continued to grip the seat anyway. "Where is Shadow when I need her to soothe me?" she mumbled to herself.

"I can do a U-turn and take you to her," Kaitlyn suggested.

"No! No U-turns on the mountain!" And besides, Josie wasn't going back, no matter how much she wanted to. Kaitlyn was wrong. This was the right choice.

CHAPTER TWENTY-FIVE

$\mathcal{T}$uck had been sitting in the car pool line in front of Maddie's school for half an hour. Now it was finally starting to budge. Maddie had asked him to pick her up today instead of making her take the bus, which she claimed to loathe. He didn't blame her there. When he was a student, he hadn't been fond of the school's transportation either.

When he got to the front of the school, Maddie walked his way. She was barely leaning on the cane now. In the next month, she might be able to say goodbye to it altogether.

"Hey," he said, his heart quickening at the sight of her. How could he love someone he only just met? He'd been asking himself that question a lot these days.

She got in, pulled the door shut, and yanked her seat belt across her body. When he heard it click into place, he pressed the gas and followed the loop that led back to the main road.

"How was school today?" he asked.

"Boring," Maddie huffed.

"I thought you liked school."

"I do but it's still boring." She folded her arms over her chest and looked out the passenger-side window.

"That just means you're not being challenged. Did your test go well?"

"I think I got a perfect score," she said with a confident smile.

"That's my girl! Things going well at home with your grandma?" he asked then. Even though they'd spent quite a bit of time together over the past several days, he hadn't thought to ask how things had been at home with Beverly recently.

"Well enough. I'm going to miss being with you and Josie when I go home."

Maddie was already in bed when Josie had left last night. She hadn't gotten the memo that there was no he and Josie anymore. His heart hadn't quite gotten that memo yet either. He'd awoken this morning dreaming about her. She'd been in his arms, and they'd been making love. It was so real that he could smell her lavender scent. He could almost feel her soft skin brushing against his. When his eyes had sprung open, he'd glanced to the other side of the bed, looking for her. Then that raw and searing pain had exploded in his chest, where it'd stayed steady all day. "Your room is always open. You're out of school in a couple of weeks. I hope you'll spend some time at Hope Cottage this summer."

"I feel like one of my friends with divorced parents," Maddie said on a laugh.

"Is that a bad thing?" He looked over.

"No. I like having two homes. That's two bedrooms and twice as much closet space."

He grinned at the comment. It sounded like something

Josie would've said. Fresh pain sprang up from its bottomless well as he pulled into Maddie's driveway and cut the engine.

"Something's wrong," Maddie said. "What is it?"

"Nothing's wrong."

"Haven't you learned your lesson yet? Stop hiding things from me."

He sighed. "You're right. Sorry. Josie and I aren't seeing each other anymore. She's actually going back to New York for a job, which was the plan all along." He tried and failed to offer a reassuring smile. Maddie was right. She didn't need kid gloves for everything. She was stronger than most gave her credit for.

"But she doesn't care about some job. She loves you. She wants you," Maddie protested.

Tuck shook his head. "It's not that simple when you're an adult. People have priorities and responsibilities. My priority is you, and Josie's is her career."

Maddie turned to look out her window for a long moment that made him wonder what was going on in her head. "This is my fault," she finally said.

"No it's not."

"Yes it is." She turned back to look at him. "In the barn when I ran away, I told Josie that I felt invisible when she was around."

"What?" Tuck's jaw dropped open. Why hadn't Josie told him this?

"And now she's gone. I didn't mean to make her go." Maddie's eyes went from dry to welling with thick tears in a quick second. He'd come to realize that wasn't so unusual for an eleven-year-old girl. "I was upset, and I was afraid that you wouldn't want me if she stayed...because you love her more than me."

Tuck reached out and took her hand. "You don't really believe that I would love you less if she was around, do you? Because I could never love you less. I love you more every day, Maddie. More than I even knew was possible. You're my daughter, and I'm so glad to have you in my life."

Maddie wiped at her eyes. "I know that now. I'm sorry. Can you find her? Can you get her to come back?"

Tuck massaged his forehead. "I'm not sure. I don't know." His thoughts swirled around, trying to make sense of everything. He'd had no reason to question Josie's decision to leave. It was always her plan to go. But she'd fallen in love with him. She didn't need to say it for him to know. Her actions spoke louder than any words. She was happy here at Hope Cottage. With him.

"Dad?" Maddie said.

He blinked her into focus. "Yeah?"

"Don't you think we've lost enough?"

He nodded slowly, heart suddenly racing. "Yeah, I do."

"Me too. So go find her." Maddie pushed the Jeep door open and stepped out. Before closing the door, she dipped inside to look at him. "My mom used to tell me that there was no limit to how much a heart can love. I must have forgotten that but I won't forget again, okay?"

He nodded and then watched her walk toward Beverly's house, slow and steady. Pride rose inside him. She was so grown, so smart...and so right. He needed to find Josie and bring her home.

* * *

Josie had arrived early at the airport so she'd sat outside in the sunshine, hoping it would lift her mood. She pulled her laptop out of its bag and opened it to an email waiting for her from *Heartfelt Media* confirming their interview tomorrow.

She pressed Reply and started typing.

Hello, Ms. Diaz,

I'm confirming tomorrow's interview. I look forward to meeting you and discussing employment.

Thank you,

Josie Kellum

Her index finger hovered over the send button. It was a lie. She wasn't looking forward to the interview. It was the dream job she would've loved to have only a month ago. But that was before she'd come to Sweetwater Springs. Before she'd gone to Hope Cottage and fallen so completely in love with a man she could never have as her own.

Her eyes burned as she stared at the screen in front of her. Leaving was the right thing to do, she told herself for the millionth time. Maybe once she got back to New York, she'd finally get that cat she'd always wanted. Her landlady liked her; she might allow it.

An alarm that she'd set on her phone started beeping. It was time to check her bag and go through security. She hit the snooze button. Then she closed her laptop without sending the email just yet—she could work on it on the plane—and pulled her messenger bag onto her shoulder. As she headed toward the front entrance, she heard a familiar voice call her from behind.

"Josie?"

She stopped walking but didn't turn. It was possible she was imagining his voice. She and Kaitlyn had watched so many romantic movies over the course of their friendship, and this would be the place where two lovers reunited. Where all was lost and then found. But that wasn't happening today. She took another step forward and froze when she heard him call her again.

"Josie?"

She turned to face Tuck. He was real and standing only a few feet away. "What are you doing here?"

"I could ask you the same question," he said with a small smile.

Her foolish heart kicked at the sight. "I'm going back to New York and taking the job just like I wanted, remember?"

"That's not what you want." He stepped closer to her.

She swallowed thickly. "It isn't?"

"Not even close." He took another step, keeping his eyes pinned to hers.

She could lose herself in those dark eyes. In fact, she already had. "Okay, then, tell me what I want."

"You want a man who will carry you when you fall down while chasing after some crazy bird."

She giggled unexpectedly.

"Someone who will pull you off life's treadmill and show you the beauty of this world and make you see the beauty in yourself, inside and out. Someone who thinks you're funny, smart, and the most loving, giving person he's ever met."

"Tuck, I'm not sure I can be the woman you think I am. The one you need me to be. You're a father now. You have Maddie, and I don't know anything about raising a child. I know how to cook her breakfast and take her shopping but I'm not sure that's enough."

Josie wasn't sure *she* was enough.

She'd spent her lifetime striving for more, and yet sometimes she still came up short. She wasn't perfect.

"You're right. Breakfasts and shopping trips aren't what Maddie needs... She just needs you. I need you too," he said, cupping her face with his hands and holding her gaze. "Josie, if you get on that plane, I'll be losing my second chance at love, something I never thought I'd get."

"Love?"

"Definitely love. I love you, Josie. So much."

A warm, gooey goodness spread from her toes to her heart. She was a lover of words, and those were the best three in the English language. "I love you too... But Maddie—"

"—has realized that my love for someone else doesn't take away from my love for her. A heart has no limit. And Maddie doesn't need you to be her mom. She just needs you to be her... Josie."

Josie laughed as tears streamed down her cheeks. "I can do that."

Tuck smiled. "I can't offer you some big, shiny office with a view of the city. Or a fancy promotion or a prestigious award. All I can offer you is my heart."

Was this really her life? It could be if she wanted it to.

"That's not enough for me, Tuck," she said, sucking in a shaky breath. Then she stepped toward him and wrapped her arms around his neck, pressing her body to his. "It's so much more."

Her phone alarm went off again. She should head inside. At least if she didn't want to miss her flight.

Tuck's gaze locked on hers. "Do you have someplace to be?"

"There's nowhere I'd rather be than with you at Hope Cottage."

"So you'll stay with me a little longer?" he asked, a big smile enveloping his face.

"As long as you want me."

He brushed his lips to hers and kissed her, long and deep. "How about forever?" he asked when he finally pulled away.

She met his eyes, seeing a lifetime of love and happiness promised there. "Forever sounds perfect."

$\mathcal{E}$PILOGUE

$\mathcal{I}$'m leaving early today," Josie told Michelle, who was less of a boss at *Carolina Home* and more of a friend. Not her only friend in town either. Josie had joined the group of women who regularly got together for Ladies' Day Out. Last week, they'd all met again at the Sweetwater Bed and Breakfast for movie night. As always, Kaitlyn and Gina had been the perfect hostesses and had served up a variety of finger foods that had tasted like heaven in her mouth.

A few weeks before that, the ladies had met at Perfectly Pampered salon and had gotten mani-pedis. Josie had gotten hearts on the tip of each nail and a few of the older women had been beside themselves over the fact that they could get polka dots and zigzags.

"I'll see you tomorrow," Michelle said. "Do you have something fun planned for this afternoon?"

"Tuck asked if I could spend the afternoon with him.

It's such a beautiful day and we're taking the horses out for a ride." And these days Josie chose people over work. She chose herself over a job.

"Sounds wonderful! Have a great time," Michelle said.

"Thanks. See you tomorrow." Walking out of the building, Josie stood for a moment and let the sun beat against her cheeks. Summer in Sweetwater Springs had turned out to be every bit as magical as spring had been. She couldn't wait to experience the town in the fall and winter months too. She wanted to experience all the seasons with Tuck and Maddie—her family.

She climbed into her car, which was a new purchase. Kaitlyn's bike was nice, but on the days that Josie had errands to run or when the weather was less than ideal, it was convenient to have an alternate form of transportation.

A short drive later, she pulled into the driveway of Hope Cottage and parked beside Tuck's Jeep. She spotted him standing down by the stables and headed in that direction. She still couldn't believe this was her life. She'd traded in her high heels for ballerina flats some days and sneakers the rest. Although some nights she dragged Tuck out on the town, which demanded her fancy red-soled heels.

"Ready for a ride?" Tuck asked when she was only a few feet away.

"I've been looking forward to it all day," she said.

A few minutes later, he helped her mount Sugar's back and then he climbed on behind her, wrapping his arms around her and holding the reins. Riding separately was fun but snuggled into the arms of the man she loved was preferable.

"Did Maddie get off to school okay?" she asked as they rode down the path that entered the woods. Josie had left home early this morning before Maddie's bus had arrived.

"Oh yeah. She was practically running," he said.

Maddie didn't need a cane these days. Half the time it was all they could do to keep up with her and her busy social life. It was a new school year and a new beginning for them all.

"She couldn't wait to get to class. Today was her big presentation," Tuck continued. "She doesn't get that excitement from me. I used to hate speaking in front of the class. I told her she must have gotten it from her mom."

Josie laughed. She respected the fact that Tuck only had nice words to say about Crystal Sanders. Maddie's birth mom had robbed him of eleven precious years with his daughter and yet he wasn't bitter. It just went to prove that he was a good and honorable man. Her man.

His arms wrapped more tightly around her waist and she couldn't remember another time when she'd felt so completely happy.

"How was work today?" he asked.

"Nuh-uh. No discussion about work. My new favorite topic is us. What do you want to do tonight?"

"Loaded question," he said, tilting his mouth to her ear and arousing all her senses. "I was kind of thinking we could celebrate though."

"Hmm. Last time we had a celebration it was because I'd just quit my job at *The Vibe*. What is it we're celebrating this time?"

Tuck pulled one arm away and shifted behind her. Then she blinked and he was holding a wood-carved box in front of her.

"What's that?" she asked, even though she had a pretty good idea. She was also guessing he'd made the box himself. It was the same wood he'd used to carve Renee's cane. Cedar.

He flipped the lid, and Josie's hands flew to her mouth. "I want to spend every day just like this," he whispered, "with you in my arms. Except I want it to be as my wife."

Josie angled herself on the horse's back so she could face him. She needed to make sure this wasn't a dream. That Tuck was really proposing to her.

"Marry me, Josie. I'm already planning to love you for the rest of my life anyway."

She laughed out loud. "Me too." She couldn't stop even if she tried. Nor would she want to. She wiped at a happy tear that slid off her cheek and then held out her left hand.

Without another word, Tuck retrieved the diamond ring accented with opals on the sides and slid it down the length of her ring finger. Then he kissed her.

"I'm hoping that was a yes," he said once he pulled away.

She grinned as she nodded. "Yes." As she faced forward, her breath hitched along with her heart. "Do you see it?"

From her peripheral, she saw his head turn slightly until he was looking in the direction of her gaze. "A purple finch."

The little sprite of a bird rested on the limb of a pine tree, seeming to watch them. She'd seen it twice behind the B&B, again in a dream, and now here. "This makes four times. I think you're right. I'm connected to that bird somehow." She glanced over her shoulder at him.

"Have you figured out what it's trying to tell you yet?" he asked.

She returned her attention to the finch. It had shown up on her second day in Sweetwater Springs. Now here it was, born to fly but resting as it stared at them. Maybe she was imagining it but the little bird seemed to be smiling at them.

"Actually, yes. I think it's trying to tell me that I've finally found what I never knew I was looking for," she said.

Tuck angled his mouth to her ear and whispered again. "And what's that?"

Tuck, Maddie, Kaitlyn and Mitch, Michelle and the magazine, Hope Cottage. They all encapsulated one word for her.

She turned to kiss his mouth softly and then pulled back to meet his gaze. "Home. I've found home."

Lula's Three Sisters Stew

When you don't have a loved one to warm you up, my Three Sisters Stew will always do the trick. It doesn't matter if it's spring, summer, fall, or winter, the three sisters—corn, squash, and beans—are always in supply. Never an empty bowl or an empty heart!

Ingredients:

- 3 cups apple cider
- 2 cups chicken stock
- ½ cup white beans
- ½ cup lima beans
- ½ cup black beans
- 2 cups peeled and cubed butternut squash
- 1½ cups peeled, diced potatoes
- 2 cups frozen corn kernels (no need to thaw)
- 1½ cups finely chopped yellow onion
- 2 tablespoons melted butter
- 2 tablespoons all-purpose flour
- ¼ teaspoon pepper
- ¼ teaspoon salt
- 1 teaspoon curry powder
- 1 teaspoon ground cumin

Directions:

1. Place the beans and potatoes into a large pot. Pour in apple cider and chicken stock.

2. Bring to a boil and then reduce heat to low, stirring occasionally for 15 minutes.

3. Sauté onions in a separate saucepan until lightly browned and then add to pot of beans.

4. Add frozen corn and cook for an additional 15–20 minutes.

5. Stir in curry powder and ground cumin.

6. Let simmer until the vegetables are soft (approximately 10 minutes).

7. Blend flour into the butter and then stir into the soup to thicken.

8. Increase heat to medium for 5 minutes or until you achieve your desired consistency.

9. Season with salt and pepper to taste, and lots of love.

P.S. Yes, this is easy but it tastes so delicious that no one will ever know!

Police Chief Alex Baker has always known that his best friend's little sister is off-limits. Except Halona Locklear is all grown up now and more irresistible than ever.

Please turn the page for a preview of *Snowfall on Cedar Trail*.

Available Fall 2019

CHAPTER ONE

$\mathcal{S}$omething crashed in the kitchen.

Halona Locklear cracked an eye as she listened and debated whether or not the sound warranted getting out of bed. Before she could decide, her alarm started to shriek from across the room. She'd put it there so that she couldn't press Snooze and make herself late for the morning school drop-off.

"Do I have to?" she groaned. Even though she already knew the answer. Yes. Even though she'd gotten up with Theo and his nightmares four times in the night, she *still* had to.

Another crash in the kitchen got her out of bed faster. She turned off her alarm, slid her feet into a pair of slippers, and scooted down the hall.

"Theo?" she called. "What are you doing?"

She blinked in the harsh kitchen light, seeing her son sitting on the kitchen counter. There was a carton of milk at his side and a box of Cheerios. Without a word, he grabbed a bowl and hopped down. There was another bowl on the floor, thankfully plastic.

"To the table," she ordered, grabbing the milk and cereal and following him. After setting him up, she got her coffee started. Then she sat down alongside her son and drank, savoring every drop of caffeinated goodness. Theo's dark eyes were underscored with blue from a fitful night's sleep.

"Hurry up," she prodded. "I've got to get you to school."

Theo lifted his gaze and started shoveling the cereal into his mouth faster than he could chew and swallow. Milk dribbled down his chin, which he quickly wiped away with the sleeve of his T-shirt.

Halona laughed despite her bone-deep fatigue. Then she retreated to her room and dressed herself before helping Theo pick out something to wear. She grabbed the lunch she'd packed for him last night, his backpack, and her own purse, and they hurried out the front door to her navy blue SUV and drove to Theo's school.

"Have a good day," she said cheerfully, hoping her son would catch her enthusiasm.

The corners of his mouth lifted just a touch.

"I love you," she added as her breath suspended in her chest, waiting and hoping this time he'd return the words.

Instead, a teacher in the car pool line opened the passenger-side door for him to exit.

"Good morning, Theo," Allison Winters said, helping him step down onto the school's curb.

To be fair, Theo didn't respond to her either. Instead, he waved to Halona and headed off. Halona watched him until the car behind her sounded its horn. Then she pressed the gas pedal and drove to the Little Shop of Flowers on Main Street. There was usually an uptick in business in the winter months heading into the holidays. People were more generous during this time of year. They looked for ways to say *I love you*, and what said it better than flowers?

She unlocked her shop and headed inside.

She knew better. Nothing replaced those three little words, not even roses. What she wouldn't give to hear her son whisper them again. These days, the only time she heard his voice was when he was having a nightmare.

She walked to the shop's back room, poured water and grinds into the coffee maker, and flipped it on. After a moment, the machine started funneling its dark brew into the pot. The coffee next door at the Sweetwater Café was far better but that would require running into half the people in town, including Chief of Police Alex Baker, who appeared to have a small addiction for Emma St. James's brew. Or maybe for the café owner herself.

When the coffee was done, she poured a cup. No sooner had she taken her first sip than the bell above the door rang with an incoming customer. Halona dutifully put on a smile and approached the front counter from the back room. Her breath stumbled along with her feet as she came face-to-face with Sweetwater Springs' own chief of police. So much for avoiding him by settling for mediocre coffee.

Alex cleared his throat. "Hey."

She had so many conflicting emotions every time she saw him. Halona had always had a thing for Alex but he'd only ever looked at her as a little kid when they were growing up. That was preferable to how he'd looked at her lately though.

"Hi," she answered. "To what do I owe your visit? Business or personal?" she asked. Maybe he was getting flowers for a special someone. Maybe for Emma next door.

"A little of both, I guess. I need an arrangement for a fellow officer's wife. Mary Beth Edwards."

"Yes. She just had surgery, right? That's nice of you to think of her," Halona said.

"Well, it'll be from the whole department."

"I'll get that arrangement for you right away," Halona said.

Alex gestured behind him. "Thanks. I thought I'd grab a coffee from next door while I wait. Would you like some?"

"No thanks. I've got a machine in the back."

"Not the same," he coaxed. "Let me grab you a coffee. How do you take it?"

She hesitated. This was another of his attempts at peacemaking. She guessed Alex still felt guilty for arresting her husband two years ago, even though she'd begged him not to. Alex didn't have all the facts, still didn't, and probably never would. Alex was the reason Ted had left her and Theo, and now her ex was dead. Yeah, coffee from the café next door wasn't going to fix that.

Alex stared at her from the other side of the counter.

"Three raw sugars and a splash of cream," Halona finally said, deciding that he probably wouldn't take no for an answer.

"You got it. I'll be back in a bit."

She watched him walk out of her store. While her mind held tight to her past grudge, her heart still clung to that girlish crush she'd had on her brother's best friend growing up.

* * *

Alex's blood felt electric, and it had nothing to do with the smell of fresh coffee and the promise of its jolt of caffeine. When was he ever going to stop reacting to Halona Locklear this way? She was his buddy's sister. He'd known her before she had curves and when she'd been a tomboy irritating him and Tuck.

She wasn't boyish in any way these days though—that was for sure.

"Hey, Chief Baker," Emma St. James said as he reached her counter. She always smiled a little wider when he was around. Why couldn't he have a thing for someone sweet like Emma? The only thing the beautiful café owner stirred for him, however, was his coffee. Halona stirred a variety of unsettling emotions: attraction, need...confusion. He didn't understand her choices or why she was so upset with him for helping her two years ago.

"Your usual?" Emma asked.

He gave a nod. "And a medium dark roast with a splash of cream and three raw sugars."

Emma lifted a pale brow. "That's the way Halona takes her coffee."

He sighed. "Do you know how everyone in town takes their drinks?"

She laughed and turned to start pouring. "It's my job to know," she called over her shoulder. A moment later, she exchanged two coffees for his debit card. She swiped it and handed it back. "Tell Hal I said hello."

Alex didn't respond. Instead, he said a polite goodbye and started toward the door just as Mayor Brian Everson was pushing through in his wheelchair. Alex held the door as a courtesy, not that Brian needed help. Brian had more strength and endurance than most men with two able legs.

"Thanks, Chief," Brian said. "You've been dodging my calls. I figured I'd run into you sooner or later."

Alex nodded. "I'm actually in a hurry this morning," he lied. He liked Brian but he knew what the Sweetwater Springs mayor wanted to discuss. Apparently, Alex wasn't the social butterfly that some expected a guy in his position to be. He focused on his job, and just the job. Heck, he'd turned the guys down for drinks at the Tipsy Tavern the last few times they'd asked because he was too busy working. Who had time for making appearances and doing volunteer work?

Brian angled his wheelchair to pin Alex with an assessing glance. "Call me. Better yet, stop by my office. This is your friend talking, not the mayor. You're good for this town, and we need to make sure everyone knows it."

Alex shifted the carrying tray of coffee in his hands. "I'll be in touch." Right after he talked to Gary Hardesty about breaking parole again and solved that cold case that had been in his desk drawer haunting him since he was nineteen years old. *One day.*

Stepping out of the coffee shop, Alex breathed a little easier as he walked back to the Little Shop of Flowers. Halona looked up from the counter as he entered her store, and Alex's lungs constricted.

"Here you go," he said, clearing his throat as he laid the cup of coffee in front of her.

"Thank you." Her gaze flitted to meet his briefly. Yeah, she was still mad about him hauling Ted off in handcuffs on that domestic call two years ago. Yet he couldn't bring himself to regret it. That's what her brother, Tuck, would've demanded if he knew. But Alex had respected

Halona's wishes and hadn't told anyone. Instead, Alex had handled Halona's ex on his own.

"Um, your arrangement is over there on the table. No charge. Send Mary Beth my best wishes."

"You don't have to do that," Alex said.

"I want to. For her," she clarified, and then reached for the coffee. "Thank you for this. Emma's brew is so much better than the stuff I have."

"I like to tell people I go so often because I'm secretly investigating her. Her coffee is too addictive to be legal."

Halona's face contorted with a small laugh that punched him as forcefully as a gunshot into his bulletproof vest. "I'll see you around."

"See you," she said.

He headed toward the arrangement of flowers and heard a cell phone ring behind him.

"Hello," he heard Halona say. Her sharp intake of breath made Alex whirl to face her. "Yes. Is he okay...? I'll be there as soon as I can."

"Everything all right?" Alex asked once she'd disconnected the call.

"No. Theo threw up at school. I need to close up shop and go get him." She hesitated. "I have a customer coming in anytime to pick up an arrangement I promised her." She nibbled her lower lip and then pulled her phone back out of her pocket. "Maybe Mom can come watch the store," she said to herself.

"Not necessary. I'll watch it for you," Alex heard himself say.

Halona looked up with surprise in her eyes. He was a little shocked at the offer too. At the Sweetwater Café, he'd just been mentally telling himself all the reasons he didn't have time to play nice in town and take on extra work. Yet here he was doing exactly that for Halona.

"I don't need your help," she bit out.

"No, you don't. I know that. But you could get to Theo's school a lot faster if you let me do this for you."

Her rigid posture softened. "That's true, I guess. Are you sure?"

"Positive. Go get Theo. I'll try not to burn the place down while you're away."

Halona smiled. "Thank you."

He watched her grab her purse and keys and hurry out. Then Alex looked around the store, completely perplexed at how the chief of Sweetwater Springs' police had suddenly gotten himself into running a flower shop.

* * *

It wasn't even two hours ago that Halona had dropped Theo off. Now here she was again, picking him up. He'd been having stomach pain a lot lately. His therapist believed it was anxiety induced, and Halona had to agree. In his short life, Theo had been through a lot. Too much.

Now he'd stopped talking and was having regular nightmares. At the parent-teacher conference last month, his teacher reported that Theo didn't have any friends. She'd described him as a good student who kept to himself.

Kids were supposed to have friends though. They were supposed to act up and get in trouble. She certainly had. She'd prefer to get called to the principal's office because Theo was misbehaving than because his emotions were eating away at him little by little.

She opened the door to Sweetwater Elementary and stepped inside, hearing the cacophony of school-related sounds: the buzzing overhead lights, the sound of children's voices and laughter, the intercom calling for a custodian.

Veering into the front office off to her right, Halona straightened her shoulders and put on a smile. Masking her feelings was something she'd come to do well. She wasn't sure if that was an attribute or a character flaw.

"Good morning, Ms. Locklear," the front office secretary said. "Theo is in the nurse's office." She pointed to a room down the hall but Halona knew her way.

"Thank you." Halona took quick steps until she was standing in the doorway.

Theo looked up. He was holding his little hands over his belly, his face scrunched up.

"Hey, buddy. Not feeling well?" She walked over and kneeled in front of him.

"He's been moaning and holding his stomach," Nurse Johnston said. "No fever though."

Halona could've guessed that much. He had been fine when he was eating Cheerios at breakfast.

"His teacher said he threw up?" Halona asked.

Nurse Johnston nodded. "Just a little bit. Could've been something he ate or maybe a little bit of nerves." She winked. "I hope he feels well enough to return to class tomorrow."

Halona stood, keeping her gaze on Theo. "Yeah, me too. Want to come work at the flower shop with me today, buddy?"

Theo's face relaxed, and a smile touched the corners of his mouth. Nerves it was. Halona almost would've preferred he had a virus that she could treat. At least then she would know what to do for him.

Grabbing his hand, she walked Theo back to her

SUV, buckled him in, and cranked the engine. "School is important, you know. You can't keep coming home just because you're not happy."

He didn't look at her. The only sign that he'd even heard her was the stubborn lift of his chin. With a sigh, Halona backed out of the parking spot and directed her vehicle back to Little Shop of Flowers. Despite her worry, a little flutter of anticipation batted around in her belly at the knowledge that Alex was there waiting for her. But hot or not, nice or not, he was enemy number one.

Theo hopped out of the car as soon as it came to a stop and darted into the store. He froze at the sight of Alex behind the counter.

"Hey, buddy," Alex said.

After a moment's hesitation, Theo took off running toward him, making Halona's heart kick hard. Theo had been too young to remember Alex coming to their door, first for the domestic call and then a few months later to break the news of her ex-husband's skiing accident and death.

"Give me five, little man," Alex said after giving Theo a big hug.

Theo gave the hit everything he had.

"Down low." As Theo tried to hit him again, Alex yanked his hand away. "*Ohhh*, you're too slow."

Theo giggled happily.

"As you can tell, he's sick," Halona told Alex, approaching the two of them.

"Oh yeah." Alex's face turned solemn. "Guess you better stay in bed all day then, buddy. And eat nothing but chicken soup. That's what my mom used to say."

Theo's eyes widened. He was no longer smiling.

She redirected her attention to Alex. "Thanks for watching the store. Did anyone come by?"

Alex shook his head. "I had it easy. Just me and the flowers. They're good listeners, you know."

Halona gave him a curious look. "You talked to my flowers?"

"Told them all my secrets. They promised not to tell." Alex winked at Theo, whose cheeks puffed back up into a small smile.

"Well, I'll see you later." Alex grabbed his flower arrangement for Mary Beth Edwards and headed out the door.

Halona reminded herself to breathe. The flowers knew his secrets, and Alex knew hers. Some at least.

About the Author

Annie Rains is a *USA Today* bestselling contemporary romance author who writes small-town love stories set in fictional places in her home state of North Carolina. When Annie isn't writing, she's living out her own happily ever after with her husband and three children.

Learn more at:

http://www.annierains.com/
@AnnieRainsBooks
http://facebook.com/annierainsbooks

For a bonus story from another author that you'll love, please turn the page to read "Last Chance Bride" by Hope Ramsay.

Stone Rhodes has always been the quiet one in his family but now he's got the whole town talking. He and his longtime high school sweetheart Sharon McKee are crazy about each other but suddenly they can't agree on their future. Sharon thought they were going to go to college and then get married. But Stone has other plans—plans he hasn't shared with anyone.

FOREVER

CHAPTER ONE

Wednesday, August 1, 1990

*S*haron Anne McKee, you quit your wiggling now, you hear?" Mother looked up at Sharon with a gleam in her dark eyes. "I'm not about to let my daughter show up as this year's Watermelon Queen with an uneven hem."

Sharon redoubled her efforts to stand still as Mother fussed with the yards of pink and green tulle that comprised her Watermelon Queen dress. She didn't need Mother going ballistic today of all days. Sharon had too much to do. And besides, when Mother got upset, the world tipped over on its side. It was easier to suck it up and do what Mother wanted.

Sharon stood there for five minutes, until she couldn't stand still anymore. She put on her sweetest voice: "Mother, I really appreciate your helping with the dress, but please remember that I'm chairing the bake sale and blood drive for Crystal Murphy this afternoon at city hall."

"I'm going as fast as I can," Mother huffed.

Which wasn't fast enough to suit Sharon. But she held her tongue, because if she said anything else, Mother would purposefully slow down. Sharon anxiously watched the minutes tick away on the kitchen clock. Mother always made her late.

Finally Sharon's patience broke. "Mother, you pinned that section already. It doesn't have to be perfect, you know. It's not like it's my wedding dress."

Mother's head came up with a glower. "This dress most certainly isn't a wedding dress," she said. "And when you get married, you'll be wearing white and marrying a man with a college degree. Is that clear?" Mother's eyebrows arched.

"Yes, ma'am."

"And I expect you to marry a young man from a quality family, like the people you come from. Why, when I was a girl in Charleston, I had at least a dozen beaux, and all of them were from the best families in town."

Oh boy, that was a bold-faced fib if Sharon had ever heard one. Unfortunately, Mother had been fibbing about her background for so long that she no longer remembered the truth. She may have been born in Charleston, but Sharon's granddaddy was a dockworker. And Sharon's daddy wasn't from a rich family either, even if he had gone to college and become a bank manager. Daddy had died from a heart attack two years ago, and Mother had never been quite the same. She lived her life in a kind of dream world in which Sharon was the next best thing to a debutante. Being selected this year's Watermelon Queen didn't help any when it came to Mother's delusions.

Sharon squared her shoulders and fixed her gaze on the wall. There was no point in trying to get Mother to see the world as it truly was. Besides, Sharon was in no hurry to get married. Not even to Stony Rhodes, her boyfriend, who would also be a freshman at Carolina this fall.

"And another thing," Mother said through the pins clenched in her teeth. "When you get to college, you will remember that you are a refined southern lady. There will be boys up there who just want to take advantage of you. Don't let them lead you down a garden path, if you know what I mean."

Sharon knew exactly what Mother meant. She had plans to encourage Stony to do a little bit of that sort of thing. Sharon had even made a secret appointment with Planned Parenthood and was now in possession of a diaphragm for the moment when she and Stony finally did the deed. But that wouldn't be until they got up to Columbia together.

Mother would have apoplexy if Sharon ever went to the Peach Blossom Motor Court, like other kids did on prom night. That was too risky, what with Lillian Bray always checking out the parking lot. Since Daddy had died, Sharon had avoided conflicts with Mother. So waiting was the wisest choice all the way around. There would be plenty of time up at Carolina.

The back screen door creaked open and slammed shut, and Stony's eight-year-old sister, Rocky, waltzed into Mother's kitchen like she owned the place.

"Hey, Miz McKee," Rocky said as she skidded to a stop. As usual, the little girl's dark, curly hair was in complete disarray, and her knees were so grubby it would probably take steel wool to clean them. She was barefoot.

Mother straightened and glared at Rocky. "Hasn't your

mother ever taught you any manners? You don't just walk into other people's houses without knocking. Can't you see we're busy?"

"Oh, sorry."

"Mother, we're not that busy," Sharon said, practicing her best Watermelon Queen smile on the little girl.

Rocky grinned up at her. "Holy moly, Sharon, you look like Cinderella."

"Well, that may be, but I don't want to become Cinderella," Sharon said.

"Why? Cinderella gets the prince, doesn't she?"

"There's more to life than marrying a prince," Sharon replied.

Mother frowned. "There is?"

"Yes, Mother. The reason I'm going to college is not to find a prince. I'm going there to get a degree in social work." The truth was, Sharon had already found a prince. Right here in Last Chance, and he lived next door.

Mother blinked. "Sharon, I'm glad you want an education, but social work? It's so demanding and depressing. Couldn't you study something a little happier? You're a talented piano student. Why not study music or liberal arts?"

"Because I don't want to be a musician. And majoring in liberal arts is like studying nothing very useful. I want to help people in trouble, Mother, and for that I need a degree in social work."

"Well, in my opinion, Miss High and Mighty, you ought to be interested in the opportunities college will give you to meet nice, eligible men."

Presumably these would be the nice men who weren't interested in leading her "down a garden path." Boy, there were some serious blind spots in Mother's worldview.

Mother just didn't understand what Sharon wanted to do with her life.

Mother took that moment to glance at the kitchen clock. "Good gracious, Sharon, it's ten minutes to one. You're going to be late for the blood drive. Although why you want to give blood as a Watermelon Queen is beyond me."

"Because Crystal Murphy needs another operation and her family has no health insurance." Crystal Murphy was six years old, and one of Sharon's Sunday school kids. She'd broken her pelvis last spring when a bad storm had hit the trailer park up in Allenberg. The Murphys were living in a double-wide because Hurricane Hugo had flooded them out last fall.

"Oh," Mother said, "I didn't know."

There was no sense in reminding Mother that Reverend Reed had made a special request for help from the pulpit last Sunday. So she kept her mouth shut and escaped down the hallway to her room. Rocky followed like a little shadow.

"I feel sorry for Crystal," Rocky said.

"So do I." Sharon smiled at the little girl. "So, what have you been up to today?"

"Nothing much. No one wants to play with me. Clay is in the backyard with Ray building a tree house. Tulane is trying to help them, but they say he's too little, and they're being mean to him. Stone's at the store. And I'm bored." She plopped down on Sharon's bed.

"It's summertime. You shouldn't be bored," Sharon said as she removed her dress and hung it on a padded hanger.

Rocky shrugged. "I don't have anything to do. And Savannah's gone home to Maryland. It's always so cool when she comes to visit. Her granddaddy lets us sit up in the projection room at the Kismet." The little girl took a big breath. "So are you and Stone going to sit in the back row tonight and kiss?"

Heat crawled right up Sharon's face. "Rocky Rhodes, that's not a nice question. And if you're bored, how would you like to help me and the rest of the Watermelon Court at the bake sale?"

"You mean it?"

"Sure, I need some help carrying cupcakes. But you'll have to put on shoes and wash your knees."

Rocky looked down at her grubby toes. "Okay. But I hate shoes." The little girl paused for a moment. "How come asking about you and Stone kissing in the back row of the theater isn't a nice question? I mean, everyone is talking about how you and Stone are going to get married. So of course you're gonna kiss, right?"

Surprise hit Sharon like a punch to her stomach. "Who told you that?"

"Everyone down at the Cut 'n Curl."

Rocky's mother, Ruby Rhodes, owned the only beauty shop in Last Chance. And naturally it was gossip central. "Everyone at the Cut 'n Curl is talking about me and Stony?"

"Well Miz Randall said something about you and Stone, so of course that means you're going to get married pretty soon. That would be pretty cool, 'cause I can't think of anyone I'd rather have as a sister."

This was not happy news. Sharon was headed off to college and a career. Sure, she wanted to get married, eventually. And she loved Stony enough to marry him. But she was only eighteen. She was way too young to be the object of this kind of talk—especially from Miriam

Randall, Last Chance's practically infallible matchmaker. Boy, when Miriam started making matches, people went kind of crazy. Sharon needed to put an end to talk like that.

"Stony and I are not getting married anytime soon," she said. "People need to quit jumping to conclusions around this town. Now, go on and put on some shoes. And then wash your hands and knees real good, with soap and a washcloth. I'll meet you on the porch in five minutes. Don't be late."

* * *

Stone Rhodes strode into the post office on Palmetto Avenue. He hurried back to the mailbox he'd rented a few months ago, when he'd decided to keep his plans secret. The manila envelope he'd been expecting had finally arrived. He took it from the box and stared at the insignia of the United States Marine Corps on the return address.

He opened the envelope and pulled out the documents. The marines expected him at Parris Island on August sixteenth—in just a little more than two weeks.

Excitement coursed through him. He wanted this challenge.

Now he just had to convince his father and mother that becoming a marine was a better choice than going to college.

Daddy would forgive him for what he'd done. After all, Daddy had served his country in Vietnam, and his Purple Heart stood on the mantel in the living room. But Momma was going to have his hide. Momma and Sharon both expected him to go to college. And, boy howdy, those two women were single-minded. But they would have to come around. First of all, there wasn't enough money for him to go to college. He hadn't gotten all the scholarships he'd hoped for, probably because of his English grades. And second of all, he was tired of school.

All that schooling was just idiotic for a guy who had no desire to be a bank executive or a lawyer or a doctor. Or even an engineer. Those were occupations Momma and Sharon had decided he should go for.

But Stone wanted to be a marine. He couldn't think of anything he wanted more.

Well, the deed was done. He didn't have to argue with anyone about it, which was fine by him. He'd been captain of the football team, not the debate club. The only issue was who to tell first. Sharon. Definitely. She'd made all these plans for the two of them, and she deserved to hear his reasoning directly—not through the Last Chance grapevine.

He was heading out the post office door, thinking about how he was going to break the news to his girlfriend, when he ran into Miriam Randall, the chairwoman of the Christ Church Ladies Auxiliary, an active member of the Last Chance grapevine. He probably shouldn't have held the door for her, but Momma had drilled politeness into him. He couldn't just walk past her without saying howdy.

"Stone Rhodes, I do declare, you are the very person I want to speak with. In fact, I was just looking for you up at the hardware store." Miz Miriam always wore pantsuits and sneakers. She had a way of perching her half-moon reading glasses up on her forehead. You didn't want to get sideways with Miz Miriam. And you sure didn't want to become the object of one of her matchmaking schemes.

"Hey, Miz Miriam," he said, trying to sidle away from her, "nice seeing you. I gotta go, because—"

"Now, Stone, you just hold your horses one minute. I have something important to tell you." Miriam grabbed him by the upper arm. She hauled him across Palmetto Avenue and right into the little vest-pocket park in front of city hall where this year's Watermelon Court had organized its bake sale and blood drive to benefit the Murphy family.

He looked for Sharon, but didn't find her.

Miriam headed away from the bake sale tables, toward the other side of the little park, where she found a bench shaded by a big oak. It was as hot as blue blazes out, but Miz Miriam didn't seem to notice.

"You sit down now, son. I have something important to say to you."

"Yes, ma'am." He was done for.

"Stone, honey, I have to tell you that I've been worried about you."

"You have?"

He looked up just in time to see Sharon hurrying across Palmetto Avenue carrying a tray of cupcakes in her hands. Rocky was shadowing her, as usual. Sharon had clearly worked her magic on Stone's little sister. For once, Rocky's knees looked almost clean, and she was wearing a pair of shoes. That was a miracle right there.

"Son, are you paying attention to me?" Miz Miriam asked.

"Oh, I'm sorry. Yes, ma'am. You've been worried about me. Why is that, Miz Miriam?"

"For a lot of reasons. It's clear that I need to tell you something very important. Something that, quite frankly, I don't think you're old enough to hear. But it seems as if the Lord wants for you to have this knowledge now. Otherwise He wouldn't have given me any signs."

A cold shiver crept up Stone's spine. He had just fallen into one of Miriam's traps. There was nowhere to run or hide.

"Now, honey, here's the thing you need to know," Miriam said. "I'm quite sure you're supposed to be looking for a woman who wants to change the world."

He almost laughed aloud as he watched Sharon take charge of the bake sale on the steps of city hall. As usual, she pulled a clipboard out of her book bag and began diligently checking off items on her list. Sharon was a champion list maker and people organizer. She bossed people around, but no one minded. Especially when she smiled. Heck, when she smiled, everyone melted and did her bidding just because she asked. It was kind of amazing, really.

"Son, your attention keeps wandering." Miz Miriam sounded a little bit annoyed.

"I'm sorry. I was just watching Sharon whip everyone into shape. I think she might have a future as a drill instructor."

Miriam snorted. "So, what's this bake sale for?"

"The Murphys. Crystal needs another operation."

"Oh, I remember Reverend Reed said something about that last Sunday. I reckon I should have known Sharon would organize something."

"She's getting the entire Watermelon Court, not to mention the Davis High offensive line, to donate blood and buy cupcakes." He felt incredibly proud of his girlfriend.

Miz Miriam leaned over and patted Stone's knee. "Well, son, I suppose it comes as no surprise that your soul mate is going to be a crusader. But, here's the important part: it's your job to be her anchor."

Stone stared at the old woman. He had no idea what that meant.

Miriam turned toward the activities at the other end of the park. "Sharon sure is a busy girl."

"I guess."

"She's chairing the paint-a-thon at the church tomorrow, isn't she? And Lessie Anderson was telling me the other day that she's single-handedly raised thousands of dollars for the Murphys. And I'm very impressed with this blood drive she's organized."

"Thanks, Miz Miriam. I get your message loud and clear." Stone stood up and tried to leave.

"Do you really?" Miz Miriam cocked her head as she looked up at him. "Stone, your life is about to change in a lot of different ways. That's what happens when folks leave home for the first time. So, I'm telling you right now that most crusaders end up returning home disillusioned. And that's why crusaders need someone to remind them of what the crusade is all about in the first place."

Okay, he could see how Sharon was a crusader, but what the heck did Miriam mean with the last part? He didn't ever see Sharon becoming disillusioned. Ever. And she sure wasn't interested in leaning on anyone. She was fiercely independent. Stone liked her independent streak best of all.

"I know you're too young for this, but I hope you'll remember what I've told you. Promise me you will?" Miriam said.

"Yes, ma'am. I'll remember."

"All right, you can go. Tell Sharon to save me one of those cupcakes of hers. And tell her I'm in for a ten-dollar donation to the cause."

Yup. Typical. Sharon was a crusader. And Stone had

no doubt that she would probably save the world, one cupcake at a time.

* * *

Sharon hurried across Palmetto Avenue with Rocky in tow. She prayed that Stony's little sister wouldn't drop the pineapple upside-down cake she was carrying. Sharon knew good and well that it was tempting fate to let Rocky carry the cake, but the little girl had seemed kind of forlorn today. Rocky had needed an "important" job to do.

Annie Roberts, Sharon's best friend, was already on the scene, thank goodness, and was supervising the hanging of the big sign that the members of the Key Club had painted last night. It looked terrific. "You're late," Annie scolded as she rescued the cake from Rocky's arms and placed it on one of the folding card tables.

"Mother decided to hem my Watermelon Queen dress. I swear she thinks I've been elected queen of something important." Sharon pulled her clipboard out of her book bag and started checking her to-do list for the event.

Everyone was there already. Emily had brought chocolate chip and oatmeal cookies, Ashley had brought an apple pie, Jessica had brought homemade fudge, and Annie had brought a carrot cake; with the pineapple upside-down cake and the cupcakes, all the food pledges were in.

"Did you get some one-dollar bills and quarters for change?" Sharon asked Jessica.

"Yes, ma'am, and Momma said she was going to make a twenty-five-dollar donation. I started a pledge form."

"Good."

"Emily, when are the football players coming?"

"Around two. Chester got the loan of his daddy's pickup, and they're going to pull the float down Palmetto. All the guys are going to be on it with signs. It should be really great."

Sharon made another check against her list then looked up. Stone was across the park, sitting with Miriam Randall in the shade of a big oak tree. "That's ominous," she said.

Rocky followed her gaze. "What's that mean?"

"It means scary," Annie said, as she looked over her shoulder.

"I told you so," Rocky said. "I heard Momma telling Miz Anderson that Miz Randall wanted to talk to Stone."

Jessica stared across the park. "Holy cow, Shar, this has to mean you're getting married."

Sharon took a big breath. "No."

"No?" Annie said with humor in her voice.

Stony stood up and shoved a manila envelope into his back pocket. He didn't look very happy with Miz Miriam. "Really, y'all," Sharon said, turning away, "you have no idea what Stony and Miz Miriam are talking about. They're probably just passing the time of day."

Emily giggled. "Ooooh, I just love weddings."

Sharon inwardly cringed, then plastered her best Watermelon Queen smile on her lips as she faced the members of her court. "There is not going to be any wedding. Not anytime soon, anyway. Today, we're going to have a blood drive. So, are y'all ready?"

Jessica looked pale. Ashley looked unhappy. Emily looked scared.

"C'mon, girls, it's not going to hurt."

"Much," said Jessica.

"And it might leave a bruise on my arm. And our dresses are strapless," Ashley said.

"Oh, for heaven's sake. Y'all agreed that we would go give blood together in Crystal's name."

"I hate the sight of blood," Emily whined.

"I'll give blood. I feel really sorry for Crystal," Rocky piped up.

Sharon squatted down to be on Rocky's level. "Oh, sweetie, that's so good of you, but kids can't give blood. You'll have to grow up some."

"I want to be like you when I grow up."

Sharon gave Rocky a big ol' hug. "Honey, you want to grow up to be your own self. Not anyone else, you hear? And I'm real proud of you for being braver and more generous than the entire Watermelon Court." She gave her friends the stink eye when she said this.

Rocky beamed. Jessica, Ashley, and Emily looked guilty.

"C'mon girls," Sharon said as she stood up, "the Red Cross is waiting on us. And Andy Jones should be there as well. He promised me he would take a photo of all of us giving blood together. Don't y'all want to have your pictures in the *Times and Democrat*?"

That did the trick. Sharon left Annie in charge of the baked goods and Rocky, then herded her Watermelon Court in the direction of city hall, where the Red Cross had set up the blood drive.

They had just reached the front steps when Stony caught up to them.

Boy howdy, he was handsome. He'd grown tall the last few years, and his shoulders had broadened so much that he looked like a man, not a boy. His worn blue jeans hung low across his hips, and his shaggy brown hair drooped across his forehead in a way that made Sharon want to push it back into place. But of all his traits, Sharon loved his eyes most of all. They were the green of the deep woods in summertime. And he had a way of looking at her that made her insides melt and her heart cinch up in her chest.

She'd felt that spark the very first time she'd gazed into his eyes. She'd been only eight years old. It never ceased to amaze her that she could still feel that tug on her heart whenever he glanced her way.

"So are you going to give blood?" she asked him. She refused to mention that she'd seen him with Miriam or that his little sister was running around town gossiping. She didn't want him to think she gave much credence to that sort of nonsense.

"Uh, well, I need to get back to—"

"It won't take a minute. And you promised me, remember? Besides, it would please me if you would come inside for just a minute."

He gave her an odd look. Like he had forgotten his promise or maybe that he was just as scared of needles as Emily. "C'mon, Stone, you were the team's quarterback. Don't tell me you're scared of a little blood."

"Uh, no, but, um, I need to get back to—"

She grabbed him by the arm. "Come on, honey, you have time to give blood. Everyone is going to do it, including every member of the Davis High Rebels offensive line. You aren't going to let the O-line show you up, are you? Especially after they protected your backside for the last two years?"

She took Stony by the arm and hauled him into city hall with her court following behind. He didn't resist all that hard. But clearly something was on his mind. Probably what he and Miriam Randall had been talking about.

That made Sharon's stomach slightly queasy—not a good thing right before donating blood.

They crossed into the air-conditioned lobby, where the Red Cross had set up a couple of cots. Several town employees were already making donations. Andy Jones, the local stringer for the Orangeburg *Times and Democrat*, was there as well, taking photos. He hurried up to Sharon as she entered the lobby.

"Well, hello, Sharon. I see you've got your court in tow." He smiled at Ashley, Jessica, and Emily.

"We're all going to give blood. And when you write up the story, you'll be sure to mention that we all feel that it's our duty as members of the Watermelon Court to help out people in need."

Mr. Jones smiled at her. "Yes, ma'am. But that's not what I really came here to talk about."

"No?" she asked.

"No. I got a call from John Murphy last night. He told me about what you did, and I want to do a story about it. I can't believe your generosity."

Sharon's face grew hot.

"What did you do?" Stony asked.

Before Sharon could answer, Mr. Jones spoke again: "She's donated the entire one thousand dollars of her Watermelon Queen prize to Crystal's medical bills."

"Oh my goodness," Ashley said, "you didn't. What is your mother going to say?"

"My mother doesn't know about it. Besides, I don't need that thousand dollars the way Crystal does. The way I look at it, God has blessed me in so many ways. He had a plan in mind, and I'm sure that's why I was selected as this year's Watermelon Queen. I wasn't the prettiest girl in the competition, not by a long shot."

She smiled up at Stony when she finished speaking. The spark in his eyes pulled at her soul. Mother would have a conniption when she learned what Sharon had done. But it didn't matter, because Sharon could see that Stony was proud of her. And that made her feel warm all over.

* * *

Later that evening, Sharon sat in the back row of the Kismet and dashed a tear from her eye. She gave Stony a brief glance. He would laugh at her for getting all teary-eyed. But, darn it, the movie was sad.

The heroine, Demi Moore, had to let go of her dead boyfriend, Patrick Swayze, and go on with her life. And, boy, Patrick Swayze made one handsome ghost. Sharon would have a lot of trouble letting go of a guy like him. Of course, Stony was just as handsome. But Patrick was a much better dancer.

Stony gave her a little squeeze. He draped his arm over her shoulders during the scene where Demi and Patrick made a clay bowl. Who knew pottery could be so... well, she didn't know what, but she practically combusted during that scene, especially when Stony moved his hand down to her breast. She was leaning into him so hard her ribs came up against the metal armrest between them. Her insides melted when his thumb brushed over her nipple.

Once they got in Stony's truck, there wouldn't be any barriers.

Sharon was looking forward to it. Mother would be shocked to know that Sharon liked it when Stony touched her breast, or all the other things Sharon had fun doing in Stony's truck. She especially enjoyed touching him. It was pretty exciting when he lost control.

The house lights came up. "Well, that was a different kind of ghost story," he said as they stood up. "I was expecting something scary."

"I liked it. It was sweet."

"It was girly." He took her hand and pulled her up the aisle. The crowd was pretty sparse, it being a Wednesday night. It was a wonder Mr. Brooks managed to keep the Kismet going, especially since he was always a few weeks behind other theaters in showing the newest movies. *Ghost* had been playing up in Orangeburg for weeks. Annie had seen it up there and raved about it.

Five minutes later, they were riding in Stony's old truck, heading out to Bluff Road. George Strait was singing about love without end on the radio. Stony didn't say much as he drove, which wasn't all that unusual. But tonight Sharon got the feeling he might be brooding on something. Maybe he wasn't so proud of her for giving up her prize money.

She studied her boyfriend as he drove, his wrist over the steering wheel. He looked so competent behind the wheel. And the dash lights seemed to highlight the hard angles of his face. He might be a quiet boy, but she would much rather be with Stony than with the other boys and their constant chatter.

There was something really solid about Stony. She had once overheard Miz Randall telling Miz Polk that Stony was the kind of boy who would grow up to be a man a woman could depend on. Kind of like Daddy had been.

Stony stopped the truck at the end of Bluff Road. He set the brake and turned down Garth Brooks, who was singing about friends in low places. She slid across the bench seat and ran her hands up through his hair, repositioning the lock that always wanted to curl down over his forehead. It had been a while since he'd been to the barber. The long, silky strands slipped softly through her fingertips. "When we get to Carolina, we should take a pottery course," she whispered into his ear. "We could re-create that scene in the movie." She licked his ear, then linked a trail of kisses across his hard jaw to his soft mouth.

"Honey," he said when she tried to interest him in a kiss, "we need to talk about that."

"What's wrong?" She pulled away and searched his face in the pale green dashboard lights. What the heck? He had never responded like that when she'd kissed his ear before. Usually a kiss on the ear turned him into jelly. Well... not all of him, of course. And Stony was not the kind of boy who would stop fooling around to talk. About anything. He really liked fooling around. His lack of reaction was like a flashing danger sign.

He turned his gaze toward the dark pine woods that grew at the end of the road. "Um, look," he said. "I care about you, Sharon. I... well, I can't imagine being with any other girl. But, the thing is, I can't go to Carolina with you." When he turned back, his green eyes were filled with emotion.

"What are you talking about? We've been planning this for a year. We were both accepted." She slid to the far edge of the bench seat.

"I can't afford college. And I can't ask my folks to pay for it. Momma and Daddy aren't rich, and I have two little brothers and a sister. I've seen Momma sitting up late at night sometimes doing her bookkeeping. She worries all the time about making ends meet."

So this was about the scholarship he hadn't gotten. Her heartbeat steadied a little as relief washed through her. He could get a job. He could apply for work-study. He could take out a loan. "Stony, come on, we can find solutions to this problem. Money should never be an obstacle to education. You could—"

"No, I can't. It's more than the money."

"What are you talking about? Are you upset about what I did with my prize money?"

Muscles bunched along his jaw. "No, Sharon, I love what you did with your prize money. That's not it. It's something else. See, well, I've joined the marines."

She laughed. "Okay, you can quit with the joke. I know you didn't join the marines. You're just trying to get a rise out of me."

"But I did. I have to report to Parris Island on August sixteenth."

Sharon's stomach heaved, and for an instant, she thought she might be sick right there in his front seat. "You're leaving in two weeks? You aren't coming to Columbia with me?" Pain swept through her like a raging river. She couldn't breathe. Stony was abandoning her.

"I'm sorry, honey," he said in answer to her shock. "I know you made plans for the two of us. But I don't want to go to college."

"But we've been over this a million times. Mother is never going to accept you until you finish school."

"Right." He sounded angry.

"But you know how she is."

"I do. But I don't care about your mother. I care about you."

"But we made plans and—"

"We can still be together. I mean, you'll be at college, and I'll be at boot camp. But we could still be…you know…"

"What? What could we be?" She was angry now. She had planned it all out in her head. They were supposed to be living in the same co-ed dorm. She had her packing list all done, and Stony's, too. They would be together and see each other every day. They would share this time in their lives like they had shared everything since they were eight. And, most important, they could find some privacy.

"I thought we were going to be together."

"But we will be. Like we've always been."

"With you God knows where and me in Columbia? That's not together, Stony."

"Well, I know, but we'd still be going steady."

"That's a heck of an assumption," she said in anger.

He stared at her for a long moment. "Sharon, come on, don't you even care about how I feel?"

"I do, but why didn't you say something before I made plans? I have whole pages of plans."

He stared at the dashboard, as if gathering his arguments. "I know. I never saw a person make lists the way you do. And I feel bad about it. I've been trying to find a way to tell you and my mother how I feel, but you never give me a chance to explain. Y'all are always talking and planning. It's hard to get a word in edgeways. I don't think I'd be that good in college." He finally turned back toward her, but he wouldn't meet her gaze.

"Why do you always sell yourself short? You're smart. You could be anything you want to be."

"Except a marine? Do you think being a marine is selling myself short?"

"Stop twisting my words like that."

His gaze finally met hers, and she could tell he was angry. "I didn't twist them, honey. That's the way they sounded when they came out of your mouth." He paused for a moment, the corner of his mouth twitching upward. "Just listen for one second. Miriam Randall tackled me at the post office today and told me I should be looking for a crusader—you know, someone who wants to change the world. And I thought about you the minute I heard that. I admire you so much. And I always thought you admired me. I thought we were, you know, like a pair, no matter where we are."

Sharon's head felt like it was about to explode. "What are you saying? Are you saying you want to get married just because Miriam Randall gave you some lame forecast? And then you want to go off and join the marines while I go to college all by myself?"

A truly stunned look crossed Stony's face. "No. We're too young to get married. But I guess I thought, what with Miriam saying what she said and you always talking about us being together in Columbia, well, I thought maybe we could move things up a little bit. Maybe we could go to the Peach Blossom Motor Court or something before I ship out. I don't want to get to boot camp and still be a virgin."

"Take me home," she said.

"But Sharon, I—"

"I'm not sleeping with you at the Peach Blossom Motor Court so you can cross that off your to-do list. And I don't want to marry you." She took Stony's high school ring off the chain she wore around her neck, turned in her seat, and hurled it at him. It hit him in the face, and she was glad. He'd wrecked her carefully laid plans. Everything she had been dreaming about was undone. She was going to be in Columbia all on her own. And he wanted to take her to some seedy motel instead of finding a nice, private place where they could actually sleep together. She could almost hear her Mother saying, "I told you so."

"Damn, Sharon," he said, touching his cheek, "That hurt."

"Good, because you joining the marines without telling me hurt, too. And I don't even want to talk about the suggestion you just made about that seedy hotel."

"Ah crap, are we breaking up?"

"I guess so."

CHAPTER TWO

$\mathcal{T}$he next day, Sharon had to help at the church paint-a-thon. She wasn't feeling very charitable that morning as she dipped a roller in the pan of paint and vented her emotions on one of the plaster walls in the fellowship hall.

"Hey, quit rolling so hard. You're getting speckles all over the floor," Annie Roberts said. "You're mad at Stone, not the wall."

"I am not angry," Sharon said, dropping the roller into the pan. She grabbed a clean rag and began to blot up the paint speckles. As she worked, the tears she'd been holding back began to leak from the corners of her eyes.

Her world was unraveling at the seams, and she didn't know what to do about it.

In a few weeks, she'd be going off to college in Columbia. Annie would be leaving for Ann Arbor and the University of Michigan. Nick, Annie's boyfriend, had joined the army and was already gone for basic training. Everyone was leaving.

A knot lodged in Sharon's throat, and she swallowed it back. She'd known Annie and Nick and Stony practically all her life. The four of them had been a tight-knit group since middle school. It had been easy to let go of Annie and Nick, knowing that Stony would be coming to Columbia with her. But now he was going off to Parris Island, and his suggestion about that no-tell motel made her so angry every time she thought about it.

"Aw, honey, don't cry." Annie dropped to the floor and put her arm around Sharon. "Stone still loves you, you know. It's not like he broke up with you. You broke up with him."

"He went off and made a life-changing decision and didn't even consult me. Then he made a rude suggestion that really hurt. Nick did the same thing to you." She paused for a moment, searching her best friend's face. "Didn't you feel like your world was unraveling when Nick tried to get you to sleep with him and then left for basic training?"

Annie smiled, her eyes full of empathy. "Nick and I were a habit. And I left him panting at the Peach Blossom on prom night. But you and Stone—that's a whole different story."

"How? He sabotaged me and everything I had planned."

"Well, that was pretty crappy of him."

"It was. And the worst thing about it is that we've been discussing things all summer. You know, about how things are going to be when we get up to Carolina. I've been holding off sleeping with him until we get up there and can have a little more privacy. I didn't want to go with him to that nasty motel."

Annie gave her shoulders a squeeze. "Are you sure he was listening?"

"Who knows. But I had already told him dozens of times that I was never, ever going to the Peach Blossom Motor Court with him. So you can imagine how angry I was when he suggested it. And to use Miriam Randall as an excuse for moving his plans up. That really hurt."

"Right." Annie sighed.

"What? It sounds like you're taking Stony's side."

Annie shook her head. "I guess maybe a little bit. See, everyone is talking about how Miriam Randall has predicted that you and Stone are going to get married. And Stony is going into the marines whether you like it or not. So I'm just putting two and two together, you know."

"No, I don't know. Are you saying I should marry him or sleep with him? I'm only eighteen."

"Yeah, I know. But on the other hand, what if Stone ends up in a shooting war in some godforsaken place? I just can't shake the notion that if he were married to you, he would be protected in some way. I mean, Miriam Randall is like magic, isn't she? Everyone she matches up lives forever and has lots of kids. Just look at Millie Polk or Thelma Hanks."

Sharon stared at her friend. "You're insane."

"Am I? Miriam Randall never misses. You should be trotting down to the hardware store to forgive Stone. You should tell him you're proud of him. You should marry him, and then he can take you to some nice hotel up in Columbia or something."

"I'm not ready to get married." Sharon pulled her knees up and rested her forehead on them. But she wasn't really ready to give up Stony, either. The idea of being at college, or anywhere, without him scared her to death.

Still, she didn't like being put into this cage where she either had to marry him or sleep with him before he disappeared from her life. She didn't want to do either of those things.

A sob rose in her throat. Annie gave her a little hug and patted her back while she struggled to regain control of her emotions.

"You know," Annie said, once Sharon had sniffled back her tears, "it would be a shame if you got so angry or selfish that you missed out on getting married to your soul mate. And the thing is, Sharon, you almost never get angry, and you are the most unselfish person I know."

Sharon straightened up. "I'm not getting married to Stony. I'm not some crusader. I'm just a good Christian. Giving my prize money to Crystal won't change the world. It might help her get better." Her voice wavered again. "And the fact that he joined the marines in secret, without even talking to me about it, suggests that maybe it's a good thing we broke up. I mean, I don't want to be with someone who isn't honest with me. And Stony wasn't honest."

"Sharon Anne McKee, you're being stupid."

"Am I? How many people do you know in this town who are married to cheating husbands?"

"Okay, there are some. But Stone isn't like that."

"He didn't tell me the truth. He let me go on planning our life at college while he knew he wasn't ever going to be up there with me. And then he drops his bomb two weeks before he has to leave. And the thing is, he didn't ask me to marry him. He just used Miz Randall's advice as an excuse for trying to get me to the Peach Blossom. I'm not sure I can ever forgive him."

* * *

Stone dealt with all the crises in his life by going fishing. He reckoned that his fishing time might be severely limited once he got to Parris Island, and with Sharon on the warpath, along with Momma, Daddy, and Uncle Pete, disappearing seemed like the right thing all the way around.

He paddled his canoe up the Edisto River, dropped anchor, and sat for hours. Since it was hot and late in the afternoon, he didn't catch a blessed thing, but he sure did have time to think. He didn't like Sharon being angry at him. He didn't want to go off to boot camp without knowing that she would be waiting for him. And, yeah, he wanted to sleep with her before he left.

In short, he didn't want to let her go.

But, of course, her mother had filled her head with a lot of crap about college boys. He should have figured out that Sharon would break up with him the minute he decided not to get a degree. He stewed over this for a long time and got nowhere. It hurt, down deep. Did she really believe he wasn't good enough for her?

She thought he was selling himself short. And so did Momma. In fact, everyone thought he was selling himself short by choosing the marines.

How could everyone be wrong?

It was late by the time he hauled in his anchor and headed back to the public boat ramp. He had missed dinner, but he didn't care. He was already so deep in the doghouse he would probably never see the light again. He didn't care about much of anything. And the people he loved didn't seem to care about him.

So he was flat-out stunned to discover Aunt Arlene at the boat ramp, lounging in a lawn chair with a beer in her hand and a cooler at her feet. She had a line in the water too, which was typical. Aunt Arlene loved fishing even more than Uncle Pete, and that was saying something right there.

"Hey," she called, raising her Bud can. "You want one?"

"I'm only eighteen, Aunt Arlene."

She snorted. "Like you haven't ever had a beer." She got up and helped him carry the canoe to the bed of his truck. "I figured you were hungry. I brought some pimento cheese sandwiches."

She gestured to a second lawn chair that was evidently waiting just for him.

"Are you going to bawl me out, too?" Stone asked as he settled into the chair and opened the cooler. He took out a Dr Pepper and a baggie with three cheese-spread sandwiches. Aunt Arlene sure did know what he liked.

"Nope. I wanted to come out here and let you know I'm proud of you."

Stone stopped chewing his bite of sandwich. "Really?"

"Yes, I am. Near as I can tell, you have taken a stand for yourself. I admire that. I can think of a few ways you might have improved your communication skills, but I'm still proud of you for joining the marines. I think you're going to be very successful. And if your momma would stop for just one minute and think this thing through, she'd realize you are not the one she should be sending off to college. Clay would make a better college boy. Tulane's going to grow up to be a mechanic."

"Rocky's the smart one," Stone said.

"She sure is. But so are you."

"No, I'm the child who is an idiot."

"I don't think so." Arlene took a slug of her beer. "But you are the talk of the town."

"I am?"

"Yup. Olivia McKee is delighted that her daughter has thrown you over. This news has also pleased Lillian Bray, who thinks Sharon is too good for you. And, of course, whatever Lillian thinks is sure to be a matter of discussion down at the Cut 'n Curl. Thelma and Millie are on your side, in case you're interested." She snorted a laugh. "Miriam is being quiet, as usual."

"She wasn't quiet yesterday."

"Oh, I know that. She drops her little matrimonial bomb-shells, and everyone runs around like headless chickens. Then she just stands back and watches the show."

"Sort of like you."

"Well, that's true. But I don't drop any bombshells."

Stone leaned back in his chair and stretched out his legs. This was nice. He always enjoyed fishing with Aunt Arlene. She was one of the most sensible women he knew.

"So I'm dying to know," Arlene asked. "Did you get that bruise on your cheek because Sharon slapped you?"

"No. She brained me with my high school ring."

"Hmmm. I see. She must have been upset."

"She *was* ticked off."

"Well, I reckon Sharon is sort of like your momma. She had a few dreams about the both of you being up at Carolina this fall."

In the distance, the birds began their twilight serenade. "I guess," he said lamely. "The thing is, Aunt Arlene, I don't see why my going into the marines means she can't go to college. I just thought, well, we could still be together, and each of us could have the future we wanted. I guess I'm just stupid."

Arlene cocked her head. "No, that's not it. So did you ask her to marry you?"

The question jolted right through him. "Uh, no, I didn't. I just explained that we could, well, you know..." His voice faded out. He remembered exactly what he'd suggested. Heat crawled up his face.

Arlene studied him for a long moment as she drained her beer. "Son, I have a good idea what you suggested. And to be honest, I don't blame Sharon for braining you with her ring. Honey, if Miriam tells you a woman is your soul mate, then you have to marry her. You do understand how it works, don't you?"

"Sharon doesn't want to get married. She's always talking about how she wants to be independent. And besides, she wants to marry a college man. You know, like her daddy was."

"Oh, I don't know about that. Her momma wants her to marry a college man. And as for her independence, well, she can't run from Miriam's forecast. If there was ever a crusader in Last Chance, I'm thinking it's Sharon McKee."

"We're only eighteen, Aunt Arlene. We can't get married."

"Why not? You're old enough to join the marines and fight for your country. You made that decision all on your own. And from the red on your face, you seem to think you're old enough to do some other things, too."

He didn't answer. He simply picked up Arlene's fishing rod and cast out into the middle of the channel. He slowly reeled the line in.

Arlene let go of a sigh. "Stone, you've made a man's decision. That makes you old enough to get married. Don't you want to marry Sharon?"

He focused on the bobber at the end of the fishing line. It danced in the water like something was thinking about taking the bait.

"Stone, are you paying any attention to me?" Aunt Arlene asked.

Yeah, he was paying attention. She wanted to know if he wanted to marry Sharon, and he was thinking about the way Sharon touched him in the dark. The way she kissed him with her entire body. He thought about the way she was always ready to help, the way she made lists, the way she baked cupcakes every time someone died or got sick. He loved the way she laughed. He was so proud of her for giving up her prize money. She was the most determined person he knew. He really loved that about her. The idea of her being someone else's girlfriend made his skin crawl.

The high school ring on his finger seemed to get heavier by the moment.

"I can't imagine being with anyone else," he finally said. "Sharon is my best friend. I...I love her." His voice got kind of wobbly. He stopped talking and reeled in the line. The hook came up empty. The fish had taken the bait.

"Well, then, I reckon you'll need to court her. And you don't have much time," Aunt Arlene said.

He put the rod down on the ground and turned toward his aunt. "Court her? Aunt Arlene, how many beers have you had?"

She laughed. "Not many. I'm as sober as a judge. I'm serious, Stone—you can't just let her walk away. You have to fight for her."

"How? She's got it in her mind that she wants a college boy, not a marine. How do I change that?"

"Honey, this has nothing to do with you being a college boy, so put that out of your mind. This is about trust."

"Trust?"

"Yes. She trusted you, and you didn't play fair. That's a hard thing for a woman to forgive. I'm afraid you're going to have to grovel. So I suggest you get some flowers, and go over there, and tell her you're sorry and that you want to marry her. And while you're at it, you tell her all the things you admire about her—there must be a lot because you were sure doing some heavy thinking just now."

Stone could almost understand what Arlene was saying. Maybe Sharon was just angry because her plans had been upset. And because he'd been an idiot last night about the Peach Blossom Motor Court.

"Oh, and one other thing," Arlene said. "You're going to need a ring."

"A ring? I've got my high school ring."

"No, silly, a ring she can actually wear on her finger. I've got just the thing. It belonged to your great-grandmother. Pete wanted me to wear it, but it's not my style. I think it would do just fine for Sharon, though." She pulled out a little square leather box.

"Uh, Aunt Arlene, I can't—"

"And you'll need to dance with her at the barbecue. You get yourself all dressed up, and you dance with that girl. Ain't nothing makes a girl fall in love faster than a dance with a handsome young man. You're just going to have to sweep her off her feet. And you're going to have to convince her that even if you're halfway around the world, your heart is always where she is."

"Uh, okay." He could do the flowers and the groveling. He could even see himself getting down on one knee and begging Sharon to marry him. But there was no way in hell he was going to make himself a laughingstock by dancing with her.

CHAPTER THREE

The next day, Sharon sat in one of the chairs at the Cut 'n Curl with Mrs. Rhodes fussing over her hair. The situation couldn't have been more awkward. Sharon would have avoided it if she could have. But the Watermelon Festival kicked off tomorrow, and that required the reigning queen to visit the local beauty shop.

So she had to sit there, trying not to show any emotion, which was impossible. Mrs. Rhodes was levelheaded and never fibbed about her background. She was the kindest person Sharon had ever known. Losing Mrs. Rhodes's friendship would suck. And really, after a day of being angry and depressed, Sharon had come to the conclusion that breaking up with Stony was like having her arms cut off. It hurt. Bad.

Mrs. Rhodes was taking the rollers out of Sharon's hair when she stopped, looked in the mirror, and said, "Honey, I know exactly how you feel."

"You do?"

"Yes, I do. I wanted Stone to go to college."

"Oh." Sharon wasn't sure what to say, because after sleeping on the situation for a night, she had come to the conclusion that she wasn't angry about that. She didn't want to force Stony to go to college if that didn't suit him. His getting a college degree would make Mother happy, but so what. Mother was rarely happy about anything. She would find something else to harp on.

The heart of the problem wasn't whether or not Stony got a degree; it was that he'd gone behind her back to join up. And then there was that comment he'd made about losing his virginity. Sharon was still angry about that one.

But how could she explain any of this to Mrs. Rhodes?

"I'm really disappointed in Stone," Mrs. Rhodes continued. "And for a while, I was angry. But I'm getting over it."

Sharon sat there wishing to God Mrs. Rhodes would stop talking.

"You know," Mrs. Rhodes said, "I was so angry that he went behind my back. But then I thought about it, and I came to the conclusion that he just didn't want to hurt me. And he's never been the kind to pour out his feelings. He doesn't argue about things, the way Tulane does. He avoids confrontation if he can. I didn't even see that he was hurting in his own way. I just took his silence for his acceptance. And that was wrong."

Sharon looked away from the mirror. The beauty shop settled into silence for an interminable moment, and then, out of the blue, Mrs. Rhodes swiveled the chair around so that the two of them could talk face-to-face. Sharon had no other option except to look Mrs. Rhodes in the eye.

Stony's mother spoke again, her voice soft and kind: "Mr. Rhodes told me last night that he thought Stone would make one heck of a marine but maybe only a so-so college boy. I have to admit that I argued with Bert when he said that, but Bert won the argument. Because once I started thinking about it, I realized Stone would make a heck of a soldier. Just like his daddy and his granddaddy. I reckon it's in his blood or something. Now, mind, I know for a fact Clay would make a terrible soldier."

Sharon managed a tiny smile. "He'd have to grow a few inches and lose a few pounds."

Ruby gave her a no-nonsense look. "Just you wait. He's going to sprout up one of these days, just like Bert did." She took a big breath. "But, see, I think you and I have been determined to turn Stone into something he's not. And even though I don't agree with the way he went behind our backs, maybe that's just the way he is. Honey, Stone doesn't talk about things. He just does them. He's always been that way. It's part of why everyone admires him."

Sharon sucked in a deep breath. "But I'm not mad at Stony because he's given up on going to college," she whispered. "I may have given that impression at first, but I've thought about it, just like you have."

"Oh, thank goodness. I thought you had broken up with him because of that."

"No. My mother is the one who's hung up about college."

"Then why did you give him back his ring?"

"I got mad."

"Because he messed up your plans?"

She shrugged. "Among other things."

"What other things, honey?"

She couldn't tell his mother why. It would be too embarrassing. "Well, after what he pulled, I'm not sure I can trust him, you know? And you've just pointed out that he does stuff like that all the time. So maybe we aren't right for one another. And then I don't want to be rushed into something just because Mrs. Randall is gossiping. I'm only eighteen."

"Oh my goodness. Did Stone ask you to marry him?"

"No, of course he didn't."

Mrs. Rhodes stared down at her for a long moment, one eyebrow arching. Sharon got the feeling that Stony's mother was looking right through her. "Oh, I see." She let go of a deep sigh.

Sharon had the horrible feeling that Mrs. Rhodes actually did see—all of it—because a kind smile touched her lips. "Honey, I think maybe you and Stone need to talk. I'm sure he's confused about why you're so mad at him."

Sharon looked down at her lap. "But, see, that's part of the problem. I'm not sure he listens. And he hardly ever talks. Which I don't mind, because I don't like boys who chatter. But sometimes he does talk and then..." Her voice trailed off.

Mrs. Rhodes sighed. "And then he says stupid stuff that makes you furious?"

"Yeah."

"Well, I'd love to promise you that Stone will never ever say anything stupid again. But I'm afraid I can't. Bert says stupid things all the time. But somehow we manage to forgive each other, since I've been known to say dumb things, too. If it makes you feel any better, Stone's completely torn up about what's happened between you two. He's been fishing nonstop since you gave him back his ring. And when he does that, you know he's hurting real bad about something."

"Mrs. Rhodes, I don't want him to hurt. But if he can't understand how it hurt me when he went behind my back, or how angry I was when he—" She stopped before she said too much, then quickly continued to cover up her near blunder. "I know the Lord values forgiveness, Mrs. Rhodes. But I'm struggling with it right now. I guess that makes me a lesser person, but I can't help but feel I deserve an apology."

* * *

Stone clutched the bouquet in a death grip as he marched up the walk to Sharon's front door. He had to be crazy to come up here with these flowers. Sharon was going to throw him out on his backside.

The little ring in his pocket grew heavier. He was not entirely sure this was the right thing to do. But he was doing it. He couldn't stand the idea of Sharon going to college and being with some other guy.

He knocked on the door and waited. A trickle of sweat inched down his back. It was still ninety-five degrees and muggy as all get-out. The frogs were starting their evening song. Pretty soon the mosquitoes would be out in full force.

The door opened, spilling light onto the darkening day. Mrs. McKee looked down her straight, narrow nose and managed to make Stone feel about three feet tall. Sharon's mother was some kind of high and mighty.

He cleared his throat. "Is Sharon home?"

"She is, but she's gone to bed early to get her beauty rest. Tomorrow is going to be a big day for her, you know.

She has to be up at five-thirty to get ready for the Watermelon Festival parade." Mrs. McKee's disapproving stare made Stone feel like an idiot for not realizing how busy Sharon was. Of course, he would have known all of this, if he'd been thinking straight.

But he hadn't really been thinking straight since Sharon threw his ring at him.

He held out the flowers he'd just bought at the florist shop in the Bi-Lo supermarket. They were pink. He had no idea what kind of flowers they were, but they seemed to be wilting in the heat. Or maybe he was holding them so tight he was strangling them. "Uh, could you give her these, please. And tell her I want to talk to her."

Mrs. McKee gazed at the flowers as if they were something nasty. "You know, when I was a girl in Charleston, the young men who courted me brought roses, not carnations. You really don't want me to give her those, do you? I mean, tomorrow she's going to have people throwing roses at her feet."

He stared at the flowers. They suddenly seemed pitiful. He pulled back his hand. "Well, uh, could you tell her I stopped by?"

Mrs. McKee folded her arms across her chest. "Stone, I don't think she wants to talk to you. She gave you back your ring, didn't she? She's going to college. She's going to better herself."

The stems of the flowers snapped. There was no point in arguing. Sharon wanted a college boy, and he would never be that.

"Good night, Mrs. McKee," he said between his clenched teeth.

He threw the broken flowers down on the porch, turned, and stalked off to his truck. He fired it up and took it out to Route 70, where he turned all 350 horses loose. That was almost fun until Sheriff Bennett pulled him over, made him take a sobriety test, and then threw the book at him just because he hadn't been drinking and therefore should have known better.

CHAPTER FOUR

$\mathscr{I}$t was oh-dark-thirty on Saturday morning. Mother tuned the car radio to the all-news station as she and Sharon drove to the parade staging area at the high school. The announcer came on talking about trouble in the Middle East. Iraq had invaded Kuwait, and President Bush said the United States wouldn't let the aggression stand. The secretary of state said the United Nations would take up the issue. The secretary of defense suggested that the United States would send in the air force and the marines.

Sharon's stomach dropped, and not with anticipation for her big day ahead.

Mother didn't miss a beat. "See," she said as they pulled into the school's parking lot, "there's a good reason not to get involved with a marine."

Sharon pressed her lips together. What was the point of arguing with Mother? She didn't get it. Not like Mrs. Rhodes.

Sharon had been thinking a lot about the things Mrs.

Rhodes had said yesterday. In fact, she had spent a sleepless night, thinking and worrying about Stony. She hated the idea of him hurting. It made her insides feel all funny and bad.

So she did what she had been doing for the last few years, ever since Daddy died. When she got that funny feeling in the pit of her stomach, she prayed. And when prayer didn't help, she would pull out her Bible and randomly pick a passage to read. Nine times out of ten she found comfort there. And often she found remarkably good advice.

Last night she'd opened her Bible right to Corinthians and found Saint Paul's beautiful words about how love is always patient and kind. How it doesn't insist on its own way. How love is never resentful. And how, most of all, love bears all things, believes all things, hopes all things, and endures all things.

The minute she read that Bible passage, Sharon realized that whatever was wrong between her and Stony wasn't only his doing. She had a part in it, too. She had said some terribly unkind things about his goals. She needed to remember Saint Paul's words: Love does not insist on its own way.

She saw clearly now how Mother had been insisting on her own way for a very long time. And Sharon had been going along with her, in the name of love. But she couldn't do it anymore. She wanted to be a better person. The kind of person who could love without preconditions.

The minute the car rolled to a stop, Sharon opened the door and jumped out. She didn't think she could spend another instant in her mother's company.

"Be careful or you'll tear your dress."

"Mother, please, I don't care about my dress," Sharon

replied. "What I care about is Stony. He could be heading right into a war zone, and your ugly comments are beyond insensitive. Stony is a human being, same as you and me. More important, he's my friend. Maybe my best friend in all the world." She stopped before she worked herself up into a full yell.

She turned and walked toward the people staging the parade floats. Mother yelled at her back as she walked away: "You'll thank me one day, missy. That no-account boy came by last night looking for you. He brought you carnations. Can you imagine? Carnations instead of roses. That pretty much says it all. His mother is a hairdresser, and his daddy is a laughingstock. And he's going into the marines because he can't even afford college. You're well rid of him."

"Stony came by last night? When?" Sharon turned and asked her questions in a surprisingly calm voice, given her fury. She needed to take this confrontation with Mother down a notch. People in the staging area were starting to stare.

"He came by around nine," Mother said. "You were taking a bath. I sent him away. I told him you didn't ever want to see him again."

"How could you?" Sharon hissed the words.

Mother blinked. "How could I what? You broke up with him, didn't you?"

Sharon didn't argue. She *had* broken up with him. She had gotten angry when she hadn't gotten her way. And how did that make her any different from Mother? She'd been silly and selfish.

If only she'd known that Stone had come to see her last night. She would have apologized. Clearly, if he'd come bearing flowers, he'd intended to make his own apologies.

Sharon turned away from her mother and walked toward the queen's float. Within minutes, she was hoisted up onto her throne, but it was the last place on earth she wanted to be. She wanted to be free to find Stony and get things straight between them.

Instead, she had to plaster a smile on her face and ride in the parade. She had to kick off the barbecue at the country club with a small speech. She had to taste the hash and proclaim it the best ever. She had to pose for photos with the mayor and the men who cooked the pigs. She had to eat with the members of her court. She had to smile and sign autographs for the little girls who looked up to the Watermelon Queen. She had to shake hundreds of hands. She had to listen to people talk about how unselfish she was for giving up her prize money, knowing just how wrong those people were. She had to endure everyone looking at her as if she were something special.

And every minute of it was torture because Stony wasn't at her side. Without him there, it all seemed superficial. She felt like a complete fraud.

Sharon finally managed to escape, late in the day. After visiting the little girls' room, she snuck out of the dance pavilion's back door. The country club was situated right on the banks of the Edisto River. She slipped out of her heels and let the sword grass cool her aching feet as she walked down to the riverbank.

What was she going to do about Stony? She'd obviously hurt him badly if he hadn't even shown up at the barbecue. Everyone came to the barbecue.

She walked along the riverbank toward the downstream pier, deserted now that the day was nearly done. She sat on one of the benches and gazed upriver.

And there he stood on the upstream fishing pier with a line in the water.

Of course. What an idiot she had been. His mother had told her that he'd been fishing nonstop. She should have come looking for him sooner.

She watched him cast his line. He was graceful and powerful, and she never tired of watching his hands in motion. They were broad in the palm and long in the finger. They could be strong and gentle, just like him.

Heat flushed through her as she thought about what those hands could do to her body.

She got up and marched toward him, a woman with a mission, her heart hammering against her ribs and the words of Corinthians spinning in her head. He turned at the sound of her footsteps, a surprised look on his face.

She didn't wait for him to put down his fishing rod. She simply threw herself into his arms. The rush of relief was strong and almost earthshaking. There was no place she fit as well. She had been a fool to get so angry with him. She promised herself never to get that angry with him again.

* * *

Nothing had been right that day for Stone until Sharon came rushing down the pier and into his arms. And then the pressure of her body against his made everything seem extremely clear. Which was kind of funny because holding Sharon usually made his head go fuzzy. But not this time. She felt soft and curvy, and her incredible dress left her shoulders bare. He pressed his lips to her throat. A buzz of desire filled his head along with her sweet scent.

He linked a series of kisses up her neck and across her cheek, and all the way to her sweet, soft mouth. She tasted of forgiveness and sex. She wrapped her arms around his neck and squirmed a little against his front. Boy, she was really hot and willing.

"Honey, I need to talk to you," he murmured against her cheek.

She looked up at him, the lights from the distant pavilion dancing in her dark eyes. "It's okay, Stony. I forgive you. And I'm sorry for being so silly. Real love isn't selfish. Real love is forgiving. Your mother told me that yesterday, but it took a while to sink in." Her voice sounded strained and shaky, like she might cry. He had never seen her cry before, and it slayed him to think that he might have put tears in her eyes. He never wanted to do that again.

"Honey, listen. I gotta say something here."

"Okay."

"Well, the thing is, I want you. Bad. And, well..." He exhaled in frustration and stopped. "I didn't start that right. Let me try again."

Sharon pressed her fingers across his lips. "No, Stony, you don't have to explain. I just haven't been listening is all. I needed to close my mouth and open my eyes and listen to you."

He gently moved her fingers away. "Honey, let me finish, please. I got a heap of things to say."

She smiled up at him. "Okay. I'm listening."

He took a deep breath. "I don't think I'll ever be the person you want, but, see—"

"Stony, for goodness' sake. You are precisely the person I want. I know I said some stupid things about you going to college, but I don't want you to go to college if it's not what you want. And I'm not like Mother. I love you for who you are, not something I think you are. And as for the rest, well, I want you so bad. I think you maybe started out better the first time."

"Sharon, you're not listening."

"Oh, sorry, I just meant that I don't want to wait any longer. I want to—"

"Shhh." He stared at her for a long time. Was she saying yes before he even got to ask? No, that wasn't right. She was saying yes to the wrong thing. And he wasn't about to let her do that, as much as he really wanted to drag her off somewhere and get her naked. If he did that, she wouldn't respect him—or herself—in the morning. And that mother of hers would never let her hear the end of it.

"I'm not taking you to the Peach Blossom Motor Court."

She startled and dropped her arms from around his neck. She stepped back, her brown eyes widening. "But on Wednesday you said—"

"I know what I said, and it was shameful. Really. You've made it clear that you don't want to do that. I don't know why I suggested it. I've been going over it again and again, and I realize that I got it all wrong on Wednesday, too. I'm just not good at this."

He dug into his pocket and pulled out the little box Aunt Arlene had given him. He dropped to one knee. "Sharon McKee, will you marry me?"

She looked a little scared, so he figured he should keep talking.

He sucked in some more air and continued: "I know you really value your independence, and I guess we could go somewhere or something, but I want more. I mean, I know that you want more. And I respect you for it. I want you to be mine even if you are independent. I know that doesn't make any sense, but it does if you think about it long enough.

"I'll be gone a lot. And you wanting to be independent is probably a good thing. But, see here, you'll still be my wife. And I want it that way.

"And I did a little research. We can't get married in South Carolina without waiting a bunch of days, but we could drive to Georgia and get married tonight."

He'd run out of words and air. He gazed up at her. She was kind of smiling, but her eyes looked all watery too, like she might cry. His heart raced. He didn't know what else he could do to talk her into marrying him. But he was determined to do it even if he had to stay here on his knee for the next three hours.

She got down on her knees, too. "You planned this out?"

"Yeah, I guess."

"Did you come to the house last night to say this?"

He nodded. "Your mother said you didn't want to see me."

"Mother didn't ask. She just assumed."

"After she sent me away, I got really mad. And then Sheriff Bennett gave me a speeding ticket. Shoot, honey, I didn't know that carnations weren't as good as roses. I've been out here fishing all day and worrying that you might think I wasn't—"

"Oh, for heaven's sake, my mother told you that carnations weren't good enough for me? She said that to your face last night? Good grief. Stony, honey, I don't deserve you, but I love you with all my heart. These last few days have made me realize it. I don't ever want to be away from you. You're like my anchor or something."

A fountain of pure joy sprang up inside him. "You think I'm your anchor? Really?"

"Yes."

"Miz Miriam said that exact same thing to me. She said I was supposed to be your anchor. And I want to be that for you, Sharon. I love you so much. I'm going to love you until the day I die."

She gave him a fierce hug. "Don't you say that, Stony Rhodes. I'm so scared for you. Have you heard the news about Iraq?"

"Yeah."

"Well, if you get sent there, just remember that I plan for us to grow old together."

He laughed. "Are you going to make a list to go with that plan?"

"Don't you laugh. This is not funny. You come home to me."

"I promise. We're going to be together forever, honey. We've got Miz Miriam Randall to thank for that."

She kissed him, and her mouth was like a hot summer night, full of stars and moonshine and first-time love. She never really said yes. She just kissed him until he couldn't breathe. And that's when he got off his knees, and carried her all the way to his truck.

* * *

"Oh crap, Mother's home," Sharon said as Stone pulled his truck to the curb. He responded to this news with a truly filthy curse word, and for once, Sharon wasn't of a mind to object.

"You're sure I need my birth certificate? Wouldn't my driver's license be good enough?" she asked.

"Not according to what the Georgia authorities told me on the phone. Do you know where your birth certificate is?"

She nodded. "Yeah, it's in a file in Daddy's study. Mother doesn't go in there very often. The room is kind of a shrine to Daddy. But still, if she hears me, I'm dead. She thinks I'm at the barbecue, and it won't be long before I'm missed."

"Are you sure you want to do this?"

She smiled at him. "Getting cold feet?"

"No, but I don't want you to get into trouble with your mother. She already hates me."

"She's going to really hate you after we elope, but I don't care. That's her problem. You stay here. I'll be back in no more than ten minutes."

"And if you're not?"

"Then you come busting in like the marine you want to be. Give me ten minutes."

Sharon headed to the front porch, walking on her bare feet, her Watermelon Queen dress swishing with every step. She opened the front door.

All was dark in the house except for Mother's room, down the hall. She could hear Mother stirring around in there, waiting for her.

Sharon turned the other way, toward Daddy's study. She sat at her father's desk and opened the top drawer. He always kept the key to the file cabinet there. She found the key without any problem. But she hesitated when she saw the little leather ring box sitting right there in the middle of the drawer.

She didn't remember the ring box being there the last time she'd looked for the filing cabinet key.

She opened the box and gasped. It was Daddy's wedding band.

She closed the box and pressed it to her heart for a moment. Daddy had always liked Stony. Maybe this was his way of giving her away.

She quickly opened the file cabinet and found her birth certificate. Daddy had been a very organized man during his lifetime.

Now all she needed was to sneak into her bedroom to collect a few necessities, including the diaphragm she'd gotten from Planned Parenthood. But to get to her room, she would have to walk down the hall right past Mother's bedroom. That would never work. Mother's bedroom door was open. She was clearly waiting up for Sharon's return.

Sharon stood there weighing her options. She decided against going down the hallway. The very last thing she wanted was a big confrontation between Stony and Mother on the day she planned to get married. She would leave Mother's house with nothing but her birth certificate, her Watermelon Queen dress, and Daddy's wedding ring.

Somehow that seemed appropriate.

* * *

Justice Henry J. Pearsall had a little house with a room set up as a wedding chapel of sorts. He lived on the outskirts of Augusta and assured Stone that he was quite used to being awakened in the middle of the night for drive-by weddings.

The license cost less than twenty bucks.

And now Stone stood in an itty-bitty room wallpapered in pink roses and containing a dozen folding chairs arranged to make an aisle. Mrs. Pearsall, wearing a Georgia Bulldogs sweatshirt and a pair of flannel PJ bottoms, banged away at the upright piano, playing the wedding march. The door at the other end of the room opened.

And suddenly the slightly tacky surroundings faded to gray.

Boy, Sharon looked like an angel wearing that Watermelon Queen dress. It wasn't exactly the standard-issue white, but the cascading shades of pink and green suited her tanned skin. She had a carnation in her hair, and a bunch of them clasped in her hands.

Carnations were the only flower they could find at the all-night Bi-Lo. He would have bought her roses if he could have found some. But Sharon said that carnations were good enough for her, and besides, they were just the right shade to match her dress.

He didn't know about that. He really didn't know about much of anything, because one glance at her and his heart took flight. If he lived to be a hundred, he would never forget the way she looked right at this moment, walking so slowly and softly toward him with a tiny smile on her pink lips.

He caught her spicy scent as she drew near. His heart nearly burst as she gazed up into his eyes. She was his— his beautiful, amazing, wonderful bride.

Mr. Pearsall started speaking words that floated beyond Stone's complete comprehension. But when it came time for him to speak his vows, he said them solemnly and with his whole heart. He would honor and protect and keep her all the days of his life.

He put the ring on her finger.

And then she spoke to him, her eyes dark and wide and liquid. And when she suddenly came up with a wedding ring, it seemed almost like a miracle. She took his hand in hers and slipped the plain gold band over his knuckle.

It fit perfectly. He smiled down at her. It was a comfort to know that he would wear that ring all his life.

And then it was time to kiss the bride. And time stood still until he carried her back to his truck and drove like a demon all the way back to Allenberg, where they rented the honeymoon room at the Magnolia Inn.

It wasn't much better than the Peach Blossom Motor Court, but he wasn't paying that much attention to the decor. He was too busy taking off that incredible dress and discovering the wonderful woman underneath.

$\mathcal{E}$PILOGUE

August 16, 1990

$\mathcal{S}$haron wrapped her arms around Stony and hung on for all she was worth. The hot summer sun beat down on her shoulders as she buried her nose in the soft fabric of his polo shirt. She looked up at him and gently pushed the lock of hair away from his forehead.

She was not going to cry.

"I guess the next time I see you I won't have to worry about your hair."

He nodded. His green eyes sober. "I'm going to be okay."

"Of course you are," she said, her voice oddly bright. But she wasn't a fool. Just yesterday the U.S. Marine Corps had sent more than forty thousand troops to the Persian Gulf. The United States already had a naval blockade in place, and everyone was talking about the possibility of reservists being called up for active duty.

"I'm going to be fine, honest. You'll come to my graduation ceremony in November?"

"Of course I will. I can't wait to see you all spit and polished." She ran her fingers through his hair again. "But I'm going to miss your cowlick."

"You know I won't be able to contact you much during boot camp."

"I know. I'll be busy at Carolina."

He gave her a sober-eyed look. He was completely fine with her going to college, but she knew he didn't like the idea of other guys hitting on her.

"I'll be studying," she said.

"I'll be able to call you this afternoon to let you know I got to Parris Island, but I won't be allowed to say anything else."

"I know, Stony, I've read all the material the Marine Corps sent about the first call home."

"Okay. Just so you know. I love you. I'm going to be okay. You have fun at Carolina, okay?"

She nodded and choked back the tears. She was not going to let him see her cry. She was not going to let him know how scared she'd been by the news reports on CNN.

Of course he knew that already; otherwise he wouldn't keep saying he was going to be okay. He was probably scared himself, but Stony would never show that.

She rose up on tiptoes and gave him the hottest kiss she could muster. She hoped with all her heart that her kiss told him what he needed to know. She would be waiting for him when he got home.

She let him go. It was the hardest thing she'd ever done.

His mother, father, little brothers, and sister were there. He hugged them all, even picking Rocky up and giving her a toss into the air that had her giggling. Boy, that little girl adored her brother. God keep him safe, Sharon prayed.

"I'm going to be okay, everyone. Stop with the long faces." He grinned. Then he squared his shoulders, turned, and walked purposefully toward the waiting Marine Corps van, which would take him from the Orangeburg recruiting office to Parris Island.

He didn't look back.

Sharon's stomach lurched. She was afraid she would be sick, like she had been this morning. She swallowed back her emotions along with the bile.

They were going to be okay. Miriam Randall had matched them up, and that meant they would have their happy-ever-after ending. It was guaranteed. In fact, they were already the talk of the town. No one had ever run off with a Watermelon Queen. No one had ever gotten married in a Watermelon Queen dress.

Their happy-ever-after ending was guaranteed. And besides, everyone in Last Chance was expecting it.

Sharon and Stone would just have to wait a little bit for it. But it would come. She had no doubt.

About the Author

Hope Ramsay is a *USA Today* bestselling author of heartwarming contemporary romances set below the Mason-Dixon Line and inspired by the summers she spent with her large family in South Carolina. She has two grown children, a demanding lap cat named Simba, who was born in Uganda, and a precious cockapoo puppy named Daisy. She lives in Virginia, where, when she's not writing, she's knitting or playing her forty-year-old Martin guitar.

Fall in love with these charming small-town romances!

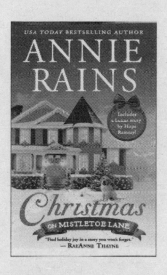

CHRISTMAS ON MISTLETOE LANE
By Annie Rains

Kaitlyn Russo thought she'd have a fresh start in Sweetwater Springs. Only one little problem: The B&B she inherited isn't entirely hers—and the ex-Marine who owns the other half isn't going anywhere.

THE CORNER OF HOLLY AND IVY
By Debbie Mason

With her dreams of being a wedding dress designer suddenly over, Arianna Bell isn't expecting a holly jolly Christmas. She thinks a run for town mayor might cheer her spirits—until she learns her opponent is her gorgeous high school sweetheart.

Discover exclusive content and more on read-forever.com.

CHRISTMAS WISHES AND MISTLETOE KISSES
By Jenny Hale

Single mother Abbey Fuller doesn't regret putting her dreams on hold to raise her son. Now that Max is older, she jumps at the chance to work on a small design job. But when she arrives at the Sinclair mansion, she feels out of her element—and her gorgeous but brooding boss Nicholas Sinclair is not exactly in the holiday spirit.

THE AMISH MIDWIFE'S SECRET
By Rachel J. Good

When *Englischer* Kyle Miller is offered a medical practice in his hometown, he knows he must face the painful past he left behind. Except he's not prepared for Leah Stoltzfus, the pretty Amish midwife who refuses to compromise her traditions with his modern medicine...

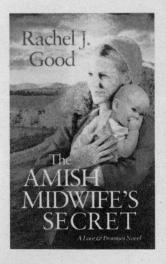

Find more great reads on Instagram with @ReadForeverPub.

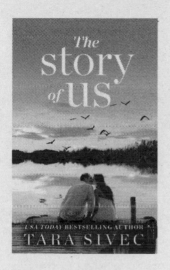

THE STORY OF US
By Tara Sivec

1,843 days. That's how long I survived in that hellhole. And I owe it all to the memory of the one woman who loved me more than I ever deserved to be loved. Now I'll do anything to get back to her...I may not be the man I used to be, but I will do whatever it takes to remind her of the story of us.

THE COTTAGE ON ROSE LANE
By Hope Ramsay

Jenna Fossey just received an unexpected inheritance that will change her life. Eager to meet relatives she never knew existed, she heads to the charming little town of Magnolia Harbor. But long-buried family secrets soon lead to even more questions, and the only person who can help her find the answers is her sexy-as-sin sailing instructor.

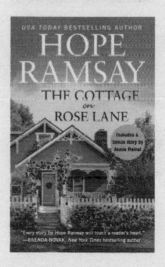

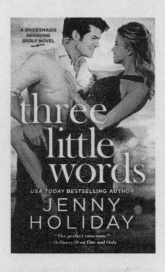